# LISA JACKSON

# UNSPOKEN

KENSINGTON BOOKS
www.kensingtonbooks.com

KENSINGTON BOOKS are published by

Kensington Publishing Corp.
119 West 40th Street
New York, NY 10018

All Kensington titles, imprints, and distributed lines are available at special quantity discounts for bulk purchases for sales promotion, premi-
ums, fund-raising, educational, or institutional use.

Special book excerpts or customized printings can also be created to fit
specific needs. For details, write or phone the office of the Kensington
Sales Manager: Kensington Publishing Corp., 119 West 40th Street,
New York, NY 10018. Attn. Sales Department. Phone: 1-800-221-2647.

Kensington and the K logo Reg. U.S. Pat. & TM Off.

First Zebra Mass Market Printing: November 1999

ISBN-13: 978-1-4967-1730-6 (ebook)
ISBN-10: 1-4967-1730-9 (ebook)

ISBN-13: 978-1-4967-1729-0
ISBN-10: 1-4967-1729-5
First Kensington Trade Paperback Printing: April 2019

10 9 8 7 6 5 4 3 2 1

Printed in the United States of America

# Books by Lisa Jackson

## Stand-Alones

SEE HOW SHE DIES
FINAL SCREAM
RUNNING SCARED
WHISPERS
TWICE KISSED
UNSPOKEN
DEEP FREEZE
FATAL BURN
MOST LIKELY TO DIE
WICKED GAME
WICKED LIES
SOMETHING WICKED
WITHOUT MERCY
YOU DON'T WANT TO
   KNOW
CLOSE TO HOME
AFTER SHE'S GONE
REVENGE
YOU WILL PAY
OMINOUS
RUTHLESS
ONE LAST BREATH
LIAR, LIAR

## Anthony Paterno/Cahill Family Novels

IF SHE ONLY KNEW
ALMOST DEAD

## Rick Bentz/Reuben Montoya Novels

HOT BLOODED
COLD BLOODED
SHIVER
ABSOLUTE FEAR
LOST SOULS
MALICE
DEVIOUS
NEVER DIE ALONE

## Pierce Reed/Nikki Gillette Novels

THE NIGHT BEFORE
THE MORNING AFTER
TELL ME

## Selena Alvarez/Regan Pescoli Novels

LEFT TO DIE
CHOSEN TO DIE
BORN TO DIE
AFRAID TO DIE
READY TO DIE
DESERVES TO DIE
EXPECTING TO DIE
WILLING TO DIE

Published by Kensington Publishing Corporation

*This book is dedicated to my sons,*
*Matthew and Michael Crose,*
*who are, without a doubt,*
*the lights of my life.*
*Thanks, guys! You're the best!*

# Acknowledgments

I would like to express my thanks and appreciation to all the people who helped in the research and structuring of this book. Without their help and support it would not have been written. Thanks to my friends and family and especially Ann Baumann, Nancy and Ken Bush, Matthew Crose, Michael Crose, Alexis Harrington, Mary Clare Kersten, Ken Melum, Betty and Jack Pederson, Sally Peters, Tess O'Shaughnessy, Robin Rue, John Scognamiglio, Linda and Larry Sparks, and Mark and Celia Stinson. *Muchas gracias!*

# PROLOGUE

*Blanco County Courthouse*
*Texas*

From his seat at the defense table, Ross McCallum sent a prayer to Heaven, to a God he'd never trusted, and silently bargained for his freedom. In his hasty words with God, Ross vowed that if he was found innocent of the murder conviction, he'd turn over a new leaf, walk the straight and narrow, go door to door giving out Bibles, even become a preacher, a reformed sinner who had quit his lawless ways.

Shifting in his chair, his leg shackles clinking loudly, he was reminded that his chances of beating this trumped-up charge were slim to none. Not after Caleb Swaggert's damning testimony. The old son of a bitch had sat right up on the witness stand and lied through the few teeth still in his mouth.

He'd only hoped that the jury, at least one damned person, would see through Swaggert's lies. The juror he'd pinned his hopes on was an older woman, well north of seventy, from the looks of her, with white, kinked hair and deep grooves in skin tanned by years in the sun. During Caleb's testimony, juror seven had seemed to dislike what she'd heard, wrinkling her nose and shaking her head, just slightly. She'd even sent McCallum worried, but encouraging, glances. She, alone, seemed to be on his side.

That was enough. Just one vote in his favor.

The decision to find him guilty had to be unanimous.

He was counting on juror number seven.

Now, the courtroom was sweltering, here in this county courthouse where the air-conditioning had given out, and the lazy Texas sun was beating down with a ferocity that melted the tar in the streets and burned through the windows of this hundred-year-old building.

He felt a trickle of sweat roll down from his temple, but didn't lift his hands to swipe it away as his wrists, too, were bound. Behind him, in the seats positioned behind the railing, he heard the whispers and felt dozens of pairs of eyes staring at the back of his head, their accusatory gazes drilling through his skull. The courtroom was filled to capacity and he imagined there were people waiting outside on the steps, in the shade, in cars. Newspeople as well as the curious, all wanting to see him punished for this crime.

*Well, let 'em look!*

Of course, *she* was among those who hoped his soul rotted in hell.

Shelby Cole, daughter of Judge Jerome "Red" Cole, who probably played cards with the bastard who was presiding over his case, the Honorable Judge Leonard Fry. McCallum didn't glance behind him, just kept his eyes fixed straight ahead to the carpet in front of the bench.

The members of the jury filed in and the courtroom became quiet—deathly quiet. Every muscle in McCallum's body tensed, but he forced his face to remain calm, emotionless. The jurors wouldn't look his direction, not even the little granny with the kinky white hair and the weathered face. He'd counted on her, but she avoided eye contact with him, as did all the others.

Not a good sign. Was it possible? Had they really decided to convict him on the flimsy, circumstantial evidence that the prosecution had thrown at them? No murder weapon had been found and nothing linked Ross McCallum to the crime except the flimsy testimony of an old geezer known for his love of whiskey.

And yet, he felt his guts clench with a new desperation.

"Has the jury reached a verdict?" Judge Fry, a beanpole of a man in heavy black robes, asked the foreman of the twelve men and women who'd been chosen to determine the course of Ross Mc-Callum's life.

"We have, Your Honor," the foreman responded. Wearing glasses that were always tinted gray, the heavyset man in his Western-cut suit handed the bailiff the paper that would change the course of Ross McCallum's life forever. Ross followed the motion without any expression. But his heart pounded with dread, and sweat drizzled down the side of his face.

Reading over the tops of his half glasses, the judge read the papers and the next few minutes were a blur as McCallum was urged to his feet by his court-appointed attorney, a snot-nosed kid fresh out of law school who was smart enough, just unwilling to bend the rules, and the foreman read the verdict of "Guilty."

The word echoed through the courtroom and around him, people began to talk. Like bombs exploding, the verdict blasted through his head. *Guilty! For the murder of Ramón Estevan, a miserable bastard who deserved to die! Oh, Jesus. No! No! No!*

Vaguely conscious of each member of the jury being polled, he somehow remained standing, his jaw set, his legs feeling as steady as sand. He only realized it was time to move when the guards came to usher him away.

For the rest of his miserable life.

If he let them.

But he wouldn't.

He glanced over his shoulder and saw the spectators, all staring back at him and, sure enough, Shelby Cole was there, looking down her straight nose at him, defying him, feeling a glimmer of satisfaction at his doom. He forced a grin he knew was a leer, and felt the same heat rise in him that he always did when his gaze landed upon her.

"I'll be back," he whispered under his breath. "I'll be back and when I do, I'll find you."

As if she'd heard him, she visibly started and for the briefest of seconds, she remembered. Just as he did. All that had happened between them. The hot night. The hotter sex. The fear.

His grin widened and she turned ashen, as if she might just faint.

That was a good start.

A damned good one.

"Hey!" One of the guards pulled at him, but not before he lifted his hands, clasped together, only his two index fingers pointing outward. He aimed them straight at Shelby Cole, then blew her a kiss.

The bitch had the audacity to shake her head at him, as if she wasn't afraid. But he knew better. And his cock threatened to get hard just at the thought.

"Let's go, McCallum!" the burly guard in the sweat-stained uniform ordered as he pushed his charge roughly toward the side door.

*Oh yeah,* McCallum thought in silent fury, *I'll be back, you fuckers! And when I return, I'm gonna extract my vengeance... slowly, and surely, on each and every one of you who set me up. Get ready. 'Cause you'll see me coming. You'll know your fate, you sorry sons of bitches. And Shelby-girl, you better take note. You're at the top of my list.*

*I swear to God, Bad Luck, Texas, will never be the same!*

Escorted out of the courtroom, he realized that his prayers at the defense table had been for naught.

As it turned out, once again, God wasn't listening.

# CHAPTER 1

*Bad Luck, Texas*

Heat sweltered over the dry acres of range grass. Shade was sparse, the smell of dust heavy in the summer air. Nevada Smith took aim. Closed his bad eye. Squeezed the trigger.

*Bam!*

The old Winchester kicked hard against his bare shoulder, and his target, a rusting tin can, jumped off its fence post to land on the hard ground. The longhorns in the next field didn't so much as twitch, but a warm feeling of satisfaction stole through Nevada's blood as he took a bead on the next target, an empty beer bottle he intended to shatter into a million pieces.

He hoisted the rifle again. Cocked it. Set his jaw and narrowed his eyes. His finger tightened over the trigger, but he hesitated.

He sensed the truck before he heard it. As he craned his neck, he spied a plume of dust trailing the fence posts along the lane just as he heard the rumble of a pickup's engine. Squinting through scratched Foster Grant lenses, he studied the make and model and recognized Shep Marson's red Dodge.

Shit.

What the hell did that old bastard want? Shep was a deputy with the Sheriff's Department, a hard-ass who was leaning heavily toward running for county sheriff. As crooked as a crippled dog's hind leg, Shep was a nephew of a county judge, was married to the daughter of a once-rich cattle rancher and was about to be elected by a landslide. Crime in this neck of Texas Hill Country was about to take an upswing.

Nevada's nerves were strung as tight as bailing twine, and it wasn't just because Shep was one mean, bigoted son of a bitch who had no business being this far out of his jurisdiction.

The simple fact of the matter was that Shep just happened to be Shelby Cole's shirttail cousin, a man with whom Nevada had worked briefly and a man who had once threatened him at gunpoint. Nope, there never would be any love lost between Nevada and Shep.

Hauling the rifle in one hand, Nevada walked past an old rose garden with overgrown bushes going to seed. He snagged the worn T-shirt he'd hung over a fence post and hooked it with one finger, slinging the faded scrap of cotton over his shoulder.

A wasp was working busily building a nest in the eaves of the two-room cabin he called home, and his crippled old dog, a half-breed with more border collie than Lab in him, lay in the shade of the sagging front porch. His tail gave a hard thump to the dirt as Nevada passed, and he lifted his head and gave off a disgruntled "woof" at the sound of the Dodge.

"Shh. It'll be all right," Nevada lied. He tried and failed to ignore the throb of a hangover that had lingered past noon and seemed to get worse rather than better as the sun rode high in the western sky and heat shimmered in undulating waves as far as the eye could see. Nevada's stomach clenched as the truck roared closer. His bad eye ached a bit, and he swatted at a stupid horsefly that hadn't figured out that the herd was three hundred feet west, huddled behind a thicket of scrub oak and mesquite trees, each lazy horse standing nose to buttocks with another and flicking at flies with its tail.

Marson's truck slid to a stop in front of the old toolshed and he cut the engine.

The muscles at the base of Nevada's neck tightened—the way they always did when he was confronted by the law. At one time he'd been a member of the ranks; now he was an outcast.

Shep climbed from behind the wheel. A big bear of a man whose

lower lip was always extended with a chaw of tobacco, Shep sauntered around the front of his bug-spattered truck. In snakeskin
boots, faded jeans and a Western-cut shirt that was a little too tight
around his belly, Shep made his way up the dusty path leading to
the cabin. Two cans of Coors, connected by plastic strapping that
had once held six sixteen-ouncers, dangled from his thick fingers.

"Smith." He spat a stream of black juice through his front teeth
as he reached the gate. "Got a minute?"

"Depends."

"On?"

"Is this official business?"

"Nah." Shep wiped the back of his free hand over his lips. The
beginning of a mustache was visible on the freckled skin over his
upper lip. "Just two old friends chewin' the fat."

Nevada didn't believe him for a second. He and Shep had never
been friends—not even when they'd been part of the same team.
They both knew it. But he held his tongue. There was a reason
Marson was here. A big one.

Shep yanked one can from its holder and tossed it to Nevada,
who caught it on the fly. "Hell, it sure is hot," Shep grumbled, popping the top and listening to the cooling sound of air escaping.
With a nod he hoisted the can and took a long draught.

"It's always hot." Nevada opened his beer. "Summer in Texas."

"Guess I forgot." Shep chuckled without a drip of humor.

"C'mon, let's sit a spell." He hiked his chin toward the front
porch where two plastic chairs were patiently gathering dust. Sweat
trickled down the side of Shep's face, sparkling in skinny sideburns
that were beginning to gray. "Y'hear about old Caleb Swaggert?"
he asked, eyeing the horizon where a few wisps of clouds gathered
and the dissipating wake of a jet sliced northward.

The warning hairs on the back of Nevada's neck prickled. He
leaned against a post on the porch while Shep settled into one of
the garage-sale chairs. "What about him?"

Shep nursed his beer for a few minutes while looking over the
eyesore of a ranch Nevada had inherited. With a grunt, he said,
"Seems old Caleb's about to die. Cancer. The docs up in Coopersville give him less than a month." Another long swallow. Nevada's
fingers tightened over his Coors. "And lo and behold, Caleb says

he's found Jesus. Don't want to die a sinner. So he's recantin' his testimony."

Every muscle in Nevada's body tensed. Through lips that barely moved, he asked, "Meanin'?"

"That Ross McCallum is a free man. Caleb's testimony sent the ol' boy to prison in the first place, his and Ruby Dee's. Ever'b'dy in these parts knows what a lying whore Ruby is, and now it looks like she might admit that she was just settin' Ross up."

Nevada felt sick inside. A bit of a breeze, hot as Satan's breath, brushed the back of his neck.

Shep hoisted his can again, nearly drained it. "Now I know it was you who arrested the sum-bitch, Smith, you who sent him up the river, but I thought I should let you know Ross's gonna be out in a couple a days, dependin' on who's reviewin' the case, and I don't have to tell ya that he's got a short fuse. Hell, he was in more fights around here when he was growin' up than you were. Half the time they were with you. Ain't that right?" When Nevada didn't answer, Shep nodded to himself and took another long swallow, finishing the Coors. "When he gits out, he's gonna be mean as a wounded grizzly." Holding the can, he managed to point an index finger at Nevada. "No doubt he'll come lookin' fer you." Crushing the empty sixteen-ouncer in one meaty fist, Shep added, "The way I figger it, forewarned is forearmed. Y'know what I mean?"

"Yeah."

"Good." He tossed his empty onto the half-rotten floorboards of the porch and stood. "Y'know, Nevada, I never did understand it much. You two were best friends once, right? He was the quarterback on the football team and you his wide receiver. Well, before he got throwed off. But what happened between you two?"

Nevada lifted a shoulder. "People change."

"Do they now?" Shep's lips flattened over his teeth. "Maybe they do when a woman's involved."

"Maybe."

Shep walked down the two steps of the front porch and then, as if a sudden thought had struck him, turned to look over his shoulder. "That's the other news, son," he said, and his tone was dead serious.

"What is?"

"There's a rumor that Shelby's headin' back to Bad Luck."

Nevada's heart nearly stopped, but he managed to keep his expression bland.

"That's right," Shep said as if talking to himself. "I heard it from my sister. Shelby called her this mornin'. So, if she does happen to show up, I don't want no trouble, y'hear? You and Ross did enough fightin' over her years ago. I remember haulin' both of you boys in. You were cut up pretty bad. Lost your eye. Ended up in the hospital. And Ross, he had a couple a cracked ribs and a broken arm after wrasslin' with ya. Seems to me he swore he'd kill ya then."

"He never got the chance."

" 'Til now, son." Shep glanced around the sorry yard and drew a handkerchief from his back pocket. He mopped his face, and the grooves near the corners of his eyes deepened as he squinted. "Like I said, I just don't want no trouble. I'm gonna run fer sheriff of Blanco County next year, and I can't have my name associated with any wild-ass shit."

"Don't see how you'd be."

"Good. Let's just keep it that way." He started toward his truck again, and Nevada told himself that he should just let sleeping dogs lie, pretend no interest, seal his lips. But he couldn't.

"Why's Shelby comin' back to Bad Luck now?" he asked.

"Now, that's a good question, ain't it?" Shep paused and rubbed his chin thoughtfully. Sweat stained the underarms of his shirt. "A damned good question. I was hopin' you might have an answer, but I see ya don't." He looked off into the distance and spat a long stream of tobacco juice at the sun-bleached weeds growing around the base of a fence post. "Maybe Ross knows."

Nevada's headache pounded.

"Seems odd, don't ya think, that both he and Shelby are gonna be back in town at the same time? Kind of a coincidence."

*More than a coincidence,* Nevada thought, but this time, he held his tongue as the older man ambled back to his truck. As far as Nevada could see, Shelby Cole—beautiful, spoiled, the only daughter of Judge Jerome "Red" Cole—had no business returning to the Texas Hill Country. No damned business at all.

\* \* \*

Shelby stepped hard on the gas pedal of her rented Cadillac. Brush, scrub oak, dying wildflowers and prickly pear cactus flew past as she pushed the speed limit. Road kill, predominantly armadillos with a few unlucky jackrabbits thrown in, was scattered along the gravel shoulder of the highway. It reminded her that she was closing in on Bad Luck, a tiny town not far from Austin, a town she'd sworn she'd never set foot in again.

The sunroof was open, harsh rays beating down on the top of her head, strands of her red-blond hair yanked from the knot she'd twisted to the base of her skull. She didn't care. She'd kicked off her high heels at the airport and was driving barefoot, her eyebrows slammed together in concentration, the notes of some old Madonna song barely piercing her consciousness.

She took a corner a little too fast, and the tires on the Caddy screeched, but she didn't slow down. After ten years of being away, ten years ostracized, ten years of living life her way in Seattle, she couldn't wait to pull up to the century-old home where she'd been raised. Not that she'd stay long. Just do her business and get the hell out.

Her fingers tightened over the wheel. Memories flooded her mind, memories that were trapped in another time and space, recollections of promises and lies, making love in a spring thunderstorm and feeling the aftershocks of betrayal. And then the grief. The soul-shattering grief that still in the long lonely nights returned to scrape at the hollow of her heart. She swallowed hard. Refused to walk down that painful path.

She snapped off the radio and shoved a pair of sunglasses onto the bridge of her nose. Right now she didn't need to hear anything the least bit maudlin or romantic. Not today. Probably not ever. She glanced at the bucket seat next to her, where she'd tossed her briefcase. From the side pocket, the corner of a manila envelope was visible; inside was a letter—written anonymously—with a San Antonio postmark. It was the reason she'd demanded a leave of absence from the real estate company where she was employed, packed one overnight bag, driven to Sea-Tac Airport and taken the first available flight to Austin.

Less than twenty-four hours from the time she'd received the damning letter, she was driving through the grid of streets in the center of the small town she'd called home for the first eighteen years of her life.

Nothing much had changed in Bad Luck.

The drugstore looked the same, down to the original hitching post still planted in front of the side door. With a wry smile, she remembered carving her initials in the underside of that same post and wondered if they were still there, aged by time and weather, a silly little carving that proclaimed her love for a man who had ended up breaking her heart.

"Fool," she muttered, stopping at the single red light in town and waiting as a pregnant woman pushed a stroller with a crying toddler across the street. Heat rose from the pavement, distorting her vision and threatening to melt the asphalt. Lord, it was hot here. She'd forgotten. Sweat prickled her scalp and the air seemed heavy as it pressed against her cotton blouse. Beneath her khaki skirt her skin was moist. She could close the damned sunroof, roll up the windows and blast the air-conditioning, but she didn't want to. No. She wanted to remember Bad Luck, Texas, for the miserable scrap of ground it was. Named appropriately by an old prospector, the town had grown slowly and only a few of the citizens had prospered—her father being the most visible. Once she'd shaken the dust of Bad Luck from her heels, she'd sworn she'd never return.

And yet she was back.

With a vengeance.

Unerringly she drove down sun-baked side streets and turned the corner at a cement-block motel boasting low rates, air-conditioning, Wi-Fi and cable TV, then nosed the Caddy past a mom-and-pop grocery where scattered cars glinted in the pockmarked lot. Farther on, past small bungalows, some with FOR RENT signs in the windows, the street curved around a statue of Sam Houston in the park and wound through a residential area where shade trees offered some relief from the sun and a few of the older homes had a veneer of nineteenth-century charm.

Far from the center of town, closer to the hills, were the more prestigious and widely scattered homes.

Her father's Victorian was the grandest of the lot, a mansion by Bad Luck standards. Nestled on five acres in the sloping hills a mile from town, with a creek meandering through ancient pecan trees, the house was three stories of cut stone and brick, flanked on all sides by wide, covered porches. Ornate grillwork and tall windows were graced by hanging baskets of fuchsias exploding with color. The grass was cut, green and edged, the flowering shrubs trimmed, and she imagined that the kidney-shaped pool in the back was still a shimmering man-made lake of aquamarine, a testament to Judge Red Cole's wealth, power and influence.

Shelby frowned and remembered the taunts she'd heard as a child and teenager, the whispered words of awe and scorn that she'd pretended had never been uttered.

"Rich bitch."

"Luckiest girl west of San Antonio."

"Can you imagine? She has anything she ever wanted. All she has to do is ask, or blink her baby-blues at her daddy."

"Rough life, eh, darlin'?"

Cringing even now as she had then, Shelby felt her cheeks burn with the same hot shade of embarrassment that had colored them when she'd been told not to play with Maria, the caretaker's daughter, or warned that Ruby Dee was a "bad girl" with a soiled reputation, or learned that her Appaloosa mare was worth more than Nevada Smith had made in a full year of working overtime at her father's cattle ranch located eight miles north of town.

No wonder she'd run. She braked at the garage, slipped on her heels, cut the engine and tossed the keys into her briefcase. Muttering, "Give me strength," under her breath to no one in particular, she climbed out of the car, ignored the fact that her blouse was sticking to her back and marched up the brick walk to the front of the house. She didn't bother raising the brass knocker that was engraved proudly with the Cole name as she remembered the sickening spoof of a nursery rhyme she'd heard in grade school.

> *Old Judge Cole*
> *Was a nasty old soul*
> *And a nasty old soul was he.*
> *He called for his noose*
> *And he called for his gun*
> *And he called for his henchmen three.*

The front door opened easily and the smells of furniture polish, potpourri and cinnamon greeted her. Italian marble, visible beneath the edges of expensive throw rugs, gleamed as sunlight streamed through tall, spotless windows.

"*Hola!* Is someone there?" an old familiar voice asked in a thick Spanish accent. From the kitchen, soft footsteps sounded, and as Shelby rounded the corner to the kitchen she nearly ran smack-dab into Lydia, her father's housekeeper.

Dark eyes widened in recognition. A smile of pure delight cracked across her jaw. "Señorita Shelby!" Lydia, whose once-black hair, neatly braided and wound into a bun at the base of her neck, was now shot with streaks of silver, smiled widely. Wiry strands that had escaped their bonds framed the face that Shelby remembered from her youth. Lydia's waist had thickened over the years but her face was unlined, her coppery skin stretched over high cheekbones as smooth as ever.

"*Dios!*" Lydia threw her arms around the woman she'd helped raise. "Why did you not tell anyone you were coming home?"

"It was kind of a quick decision." Unwanted tears burned the back of Shelby's eyes as she hugged Lydia. Black dress, white collar, white apron and sensible sandals—Lydia's attire hadn't changed in all the years Shelby had been away. And she still smelled of vanilla, talc and cigarette smoke. "It's . . . good to see you."

"And you, *niña.*" She clucked her tongue. "If I had known you are coming, I would have cooked all your favorites—ham and sweet potatoes and for dessert pecan pie. I'll make it this day! It is still your favorite?"

Shelby laughed. "Yeah, but please, Lydia, don't go to any trouble—I don't know how long I'll be staying."

"Hush. We will not talk of your leaving when you just walked through the door. Ahh, *niña!*" Tears brightened the older woman's eyes. Blinking rapidly, she said, "You are like a *fantasma,* the ghost of your mother." Sighing, Lydia held Shelby at arm's length and looked her up and down. "But you are too skinny—*Dios!* Do they not know how to cook up north?"

"Nope. No one does," Shelby teased. "Everyone's skin and bones in Seattle. They just drink coffee and huddle against the rain and climb mountains. That sort of thing."

Lydia chuckled. "This, we will fix."

"Later. Right now I want to see the Judge," Shelby said, refusing to be deterred by the housekeeper's kindness or any ridiculous sense of nostalgia. She had a mission. "Is he at home?" She extracted herself from Lydia's embrace.

"*Sí*. On the veranda, but he is with clients. I will tell him you are—"

Too late. Shelby had already started for the French doors leading to the backyard. "I'll do it myself. Thanks, Lydia."

She walked past the shining mahogany table that, with its twelve carved chairs, occupied the dining room. A floral arrangement of birds of paradise, her mother's favorite flowers, graced the lustrous table, just as a new arrangement had every week since Jasmine Cole's death over twenty years earlier. Crystal and china, sparkling and ready for a sit-down party, were visible through the glass panes of a massive china closet.

Nothing seemed to change in Bad Luck, Shelby decided as she opened the French doors and stepped onto the tile veranda that overlooked the pool. Fans mounted in the ceiling of the porch swirled the air lazily, and shade from the live oaks and pecan trees eased some of the summer heat that rose from the terra cotta that skirted the pool and reflected in sharp rays off the shimmering blue water.

Her father was seated at a small table. Dressed in a black suit and white shirt, a black Stetson on the table, his cane with its carved ivory handle lying across his lap, he was deep in conversation with two men. Not three henchmen, but, she supposed, two yes-men dressed in jeans and shirts with their sleeves rolled up. One had a brown mustache and thinning hair, the other wore a silvering goatee and dark sunglasses.

At the sound of the door closing behind her, they all looked up. Two faces scowled slightly, then gave her the once-over as if in tandem. Their sour expressions ebbed slowly to interest.

She ignored them both.

Her father looked over his shoulder. "Shelby!"

She ached inside when she saw the pure joy that lit his face. God, he'd aged. His face had become jowly with the years, his belly larger than it had been. His eyelids had sagged a bit and lines weaved through his neck and across his forehead. His red hair had faded and grayed, but he was still an imposing man, and as he pulled himself to his full height of six feet, three inches, she remembered how intimidating he'd been on the bench.

"My God, girl, it's good to see you." He opened his arms wide, but Shelby held her ground and stood away from him.

"We need to talk."

"What the hell are you doin' here, darlin'?" Disappointment clouded his blue eyes, and a part of her wanted to run to him and throw her arms around his neck and say *oh, Daddy, I've missed you.* But she didn't. Instead she swallowed back the urge to break down altogether and stiffened her spine. She was no longer a frightened little girl.

"Alone, Judge. We need to talk alone." She stared pointedly at his latest gofers.

The men, dismissed by a nod from their boss, kicked out their chairs, and with muffled words and hasty assurances from Judge Cole that they'd get together later, walked stiffly around the back of the house and through a gate. In the ensuing stillness, when the sound of bees humming and a woodpecker drumming were all that could be heard, Shelby didn't waste any time. She reached into her briefcase, pulled out the manila envelope, ripped it open and spilled its contents onto the glass-topped table where the ice in three half-consumed drinks was still melting.

The black-and-white photo of a girl of nine or ten stared up at them, and the Judge sucked in his breath as he slowly sat down again. Shelby noticed that his wedding band had cut a groove in the ring finger of his left hand, a ring that hadn't been removed in over thirty years, and on his right, he sported a flashy diamond that most Hollywood brides would envy.

Shelby leaned over the table so that the tip of her nose was nearly touching her father's. With one finger she pointed to the black-and-white picture. "This is my daughter," she said, her insides quaking, her voice unsteady. "Your granddaughter."

She looked for any sign of recognition in the old man's face. There was none. "She looks just like me. Just like Mom."

The Judge glanced at the photo. "There's a resemblance."

"No resemblance, Judge. This girl is a dead ringer. And here"—

she edged a piece of paper from beneath the photograph—"this is a copy of her birth certificate. And this...the death notice of her as a baby. Read it—Elizabeth Jasmine Cole. She was supposed to have died, Judge—of complications, heart problems—right after birth. You...you told me she hadn't made it. That those ashes I spread in the hills...oh, God, whose were they?" she asked, her voice cracking, the immense pain rising up again. Shaking her head, not wanting to hear any more lies, she said, "Don't...oh, God." Shelby's throat was clogged and she thought she might throw up. "You lied to me, Dad. Why?"

"I didn't—"

"Don't! Just don't, okay!" She held both her palms outward, in his face, and stepped back. Bile roiled in her stomach. Beneath her skin, her muscles were quivering in rage. "Someone, and I don't know who, sent me all this. I got it yesterday, and so I came back here to clear it up. Where's my daughter, Dad?" she demanded through teeth that were clenched so hard her jaw ached. "What the hell did you do with her?"

"Now, darlin'—"

"Stop it! Right now! Don't call me darlin', or sweetie, or kiddo, or missy or any of those cute little names, okay? I'm all grown up now, in case you hadn't noticed, and you can't smooth-talk your way out of this, Judge. I'm not a little girl. I know better than to believe a word that passes through your lying lips, and I only came back here to find my child, Judge—*my* daughter." She thumped her chest with her thumb.

"Yours and who else's?" he asked, his smile having disappeared and the old, hard edge she remembered coming back to his voice.

"That—that doesn't matter."

"Doesn't it?" The Judge scattered the papers across the table and frowned, his eyes narrowing behind wire-rimmed reading glasses. "Odd, don't you think? You get proof that you've got a kid during the same week that Ross McCallum is going to be released from prison."

"What?" Her knees nearly buckled. McCallum couldn't be given his freedom. Not yet. Not ever. Fear congealed her blood. She was suddenly hot and cold all at once.

"Oh, so you didn't know?" The Judge settled back in his chair and played with the ivory handle of his cane. He looked up at her over the tops of his glasses. "Uh-huh. Ross is gonna be a free man. Oh…and Nevada Smith, he's still around."

Her stupid heart skipped a beat, but she managed to keep her face bland, her expression cool. Nevada was out of her life. Had been for a long, long time. Nothing would change that. Ever.

"Yep," the Judge went on, fingertips caressing the smooth knob, "inherited a rocky scrap of land that he's tryin' to ranch. No one knows how he'll handle Ross's freedom, but the word is that there is certainly gonna be hell to pay." He bit his lower lip and scowled thoughtfully, as he'd often done while hearing long-winded summations when he was on the bench. "And now someone sends you bait—a little chum in the water to lure you back to a town you've sworn you'd never return to. Someone's playin' you for a fool, Shelby," he said, slowly nodding his head, as if in agreement with himself, "and it ain't me."

For once she believed him.

She'd flown back here on a cloud of self-righteous fury and determination to find her child. That hadn't changed. But now she felt manipulated, and yes, as her father had said, played for a fool. Unwittingly, she'd stepped into a carefully laid trap set by an unknown individual with purposes of his own.

Well, tough!

Beneath the blouse that stuck to her skin, her shoulders squared.

She'd find a way to get herself out of this damned snare. Come hell or high water, she'd leave Bad Luck, Texas, and the pain it wrought behind her once and for all.

And this time, by God, she'd take her daughter with her.

# CHAPTER 2

"But you can't leave. *Niña,* please, you just got here!" Lydia was nothing if not persistent. It was her one quality that hadn't changed over the years. Oh, her hair may have grayed and a few pounds had thickened her waist and ankles, but she was just as determined as she had been for as long as Shelby could remember. "The Judge, he needs you," she said, puffing to keep up with Shelby's quick steps as she marched through the house to the front door.

"He doesn't need anyone."

"I thought you were here to visit."

"Nope. Business." Shelby shook her head; she couldn't stay here, not in this house, this huge tomb where her own mother had taken her life, where she'd grown up an only child with the stern Judge as her father, where faceless people with special requests of the Judge had slunk in and out of the house at all hours, unaware that Shelby had watched in the shadows of the upper landing, hidden in a niche near the linen closet behind the ficus tree and peeking through the lacy branches to the foyer below.

"But Shelby…" Her voice broke, and Shelby stopped as she reached the door. Turning, she saw genuine sadness in Lydia's dark eyes. "…I've missed you, *niña.* The house has been cold since you've been gone."

The ice around Shelby's heart cracked, for this was the woman who had raised her from the time that Jasmine Cole had made the decision that she preferred death to the dishonor of divorce. It was Lydia's arms that had surrounded her when she'd been scared, Lydia's ample breasts on which she'd cushioned her head and heard the steady beat of a true heart, Lydia who had encouraged her to be anything she wanted to be and comforted her when she'd failed. Lydia Vasquez had applied iodine to her scraped knees and scolded her in rapid-fire Spanish when she'd made a mistake and winked, then turned a blind eye, when she'd "borrowed" the keys to her father's 1940 Pontiac for a joyride.

"I can't stay here," she said now, holding Lydia's fleshy upper arms in her hands.

"Not forever, no. But for a few days? It would bring such comfort...such joy to him." She cocked her head toward the back of the house and the patio where the Judge still sat by the pool. "And, to me, as well. *Por favor.* A few days. A *semana.*"

"A week?" Shelby said. "No way. I can't."

"What would it hurt? Your father, he would like it and I...I would see to it that you gained a little weight. Things have changed since you've been gone." Her lips pursed, little lines visible around the edges. "He is not the...the...what did you call him? The *monstruo.*"

Shelby couldn't help but smile. "Ogre, Lydia. Not monster. Get it right."

"*Sí.* Ogre."

"I'll...I'll think about it."

"Do and I will pray. To the Holy Mother and—"

"She'll do fine. You don't have to call up all the saints," Shelby said, and at the look of sheer horror on Lydia's round face at the sound of her blasphemy, Shelby laughed and gave the older woman a quick kiss on her cheek. "Just let me handle this my way, okay? I don't need you or the Sacred Virgin, or God Himself, to try and tell me what to do."

As Shelby reached for the handle of the front door, Lydia crossed herself with the dexterity and fervor of the truly religious and was muttering in Spanish about headstrong, irrational young women who didn't know their rightful place on this earth. Shelby only understood half of it. But she got the gist and closed the door with finality.

She didn't want to stay in the same house as her father, couldn't imagine reliving all the hopes, dreams and disappointments that she'd endured during the first eighteen years of her life, and yet it would only make sense to stay here, in close proximity to the man who had so callously destroyed her life—to find out exactly what had gone on ten years ago, to find out how involved he was in this mammoth deception. The ache in her heart, the agony of losing her child still remained and reminded her of the horrendous deception of which her father was a part.

Her legs were a tad wobbly as she made her way to the Cadillac, but she didn't falter and slid behind the wheel, the bucket seat hot against the backs of her legs. Twisting on the ignition, she glanced at the house and swore a curtain moved in the den. Her father? Lydia? Someone else?

Not that it mattered. Slipping her shades onto the bridge of her nose, she nearly backed into the corner of the garage, then threw the car into drive and gunned the engine. In some ways it would be easier to stay with her father, and yet she wasn't ready to eat that kind of crow. Not yet.

*Where better to uncover his secrets? To talk to him, hope that he'll open up and tell you the truth?*

"Damn it all," she muttered under her breath and guided the huge car toward the heart of town and the old stone building where Doc Pritchart had once housed his practice. As she drove, her head pounded. Ross McCallum was going to be out of jail.

Her fingers were suddenly clammy over the wheel, her heart a drum. The bitter taste of bile rose in the back of her throat, and she clenched her jaw tight. Desperately she tried to concentrate on driving into the heart of Bad Luck and the clinic where she'd once been treated for everything from bronchitis to pink eye.

The building hadn't changed. It rose four stories from sidewalks where bits of glass winked in the sunlight. The windows were paned, the glass reinforced by wire. An ash canister stood near the front door as it always had. Air-conditioning had been added; inside, the once-linoleum hallways had been carpeted with a brown industrial weave. On the second floor, the glass door that had once been the portal to Pritchart's office now was lettered with the name of an insurance company.

Disappointment settled over Shelby's shoulders, but she twisted the knob and stepped inside to a cool reception area decorated in shades of blue. A pert receptionist with hair that matched the silvery blue of the walls and enough jewelry to put Mr. T to shame, looked up from her computer as Shelby entered. The name plate on the desk read Roberta Fletcher.

"I'm looking for Dr. Ned Pritchart," Shelby said, before the woman could ask to help her. "I was a patient of his years ago, when he occupied this office."

The woman's smile was sugary sweet, though her eyes, wide with contacts, held little warmth. "Doc Pritchart? He's been gone a long time, nearly ten years, I think. We've been here six and before that there was a lawyer—a Mr. Blackwell. Arthur Blackwell."

"Do you know who took over his practice, or where I might find him?"

Ms. Fletcher shrugged, rolling her palms to the ceiling. "No idea. But I heard he'd quit working, moved away, though I can't recall where. I never really knew him, at least not to speak to him. Just saw him around town occasionally." She paused for a second, her eyes appraising. "Say, aren't you Judge Cole's daughter? Shelby? I remember you . . . oh, my but you're the spitting image of your mama, may she rest in peace."

"Yes. Thank you." So this was how it was going to be; everyone in Bad Luck would recognize her.

"A pity about her. You know, honey," she said, suddenly Shelby's friend, "she was a wonderful woman."

"Yes. I do know. I remember."

"How's your father? I haven't seen him for a while."

"Fine. He's—uh, fine," Shelby said.

"How long are you in town?"

"A while," Shelby hedged, remembering one of the pitfalls of a small town: everyone knew everyone else's business. "I'm not sure exactly."

Realizing she was getting nowhere on her quest and not wanting to answer any more questions, Shelby thanked the receptionist, made her way downstairs and threw open the front door to the scorching heat of midafternoon. Across the street was the only pharmacy in town, originally a Rexall drugstore complete with soda fountain in the back. She'd hung out there as a preteen in that netherworld between childhood and adolescence. Shelby hated to think how many cherry Cokes she'd sipped there while rotating on the red-topped stools, swinging her legs and dipping French fries in catsup laced with lemon and Tabasco sauce, while dreaming of some teen idol or TV heartthrob whose name she could no longer remember. It seemed a lifetime ago, a carefree time before all the trouble began.

She jaywalked as there wasn't much traffic and rounded the corner to the side entrance where the hitching post, battle-scarred and glorious, stood guard. Cigarette burns marred its smooth, time-worn wood, and as she felt beneath the log, she traced the etched-in heart with the tips of her fingers—still there after all these years.

God, she'd been a fool over Nevada Smith. She'd been in high school at the time but he'd been older, home from a short stint in the army when she'd fallen for him.

"Not the smartest move of your life," she reminded herself now as she straightened and dusted her hands. She wasn't about to be caught up in silly reminiscence, not when she was pressed for time. And pressed she was. Each day that slipped through her fingers was another twenty-four hours gone without meeting her daughter.

As she had before, she accessed the Internet on her smartphone and tried once again to locate Dr. Ned Pritchart. Googling him, she found a few old articles about him, but nothing of interest or any reference at all within the past ten years. Certainly, there was no phone number or address for the man. It was as if he'd become a ghost.

She decided, when all else failed, she'd have to go "old school."

Setting her jaw, she crossed an alley to a solitary phone booth and flipped through the torn and crinkled yellow pages of the directory, searching through the listing for physicians, hoping to find Dr. Ned Pritchart's name.

No such luck. She ran her fingers down the columns of names, hoping that she might remember a partner or underling, or someone connected with Pritchart, but none of the listings rang any bells in her mind. The wind kicked up, hot as a blast furnace, pushing scraps of paper and dry leaves down the street. A mottled gray cat slipped from a doorway to the shade beneath a sun-baked Chevrolet that looked as if it had been parked in that same spot for the last twenty years.

Yep. The lazy pace of Bad Luck was a far cry from the bustle of Seattle, where pedestrians, bikes, cars, trucks and buses clogged the steep streets leading to the waterfront. Seagulls wheeled and cried over crowds of tourists, harbor seals threatened the salmon runs and huge ferries chugged through the choppy gray waters of Puget Sound as sailboats, their sails filled with a rough, northern wind, skimmed across the surface. That city was alive, filled with a raw, vibrant energy drawn from an eclectic blend of citizens who inhabited, worked or visited that Northwest town where skyscrapers clustered near the shoreline as they knifed toward the sky. The air there was fresh, smelling of the brine of the ocean, the streets often rain-washed, pedestrians huddled in raincoats and parkas as they walked briskly, heads bent against the brace of the wind, in stark contrast to the slow tempo of summer in Bad Luck.

As she stepped out of the phone booth and walked to the pharmacy, she wiped the sweat from her forehead with her fingers and sensed eyes watching her. She looked down the length of the street to a far corner, where a battered pickup was parked and a man tossed a bag of grain into the bed. But his eyes, hidden by sunglasses, were focused directly on her.

She'd recognize him anywhere.

Her breath was lost for a second, stopping as memories, some bitter, some sweet, seared through her brain like flashes of lightning. Nevada Smith. He didn't so much as smile, just started walking her way in that same easy, athletic gait that was so deceptively quick. In worn, sun-faded Levi's, dusty boots, a frayed, once-dark green T-shirt, he didn't stop until he was standing in the shade thrown from the pharmacy, just inches from her. Sweat dampened his hair.

"Shelby Cole." Distaste laced his voice. "Well, well," he drawled, giving her a slow once-over. "I heard a rumor you were comin' back here."

"Did you?" Why was her heart pumping so wildly? What they'd

once shared was over. A long time ago. And that was the way she intended to keep it. This rugged cowboy was a stranger to her.

"Bad news travels fast in Bad Luck." He rested a lean, jean-clad hip against the hitching post.

"Bad news travels fast anywhere."

"S'pose so." Behind his lenses he surveyed her. His chin was still strong, blackened by the stubble of a few days' growth of beard, his arms muscular, covered with bronzed skin, his attitude still irreverently sarcastic. "What brings you back to Bad Luck?"

She'd actually considered confronting him. After all, he had the same right to know that she did. Somewhere he had a daughter, one he'd never known existed, a nine-year-old he hadn't had the chance to love or reject. At least she'd convinced herself over the years that the child was his. There was a slim chance . . . Her stomach roiled at the horrid thought, the unthinkable possibility.

A minivan cruised past, windows open, a frustrated mother yelling at her children, and farther up the street a crow with shiny black wings was nervously strutting along the gutter, looking for a morsel.

He was still waiting. Insolently. She cleared her throat. "I came back for a couple of reasons," she admitted, squinting up at him and deciding it was now or never. "One involves you. When you've got a minute, we should talk."

"That all it'll take? A minute?" He regarded her through those damned glasses and she wanted to rip them from his face.

"Ten . . . twenty at the most."

"How about now?"

Her throat closed for a second. So many nights she'd wondered if she'd ever approach him, tell him the secret she'd buried in her heart for nearly ten years. She'd never come up with a viable answer. Until now. Probably because she had no choice. Well, in for a penny, in for a pound. Better to get this off her chest and let the chips fall where they may. "Okay. Yeah, why not now?" she said, then glanced down the hot asphalt street.

"I'll buy you a drink. You're legal now, right?"

"Well past," she said.

Hitching his chin toward the Last Stand Saloon, he started walking and Shelby screwed up all her courage to tell him the truth. He held the door open for her; it creaked on ancient hinges and she walked into a dark, tomblike room where the exposed crossbeams were black from years of cigarette smoke, and the antiquated air-conditioning system hummed and wheezed noisily as it fought a losing battle with the heat. Overhead a few lazy paddle fans pushed the thick, warm air around while tinny music flowing from hidden speakers vied with the distinctive click of pool balls in the back corner. Ice cubes rattled in glasses, and the stale odor of booze filled Shelby's nostrils. As she passed the length of the bar, she felt more than one set of interested eyes follow her to a back booth.

"Beer?" Nevada asked as she sat.

"Fine." It didn't matter. As she dropped her sunglasses into a side pocket of her purse, he walked back to the bar and motioned with two fingers to the bartender, a thin, brittle-looking woman with fried blond hair, exaggerated eyebrows and faded lipstick.

"Two, Lucy."

"You got it."

He slid onto the bench across from her and tossed his sunglasses onto the table. In the dim light she noticed that his eyes were slightly different, one pupil larger than the other—the result, she remembered, of his run-in with Ross McCallum a long time ago. "Shoot," he said. "What is it, Shelby? What's suddenly so important that you high-tailed it back here?"

Anxiously she glanced over her shoulder and told herself that she would have to face this day sooner or later. It was best to get it over with. "There's something I should have told you a long time ago," she admitted and saw the cords in the back of his neck tense. "Something important."

"What?"

Lucy came, dropped a couple of paper coasters decorated with a map of Texas on their table, then placed two long-necked bottles of beer and a couple of glasses in front of them. As an afterthought, she reached across the bar and slid a small basket of peanuts in shells across the battle-worn tabletop. It stopped a hairbreadth from the napkin holder. "Anythin' else?" she asked.

"Don't think so," Nevada said.

"Y'all let me know if ya change yer minds."

"Will do." Nevada poured his glass as she sauntered off and his eyes found Shelby's. "Go on."

She felt her spine stiffen and she kept her voice as low as possible. "You and I. We...we had a baby," she admitted.

He was reaching for a peanut, but his hand stopped in midair. Every muscle in his body froze. His eyes narrowed on her with the same intensity as if he was sighting through his rifle. "What?" he demanded, his voice harsh.

"It's true." *Oh, God.* "A...a girl."

For a second there was silence. Deafening, condemning silence. His eyes sought hers, looking for a hint of a lie.

"And you didn't tell me?" he finally whispered, the skin over his face stretched taut. Thunderclouds gathered behind his eyes.

"No."

"Where is she?" His lips barely moved.

"I don't know."

"You don't know?" The peanut and his drink were both forgotten. He looked as if he were about to climb over the table and shake her. "What do you mean?"

"I...I thought she was born dead," she stammered, trying to stay calm.

"What? You *thought?* Weren't you there?" he demanded, stunned, silently accusing her of lying through her teeth.

Oh, it all sounded so feeble now and inside she felt the crushing weight of her pain. "That's what I was told by everyone, but now... now I think I was lied to, and that she's alive, but I don't know where. She was probably adopted through the black market."

"Wait a minute!" One of his hands shot up, palm out, silencing her. He glanced toward the bar, and Shelby realized that Lucy, obviously eavesdropping, was mopping the long, glossy surface of the bar and had inched closer.

With a silent warning Shelby didn't mistake, Nevada reached into his pocket, found his wallet and threw a couple of bills onto the table. "Come on," he ordered, half dragging her from the booth and sweeping up his sunglasses. "Keep the change," he shot at Lucy while propelling Shelby toward a narrow back hallway wedged between the restrooms and the kitchen. He shouldered the door open.

The heat was a hellish blast; the sunlight blinding. Flies and bees swarmed around a Dumpster pushed against the back of the building. A parade of slow-moving cars and trucks rolled along the alley.

Strong, determined fingers surrounded the crook of Shelby's elbow as he propelled her across a pockmarked asphalt parking lot.

"Where are we going?" She yanked hard on her arm, but his grip only tightened.

"To my place."

"And where's that?"

She realized that he was shepherding her toward his truck. "Outside of town a few miles."

"No way."

"You'd rather talk here?" he asked, stopping short on the sidewalk where two kids rode their bikes past a row of parking meters and half-a-dozen cars and trucks were pulling away from or easing up to the curbs. Several curious glances were cast in their direction.

One man wearing aviator sunglasses and a Dallas Cowboys baseball cap pulled low over his eyes stared with undisguised interest from the open window of his flatbed truck.

Shelby felt suddenly as out-of-place as she looked.

"People do recognize you, you know," Nevada warned.

"Oh, I know." She hesitated only a second. "Let me take my car, okay?"

He dropped her elbow. "Follow me."

She didn't need any further incentive. As the guy in the flatbed shot a stream of tobacco juice onto the pavement, Shelby hurried to the rented Caddy and unlocked the door. The interior was blistering. Cranking the air-conditioning to high, she rolled down her window, then pulled a U-turn. As Nevada's old truck eased away from the curb, she tucked in behind him.

Right on his tail and swearing under her breath, she donned her sunglasses again. *This is insane,* she told herself. *What do you think you're doing, going to Nevada's place, for crying out loud?* Teeth clenched, she followed him through town and west into the open hill country, where the air-conditioning finally kicked in.

The surrounding ranch land was guarded by barbed wire, and sumac trees vied with the live oaks. Herds of goats, sheep and cattle roamed the dry, dusty acres grazing on sparse grass and weeds.

Miles flew by. Past a dry gulch where there had once been a stream, Nevada turned his pickup into a thicket of live oaks. Down a lane of gravel and potholes she followed his truck to the heart of his ranch.

The Caddy bounced over weeds that grew between the twin ruts and scraped the underside of her car.

"Great," Shelby muttered under her breath, her hands clenched over the wheel.

*So this was where Nevada had ended up.* A scrap of a ranch with a cabin that defied the definition of rustic and a few hundred fenced, dry acres. A smattering of longhorns ambled through the fields and a few horses sporting dusty hides tried to graze while their tails switched at the ever-present flies.

Not exactly heaven on earth.

She ground the Cadillac to a stop by a small pump house and rammed it into park. While the dust from her car was still settling and before her confidence could flag, she dragged her briefcase with her and climbed out of the Caddy.

Nevada was waiting for her.

So was the dog. He started barking his fool head off.

Nevada leveled his shaded eyes in the animal's direction.

"Crockett, hush! It's all right." The mutt of a dog stood, legs apart, the hairs at the scruff of his neck bristling, his teeth flashing as he growled low in the back of his throat. "Enough!" The snarling abated, but dark, suspicious eyes didn't leave Shelby. Every muscle beneath his rough black-and-white coat was still stiff and taut, ready should he be given the command to spring. "I mean it," Nevada warned, then reached down and scratched the dog behind his ears. "Come on in," he said, opening a screen door. The mesh had been patched and the paint was beginning to peel.

Shelby walked into a house that wasn't any cooler than outside. The furniture was worn and tossed haphazardly around a rag rug that covered a linoleum floor. Nothing matched. Everything was secondhand. If Nevada Smith had a dime to his name, it wasn't invested in creature comforts. A few magazines were strewn across a coffee table that had seen better days but didn't have enough class to be called retro.

He walked her past a postage stamp of a kitchen and through a back door. The porch was shaded, enclosed with screens and gratefully cooler by at least ten degrees. A faded Burma-Shave sign that had to be nearly a century old was tacked to the siding on one side of the door, and next to it a thermometer, starting to rust, registered a sweltering ninety-three degrees. "Sit," he suggested, and she slid into a plastic chair near a small table. "Iced tea?"

"You got?" She was surprised. She really didn't want any bit of hospitality from him, but her throat was parched and she was as nervous as a bumblebee landing on a Venus flytrap.

"I can make it. Instant."

"Fine."

He disappeared inside and Shelby had a chance to scan the backyard, where scattered patches of dry grass surrounded a horseshoe pit and a stone barbecue that was beginning to crumble. A clothesline stretched from a corner of the house to a pole in the yard. Beyond the fence a couple of horses, coats gleaming in the sun, were drinking from a cement watering trough. The screen door creaked, the old dog thumped his tail and Nevada emerged from the kitchen. He carried two mismatched glasses filled with ice and a cloudy amber liquid that she doubted most people would consider any relation to tea.

He handed her a glass. "Now, you were telling me about your baby." Expression unforgiving, he settled into a chair and rested the worn heel of his boot on the top of a barrel near the door. "*Our* daughter."

Shelby's shoulders stiffened a fraction. She wasn't going to be intimidated and plowed on. "That's right, Nevada. As I said, I thought she was dead."

"Weren't you there—didn't you see her delivered?"

"I . . . I was medicated."

"Hell." He tossed her a look that said volumes, then rotated his wrist quickly, indicating that she should continue.

Shelby cleared her throat. "I have copies of a birth certificate and a death certificate."

"Who gave 'em to you?"

"I got both signed by Doc Pritchart at the hospital."

"The guy's a crook."

"The guy's missing," she replied, then took a sip from her tea.

Condensation dripped down the sides of the glass. "I've searched the Internet, looked everywhere I think he might be, and can't find a trace of him."

"He left town not long after you did."

"Figures." Fishing in her briefcase, she found the manila packet that had changed her life. "Take a look at these," she said, handing him the file and wondering why she was making the mistake of letting him look over the documents, letter and picture of Elizabeth Jasmine Cole, the name she'd given her daughter.

"You never saw the baby?" His voice held no inflection, but a muscle worked near the corner of his jaw.

"Never."

"Why not?"

"I told you. I was drugged, not conscious when the baby arrived." Tears of outrage stung the back of her eyelids, but she refused to break down. She didn't have time for self-pity. Not now.

His eyes narrowed. "You're saying that there was some kind of conspiracy against you, that—what? Doc Pritchart slipped something into your IV?"

"No...I don't think so. I mean..." She didn't want to go into the details and slid her jaw to one side. "I was stupid, all right? I went horseback riding in my eighth month, took a spill and the baby decided to come early." She looked away to the haze gathering over the low hills and a solitary hawk circling over a cropping of mesquite. No reason to explain about the pain, the fear, the river of blood that had scared her to death. He didn't need to know about the ambulance ride that her father hushed up or the fact that Doc Pritchart had smelled of alcohol, or the simple truth that for ten years she'd felt as guilty as sin for the death of her child.

"When I woke up, everyone told me that the baby was dead, and my father, who was still my legal guardian as I was underage, had ordered the autopsy and cremation."

"And you didn't question it?"

"I was seventeen." Turning, she pinned him in her furious glare. "I didn't think he'd lie."

"That was your first mistake."

"Not my first." Frost chilled each one of her words, and she noticed the muscles at the base of his neck constrict. "I seem to have made more than my share back then."

"Didn't we all?"

Her heart twisted, but she hid it. She'd come to tell him the truth and having done that, there wasn't a lot more to say.

He studied the glossy picture in his hands as if looking for some kind of evidence that the child was his. "Have you talked to the Judge?"

"You bet."

"And?"

"He denies it all."

"But you don't believe him."

"Not for a second."

"You're learning."

"Let's hope so." She finished her drink in one swallow and set her empty glass on the table. "I've grown up a lot since this all happened." Standing, she reached for the snapshot and papers.

"Who sent these to you?" He took one last look at the smiling girl in the photograph, then slid the photograph and other papers into the envelope.

"That's why I'm here. To find out."

Eyebrows coming together thoughtfully, he flipped the packet over and eyed the postmark. "San Antonio."

"Yep. Not far from here."

He slapped the envelope into her waiting palm.

"So I can't help but wonder if she's around Bad Luck...if by any chance Elizabeth grew up here or in the next town, or on some ranch in the country, or if the postmark was a deliberate red herring meant to bring me back here when really she's in California or Mexico or Quebec or God only knows where...." The painful old lump filled her throat again, the same thickness she'd felt throughout the years when she'd thought of the daughter she'd lost. But falling apart now would solve nothing. She slipped the envelope into a side pocket of her briefcase.

"You gonna talk to the police?" He stared up at her from his insolent position in the chair, but, she guessed, despite his outwardly calm demeanor, he was turning every piece of this new information over in his mind.

"The police? I don't know," she admitted. "I just received the envelope yesterday. Who would I contact? The San Antonio police? The Sheriff's Department? The Rangers?" Her headache throbbed as she thought about it. "No... I think I'll handle this on my own right now. I don't want the press involved until I do some checking on my own. I only told you because I ran into you."

"Surprised you did."

"Why?"

One arrogant eyebrow raised. "I really didn't think you had the guts."

"Then you don't know me very well, do you?"

Crossing his arms over his chest, he leaned his chair back against the weathered siding beneath the porch light and gave her the slow once-over. Down. Up. His gaze finally ended up where it had begun, at her eyes. "I know you well enough."

"Did, Smith. Did. I was just a kid then."

"A pretty nice kid, if I remember right."

"I was certainly naive," she said, refusing to be seduced by his words, "and probably stupid."

He stood and rubbed the stubble of his chin. "You didn't waste much time gettin' here."

"Nine years. Long enough." She picked up her briefcase as if to leave.

"You stayin' with your pa?"

She hesitated. "Don't know."

"Call me when you make a decision."

Her spine stiffened and she glared at him through her dark lenses. "Why?"

"I'd like to keep in touch."

"I don't think that would be such a hot idea. Really."

"Well, I don't see how it can be avoided."

"The town isn't that small."

"That's not what I'm talking about and you know it. You just breezed into Bad Luck and dropped a bomb at my feet—told me I might have a kid somewhere. If that's true—"

"It is," she said vehemently, feeling her cheeks burn.

"If that's true, then I'd say I have a stake in it." Steely eyes assessed her. "I'll want to meet my daughter."

"I've got to find her first."

"Correction: we've got to find her."

"But—"

"And we will." He said it so matter-of-factly. "I want copies of everything you've got."

A drop of dread slid down her spine. She didn't want to get caught up in the trap that was Nevada Smith again. No way. No how. The man was a loser—still sexy, she'd grant him that, but no one she wanted to deal with. And yet he seemed as immovable as granite, standing in front of her, all male, muscle and determination. "I'll see what I can do."

"No, Shelby. You'll do it."

Her back teeth clenched. The man's gall was unbelievable. But then, it always had been. "Let's get one thing straight, Nevada. You can't order me around."

One side of his mouth lifted—as if he enjoyed the challenge. "Wouldn't dream of it," he drawled. "Could I have copies of everything." A pause. "*Please?*"

Blatantly mocking her, he smiled with that thousand-watt Texas grin she'd fallen victim to so many years before. Pinpoints of amusement suddenly lighted his eyes.

"I'll think about it."

"Do."

She reached for the door handle and hesitated. There was business between them yet undiscussed. Cringing inwardly, she said, "The Judge said something about Ross McCallum getting out of prison soon."

"Real soon." Nevada's nostrils flared slightly. "Seems as if ol' Caleb Swaggert is recantin' his testimony and claims Ross didn't kill Ramón Estevan after all."

"So who did?"

"That, Shelby-girl, is the million-dollar question."

"One of them."

"Right. Here's one that's bothering me: Why is it, on the very week McCallum is to be released, you get all this information about a child you thought was dead?"

"I don't know," she admitted.

"Maybe we should find out."

*"We?"* She was instantly wary. There it was again. That word binding her to him.

"Oh, yeah." He placed one arm on the door, holding it closed and cutting off all chance of her leaving. Close enough that she could smell him—mingled scents of sweat and soap and dust—he leaned even nearer. Her heart pumped stupidly and she noticed the few dark hairs on the backs of his hands and the irregular shape of the pupil of his bad eye. His breath was warm and featherlight. Beads of sweat ran down her back. Coming here, being alone with him, had been a mistake. A huge mistake. She swallowed hard and tried not to stare at his lips as he continued, "If the girl in the picture is my daughter, you damned well know that I'm gonna be involved."

"You don't have to—"

"I know I don't *have* to do anything. It's not about obligation, Shelby," he said firmly, his gaze locking fast with hers. "It's about blood."

# Chapter 3

Shep Marson parked the cruiser in the shade of a solitary live oak and mopped the sweat from his brow. The little house he'd called home for the past ten years—a three-bedroom ranch with one bath—appeared shabby in the sun's unforgiving rays. Light green paint peeled near the front door, an old, unused television antenna listed to one side and the shingles on the roof had been patched more than once. But there wasn't a lot of extra money these days, not when there were six mouths to feed. And that wasn't the worst of it. He could stretch his salary to cover expenses—after all, he'd bought his house on the G.I. bill—but there were other secrets that seduced the cash from his pockets.

He felt like a damned fool—hell, he was one, but maybe he'd find a way out of this trap. He had to. Before he bled to death. At one point, he'd hoped his wife's parents would bail them out, but then the old man had lost most of his money when the cattle market collapsed.

Scratching his neck, Shep walked around the house to the backyard, where Skip, his hunting dog, lying in the shade, barked like crazy.

"Hush!" Shep yelled, then noticed a neighbor's calico cat slink under the porch. He yanked the knot in his tie and loosened the top two buttons of his shirt.

The scents of cinnamon and nutmeg greeted him as Shep hung his hat on a peg near the back door and was about to step into the kitchen.

"Boots on the back porch! Shep, you hear me?" Peggy Sue yelled from somewhere near the living room over the din of the television and the squabble of the kids. Two of them ran toward him, their bare feet slapping the worn linoleum. "Daddy, Daddy!" Candice yelled, her blond pigtails bouncing over her ears, her younger brother right on her tail.

"Hey there, little missy," he said, scooping up the six-year-old as Donny pointed a water pistol at her and squeezed the trigger. A squirt of tepid water stained the front of Shep's uniform. "None of that in the house," Shep reprimanded him sharply.

His wife, Peggy Sue, wearing faded jeans, a checkered blouse tied under her breasts and a sorry expression marring what had once been a fresh and beautiful face, appeared from the hallway. Her hair was scraped back, showing off cheekbones that other women had said they'd "die for." A few freckles still bridged her pert nose, the tiny spots he'd once thought were so damned cute.

"What did I say about yer boots?" she asked, walking to the oven and blowing her bangs out of her eyes. A ponytail swung behind her head, and the first few strands of gray were visible in her brown curls as she leaned over and opened the oven door. Her butt filled out her jeans more than it used to, and Shep hated the thought that his wife, Peggy Sue Collins Marson, once the premiere baton twirler in the county and the cutest piece of tail he'd ever had in the backseat of his old Ford wagon, was beginning to appear shopworn.

Shep set Candice on the floor and wrestled Donny's water pistol from him, then nudged off one boot with the toe of the other. "Where're Timmy and Robby?"

Using two frayed oven mitts, Peggy Sue pulled out a bubbling peach pie and set it gingerly on the top of the stove. "Timmy's fillin' out applications over at Al's Grocery. Then he was going to see if they're hiring at Cole's mill, I think." She picked off the tinfoil that rimmed the pie plate. "And Robby, he mumbled somethin' about goin' swimmin' with Billie Ray and Pete Dauber."

"I don't like him hangin' out with the Dauber boys. They're always into trouble." He reached into the refrigerator and found a chilled can of Pabst Blue Ribbon. "Prob'ly out smokin'—"

"Ah, ah, ah," Peggy Sue cautioned, throwing a warning glance over her shoulder, then looking pointedly at the younger kids. "We'll talk about this later."

"He should be tryin' to find him a summer job."

"He bucked hay last month."

"And he could be doin' it still if he hadn't messed up with old man Kramer." His bad mood worsening, Shep popped the top of his sixteen-ouncer and smiled as he heard that soft, familiar hiss.

"Water under the bridge."

"I wants pie!" Donny announced.

"After dinner. Now you run along, pick up them Legos and you, Candice, you help him." To her husband she added, "Why don't you fill up the wadin' pool for 'em?"

"In a minute." He just wanted to settle into his recliner and watch the news, but the look she sent him would have skewered an angry rattler and he didn't want to get into an argument, not now. He liked to pick his fights with her later at night and then spend some hours making up in the sack.

When she wanted to be, Peggy Sue could be a wildcat in bed, the best damned fuck in the county. And she was his wife. For whatever reason he felt a sense of pride knowing that she was as horny as a wild mare in season, bucking and screaming on a Saturday night, only to rise early Sunday morning, get the kids cleaned up for Sunday school and lead the church choir with all the piety of an angel. He gave her a playful slap on the rump as he passed, and she turned on him. "Stop that and go fill the wadin' pool. Now." Shaking her head, she reached into a cupboard.

"I will," he promised and killed the Pabst, then tried to wrap his arms around her waist and cop a quick feel of her breasts. He nuzzled the back of her neck and pressed his cock, always at the ready, into that nice little crease in the backside of her jeans.

"Stop it, Shep! I don't have any time for this!" She wheeled to face him. Her mouth, where only traces of lipstick remained, was set, her jaw hard.

"All right, all right. Hell, you'd think a woman would like a little attention now and again."

She muttered something under her breath as he found his old pair of sneakers. *Neanderthal?* Is that what she'd said? Not bothering with the laces, he walked outside and frowned.

Skip put up a ruckus.

"Shut up!" Shep growled. Then, feeling a twinge of conscience as the retriever was just hoping for some sign of attention, Shep sighed and walked down the dusty path the dog had worn in the lawn to pat his head. "We'll go out huntin', you and I. Soon, ol' boy," he promised, then ambled to the hose bib, where wasps were hovering over a circle of mud from the leak in the faucet he'd planned to fix for weeks. Swatting away the pests, he pulled out the hose and walked to the pool. Week-old water stagnated, and blades of grass, weeds and dead bugs had collected on the surface. He dumped the old water, filled the pool and figured he'd earned his spot in the recliner for the night.

Donny and Candice clamored down the back porch and squealing in delight or anger, splashed into the clear water. Candice was a beauty—would look just like her ma, he suspected—but Donny, he was a skinny kid with a nose that was forever running and big, watery eyes. Truth to tell, Shep wasn't that fond of his youngest son and he felt guilty about it, but there it was. Donny was a whiner, a complainer, and Peggy Sue babied him, wouldn't ever let Shep put a strap to the boy's behind when he needed it.

He twisted off the faucet and straightened, then looked past the side yard to the street where an aging El Camino glided past. Behind the wheel, her black hair blowing in the breeze, a cigarette wedged between moist-looking red lips, was Vianca Estevan, daughter of the man everyone assumed Ross McCallum had put into an early grave. Oversized sunglasses hid eyes that Shep knew glowed like dark coals. In one short glance he caught a glimpse of the tops of her breasts, visible over the low-cut scoop of a white T-shirt.

As he turned back to the house, his damned cock tightened all over again and he clenched his jaw tight.

Inside, Peggy Sue was chopping onions while bacon sizzled in a skillet on the stove. Grease, crackling and popping, spattered over the edges of the pan.

"Smells good."

She didn't respond. Lately she'd been testy, he thought, as he reached into the fridge for another beer. She shot him a glance, her lips tightened, but she didn't nag. She knew better. He watched her work and got hard. How long had it been since they'd gone at it? A week? Two? It had been a while. He'd tried to cuddle up to her each night and she'd told him she wasn't in the mood, then rolled over in their double bed with the sagging mattress and offered him no more flesh than a severely cold shoulder.

"You runnin' for sheriff?" she finally asked, tossing a handful of chopped onions into the skillet. They sizzled instantly in the hot grease.

"Yep."

"You filed?"

"Nope."

"Don't you think you ought to?"

"I will."

"What's holdin' you up?" She didn't so much as glance at him as she scraped up the remains of the onions with her knife, cleaning off the scarred chopping block.

"Work." He wouldn't go into it now. She really didn't want to know.

"It's because Ross McCallum's gettin' out, ain't it?" she asked, and he was surprised she understood. "My guess is that the D.A. wants to reopen the case because he's gettin' some pressure from the townsfolk and them Chicanos or Latinos or whatever they call themselves now."

"That's about the size of it." Leaning a shoulder on a cupboard, he sized her up. She never ceased to amaze him. Sometimes she was dumb as a stone, other times he noticed a hint of brains she'd spent over thirty years hiding. "I already had myself a talk with Smith."

"Nevada?" Her shoulders stiffened just a mite, but he caught it. She'd always had a thing for the half-breed. Hell, half the women in the county did.

Shep had never understood it, why seemingly sane women hungered after a no-account, worthless rancher with a black reputation, who, unless Shep missed his guess, knew a helluva lot more about the Estevan murder than he'd ever let on.

"Yep. Smith's the one who put McCallum behind bars, back before he was thrown off the force."

"Railroaded, you mean."

"He had his chance to clear his name. Didn't take it. Some people think he knows more about Ramón Estevan's death than he's sayin'."

"Do they?"

"I thought maybe I'd just lean on him a bit and see if he'd break."

"He won't."

She was so damned certain of it. Using the knife, she mixed up the ingredients in her fry pan.

"Shelby Cole's back."

This time she turned to face him, and her face had gone as white as old Etta Parsons's vintage Mercedes. "You don't say." The onions had turned opaque, the bacon sizzling.

"Yep. Saw her in town today, and boy, howdy, who's the first person she ran into?" He saw the understanding in her eyes. "That's right. Nevada Smith himself. Had themselves a little talk over at the Last Stand."

"Who told you this?"

"Lucy. But half-a-dozen folks saw 'em walk in together, then hustle out the back door before they even had a sip. The way I heard it, Badger Collins drank both beers before Lucy could snatch 'em up." He chuckled to himself, but Peggy Sue didn't even smile.

"Shit." She stopped her work, fastened him in eyes that seemed twice her age.

"Somethin' buggin' you?"

"You might say that." Her shoulders rose and fell.

"What?"

"I'm pregnant again, Shep." She blinked hard and sniffed.

"Oh, hell." His world started to collapse. How could he feed one more mouth? Money was stretched too tight as it was. He finished his beer, tossed the empty into a trash can and walked toward her, but she cringed and held the knife between them. The blade flashed in the dimming light.

"Don't you come near me, y'hear."

"But—"

"I mean it. You go to the clinic and make an appointment to git yourself fixed and don't you even think about touching me again or

I'll take care of it myself." She wasn't kidding. "You and me both know we can't afford another kid."

"We don't have to have it," he said slowly.

"Oh, yes we do. You know how I feel about that."

Of course he did. They'd had the discussion before Candice and Donny were born. She hadn't budged. He'd promised to get a vasectomy. Twice. It would never happen. No surgeon was gonna get a knife anywhere near his balls. Hell, he could end up a soprano in the church choir that Peggy Sue was so proud of.

"We'll find a way."

"You mean you will." She twitched her wrist, and the knife wiggled near his chest. "Git fixed, Shep, and get that sheriff's job, 'cause I'm tired of just scrapin' by. Believe me, I ain't sleepin' with you 'til you do."

"Now, honey—"

"Don't." Her lips curled angrily. "Don't you even think about touchin' me. Got it? I ain't changin' my mind. Not ever, so unless you want to spend the rest of your days horny as Judge Cole's prize bull, you'll go make yerself a damned appointment."

At that moment a wail loud enough to wake the dead in the next county ripped through the house, and Candice, red-faced and screaming to high heaven, ran in with Donny right behind her. "She got stunged," he said, and Shep saw the two bright red circles that were rising on his daughter's forearm. Candice howled and cried. Donny with his watery eyes melted into a corner. Peggy Sue picked up her daughter and glared wearily at her husband. "Do it, Shep," she mouthed as the bacon sizzled and burned, smoking up a house already dark with silent accusations and dying dreams.

What in the name of Jesus was he getting himself into? Nevada carried his sack of feed to the barn and threw it onto the floor. It landed with a thud. A cloud of dust rose and a rustle in the straw indicated that a denizen of the local mouse population was hurrying into a hidden crevice.

He whistled to the horses, slit the burlap sack with his jackknife and, using an old Folgers coffee can, measured a ration of oats into each stall. Two mares appeared—his best, the only two worth any real money. Ears upright, nostrils quivering, bright eyes expectant, they trotted into the dimly lit interior. Outside, he heard an expectant nicker and the thunder of anxious hooves as the rest of the herd made its way inside.

Crockett sniffed at the corners of the old corncrib and Nevada felt tense. Anxious. Restless. The way he used to feel whenever Shelby Cole was within driving distance. His jaw slid to the side as he thought of how many moonlit nights he'd coasted his old truck down the lane to the Judge's house, his heart thudding, his hands sweaty on the steering wheel, his cock hard against the fly of his jeans as he'd thought about Shelby.

Now his throat tightened at the memory of making love to her.

Her breasts had been small, rosy-tipped and white in the moonglow, the thatch of curling hair at the juncture of her tanned legs a soft red color. God, he'd wanted her, though he'd tried to deny it.

"Shit." He was hard now, just thinking of their lovemaking late at night, before the storm, before all hell had broken loose.

He finished with the feed, checked the water in the troughs and, with Crockett ambling behind, walked back into the house. He couldn't think of Shelby now, not that way. There was too much to do. Peeling off his clothes, he took a cold shower, if that was what you'd call the thin trickle of water that drizzled from the showerhead. This time of year the well wasn't all that reliable, and he figured he'd have to drill another one.

In twenty minutes he'd toweled off, slapped on some deodorant and cologne, thrown on a clean shirt and pair of jeans and was striding to his pickup. The memory of Shelby Cole still lingered, like the scent of her perfume still hanging in the air of the cabin, but he determined that he wouldn't dwell on her, not now. He had serious business to deal with. Whether she liked it or not, he was going to do his own digging into the birth of her daughter—find out if the girl was alive and if she was his. He opened the door of his truck and climbed into the sun-baked interior. Then there was that business with Ross McCallum. Nevada couldn't let that lie.

It just didn't smell right.

"Don't be a fool," Shelby told herself as her rental car idled in the parking lot of the Well Come Inn. The cinder-block building with its broken neon sign advertising vacancy and color TV didn't deter her, nor did the fact that the building had once been condemned, but the simple truth of the matter was that if she really wanted to find out the truth, she would be more likely to ferret it out from her father if she lived with him for the next week or so.

"Damn, damn and double damn," she muttered, backing up and spinning the steering wheel. She drove away from the single-storied building as the sun was beginning to settle behind the western hills. It was still as hot as Hades, but soon, with the coming of dusk, the temperature would drop, the wind would kick up and the sweet lullaby of insects would sing through the night. Somehow that thought was calming, though why she didn't understand.

She drove by rote, as she had hundreds of times before, and reminded herself that eating crow wasn't the worst meal she'd ever consumed—there was that serving of humble pie still out there, waiting for her.

The Caddy rolled to a stop near the brick garage and she climbed out in the shade of the live oaks that guarded the house. The garage door was open and her father's Mercedes was missing. She wouldn't have to deal with him for a while.

Hauling her laptop in its case, her purse and a single bag, she climbed the front steps and didn't bother with the bell. As she entered, she heard Lydia singing softly in Spanish. An unwanted sense of homecoming enveloped Shelby, and she told herself she was being foolish. This house, cold as it was, had never really been her home—not since her mother had decided she could no longer live with the tyrant who had been Jerome Cole.

*"Niña?* Is that you?" the older woman called from the back of the house.

"Yeah, Lydia, I came back. The prodigal daughter."

"I knew it." Lydia emerged from the wing housing the kitchen. Her smile was wide, her dark eyes bright.

"Okay, okay, you won. I admit it," Shelby said, shaking her head. "I should know better than to argue with you."

"This is true. Now, come on in. The Judge, he will be back in an hour or so and you will have dinner."

"Wonderful," Shelby said, unable to hide her sarcasm.

"It is. *Fabuloso!* Now, go! Freshen up. I have work to do." With a wink, Lydia shooed her toward the back stairs and swatted at her rear.

As Shelby climbed to the second floor, she remembered the nights she'd left the French doors unlatched and waited on her bed, her ears straining to hear the sound of a footstep on these worn steps, hoping Nevada would sneak into the house and along this very hallway, where pictures of generations of Coles stared out of gilded frames, and freshly cut flowers graced the tables under the windows. It had never happened.

She opened the door to her bedroom, expecting it to smell of dust and disuse, but Lydia had already turned down the bed, polished the rosewood desk, dresser and bed with lemon oil, raised the blinds and cracked open the bay window. A slight breeze, aided by the slowly whirring paddle fan over the bed, sifted past lace curtains. Shelby dropped her bags on the foot of the four-poster and walked to the window seat overlooking the pool. The water shimmered seductively and reflected the last rays of sunlight. As she stared into the aquamarine depths, her mind swam back to the reason she'd returned to Bad Luck, the questions she couldn't yet answer.

Who had sent her the pictures of Elizabeth? she wondered for the millionth time. Who had known the truth and what, exactly, was it? She bit her lip and frowned as the most painful question of all assailed her. What if this all turned out to be a wild-goose chase, a hoax, a cruel practical joke? She had plenty of enemies in this town, people who had envied her privilege and station as she'd grown up. As for her father, the list of people who hated him was endless. On his climb to the bench, Jerome Cole had crushed his share of friends and opponents under his silver-toed boots. Once he'd donned judge's robes, he'd sent hundreds of men and women up the river.

> *Ol' Judge Cole*
> *Was a nasty old soul*
> *And a nasty old soul was he . . .*

The poem made her cringe inwardly, but she refused to let it get to her. Right now all she could think about was finding Elizabeth.

*And what about Nevada?* her mind taunted, but she wouldn't fall victim to those old feelings again. Nevada was a man whom she had to deal with—the father of her child. Nothing more. Until she located her daughter, nothing else mattered.

Nothing.

Caleb Swaggert was nearly asleep when Nevada entered his hospital room. A once robust man, he was now a skeleton of himself, his fleshy face having withered away, his skin pasty, his hair nearly gone. The room was lit by fluorescent lights mounted on either side of his bed, and one dying bouquet of flowers was crammed onto a small table that also held a box of tissues, a Bible and a water glass with a plastic straw. Sterile. Quiet. A room where some people came to heal, others to die.

"Smith," the old man croaked, blinking rapidly.

"Hi, Caleb," Nevada said, noting the IV that stood at Caleb's bedside and the clear fluid dripping into the back of the old man's arm, positioned near a computer screen registering some of Caleb's bodily functions.

"What you want?" Caleb's words weren't clear, either from medication or the fact that his dentures were missing.

"I heard you recanted your testimony." Nevada stood at the foot of the bed, arms folded over his chest, eyes searching for any signs that Caleb was lying.

"Got to do what's right."

"You told me Ross McCallum was at the store when Ramón was killed."

"I said I thought I saw him. I was wrong." Caleb's voice had risen an octave.

"You lied?"

Caleb opened his mouth, shut it again, then pursed his lips together. A proud man at one time, he had trouble admitting that he'd been wrong. "Yep."

"Why?"

" 'Cause you were leanin' on me," he said, looking through the window. "And I was a sinner, but now I've taken Jesus into my heart and—"

"Can it." Nevada didn't make a move toward the bed, but he

was disgusted. "Maybe Preacher Whitaker believes you, but I don't. I know you too well, Swaggert. I saw what you did to your first wife."

"I—I was a sinner, but I've changed, Smith, swear to God—I mean, I've found the Lord."

"Bull."

"It wouldn't hurt you to take Jesus into your heart, Smith. He might just chase all the hatred from that tar-black soul of yours."

"I'll take that under consideration," Nevada said, unable to hide his cynicism.

"You come here to harass me?"

"I just wanted to hear the truth." He scratched his chin thoughtfully. "You know what they say, Caleb, 'the truth will set you free.' "

"Well, that's what I'm doin', ain't it? Finally tellin' the truth. If Ross McCallum was in Estevan's store the night Ramón got himself killed, I didn't see him."

Nevada stepped closer to the bed. "But you lied and helped send him to prison ten years ago. Why?"

A muscle worked at the corner of Caleb's jaw. He blinked rapidly.

"Why?"

The old man's eyes regained their fervor, and his lips pulled back into an ugly snarl. "Because he's a mean sum-bitch, and even if he didn't kill Ramón, he needed to be put away."

"So you lied."

"I wouldn't do it today."

Nevada shook his head slowly. "Y'know, Caleb, the only reason a man would lie about something like that and frame someone for a crime he didn't commit would be to save his own sorry neck—"

"I didn't kill the old man and you know it!" Caleb was suddenly agitated, his pasty face showing signs of color.

"—or if they were paid by someone else to lie." He stared straight at the old man. "I've heard some talk around town, Caleb, talk that you're sellin' your story to a reporter of some kind."

Caleb's face fell.

"I was wonderin' if you were gonna tell the reporter some pack of lies just to make some cash."

"You're a sorry bastard," Caleb sputtered.

"No doubt."

"Get out, Smith," the old man hissed. "I'm sick and dyin' and I decided to clear my conscience before I meet my maker. That's all there is to it. Now leave here before I call the nurse and have you thrown out."

There was nothing more to be accomplished. Caleb Swaggert was going to take whatever secrets he had to the grave with him. "If your memory clears up any more, call me."

"Get out."

Nevada walked to the door.

"And Smith?"

He turned and found a sickly smile curving Caleb's thin, dry lips. "May the Lord be with you."

# CHAPTER 4

*Bang!*

The doors of the prison clanged shut.

Ross McCallum was finally a free man.

*About time.*

It had been ten years of his life—a damned decade of this nightmare, time he could never retrieve. One part of him wanted to find the nearest bar and a hot-blooded woman. A fifth of José Cuervo and a cheap motel would round out the night. Another part of him wanted vengeance and wanted it bad. Just as he'd vowed in the courtroom as he was being hauled away to prison.

He drew in a deep breath of fresh air. God, it felt good. Looking over a shoulder, he flipped off the guard in the watchtower and thought *fuck you* to every last sorry-hided inmate, every shit-head of a guard and especially *fuck you* to the bastard of a warden who ruled the place like he was some kind of a goddamned king.

"Stop it," he growled under his breath, then spat hard on the pockmarked concrete of the drive. He was out. That was all that mattered. He'd never go back. He'd promised himself that each and every morning when he woke up and found himself staring at the ceiling and smelling the stench of the place. Nope. He'd die first.

Hauling a grimy duffel bag filled with his meager belongings, he swaggered to the beat-up station wagon that idled in the shade of the tower wall. Behind the wheel, smoking a cigarette and listening to some whiney-ass country song sat the one person on this earth he could count on: Mary Beth Looney, his twice-divorced younger sister. With the fingers of one hand she was tapping out time on the steering wheel, while the other held her cigarette. She wasn't wearing a wedding ring. That was probably good news, considering her taste in men.

"'Bout time," she said through the open window. Her hair was the color of straw and cut in shaggy layers round her face, but it was shiny and soft-looking, no hint of a dark root showing, and she watched him through a fringe of bangs.

"Hey—the government don't move fast. How're ya, Mary Beth?"

"Tired."

"You look good."

A ghost of a smile crossed apricot-tinged lips as she tucked her cigarette into the corner of her mouth. "Wish I could say the same for you."

He threw his duffel bag onto the backseat that was littered with paper wrappers from McDonald's and Taco Bell. A few used packets of hot sauce lay forgotten, the remnants of red goop congealing on the tufted vinyl where half-a-dozen rock-hard French fries were scattered.

"Where're the kids?" he asked, sliding into the passenger seat next to her.

"With their dads."

"Didn't think your exes were around much."

"They're not." She yanked the wagon into gear. "I guess I just got lucky." Smoke escaped from her nostrils as she gunned the accelerator.

In a spray of gravel, they were off.

Ross rolled down his window, felt the air rush through the interior and felt ten years of vengeance burn through his brain. He'd fed his hatred each and every day, vowing retribution, and now his time had come. Names whirled through his head, the names of those he'd get even with. Ruby Dee, Caleb Swaggert, Shelby Cole, the Judge, Nevada Smith. Especially Smith.

Cracking his knuckles, Ross stared through the dusty, bug-spattered windshield and studied the vast Texas countryside with new eyes.

The sumacs and prickly pear he'd once taken for granted seemed to display a newfound beauty. The rolling hills of dry range grass were scaled by sheep and goats he'd once ignored, and the sky— Christ, the sky went on forever. His throat threatened to close and he gritted his back teeth together. No reason to get maudlin and start blubbering like a baby. He was a free man and he'd never live again behind concrete walls topped with barbed wire and guarded by silent, humorless men wearing reflective glasses and toting rifles they itched to use. No, sir.

"Where to?" Mary Beth asked as they sped along the highway and crossed the slow-moving Guadalupe River.

"Bad Luck."

Mary Beth slid him a look from the corner of her eye. "Don't you think you should start over somewhere else?"

"Nope."

"Where you goin' to live?"

"In the folks' place."

She shook her head and her fingers gripped the wheel as if she planned to rip it from the steering column. "Hell, Ross, what's there? Grandpa's old cabin has just about fallen down. What's left is rotten and filled with termites."

"What about the trailer?"

She sighed. "The single-wide's still there, and I kicked out the renters, like you asked, but it's a pigsty, believe me."

"Couldn't be any worse than where I been." But Ross glanced into the backseat. His sister's standards on cleanliness weren't all that high. In fact, if what they said about cleanliness and godliness were true, it seemed Mary Beth might not have much of a chance of gettin' through the Pearly Gates when the Lord called her home. Not that Ross cared much. "Gotta start somewhere," he said as she squashed her smoke in an ashtray already overflowing with lipstick-stained cigarette butts.

"I guess. But there's a lot of bad blood back there." She tossed her hair over her shoulder and pretended that she wasn't watching for a reaction. "Shelby Cole's back in town." Ross couldn't swallow the smile of satisfaction that crept from one side of his mouth to the other. Shelby? In Bad Luck? Well, well, things were looking up. "Is that right? Go figure."

"Don't suppose you had anything to do with it."

"You forget where I've been."

"Well, you'd best stay away from her," she warned, then twisted on the knob of the radio, increasing the volume as a song he'd never heard before, some down-and-out country-and-western lament by a woman with a clear voice, filled the interior. Mary Beth sang along with the lyrics and she wasn't all that bad—a little flat maybe, but Ross didn't care.

But then he didn't care about much. Except getting even.

Leaning back in the seat, Ross lapsed into silence as they flew down the highway, letting memories of faces from the past—especially Shelby Cole's fresh face—surface. Blue, wide-eyed innocence, pert little nose, and a few freckles on a perfect oval of a face. Yep, Shelby was somethin'. He'd have to look her up. They had some unfinished business.

Mary Beth eased up on the accelerator only when they sped through half-a-dozen small towns on their way to Bad Luck. Yep, things were going to be better.

She shook another cigarette from the pack lying on the seat between them and punched in the lighter. He helped himself to one of her Marlboro Lights. "So where're you plannin' to get a job?"

Ross twisted the rearview mirror in his direction and rubbed the stubble on his cheeks. He'd once been a handsome man, but the years behind bars hadn't been kind. Deep grooves etched his forehead and the corners of his eyes. He had a few scars from more than one fistfight, a knife wound in his right thigh and if he moved his right arm just so, he could still feel a knot and tight little pain where Nevada Smith had broken his ribs in their last bout.

The lighter clicked and they each lit up. Smoke laced with nicotine filled his lungs. "Don't suppose you have anything to drink on ya?" he asked. "Hell, it's been a long time since I had a shot of whiskey or tequila or even a damned beer."

"Stay away from liquor, okay?" Mary Beth turned the mirror back so she could look into it. "Keep your nose clean, Ross. I don't intend to make a career out of pickin' you up from jail."

"You won't," he said fervently, feeling himself key up a bit as they crossed the river that was barely more than a creek this time of year, then sped by the cemetery east of town. Headstones, some beginning to crumble, stood like odd-shaped sentinels beneath a few scattered shade trees. Ross wondered how many new souls had been interned since old Ramón Estevan met his maker. He didn't bother to ask.

Bad Luck was just over the next rise.

Taking a final drag on her filter tip, Mary Beth glanced in the rearview mirror. "Oh, shit."

"What?"

"Looks like you already attracted your share of attention. It's the cops."

"Damn it all!" He twisted in the seat and spied a county cruiser, lights flashing, behind them. "I ain't goin' back, Mary Beth. No matter what, I *ain't* goin' back. They'd have to kill me first!" Adrenaline fired his blood. His heart went wild, beating furiously.

"Just hold on!" She steered the wagon over to the shoulder and the cop's car, lights still flashing like the goddamned Fourth of July, followed them.

"What the hell did you do?"

"Nothin', okay? I did nothin' wrong!" she insisted. "Oh, crap, it's Shep Marson."

Ross's stomach turned instantly sour. He glanced through the grimy back window and saw a face that was etched in his memory. Shep's features were grim, shaded by the brim of his hat, and a little jowlier than Ross remembered. "What's he want?"

"We're about to find out." She squashed her cigarette into the tray, fluffed her hair with nervous fingers, then stuck her head out the window and called, "What's up, Shep?"

Ross heard the crunch of boots on gravel. Sweat prickled his scalp and ran down the back of his neck and he wished to God he had a shotgun in the backseat. He'd blow Marson, his badge and his cocky, self-righteous attitude five miles south of hell.

Damn it, no! He couldn't think like that. A dull roar swelled in his brain. His palms began to sweat and itch. *Hold tight. Just play it cool.* Through clenched teeth, he managed to take a drag.

A shadow passed over Mary Beth's face, and Ross trained his eyes on the open driver's-side window. All he saw was the uniform— a torso covered with a tired-looking and stained county-issued shirt.

"Do you know your tags are expired?" Shep asked over the thunder in Ross's ears. The deputy leaned down so that his face was framed by the window, the brim of his hat nearly brushing Mary Beth's cheek.

"No—I mean, I just haven't gotten around to—" Mary Beth shrugged and Ross wanted to strangle her. What was she thinking, picking him up in a car with expired license plates? Shit, was she a moron?

"Well, now, I just thought I'd give you a verbal warnin' this time," Shep said, and he looked past Mary Beth to her passenger. The weight of his gaze behind those damned reflective sunglasses was almost more than Ross could bear. Almost. "Well, look who you've got with you." With a friendly nod, he said, "I'd like to say it's good to see you again, McCallum, but we both know that it'd be a lie."

Ross didn't respond.

"I don't want no trouble from you," Shep said. "This ain't just a warnin' to your sister, you understand." His smile was as tight as his ass. "You. McCallum. You're walkin' a thin line, already, son. This here's my county."

"I remember," Ross ground out.

"Good. That's good. Don't you go forgettin'." Shep tipped the brim of his hat at Ross's sister. "And you, Mary Beth, you take care of them tags."

"I will," she said sweetly as he sauntered back to his cruiser. She slapped the old Ford into drive and waited for a truck filled with Mexicans in the cab and piled high with hay to swoosh past. As she gunned the engine, she grumbled, "It's already startin', Ross." Her face was pale beneath her tan, and her lips drew into a line of disapproval. "Goddamn it, it's already startin'."

*Yep,* he thought, tossing the butt of his cigarette out the window. And he couldn't wait.

Shelby snapped off her laptop computer. Curled into a striped chair that was tucked between the window and the bed in her room, she'd been online for hours, once more searching websites that promised to find missing people, posting inquiries on message boards, wracking her brain in her ongoing efforts to locate Dr. Ned Charles Pritchart. Her back hurt, her neck ached and her head pounded. Frustration was fast becoming her closest companion.

And then there was Nevada. His image kept floating in and out of her mind, bothering her like a pesky insect that wouldn't go away. The worst of it was, she still found him attractive—in an earthy, Texan kind of way. Though she'd told herself time and time again that soon she'd need to settle down, that she wasn't getting any younger, that she needed a rock-steady man who worked nine to five or even longer, a businessman with an easy smile but a hard edge, one who wanted children, a family, a house in the suburbs of Seattle...certainly not some broken-down cowboy who had walked on both sides of the law.

Just because they'd been lovers, had a child...and he was as sexy as all get-out didn't mean... "Stop it," she growled, stretching her legs onto the ottoman. She had work to do. She wasn't about to be distracted. Not by anyone. Including Elizabeth's damnably sexy father.

The trouble was, she was no closer to finding her daughter this afternoon than she had been when she'd first gotten the envelope two days earlier. "Get a grip, it's going to take time," she said to the pale ghost of her reflection in her bedroom window. Yet she couldn't shake the feeling that time was running out. She'd already missed nine years of her daughter's life; how much more could she risk?

She considered hiring an online private investigator, but didn't know which of the dozens listed would be reliable. As for her own efforts, she'd managed to locate a handful of Dr. Pritcharts flung far across the United States—none of whom had turned out to be the Ned Pritchart who had delivered her baby.

He could have hidden himself anywhere. Europe. South America. Or he could be dead.

*Don't think that way.*

She glanced down to the backyard and the shimmering aquamarine water of the pool. Inviting. Cool. She hadn't brought a swimming suit with her, but she could probably scrounge up something she'd left here years ago.

She was on her way to the bureau when she heard her father's car roll into the drive. A glance at her watch told her it was after three. A busy man, the Judge. He'd come in late last night and hadn't bothered to tap on her door as she'd expected, though, tossing and turning, she'd heard him arrive. He was gone again at the crack of dawn.

Shelby had been relieved not to have to deal with him at dinner after all, but she couldn't put it off forever; nor did she want to. She was back in Bad Luck with a purpose, and her father was keeping secrets from her.

Sliding into a pair of sandals, she scooped a rubber band from the bureau, snapped her hair into a haphazard bun and took the back stairs to the kitchen.

*"Niña."* Lydia, determined to fatten her up, had a tray of fruit, cheese and crackers sitting on the center island. "I was just fixing your father a drink." She smiled widely, showing off a bit of gold edging one front tooth. "What would you like?"

"I'll get a glass of iced tea," Shelby said, her sandals slapping as she crossed the terra-cotta tile of the floor to the refrigerator.

"Let me slice you a lemon—"

"Thanks, Lydia, really. I appreciate it. But I can do it myself." Much as she loved the woman who had raised her from the time of her mother's death, Shelby couldn't stomach the thought of Lydia doting on her, as if she were a helpless child—or worse yet, the pampered, princess-daughter of a rich man. She'd been independent too long, lived alone and was used to taking care of herself. Ignoring the wounded look in Lydia's eyes, she tossed a handful of ice cubes into a tall glass, poured tea from a chilled pitcher and sliced her own wedge of lemon before following Lydia onto the back veranda, where her father was already sipping a martini.

"So you decided to stay," he said, obviously pleased, as she took a chair on the opposite side of the glass-topped table and the paddle fans that whirred overhead.

"I thought it would be easier to talk to you." She swirled her drink.

Lydia, grumbling about the gardener, pinched off a couple of wilted petals of the petunias overflowing from the huge pots standing near the back door, then hurried into the kitchen as a timer buzzed loudly.

"I thought you didn't want to talk to me."

"I didn't." She took a sip from her glass. It was lots stronger and clearer than the cloudy liquid Nevada had passed off as tea yesterday. "I changed my mind." She stared at him over the rim of her glass as she took another bracing swallow. Never a shy child, she was nonetheless intimidated by her father. Some things didn't change over the years. "I hope you can help me."

"I'll give it my best shot." Plucking a plastic toothpick from his drink, he sucked off one of the olives.

"Good. Then you need to tell me about Elizabeth." She was calmer this afternoon, though no less determined.

"I don't know anything about your child."

"Don't lie to me, Dad. I'll go to the police."

He chewed on the olive, then swallowed. "With what? A picture of a kid who looks like you? An anonymous note?"

"Yes."

"You'd be opening a can of worms."

"Already opened."

He shook his head from one side to the other. "There will be lots of questions asked. Some of 'em you won't like."

"I'm not worried. Get this, Judge. I'm not a scared, confused little girl of seventeen who was ashamed that she was pregnant and not married. Not anymore."

"This is a small town."

"Amen."

"It's not like the city, where you can hide."

"I'm not hiding, Judge, and I want the truth. You know what happened the night I had the baby. You had to have orchestrated it. No one, including Doc Pritchart or anyone else in the hospital, would have had the guts to pull this off alone. You had to have bribed them or coerced them somehow."

"Bribery and coercion." he said. "Tough accusations."

She wasn't going to be derailed. "Look, either you tell me what you know and we save a whole lotta time, or I keep digging on my own and any skeleton that happens to pop out of the Cole family closet will be out in the world for everyone to see."

"You might think twice about that."

"I have—and three times, and four and probably a hundred."

He bit off another olive. "Heard you were with Nevada Smith yesterday."

"I ran into him on the street."

Graying, bushy eyebrows rose skeptically. "Fancy that, the first person you meet is the one you should avoid."

"The father of my child."

"Maybe."

She felt her skin flush scarlet as she watched butterflies and bees flit from one overflowing pot of flowers to the next.

"There's the rub, Shelby-girl. What if the kid isn't Smith's? As bad as that would be, it could be worse, y'know."

She stood slowly and leaned over the table. She couldn't, wouldn't let her father bully her. "The point is that the child is *mine*. That's really all that matters. That's why I'm back here. Now, you have a choice. Either you want to help me or you don't, but either way I'm going to find my daughter."

"And if you do?" The third olive slid easily into his mouth, and he stared at her with the same determined gaze that he'd leveled at many a recalcitrant witness from his position on the bench. "*If* the girl is alive, *if* she's yours and *if* you find her, what then? Are you going to rip her away from the parents she's known for nine years? Tear her away from a mother, father and siblings, all so *you* can rest easy? Is that what would be best for her?" He washed the olive down with a long sip from his glass and Shelby felt sick inside. "Or is it what's best for you?" The very doubts he'd voiced had plagued her from the minute she'd opened the envelope from San Antonio.

"One step at a time," she said, refusing to melt under his harsh glare. "First I find her."

"You're playin' with fire here, Shelby."

"Well, it never stopped you, did it?" She forced herself to remain cool. "Now, either you help me, or I go at this myself, but believe me, I am going at it." She finished her iced tea and set the glass aside. "Who would send me that picture?"

"Don't know." His eyes didn't leave hers and not one of his graying hairs was out of place. His suit, shirt and string tie looked as fresh and crisp as if he'd just donned them while she was sweating buckets in a T-shirt and shorts. His ivory-handled cane lay across his lap, more an adornment than a crutch.

"Okay, then who adopted my baby?" She wasn't going to leave this alone.

"Still don't know."

"How can you sit there and tell me a bald-faced lie? You *had* to know."

Slowly, his words dropping out of his mouth syllable by syllable, he said, "I don't know what happened to the baby. I didn't ask."

"But you knew she survived."

"Nope. I only knew that she wasn't born dead. Other than that, I didn't see any reason to do anything more."

"She's your granddaughter!" Even though Shelby had expected the truth, it hit her hard.

"And you're my daughter. I've always done what I thought best."

She couldn't believe her ears and then wondered why she was even trying to reason with him. He'd always been a man who played by his own rules, bent the law to serve his own purpose and rationalized his actions. "Oh, God, I can't believe this." She flopped back against the meshed caning of the patio chair. "You're insane."

"Practical."

"Manipulative. Oh, Lord." Grabbing her tumbler, she pressed the sweating glass against her forehead as the ice cubes melted. How could this man, this self-important ogre, be her father?

"What about Smith? Did you tell him about the baby?"

"I had no choice."

"You always have choices."

"Not when someone you trust manipulates you." She dropped the glass onto the table.

The Judge's jaw slackened. A sudden sadness crept into his eyes as he watched the flight of a flock of starlings taking off from a cypress tree on the far side of the pool house. "Oh, Shelby," he sighed, running big-knuckled hands through his hair. The wrinkles lining his brow and etching his mouth deepened and he seemed suddenly an old man. "You have no idea what you've done."

"Oh, yes, I do," she said firmly, refusing to be shaken. "What I've done is the right thing."

"You find out anything today?"

"Not enough. But I will," she promised as she scraped her chair back. And in a sudden inkling of insight, she knew just where to start.

# CHAPTER 5

Nevada notched the ear of the last calf, slapped it hard on its dusty rump and sent it bawling and running toward the herd. Yanking off his gloves, he glared at the setting sun and wondered why he stayed here, barely scraping out a living in a place where even in these politically correct times he'd heard himself referred to as a half-breed.

Not that he cared. It wasn't the fact that his mother was part Cherokee that bothered him; nope, it was the simple notion that she'd taken off when he was three and he couldn't remember her to save his soul. He'd never known what had become of her; he hadn't felt the need to find out.

Yet he'd decided to stay here, on the outskirts of Bad Luck. He had never fit in, and didn't really give a damn. In the back of his mind he knew that someday things would be easier.

And besides, this was home. Such as it was. He glanced to the north edge of the ranch and the land that he'd bought two years before, doubling his acreage and picking up a rock quarry and a peach orchard in the process. It had cost him big-time, but it was starting to pay off and the red ink he'd been drowning in was ebbing a bit, bleeding into black.

At the watering trough, he stopped long enough to twist the faucet and duck his head under the water, warm from the pipes. It cooled down and he splashed it over his neck and shoulders before taking a long drink. Yeah, this place, such as it was, was home.

Shaking the excess drops of water from his hair, he walked into the machine shed. There his tractor, four years older than he, lay idle, the rubber on its big tires cracked, its headlights dim. The rig's coat of paint had long since lost its luster in the endless hours of chugging up hills and pulling equipment under an unforgiving Texas sun.

But there was still life in the John Deere and he checked the oil, knowing that he'd keep the tractor until it died in a field. Wiping his hands, he considered the fact that he was now—if Shelby Cole could be believed—a father. He'd never thought he'd have any kids. Probably because he'd never found a woman he wanted to spend the rest of his life with. Wouldn't put a kid through the pain of growing up the way he did.

Now he had a daughter. Shelby's child. He'd spent a day digesting the news, even gone so far as to phone an old army buddy who had become a PI in Houston.

He'd tried to keep his mind from straying to Shelby. She was trouble just waitin' to happen. Always had been, always would be. But then, he'd never been one to back away from trouble; in fact there was a time when he'd gone lookin' for it.

Years ago.

He'd thought he was long over her, that he'd gotten her out of his blood.

But some things never changed.

One look at her and he'd felt that same old heat in his loins, that gut-wrenching tug deep in his soul. His jaw tightened, and he headed back to the house. No woman, not even Judge Red Cole's sexy daughter, was going to get to him again the way she'd done ten years ago.

Whistling to Crockett, he climbed up the back porch, kicked off his boots, took off his half-drenched shirt and used it as a towel, then downed a beer. He was about to step into the shower when he heard the sound of an engine and saw a plume of dust through the front window.

A fleck of white flashed through the live oaks lining the drive. He recognized Shelby's rented car. Long and sleek, the Cadillac sped past the copse of trees by the mailbox.

"Hell," he muttered, sucking in his breath.

Within seconds he was through the front door.

The car rolled to a stop as the sun was just settling behind the western hills. Crockett put up a helluva ruckus, but one look from Nevada silenced the mutt.

Shelby emerged from the car.

He gritted his teeth.

In khaki shorts and a white sleeveless blouse, with her red-blond hair pulled back, she was as fascinating as any woman he'd ever set eyes on. Her tanned legs were long, her waist slim, her breasts big enough to fill a man's hands, and it took all of his damned willpower to keep his thoughts where they should be.

Leaning a shoulder against a post supporting the overhang of the porch, he waited until she strode through the gate. "Back again?" he drawled.

"I think we still have a lot to discuss." She didn't bother to smile and her lips were pulled into a hard, determined line. She shoved her sunglasses onto her head. Her blue-green eyes snapped.

"And here I thought you were just slumming."

"I didn't come here to crack jokes," she said, climbing the steps and angling her face up to his. Her eyes were nearly turquoise and they reflected the last bit of sunlight.

"Shoot."

"I need your help."

He raised one eyebrow suspiciously and didn't say a word, just waited.

"You were right. *We* need to find Elizabeth."

"Is that so?" he drawled, ignoring the V of her blouse and a se-ductive glimpse of cleavage.

"Yes."

"Funny. *Now* you want my help."

"There's nothing funny about it."

"You're right," he said, his temper beginning to flare.

"Then we can get down to business and—"

"Why didn't you tell me you were pregnant?"

His question must have caught her off guard. She winced. Her cheeks and neck, even that cleft of skin between her breasts, flushed an intriguing rosy hue. "Pardon me?"

"Years ago. You could have told me."

She cleared her throat and he noticed the hesitation in her eyes—the lies—that she'd held fast to for so many years.

"There was no reason. I mean, it didn't make any sense to bother you—"

"*Bother* me? You think telling me that you were gonna have my kid wasn't something I should have been *bothered* with?" How could she stare up at him so brazenly? "If I was the father—"

"You were. Are."

He snorted in disgust. "What were you hiding, Shelby?"

"Nothing," she said, shaking her head and planting her hands on her hips. "There's nothing to hide, not anymore. And I didn't come here to argue."

"I just want to know why you didn't tell me." He couldn't let it go. Not that easily. They were talking about his kid, for Chrissakes! He'd been so shocked yesterday, he hadn't asked about it. Now, he needed to know.

"I thought the baby died."

"But you must have known for at least six or seven months that you were carrying a child."

"I was scared," she admitted, her chin jutting upward, her spine stiffening, a few strands loosening from the knot on her head to catch in the hot breeze.

"Scared of what?" he prodded.

She hesitated, and for the first time her mask of bravado slipped.

"I don't remember you being scared of much. You were pampered and rich, but you had a wild streak and a sharp tongue that you weren't afraid to use."

"That's not what I meant."

He cocked his head to one side. Waited.

She struggled, her cheeks still showing color.

"Spill it, Shelby."

"Damn." He saw her weighing a decision. "I didn't come here to discuss this."

"Discuss what?" he prodded.

"Oh, hell." Her shoulders stiffened slightly. "Okay, I was scared of you. Of my dad. Of what people would think."

"Why?"

"Because I was young."

"And?"

She looked away for a second, and he noticed the drops of sweat on her forehead. "Okay, I was scared of you because—" Her gaze swung back to his. "Because I loved you, Nevada," she admitted. Small lines puckered between her eyebrows and he wished he'd never pushed her, didn't want to hear a ten-year-old confession. "That's right. It was stupid. Foolish. Childish. But I loved you. There you have it and—oh, God, how I loved you. More than any sane woman should love a man, but...but damn it, I could never count on you, could I? I never really knew where I stood with you and then... and then I got pregnant and...and..." Her voice trailed off and she bit her lip, fighting some inner struggle. She rubbed her arms as if chilled, though the temperature was still pushing a hundred.

"Then," she whispered, drawing strength from some invisible well, "before I could turn around, all hell broke out in town and I was just really scared. Of everything."

There was more to it than that; he read it in the shadows darkening her eyes.

"I even tried to talk to you once," she conceded, and he saw her lips tighten at the corners, her shoulders stiffen. "But when I stopped by your house...you...you were with Vianca Estevan."

"Her father had just been killed."

"I—I know, but..."

"She was a friend."

"She was more to you than that and we both know it." Shelby shot him a look guaranteed to ice over the gates of hell. "Don't try any B.S. with me, okay? You and Vianca were lovers."

"Once upon a time," he allowed.

"And I was a temporary distraction."

His temper snapped. Before he knew what he was doing, he shoved her against the wall near the door. Crockett gave off a startled bark. "That's right. Shelby, you were one helluva distraction. And what was I to you? A way to get back at your old man? Someone to take pity on? One of those bad boys who were off-limits?"

"No."

"Liar."

"You—you were a deputy."

"But not for long." He tried not to notice the way her bare skin felt in his hands. "And I had a reputation—one I was trying to erase. You were with me just to rebel and get back at the Judge."

"No! I mean—"

"Oh, hell!"

Shelby gasped, and he did one of the most stupid things he'd ever done in his life. He kissed her. Hard. His lips crashed over hers, and he molded his body along the length of hers. His dusty, jean-clad legs pressed into bare calves and thighs, his hips felt the softness of hers and her mound melded naturally against his fly. He sensed her hot skin beneath the thin layer of cotton separating them and silently cursed himself for his weakness.

Pressing his tongue between her lips, he felt her tense, but she didn't stop him, nor did she kiss him back.

Perspiration dotted his back and slid down his spine. Though he was just making a point, desire fired his blood. Deep inside it sparked, then sizzled through his veins. His cock swelled, becoming thick and hard, and it was all he could do to lift his head and stare into aquamarine eyes that didn't so much as blink.

"Don't," she said with all the warmth of a Siberian winter. "Whatever you were trying to do to me, it didn't happen, okay?"

"Like hell." He pressed both palms against the rough siding on either side of her head, trapping her, but she pushed against his bare shoulders.

"Neanderthal tactics don't work with me, Nevada. Neither do Cro-Magnon, so give it up."

He almost believed her. She seemed so cool and impassive, but the pulse at the hollow of her throat was throbbing, and her fingers were curled against the cedar planks. He glanced at the curve of her neck and remembered how she had reacted when he'd kissed her there.

"Don't even think about it," she warned. "You've made your point, okay, but I don't have any time for . . . for any nonsense like . . ."

"Like what?"

"Like getting involved with you in any way, shape or form."

"No?" Folding his arms over his bare chest, he felt one side of his mouth lift in a mocking half smile.

"No." She was firm. "I came here because I thought you might want to help me." Her breasts were rising and falling a little too quickly, but he stepped back, giving her some breathing room. "Now listen." she said, her voice more breathless than it had been. "Either you're in or you're out. It's that simple. I'm going to find Elizabeth come hell or high water. With or without you. I—I thought I should let you know. So what's it gonna be?"

He sized her up. She'd matured over the years but was still just as bullheaded and tunnel-visioned as ever. Just like her old man. "I'm way ahead of you. Shelby."

"I doubt it."

"I already called in a PI."

"Without consulting me?" She had the audacity to look offended as she stood on his dusty porch.

"Yep."

"But didn't you think I'd want to know…" Her voice faded away and she cleared her throat, glanced toward the blaze of sunset—vibrant pink and gold—silhouetting the western hills. "Oh, I get it."

"Thought you might. It's not a great feeling to be cut out of the loop, is it? Now"—he backed up a couple of steps and rested his buttocks on the edge of the rail—"let's get one thing straight. We help each other out and work together to find her. That means we share information. No one goes off on a wild-goose chase alone."

She hesitated for a heartbeat. "Fair enough."

She'd agreed more quickly than he'd expected. "Good. So where are you? Are you living up at the house with your old man?"

"For now."

That bothered him, but he let it slide. "Find out what you can from the Judge."

"Believe me, I've tried." She walked to the edge of the porch and eyed the field where his best broodmares, their sleek coats shining in the last rays of light, were plucking at tufts of grass.

"And?"

"Oh, it's the old snowball's chance in hell adage."

"Then we'll have to try something else."

"I'm game."

He slid a lazy glance in her direction. "I remember."

Shelby's heart slammed against her rib cage. What the hell was he doing, flirting with her, kissing her, coming on to her? "Then let's get to it," she said, pretending not to notice the corded muscles in his shoulders, his tanned, bare chest and tight washboard of an abdomen. Nor would she react to the thatch of dark hair that arrowed down past his navel to burrow beneath the waistband of jeans that hung far too low on his hips. "And put something on, would you?"

"Bothered?" he asked, his mouth an irreverent slash of white.

"In your dreams, Smith."

"Often."

*Oh, God.* Her gaze found his. Sunlight was fading. Dusk crawled through the mesquite and cedar. Crickets had already started their night song. And in his eyes she saw seduction—raw and real and powerful. "Let's not go there," she said, wishing her voice was a little less rough, her throat not suddenly as dry as a Texas wind.

His jaw slid to one side as he eyed her. For a second she thought he would kiss her again. She caught her breath in anticipation. Her lungs were suddenly tight.

He crossed the porch and held open the shabby screen door. It creaked in protest. "Come on in, Shelby. I'll buy you a beer and we'll talk this out."

"I'll pass on the beer. Let's just come up with a game plan to find our daughter."

"Whatever you say."

She doubted it. Nevada never had been one to follow orders; that's what had gotten his badge stripped from him. She walked inside and Crockett, tongue lolling, tagged after her. Nevada followed with hardly a sound. "I've got Black Velvet or Jack Daniels," he offered, opening an antique-looking cabinet by the front door.

"Forget it."

He pulled out a half-drunk bottle of whiskey. "Perrier? Chardonnay?"

"Very funny. Let's just get down to it."

"Okay." He replaced the bottle and she glanced around the small room again. This time she took in more details. It was clean, but worn, the furniture circa 1980 or before, the coffee table strewn with copies of dog-eared magazines and newspapers. He motioned toward a once-maroon couch tucked under the window just as the phone jangled.

Nevada strode to the kitchen, snagged the receiver from the wall phone before the third ring and said a short, "Smith." Slowly lowering herself to perch on the edge of a leather ottoman, Shelby watched as every muscle in his body tensed.

"Which island?" he demanded. His gaze found hers and held.

A trickle of dread oozed down her spine.

"And he doesn't practice anymore?" Nevada demanded. Her heart thudded. Was he talking about Dr. Pritchart? On her feet in an instant, she closed the distance between them, a dozen questions on her lips.

"...you're sure. Yeah? Oh." His voice lowered a bit and irritation hardened his jaw. "I figured as much. Thanks."

"What was that all about?" she demanded as he hung up.

"Good news and bad."

"Let's hear the good."

"That was my friend, the PI. As I said, I called him and asked him to do some digging. He seems to think that the doctor who delivered your baby is in the Carribean somewhere."

"But he's not certain?" Shelby asked.

"Still trackin' it down."

"How does he know?" she said.

"Don't ask. He knows, okay?"

"Listen, Nevada, I just want to make sure he's on the up-and-up."

"Depends."

"On what?"

"Your definition of 'up-and-up.' "

"I want to know if he's legitimate."

"Does it matter?"

"Yes!"

"Why?"

"I can't believe we're arguing about this. When we find Elizabeth, I don't want any screw-ups, any...anything illegal that might prevent me...us from seeing her."

"Don't sweat it. He's an old army buddy. Worked for the CIA

for a while, now he's freelance. If anyone can locate Pritchart or Elizabeth, he will. That's what you wanted, isn't it?"

"Yes, but—"

"Then live with it."

"Who is he? I assume he has a name."

Nevada's big, calloused hands took hold of her bare shoulders. "Don't you want to know the bad news?" He was suddenly deadly serious, every muscle in his face tense.

"What?"

"Ross McCallum was released from prison." She froze. Felt sick inside. "He's already landed in Bad Luck."

Her heart plummeted. If not for the steadying hands on her shoulders, she might have started to tremble. But she forced herself to remain calm. McCallum couldn't hurt her. He wouldn't dare. "Your friend on the phone knew that as well?"

"Nope. I found it out myself, this morning. Shep Marson was kind enough to let me know."

"Shep Marson is never kind." Shelby said, shivering inside. Marson and McCallum—both bad news. She stepped out of Nevada's grasp, didn't want to feel any part of his anatomy touching hers.

"Can't argue with that. There's talk that he'll be runnin' for sheriff in the next election."

"Great," Shelby said and then walked the few steps into the living room and reclaimed her position on the ottoman. "I think I changed my mind. I could use a drink right now."

*So this was Bad Luck, Texas!*

Katrina Nedelesky jerked on the emergency brake of her Ford Escort and decided that no town on God's green earth had ever been more aptly named. Small, rural, lacking any grain of character, Bad Luck had no hope of growing.

Two or three streets of storefronts, one gas station, a handful of taverns and just as many churches collected around the heart of a town that appeared sun-baked, tired and shopworn. Bad Luck wasn't just a few hundred miles from Dallas; it was light years.

Katrina felt as if she'd been thrown back in time about half a century.

"Get over it," she grumbled, using the tiny mirror on her visor as she touched up her lipstick from a tube that was determined to melt. The air-conditioning in her Escort was on the fritz and the radiator was making strange hissing sounds, but the little car only had to hang on a few more months and then she'd trade it in on a new Porsche, or BMW, or even a Mustang convertible—something with some class, something that stated, *Watch out, world, Katrina Nedelesky has arrived!* She'd get a set of custom plates with something printed on them. And it wouldn't be Bad Luck.

Even though Bad Luck, Texas, was going to be her ticket to the big time. This lazy little dot on the map with its nearly ten-year-old murder mystery was going to bring her some well-deserved fame, get her out of debt and settle some old scores. All in one fell swoop.

And it couldn't happen fast enough!

Her clothes had wilted from the heat, and she hoped to God there was a motel somewhere. Her throat was parched, and she felt like shit from hours of driving. Fluffing her hair, she climbed out of the car. Night was beginning to fall, and a few streetlights were already glowing, attracting all kinds of insects and washing the main street with fake blue illumination.

It didn't help. Bad Luck needed more than soft lighting; it was in desperate need of a face-lift. The old saying that if you drove through and blinked, you'd miss the entire town was closer to the truth than the citizens of this part of the state would probably want to admit.

Just around the corner, by the pharmacy, she spied an old hitching post. For the love of God, hadn't anyone heard that it was a new millennium?

She crossed the street to a small grocery as a bit of wind tugged at her skirt and a couple of kids on bikes blasted past a wheezing truck carrying a load of peaches. Three teenagers with *bad attitude* carved into their expressions and tattoos blooming on their arms lounged and smoked near the front windows. They gave her the once-over as she shoved on the door. A fan mounted where there had once been a transom pushed hot air around. To the crackle of static and Spanish music, a few customers eyed shelves filled with junk food and small containers of necessities.

On the back wall was an ancient cooler where dozens of soda

and beer cans chilled. Katrina yanked out a can of Dr Pepper. Cool air rushed at her in a glorious blast that helped improve her mood.

The woman behind the counter was Hispanic, as were half the patrons within the tiny store, and that was when it hit Katrina like a blow to the head. Why hadn't she noticed it before? Talk about dumb-ass luck! She paid for her Dr Pepper and a bag of M&Ms, then walked down an aisle filled with small-sized boxes of detergents to the front door. Outside she read the hand-painted sign gracing the window. ESTEVAN'S MARKET.

As in Ramón Estevan.

As in the man who had been murdered and whose accused killer had just been absolved of the crime.

"Thank you, God," she whispered under her breath and decided that, at least for another day or two, she'd play it cool. She popped the top of her Dr Pepper and took a long swallow. No one knew who she was or that she had a personal mission here. She'd keep it that way for a while. As if she'd forgotten something, she walked into the store again and inched toward the cash register.

Ignoring copies of newspapers from San Antonio and Dallas, Katrina thumbed through some magazines, appearing to browse the glossy pages as she eavesdropped. One scruffy-looking man with a graying ponytail and too few teeth bought cigarettes and a six-pack of beer. He didn't say much, but he called the woman Vianca.

Katrina swallowed a smile. Pay dirt. Vianca Estevan, Ramón's only daughter. With gleaming black hair, expressive eyes, full lips and cheekbones to die for, Vianca flirted and laughed with the customers while making change and checking the mirror for shoplifters.

So where was the wife? Vianca's mother—what was her name? Aloise, yeah, that was it. No sign of the older woman lurking in the back or stocking the shelves. Probably at the local Catholic church or hiding out at home. Rumor had it, Aloise was a certified nut case—hadn't been the same since her husband had been murdered. But not so Vianca. Sultry and sharp-witted, she seemed to hold down the family business, though why anyone would want to was beyond Katrina.

Way beyond. She thought hard. Wasn't there a brother as well? Roberto—that was it! So why wasn't he in the store?

Katrina flipped through a month-old copy of *Cosmopolitan* and kept an ear to the local gossip as people strolled in and out. Half the conversations were in Spanish and she silently cursed *Señor* Walters, her high-school Spanish teacher, as she couldn't decipher most of the dialogue. Not that it was all that great. What she did figure out was that someone in town had just delivered twins, the fishing up at a nearby lake was pathetic and there had been a brushfire that had nearly destroyed someone's *casa*.

Big whoop.

She was about to leave when she finally heard a tidbit that interested her. Part of it was in Spanish, but the name Ross McCallum rang out as clear as a bell. Katrina glanced over her shoulder and saw the reaction she'd expected. Vianca's eyes flashed and her nostrils flared.

Katrina listened hard, but she didn't understand all the words. The undercurrents of emotions, however, were right near the surface. Vianca wasn't pleased, that much was evident. Her pretty face was suddenly overcome with thunderclouds, and other people in the store muttered their condolences.

Yep, Katrina thought, ambling up to the counter and paying for a couple of magazines she didn't want as the conversation around her died, she'd have to come back to this miserable town and interview a few people. And not just because of her job. Nope. There was more to it than the simple fact that she was here on an assignment for *Lone Star* magazine.

Katrina had her own ax to grind. And it was personal.

# CHAPTER 6

"Damn you, Nevada Smith." Shelby rolled out of bed and groaned. A headache pounded behind her eyes. She'd tossed and turned all night, her thoughts spinning with images of Nevada, her father, and a baby she'd given up long ago. Other darker, more horrifying images had assailed her as well—a kaleidoscope of ugly memories that she'd spent years trying to erase.

Her muscles were tense, her jaw so tight it ached. As she jerked an old robe off a hook on the closet door, she rubbed the back of her neck. She understood why she was anxious about her daughter, but her feelings for Nevada were unexpected and definitely unwanted.

So she'd been in love with him ten years ago. So what?

She'd been a kid and a lot of water had run under the bridge since then. She pushed her arms into the sleeves of the terry housecoat, cinched the belt around her waist, slid her feet into a pair of flip-flops, then stopped at the window.

Nevada's image still teased her—all bronze skin, hard muscles and suspicious glare. "Forget him." She stared through her window to the pool a story below. Sunlight, filtered and diffused through the branches of the pecan trees, danced upon the water.

She remembered making love to him in the rain, his hard male body joining with hers. The smell of a storm had been in the air and she'd been filled with raw, unbridled passion and the incredible naivete of youth. She hadn't known where loving him would lead. Hadn't cared.

"You were a fool. A stupid idiotic child!" She caught her reflection in the mirror above her dresser and noticed the flush of her cheeks, the dilation of her pupils. "Forget it," she told the woman staring back at her. Picking up a brush, she jabbed it emphatically at her reflection. "You're not going there ever again. Ever."

The last thing—the very last thing—she needed was to get involved with anyone from around here, especially some saddle-sore cowboy. No way. No how. She knew what she wanted in life, what kind of man she was looking for, and it wasn't a rugged, broken-down ex-cowboy in dusty jeans and a faded T-shirt. She'd gone that route before.

If and when she settled down, it would be with a successful businessman, a guy who wore a suit to the office and clean slacks or jeans at home, someone with his own business who was charming and sophisticated and educated, for crying out loud.

She brushed her hair angrily. Why was she even thinking like this? So she had a bad night, so what? So he kissed her. It happened to other women every day. Get over it. She glanced out the window again.

She needed to stretch, to unwind, to clear her mind. Swimming or horseback riding had always done the trick when she was still living at home. In Seattle, she'd taken up jogging, pounding the pavement in the early hours, ignoring the rain, reveling in the wind, and then, to reward herself, stopping off at the local coffee shop for some Northwest espresso before going into the office.

Here, with the heat, jogging was out and the pool, still and cool in the morning air, invited her.

That did it.

Scrounging in her closet, she found a swimsuit that still fit. She stripped off pajamas and robe, tugged on the one-piece and wound her hair onto her head before tossing on the terry cover-up. With a towel from the adjoining bathroom, she hurried down the back stairs and was greeted with the scent of strong coffee and the sound of rattling dishes.

"*Niña,*" Lydia said with a broad smile as Shelby appeared. "You go for a swim?"

"Yeah, I thought it would be a good idea." Shelby poured herself a cup of coffee from the glass pot on the counter.

"And then breakfast? Waffles and peaches and strawberries. Your father, he went into town to his office, but he said he would be back and I will make him something when he gets here."

"I usually just drink coffee," Shelby said with a shake of her head. Then, seeing the disappointment in the older woman's eyes, she sighed. "Sure, why not, but I've really gotten into just a cup of espresso or a latte in the morning. It's kind of a Northwest thing."

"You are home now."

"Well, for a while." She took the coffee outside with her, and the warmth of morning hit her full force. Leaving her cup on the outside table, she dropped her towel and cover-up by the pool's edge, then dived in.

Cold water embraced her, took her breath away. She started swimming, long, easy strokes, and felt her blood pumping, the headache clearing. The sky was a brilliant blue, the sun bright as it rose toward the tops of the trees. Stroke, breathe, stroke, stroke, breathe. She found her rhythm and thought about the day ahead. She'd call Nevada, get the name of his private investigator, see if they could locate Doctor Pritchart—the coward. Surely his medical license could be jerked—well, maybe it already had been. Revenge wasn't her motive. Knowledge was.

*So you'll have to see Nevada again.* Well, that was inevitable. He was the father of her child.

Or was he?

She gave herself a quick mental shake. She couldn't think like that. Wouldn't.

Stroke, stroke, breathe.

But there was a chance that Elizabeth's father was Ross McCallum.

She lost her rhythm. Her stomach turned over and she wanted to throw up. No! It wasn't possible; it just couldn't be.

*You've got to be honest, Shelby. Isn't that what you're expecting of everyone else?*

Stroke. Stroke. Concentrate on the positive.

*Ross McCallum could be—*

"Damn it, no!" She yelled as she reached the shallow end of the pool, tossed her head, flinging beads of water from her hair, and stood, leaning against the tile lip of the pool.

"'No,' what?" As she tugged the rubber band from her hair, Nevada's voice startled her. For a split second she thought she was seeing things, but there he was, big as life, standing next to the glass-topped table. A second cup of coffee steamed beside hers. Sunglasses guarded his eyes. Clean Levi's and a tan shirt with the sleeves rolled to his elbows covered the rest of him. He'd shaved, and his hair was brushed away from his face, though she didn't suspect it would stay that way for long. As she remembered, it had a tendency to fall over his eyes in boyish disarray.

"What're you doing here?" she asked.

"You took off pretty abruptly yesterday."

That much was true. After hearing that Ross McCallum was back in Bad Luck, Shelby had mumbled quick excuses, left Nevada's cabin, climbed into her rented Caddy and taken off in a swirl of dust and despair. It was one thing to deal with Nevada, quite another to have to face Ross McCallum. Though she'd known he was coming back to town, the fact that he was actually in Bad Luck turned her insides to water.

"It was upsetting," she said, placing her hands on the tile and dragging her body onto the edge of the pool. She squeezed the excess water from her hair and grabbed her towel, then squinted up at him. "You didn't answer my question. What're you doing here?"

"I thought we were partners."

"Partners?" She was instantly suspicious; then she understood. She toweled off and felt the weight of his gaze on her. "Oh."

"Right. In finding our daughter."

*Our daughter.*

"It was your idea."

"I know." She dabbed at her face with her towel and didn't consider the topic of paternity as she reached for the short terry robe.

"Do you have more news? And who's the private investigator? I assume he does have a name."

"Bill Levinson and no, not much more news. But you left yesterday without a game plan."

Pushing her arms through terry-cloth sleeves, she walked barefoot to the table. He was nearly a head taller than she, and she tried not to notice how long his legs were, how wide his shoulders, how slim his waist. She remembered how he'd grabbed her and kissed her yesterday, the way he'd pounced. Like a cougar on unsuspecting prey. The mere thought of it took her breath away. Too many hours last night her mind had strayed to that one soul-jarring kiss. She cleared her throat. "You have one—a plan?"

"I think so."

The back door opened and Lydia, carrying a tray, appeared. "I brought breakfast," she explained with an expansive smile. "For two."

Nevada was about to protest; Shelby sensed it. "Look, don't even try to get out of this. It's Lydia's personal mission to see that anyone in a ten mile radius gets more than his or her required RDAs, calories and fat grams for the day."

"But—"

"It is true," Lydia admitted, smiling proudly, her gold caps reflecting the morning sunlight.

"So stuff it," Shelby told him, and helped Lydia slap a couple of place mats onto the table. Within minutes two platters of powdered-sugar-dusted waffles, fruit and strips of bacon, as well as orange juice, water and an insulated carafe of coffee, covered the glass top. "Lydia, it looks wonderful," she said as the older woman put place settings of silver wrapped in embroidered napkins near their plates. In the middle of the table she centered a bud vase with a yellow rose.

Nevada nodded. "It does—look great."

*"Gracias."* Glowing under the compliments, Lydia started for the kitchen, then spied the gardener on the other side of a trellis where a clematis trailed a profusion of pur ple blooms. With shears in hand he was busy pruning a hedge. "'Xcuse me," Lydia muttered and bustled off, no doubt to give the poor man a tongue-lashing for mistreatment of some of the shrubbery or flowers.

"It's just safer not to argue with her about food," Shelby explained as she sliced into the waffles covered with peaches and drizzled with a syrup that smelled like cinnamon and nutmeg. "You know, I'm surprised to see you here." She glanced up at him. "Because of Dad."

"Don't tell me I wouldn't be welcome?"

"Would it break your heart?" she teased.

He hesitated. "Don't have one." His eyes held hers for a second. "Leastwise, so I've been told." He leaned closer to her as she remembered the heated conversation, the angry words she'd thrown at him. "Not that it matters a whole hell of a lot. And even though the Judge and I, we have our differences of opinion, I thought I'd better get things straight with you."

"Such as?" Suddenly she wasn't hungry.

"Assuming we do find Elizabeth—"

"We will. *I* will."

"And once you do, what then? What're you plannin' to do?" he asked, eyes narrowing on her.

"Meet her."

"You mean meet her parents."

"I mean her *adoptive* parents," she clarified, bristling as she cut into a waffle with the side of her fork and plopped the piece into her mouth.

"And then?" he asked as he pronged a peach slice with his fork. "What if they don't want to meet you? What if they want to go to court to keep you from seeing her? What if your presence would be damaging to her, or her family? Ever thought of that?" he asked as he took a bite.

The waffle turned to dust in her mouth. She forced down a swallow and felt her stomach begin to revolt as the very doubts that had kept her awake at night returned to plague her. "Of course."

"But you're going to do this your way."

"Yes." She set her fork down. "But you don't have to be a part of it, Nevada. No one's twisting your arm."

"That's not what I meant. I just wanted you to look at all the angles."

"I have. Dozens of times. Believe me. It keeps me awake at

night. But this is something I have to do." She hooked her thumb at her chest and realized that her cover-up gaped, that the tops of her breasts were bare. Lord, this was ridiculous, sitting here half-naked, eating breakfast with her ex-lover and discussing the child she'd thought was long dead. She adjusted her lapels. "It's time to set the record straight and I . . . I have to at least see her." Her voice faded slightly as emotion gripped her throat. "Look into her eyes."

"Hold her?" he asked, and she shuddered inside.

*Oh, God, yes, I want to hold my baby. Hold her and never let go.* "If . . . if it's possible."

One dark eyebrow rose over the top rim of his sunglasses, but he didn't comment. Shelby forced as much of her breakfast down as she could, but her appetite had waned and she had no choice but to face Lydia's motherly reproach.

"What does your father say?" Nevada asked, after several long minutes when the only noises that disturbed the silence were the birds fluttering in the pecan trees and the clink of their forks against their plates.

"Not much. He started out denying knowing anything about it and now avoids the subject."

"You want me to talk to him?"

"No!" she said vehemently, then bit her tongue when she saw the cords of his neck stand out above the open collar of his shirt. "I—I think I'd better handle it myself."

"Okay, but I'm willing to step in."

"Thanks." She tried to force some enthusiasm into her voice but when it came to dealing with her father, she was certain she would make more headway than Nevada Smith, a man forever branded as a useless, uppity half-breed by the Judge. A man who, as a teenager, had worked hauling hay and rounding up cattle for the Judge before he'd been fired for getting into a fight with the foreman; a man who had stood before her father in the courtroom. "I'll deal with the Judge."

"Let me know if you change your mind." Nevada stretched out of his chair, took a long, slow look around the grounds and then hooked a thumb in a belt loop of his jeans. "Keep me posted if you find anything out."

"I will. And the same goes for you." She stepped into her flip-flops and walked him through the gate. She couldn't remember the last time Nevada had been to her house. Had he ever been?

He paused near the front lawn where his pickup, a dusty, dented reminder of his own lot in life, was parked facing the main gate. "And Shelby," he added, turning and reaching up as if to touch her. But before his fingers grazed the skin of her bare arm, he let his hand fall to his side. "If Ross McCallum tries to contact you or bother you—"

"He won't!" she said emphatically.

"Maybe not. But if he does, you let me know." Nevada's jaw was suddenly rock hard, his mouth a thin, unbending line.

"I can handle Ross."

"Can you?" His eyes, behind their shaded lenses, found hers and she felt her body flush with unwanted color. "You couldn't before."

"A lot has changed in the past ten years, Nevada. Including you. And me."

"Yeah, but McCallum has been in prison. My guess is that he didn't improve with incarceration. If anything, he's probably meaner."

"Is that so?" she asked, forcing a smile and a light tone she didn't feel. "Well, here's a news flash for you, Nevada: so am I."

He barked out a laugh as he climbed into his truck. "Oh, right." he said sarcastically. Twisting on the ignition, he rested his elbow on the open window as the truck idled. "You're as mean as a wounded mama grizzly who's just been separated from her cubs."

Her smile fell away. "Exactly." How close he'd come to the truth. She'd been separated from Elizabeth for nine years, and as far as she was concerned, that was way too long.

"I didn't mean—"

"Forget it." She heard the purr of her father's Mercedes just as the car appeared at the end of the drive. Her stomach nose-dived, and Nevada, seeing her expression, glanced through his windshield. At the sight of the Judge's car, the corners of his lips pulled downward. "Just the man I was hoping to see." He cut the engine.

"No—" She shook her head. This was no time for a showdown

between Nevada and her father, but the door of the Ford opened and Nevada stepped onto the asphalt of the drive as Red Cole slowed and lowered his driver's window.

"Judge," Nevada said, nodding slightly and folding his arms over his chest.

"You lookin' for me?" Red Cole clamped the stub of a black cigar between his teeth. The familiar scent of tobacco smoke vied with the fragrances of roses and honeysuckle from the garden.

Shelby recognized her father's most patronizing grin.

Nevada stood next to her, nearly touching her but not quite. "I came to see Shelby, but I think it would be a good idea if we talked."

"Do ya now?" He glanced at his daughter, his smile flagging a little as he took in her state of undress. "Seems to me you shoulda been doin' some talkin' to me about ten years ago—some fast talkin' when you were sneakin' around with her."

"That was my choice," Shelby cut in.

But the Judge's eyes were centered on Nevada, and as he spoke his lips barely moved around his cigar. "I have nothin' to say to you, Smith. Never did have. My only regret was that I was too lenient on you when you were hauled into my courtroom. I shoulda thrown the book at you then, when you were a smart-assed kid with an attitude, sent you up the river instead of givin' you probation for all the trouble you caused and even handin' you a job at my ranch."

"I guess I forgot to thank you," Nevada drawled and the Judge's face flushed.

"That's right. With a record you never would've gotten that job with the Sheriff's Department, never would have disgraced yourself and been thrown out on your ass, never gotten involved with Shelby!" He shot his daughter a condemning glance. "Then we wouldn't be in this mess we're in now."

"Maybe we wouldn't be in it if you had told the truth to Shelby way back when. You lied, Judge. About your own granddaughter." The skin stretched tight across Nevada's cheekbones. "I just wonder why."

"I did what I thought was best."

"Seems to me, if the word got out, you would be the one in trouble. Not only your reputation but your professional ethics up for review. There're laws about falsifying legal documents such as birth and death certificates, Judge."

"I'm no longer on the bench and I don't practice law," her father said, his eyes steady.

"But you could end up in jail." Nevada didn't cut the older man a bit of slack. "The way I hear it, there's an empty cell, now that McCallum's out."

"You never did learn, did ya, Smith? All the trouble you were in and you never learned when to quit pushin', when to keep your sorry mouth shut, when to—"

"That's enough!" Shelby interjected. "Nevada just came by this morning because...because he's going to help me find Elizabeth."

Her father's nostrils flared, as if he'd just encountered a bad odor. He shifted his cigar from one side of his mouth to the other. "You're both makin' a big mistake."

Nevada nodded. "Could be. But I think we'd better try. I'd like to know if I have a daughter somewhere."

The Judge's eyes met Shelby's and she swallowed hard, fighting the doubts tearing her up inside. Silently she pleaded with him not to bring up the horrid subject of Elizabeth's paternity. *Not here. Not now.*

"So you haven't told him, eh?" her father asked. Then some of his bravado slipped and a profound sadness settled deep in his eyes. "Hell, what a mess."

Shelby's spine stiffened. She'd never been one to back down from a battle, but this was tough. Damned hard.

"You haven't told me what?" Nevada asked.

"Christ-a-mighty. You're only working on half-baked information, Smith!" Shelby's father pulled the cigar from his mouth. "But then, that seems to be your M.O. Bad information and unreliable witnesses."

"You're talkin' about Caleb Swaggert."

"Damned right."

"He lied."

"And now he's found Jesus and the truth or some variation thereof. You hear that he's sellin' his story to the press?" His balding pate wrinkled.

"What're you talking about?" Shelby demanded.

"Ol' Caleb has himself an interview or some such nonsense with *Lone Star* magazine, leastwise that's what I heard down at the coffee shop this mornin'."

"Why would he do that?" Nevada asked.

"Money."

"He's dyin'." Nevada's eyes narrowed.

"Don't matter. He ain't dead yet and now his pack of lies, the ones that sent McCallum up the river, are gonna be turned into gold." He scowled. "This is another one of your messes, Smith."

"Mine?"

"You helped nail McCallum, and now it's all fallin' apart. That's what happens when you count on derelicts and whores as witnesses. It's a wonder Ross McCallum was ever found guilty in the first place. No murder weapon ever found, and he was drivin' your truck that night."

"It was stolen," Nevada said.

"So you said."

"I filed a report."

"Easy to do when you worked for the law."

Nevada's lips thinned menacingly. "So you think Ross McCallum's innocent?" Nevada's skin was tight, the muscles beneath his shirt bunched.

"Innocent? Hell no. He's guilty as sin, but it doesn't matter now, does it, because ol' Caleb is singin' a different song and hopin' to get through the Pearly Gates. Unless I'm forgettin' the statutes, I believe a man can't be tried for the same crime twice. In the eyes of the law, Ross McCallum's a free—if not innocent—man. Hell's bells, what a mess." With that he rolled his window up and gunned the engine. The silver car eased around a final laurel-flanked curve as the garage door, clicking loudly, slowly began to open.

Nevada didn't say another word, but the brackets around his mouth were white in his tanned skin and he looked as if he could spit nails as his eyes followed the path of the Mercedes. "What did he mean, I only have part of the story?" he demanded, turning on Shelby.

"He's just mad about Ross McCallum getting out of jail," she hedged.

"Don't jerk me around."

"Wouldn't dream of it."

"Your father thought you were keeping something from me."

"My father thinks a lot of things."

Nevada seemed about to argue, but glanced at his watch and scowled more deeply. Frustration etched his features. "We'll talk later. In the meantime try and come up with a list of people who might have sent you the package about Elizabeth."

"Already working on it," she admitted. In fact she'd spent all her time on the airplane wondering who would have contacted her and why after all these years—on the very week that Ross McCallum became a free man. "I'd like to talk to your friend—the private eye you hired."

"I'll have him call you."

She swatted at a yellow jacket that hovered near her head. "I think it would be better if I called him," she said staunchly.

Nevada hesitated. "I said I'll have him call you."

"You don't trust me." She was thunderstruck at the thought.

"You're right, Shelby, I don't. And I really can't think of one good reason why I should. I said I'd have Bill call you, and I will."

"But—"

"As you so eloquently told me earlier, 'stuff it.' "

She shook her head and glared at him. "You really are a bastard, aren't you?"

"Yep."

"And probably the most irritating man in the entire state."

"Probably." He climbed into the cab, started the engine and rammed the truck into gear. "But if it's any consolation, it's taken years of practice to claim the title."

"Go to hell."

"Been there." He slashed her an irreverent grin that made her temper blister. "Matter of fact, more than one time." With that he stepped on the accelerator.

She watched as the old Ford gathered speed down the shaded lane, then, fists clenched impotently, turned on her heel. *He can't get to you, Shelby, not if you don't let him,* her mind taunted as she strode into the house and headed straight for her father's den—the sanctuary she had been taught long ago not to invade. Well, the old rules were out now.

Judge Red Cole was seated at his desk, one booted foot propped on a corner, his chair tilted back as he talked to someone on the telephone.

"... I don't care what you have to do, just sell the rest of the yearlings or ..." He glanced up and found Shelby staring at him. "Listen, I'll call you back." Replacing the receiver, he waved her into one of the cushy leather chairs on the opposite side of his desk. "Have a seat." Folding his arms across his ample middle, he asked, "What's on your mind?"

"I realize that this is kinda like beating my head against the wall, but I wanted to give you one more chance to come clean with me," she said. "It would be so much easier if you would tell me everything you know about Elizabeth."

"I already did."

"So where's Dr. Pritchart?"

"Retired. Last I heard he was in the Florida Keys. Fishing and looking for a place to settle down. He had all sorts of wild notions about a tropical paradise."

"And he never told you who adopted my daughter."

"No." The Judge was firm.

"But then, you never asked him, did you?"

"Seems to me we've had this conversation before," he said, dismissing her. "You need to move past this—get on with your life. You just heard me talking to my foreman about selling off part of the herd. There's a reason. I've been talking to my attorneys about my will, and since you're here anyway, I thought you might want to know what's in it."

"What? No. I mean, you're going to live a long time, and I don't want to even think about what will happen if you die."

"Well, missy, you're just gonna have to," he said, "because I'm not going to live forever." He reached into a drawer and she was on her feet. "I have a copy here somewhere—"

"I don't need to see it."

"Hell, where is it anyway? I guess it really doesn't matter. There are a few people who I want to take care of, you know, people who've worked for me or helped me get elected and a couple of charities that your mother was involved with . . . damn it all, where is that thing?" He sighed and pursed his lips before slamming the drawer shut. "Well, the gist of it is this—you inherit everything. I know you expected that as you're my only child, but there is a hitch."

"I don't care."

"Just listen, okay?" He was getting angry all over again, his face reddening, "I don't want you to sell this house or any of the property and—" He leveled his stern gaze on her. "I expect you to live here."

"What? Oh, Dad, why're you bringing this up now?" she asked, seeing his face light up as she acknowledged for the first time in ten years that he was her father.

"Because it's got to be said, that's why."

"I have a life in Seattle—"

"You got a husband?"

"Well, no."

"A boyfriend?"

"No . . . not any longer." She'd dated, of course, some more seriously than others, but the last man she'd been involved with had moved to San Francisco.

"Not even a pet."

"No, but my job, my friends—"

"You can work here if you want to, not that you would have to, and you have friends here and can make some more. Maybe not in Bad Luck, but in San Antonio or Austin." He was warming to his subject, his hands shifting so that his fingers tented over his belly. "In fact, I've got invitations to a few things coming up—a charity dinner and some wing-ding down in Galveston—and I want you to go with me. I'll introduce you around. Lots of men about your age. All of 'em decent-enough-lookin', some of 'em rich."

"I won't be here long," she said, a bad taste crawling up the back of her throat. "As soon as I find Elizabeth, I'm out of here."

Some of the wind left his sails. Placing his hands on the desk, he leaned across it. "Don't say it, Shelby-girl. I know I've made my share of mistakes raisin' you alone as I did, but I've missed you, honey. Oh, God, how I've missed you." He cleared his throat, and his eyes watered enough that he blinked and looked away. "You look so damned much like your mother. Oh, shit, I miss her, too. I wasn't the best husband in the world, nor the best father, but, as God is my witness, I loved your mother like no other. And you... well, know it or not, you've always been the apple of my eye, even when you were hell-bent to rebel against me."

Shelby's throat grew thick, but she reminded herself of all the lies that had festered in this house for years, secrets and innuendos that had been whispered around town. She leaned across his desk and placed a hand over his gnarled knuckles. "I came back here to find my daughter. That's all. I'd hoped that you would help me." Then she left, and as she walked into the hallway, she drew in a deep, struggling breath. Only when she passed the mirror mounted over a lacquered table in the front hall did she realize that her eyes were red and brimming with unshed tears.

"Damn it all." Dashing the foolish drops from her eyes, she silently vowed she wouldn't let her father get to her. Couldn't. She had too much to do. She climbed the stairs to her room, intent on calling her office in Seattle to check on her clients and listings, then searching for Nevada's private investigator on the Internet. But as she walked past the family portrait in the upper hall, a picture commissioned only months before her mother's death, when Shelby was barely four, her facade of strength fractured. She hardly remembered the woman who had given her life.

No, most of her memories were of another time. Those images, the ones she'd tried so hard to tamp down, assailed her now—vivid, bright, and laced with pain.

Unable to keep them at bay any longer, she walked into her bedroom and wrapped her arms around one of the beveled posts at the foot of her bed, the very four-poster where she'd grieved for months after Jasmine's death, the same bed where she'd dreamed of making love to a sexy rebel who had touched her heart and soul, the bed in which she'd lain alone, only her own arms surrounding her as she'd cried silent tears of frustration, pain and fear when she was a seventeen-year-old in the worst trouble of her life.

"Don't do this," she warned herself, but it was already far too late. Memories, long hidden away, appeared in her mind's eye, and she saw herself as she was then, fresh-faced, sassy, unaware of life's wretched ironies.

Letting her fingers trail down the smooth rosewood post, she slowly lowered herself onto the hand-stitched quilt and gave into those faraway and gut-wrenching images. Had it really been ten years? A decade of her life?

In some ways it felt like forever, but in others, it seemed like only yesterday....

# CHAPTER 7

*Ten years earlier*

"I'm tellin' you, Shelby, you can't trust him. Nevada Smith spells nothin' but trouble. He was raised wild and he still is, I don't care what you say." Her father tossed his jacket over the back of the couch in the family room and walked to the bar, where he pulled a bottle of Scotch from the cabinet. "Besides, he's too old for you."

"I'm seventeen—not a baby," she argued, kicking off her riding boots and wincing as she yanked the rubber band from her hair. She caught sight of her reflection in the beveled mirror over the liquor cabinet. Freckles, wild hair, flushed cheeks and zero make-up. No wonder her father treated her like a little kid—she looked like one.

"And he's what? Twenty-four?"

"You were twelve years older than Mom."

"Case in point." With his bare hands, he scooped ice out of the bucket that Lydia always had ready, then dropped the cubes into a short glass. "Look, Nevada Smith worked for me, you know that. I hired him and kept him on, didn't I? Even though he was hauled into my courtroom. He and some of his buddies got drunk, stole the keys to the funeral home's hearse and went out joy-riding. I fig-ured at the time it was just a case of letting off steam, you know, 'boys will be boys.' Then him and the McCallum boy were caught shootin' at mailboxes. I let that slide, too, but I don't trust him." Twisting the cap off the bottle, he eyed his glass and poured in three fingers.

"He's working for the Sheriff's Department now."

"I heard." Her father scowled and scratched his chin, then capped his bottle and stuffed it into the cabinet. "Won't last long."

"You don't know that—"

"Oh, I do." He nodded as if to himself, and for the first time in her life Shelby had a glimmer of truth, a hint that her father might not be as upstanding and honest as she'd thought, that he might actually *manipulate* others the way he did her.

"He's been in the army," she added. "Got promoted and . . ."

"Yeah, I heard all that. But a man doesn't change, missy, much as you'd like to believe otherwise. It's about personal ethics. Our boy Nevada, he doesn't have many. Not really his fault; just the way he was raised." He swirled his drink and the ice clinked softly.

Shelby wanted to defend Nevada up one side and down the other, but she knew her father well enough to know when to hold her tongue. There was no use arguing. When it came to the boys she dated, her father was a tyrant.

"So, we got that settled?" he asked, dropping into his favorite recliner. Positioned near the fireplace, the brown leather tufted and worn in spots, it was the only chair that he swore was comfortable in the entire house. He loved this room, angled as it was off the kitchen. Through a bank of windows he had a bird's-eye view of the swimming pool and gardens. Only a few steps away, on the other side of the back stairs and through shuttered French doors, was another room occupied by a sturdy billiard table covered in blue felt. Once a week the Judge's inner circle of friends came over to play cards and pool. On those nights Shelby was banished to her room upstairs, though she'd often listen through the vents to the bawdy stories that were passed around.

"Shelby?" her father said now, and she snapped back to the present. He climbed out of his chair to stare her in the eye. "We understand each other? You're not to see Nevada Smith again."

"When I'm eighteen—"

"We'll talk again. Until that time, you stay away from him." He stood in front of the cold grate of the fireplace, and the polished longhorns that were mounted on the bricks over the mantel appeared to sprout from his head. "I'd hate to have to ground you or take back your car, now. That would be a shame."

"You won't have to," she lied. She loved the car, a lemon-yellow convertible, almost as much as she loved her prized Appaloosa mare, but not nearly with the same intensity she felt for Nevada. No, the feeling she had for him defied description.

Even though a part of her realized she was rebeling against an overbearing father, knew that Nevada, with his wild streak, wasn't right for her, she couldn't help herself from going against the old man's wishes and doing what she wanted—including seeing Nevada Smith on the sly. She was sick and tired of being known as "the princess," Judge Cole's spoiled daughter, a Goody Two-shoes.

Besides, these days she wasn't even being all that wild. Nevada Smith was, except in her father's mind, an upstanding, law-abiding citizen. Though he'd been with the Sheriff's Department less than a year, he was on the road to the straight and narrow. So why did she cross her fingers as she climbed the stairs?

She paused at the family portrait and stared straight at the image of her mother—Jasmine Alicia Falconer Cole. With patrician features, ash-blond hair and eyes that were a vibrant shade between green and gold, Jasmine had been a striking woman, the sought-after daughter of an oil mogul. And she'd taken her own life a few days shy of her twenty-eighth birthday.

"Things would be different if you were here, Mom," she muttered as she headed for her room. She wished she could say that she hated to go behind her father's back, but it would've been a flat-out lie. The truth of the matter was that she was meeting Nevada tonight and no matter what her father thought, she'd gladly move heaven and earth—even hell if it got in the way—to see him.

The night was hot, the air seeming to crackle with excitement. The top of her convertible down, Shelby drove with one eye on her watch, her convertible whipping through the streets of Bad Luck as quick as the lightning the weathermen had been predicting all day.

"Watch out, Shelby, you're gonna miss the turnoff!" Lily yelled from the sliver of a backseat she shared with her boyfriend, Todd.

Lily Ingles, a waif of a girl, was Shelby's best friend, the only girl in the entire senior class of Austin High Shelby felt she could trust. "Hey—here it is!"

Shelby cranked the wheel of her convertible hard, tires screeching as she landed with a jolt in the middle of Lily's driveway.

"Jesus, Shelby, you tryin' to kill us?" Todd asked, leaning forward. He smelled of cheap wine, cigarettes and marijuana. His hair was windblown and stuck up at odd angles.

"Nope. You seem to be doin' a good enough job of that yourself."

Lily giggled and the couple, laughing, struggled out of the car. On the front lawn, Todd tried to tackle Lily, but she side-stepped and he reeled into a hedge. "You sure you're not comin' in?" Lily asked, her white dress seeming blue in the lamplight, her hair tangled as it fell over one side of her face.

"No." Shelby wasn't about to budge. Not tonight. "I already told you, I've got plans."

"But—"

"Shh. Go inside before you wake the neighbors."

Todd had climbed to his feet and grabbed Lily around the shoulders. She nearly buckled under his weight. Shelby checked her watch. Eleven thirty-five.

"If you're sure—"

"Go!" Shelby insisted.

"Okay, okay—"

Todd was nuzzling Lily's neck and clinging to her as they weaved their way under a trellis to the back door. Once they were inside, Shelby wasted no time. She kicked off her short skirt, exchanging it for a pair of cutoff jeans that she'd stashed under the passenger seat, then replaced her sandals with her favorite worn pair of boots.

She threw the BMW into reverse and backed onto the street just as the lights snapped on inside Lily's house.

Ramming the car into first, Shelby headed out of town and ignored the twinge of conscience that suggested she was about to make yet another big mistake. One of a steadily growing list. She'd already lied to her father, to Lily's folks and to Nevada. Biting her lip at that particular thought, she felt some guilt because she knew he'd been reticent about meeting with her alone, that he'd been having second thoughts about getting involved with Judge Cole's daughter.

But it was too late.

They were involved already. Well, at least Shelby was involved with him and she wanted desperately to see him, had spent the entire day waiting for the time when she could throw her arms around his neck and kiss him wildly. He was a little more cautious, didn't like the fact that they were sneaking behind her father's back. Well, too bad. That was the way it had to be right now.

She flipped on the radio as the town disappeared in her rearview mirror, but didn't hear a word of the music thrumming through her speakers.

She and Lily had gone to the high school dance and it had been a bore with a capital B. The local band had only known about five country-and-western songs, and they'd played them over and over again, grating on Shelby's already frayed nerves. She told herself now that she'd really tried to get into the mood of the dance but hadn't been able to find anything remotely romantic or exciting about the gym that always smelled faintly of overused wrestling mats. The boys were immature, the music had been dull, the ambience, if that's what you'd call it, an odd mix of desperation and redundancy.

Shelby was sick to death of high school, tired of her friends, uninterested in the cliques and social scene that everyone else seemed to find so incredibly fascinating. Yeah, about as intriguing as a tobacco-spitting contest.

Earlier in the day, as her father had been packing his garment bag for a trip to Dallas, she'd claimed that she was staying overnight with Lily, and Lily had lied to her folks, who were going out of town, about sleeping over at Shelby's house. It had been a perfect plan. Lily could spend some time alone with Todd, and Shelby could meet Nevada.

She smiled and shifted down as she stared at the twin splashes of light cast by her car's headlights. She and Nevada had been seeing each other on the sly for a couple of months. She'd known of him all her life, but she'd been too young to really care when, as her father had said, "that hellion's going into the service, thank God.

It's good news for this town but bad news for Uncle Sam." She hadn't thought a thing of it; she had always heard Nevada was wild and out of control, a "bastard too smart for his own good." Nevada had left town, and her life had gone on its unerring path.

But then he'd returned, and it was her time to rebel. She hadn't seen him until fate and her lead foot had collided one night. Driving home at the speed of light because she was late, Shelby had been pulled over by Nevada Smith. Serious and unblinking, he'd asked for her license and registration and, after scanning the documents with his flashlight, he'd turned the beam into her face. She'd blinked. "Hey, cut that out!"

"Well, isn't this some sort of sweet irony," he'd said. "You're Judge Cole's daughter."

"What of it?"

One side of his mouth lifted. "Let's just say he's a friend of mine."

"Hardly."

"What do you know about it?"

"The Judge doesn't have friends."

His smile widened, and she noticed then how good-looking he was, how ruggedly handsome, even if he was a cop.

"Well, I'm gonna let you off this time," he said, "but slow down, will ya? Speeding is gonna get you into trouble, Shelby."

That was when she caught a glimpse of his name tag and she realized who he was. Nevada Smith. The smart-aleck juvenile outlaw her father seemed to hate. "You know all about trouble, I hear."

"I did."

"And now you're a *cop?*"

"Yep." He laughed, a deep-throated chuckle that was filled with the very irony he'd mentioned. "Who would have thought?"

"Not my dad."

"Hey, not even me." He'd patted the side of her car and said, "Now you slow down and stay out of trouble."

*Never,* she'd thought and watched him walk back to the cruiser parked behind her car on the side of the road. Her heart was racing out of kilter and she was nervous as she pulled onto the road. Geez, had she really noticed his butt as he'd walked away?

From that moment on she'd been smitten, and it didn't help that she seemed to keep running into him, at the coffee shop or the old-time fountain at the drugstore. She'd spent hours daydreaming of him and then told herself she was an idiot. But the boys in school were so immature, and she found reasons to hang out wherever she knew he'd be. It was spring, she was restless and Nevada Smith, once-upon-a-time bad boy, appealed to her at a level she'd never experienced before. Maybe it was because he still got under her father's skin, maybe it was because he wasn't a boy, maybe it was because he was the sexiest man she'd ever met. Whatever it was, she thought of him constantly, even going so far as to carve his initials and a heart under the dumb hitching post by the pharmacy, and when she ran into him one night in Coopersville in a café after she and her friends had gone to a movie, she knew she had to have him.

"Hi," she'd said as he sat at a table alone, nursing a beer. In faded jeans and a clean T-shirt that pulled across his back, he sat low on his spine, long legs stretched into the aisle.

He glanced up, "Well, if it isn't leadfoot. How's your pa?"

"Same as ever." She felt the back of her neck turn red. He was baiting her. Teasing her. And it felt good.

"Whatever that is." He took a long sip and appraised her slowly, from the tips of her toes sticking out of her sandals, up her legs to her cutoff jeans and short blouse. "I figure he's still using his ranch as kind of a home for renegade boys who would rather work for slave wages than do time."

"Well, it's slowed some, now that you've gone straight."

He barked out a laugh and smiled that killer grin that caused Shelby's breath to catch and her pulse to beat a smart tattoo. "S'pose it has." He finished his beer, checked his watch. "What're you doin' out from under your daddy's thumb?"

She stared straight into his steely eyes. "Anything I damned well please."

"Oh, a sassy thing, are you?"

It was her turn to smile, "So I've been told."

He cocked a dark eyebrow. "You should be careful, Shelby. Talk like this could get you into trouble."

"Maybe that's what I'm lookin' for," she said and couldn't believe the words had leapt from her tongue. She was actually flirting with him.

"Then you'll find it. I guarantee it."

"Good."

His gaze lingered on hers for just a second and she saw a spark of desire—hot, male and raw. It was gone in an instant, but Shelby recognized it for what it was and her heartbeat began to echo in her head. "Be careful what you wish for, darlin', or you just might get it." He scraped his chair back and walked outside leaving Shelby, alone, feeling like a fool.

It didn't help when she glanced out the window of the café and spied Vianca Estevan climbing out of a truck driven by her brother and running across the parking lot to Nevada. She threw her arms around his neck and kissed him soundly right there in the parking lot for all the world and Shelby to see.

Nevada didn't respond, just helped her into his pickup and drove away, leaving Shelby silently calling herself every kind of idiot in the book. But she didn't care. She wanted Nevada, plain and simple, and she was used to getting what she wanted. However, for the first time in her life, she was going to chase after it.

As it was, that part hadn't been hard. Nevada, it seemed, was as interested in her as she in him. After bumping into her one night at the local swimming hole, he'd called and they'd met, begun secret dates away from her father's eyes. He'd broken it off with Vianca, he claimed, and the rumor in town was that Vianca was angry, but her father relieved. Ramón had never liked her dating a man who wasn't of Spanish descent, a man who had a bad reputation and was now a cop, a man who was just "using" her. But then, according to town gossip, Ramón had never approved of anyone Vianca dated.

For her part, Shelby fell in love. It wasn't hard. The excitement of it all—meeting behind her father's back, running through the dark in a fine spring mist, dreaming of Nevada at night, thinking of him during the day—made it easy.

So one night, when they were alone at the swimming hole of the river while the moon was riding high in the sky, he finally kissed her. A strong arm wrapped around her shoulders, dragged her onto his lap, and his mouth clamped over hers so hungrily that she could barely breathe.

Fire invaded her bloodstream, thoughts of denial fled and she knew at that moment that she would make love to him.

She hadn't, of course, hadn't gotten the chance, for as he began unbuttoning her blouse and kissing that oh-so-sensitive spot behind her ear, he'd stopped short.

"I can't do this," he'd said.

"W-why?" She was still sitting on his lap, still drunk from his kisses and beneath her rump, separated only by a couple of layers of denim, she felt his hard-on, which seemed to be potently arguing with his words.

"Shelby, you're too young, we're sneaking around, this isn't right. Oh, hell, there are a dozen reasons. You're a virgin, aren't you?"

She was stunned. "What does that have to do with anything?"

"Are you?"

"No. I...I..."

"Liar."

"What is this? Is it written across my face or something?" He chuckled. "Yeah. Or something. Look—" Firmly, he pushed her off his lap and stared across the night-black water. "Maybe someday this might work out, but...oh, Christ, no, it won't. We have to stop seeing each other."

*"Why?"*

"A million reasons."

"If it's the Judge—"

"There's a big one." He stood, dusted off his jeans.

"He doesn't run my life!"

"Sure he does. He runs everyone's life."

"But I won't let—"

"You don't have a choice. Really." He offered her a hand to pull her to her feet, but she refused, preferring to stand on her own and inch up her chin.

"I do have a choice and so do you."

"Oh, Shelby—"

"Since when do you care about what the Judge thinks?"

"Since I started caring for you." His smile was gone and his night-darkened eyes seemed sad. "Come on, I'll take you home."

"No." She flung her arms around his neck and kissed him fervently. "I—I can't do this."

"It's for the best." Then he wrapped his arms around her, held her tight against him and kissed the top of her head. Shelby's eyes filled with tears, but she didn't break down, wouldn't fall apart. Whether he knew it or not, Nevada Smith wasn't done with her.-

And tonight, after blowing off the dance, she was going to see him again. She'd called, insisted, and he'd agreed to meet with her though she'd heard the reluctance in his voice. Well, she'd change his mind. She could do that. After all, she was Judge Cole's daughter. Some of his determination should be in her damned genes.

She took a corner too fast and the tires squealed. She barely noticed.

Nevada's shift was over at midnight. He had promised to meet her at her father's ranch at one.

If things went right, she'd be waiting for him.

She maneuvered her little car around the corners of the country road that ran past the ranch. Wind streamed through her hair and cooled her skin, but her hands were sweating. She eased off the throttle at the turnoff, and her heart began to pound. Here was where it got tricky—where she could be discovered at any second.

Shifting down, she turned into the lane and prayed that she wouldn't meet a car coming from the opposite direction. She got lucky. No headlights bore down on her.

The moon was high, an April breeze blowing cool and soft as Shelby parked her convertible behind a tangle of mesquite at a turnout in the long lane winding through the hill country to the heart of her father's ranch. Somewhere in the distance a coyote howled and goose bumps rose on her flesh, but she ignored the feeling that something wasn't quite right, the eerie sense of electricity charging the air as she pocketed her keys.

Meeting Nevada this way, going behind her father's back, of course she would be apprehensive, have a case of nerves. That was it. Nothing more.

A few wispy clouds scudded in front of the moon as she dashed along the hillside where the grass smelled fresh. Somewhere in the distance a train rattled, and high overhead the lights of a jet winked in a sky strewn with stars. The range horses that weren't stabled at night snorted and lifted their heads as she ran past. Down a hill she raced, then picked her way across a stream and climbed over a fence to land on a short expanse of grass. She was breathless by the time she made it to the outbuildings.

Heart pounding through her brain, her pulse leaping as she ducked around a machine shed, she flattened against the weathered siding, her ears straining to listen. One of the dogs started barking and she bit her lip.

A door creaked open.

"What is it?" a deep male voice thundered.

Shelby thought she was dead.

The fool dog barked even louder, more wildly. She hardly dared breathe. "Shut up!" the man ordered. "No-good skittish mutt!"

"Somethin' wrong?" another voice, this one reedy and impatient, demanded.

"Nothin' I kin see."

"Damned dawg."

"What he needs is a bitch in heat," a third voice said, then let out a low, gravelly laugh that ended in a coughing fit. "But then, don't we all?"

She recognized the voice and her stomach turned sour. Ross McCallum. There was something about Ross McCallum she didn't trust. She'd known him for years, and lately she'd caught him staring at her with eyes that seemed cruel.

"C'mon, Jeb. We're playin' here. You in or out?"

"In. I said I was in, McCallum. Hold on to yer damned horses. I'll see your five and raise you ten." Jeb's voice was deep and smooth.

"Then get the fuck inside, would ya? We ain't got all night." McCallum was edgy.

"Hold yer horses—"

"Either piss or get off the pot!"

"Shit, McCallum, you got some bug up yer ass?" Jeb demanded.

"Yeah—you could say that."

"Meaner than a snake, that's what you are." The screen door closed with a bang. "Probably has to do with Nevada Smith making deputy."

Shelby froze. Her heart nearly stopped. What did Ross McCallum have to do with Nevada?

"Looks like Smith's walkin' the straight and narrow." The reedy voice reverberated through the yard. "Got hisself a real job, got some money tucked away—cash he saved while he was workin' for Uncle Sam—and now the biggest prize of all. He's squirin' around the Judge's sweet little daughter—man, did you ever see such a ripe piece of ass?"

"Shut up, Frank," McCallum snarled.

Heat climbed steadily up Shelby's neck. Anger fired her blood. Who did these men—these low-life cowpunchers—think they were to be talking about her like that?

"Ruby Dee, she must not be givin' ya what ya need." Jeb again.

"Leave that whore out of this."

Sniggering laughter slithered out of the window. "Cain't say as I blame ya fer wantin' to give the Judge's daughter a ride." Reedy voice—Frank—laughed and the sound was pure evil. "Man, I'd give my right arm to have a taste of that sweet pussy."

"You and me both," Jeb agreed.

Shelby wanted to run away as fast as her legs would carry her.

"But she's savin' it for Smith." A snort of malevolent glee from Frank, a whip-thin, pimply-faced cowboy she'd met only a few times before. "And boy, does that piss the Judge off."

"Enough!" McCallum's voice had an edge as rough as sandstone. "Let's play."

"Okay, okay." Frank was still chuckling. "I'll see ya—but don't try and deny it, McCallum, you've got an iron hard-on for Princess Cole that just won't quit."

*Bam!* Something hit the table hard. Probably a fist. "Shut the fuck up, Frank, or I'll knock your teeth so far down your throat they'll fly out your ass. Got it?"

"Hey, whoa, McCallum, he was only funnin' ya. Let's all jist cool down and play. All right now?" Jeb was playing the part of referee. "We've got ourselves enough Jack Daniels for another round or two, and then whoever wins can take the rest of us to the Last Stand later, okay?"

Tension crackled. No one said a word. Shelby held her breath. Sweat slickened her palms.

"Fine," McCallum said in his deep, grating voice. "I'll call."

Wishing to high heaven that she'd come up with some other meeting place, Shelby quivered inside. The ugly conversation rang in her ears and caused fear to skitter down her spine. If she had half a brain she'd turn back now, get in her car and make tracks home. She'd forgotten about the Friday night poker game that was a tradition with some of the ranch hands who drank, played cards, then sometimes hauled themselves into town.

*If you turn back now, you won't see Nevada.*

No way.

Determination squared her shoulders and she slowly eased forward, slinking in the shadows, avoiding the humming blue glow of the security lamps, creeping toward the stables where her mare, a prize-winning Appaloosa, was housed. She had to see Nevada tonight. *Had* to.

A low rumble escaped from the dog's throat, but Shelby edged around the machine shed. Her heart pounded in her ears and her nerves were strung as tight as bowstrings. She cast a worried look over her shoulder to the bunkhouse, but the door didn't open again and the dog—oh, damn, where was the dog? Squinting hard, she didn't see him sitting on the porch, but it was shadowed there. He could be anywhere, ready to start barking and growling.... There he was, crouched by the fence, where a few scattered trucks and Jeeps were parked. The hackles on the back of his neck were raised and his yellow canine eyes, illuminated evilly in the glow of the lamps, were following her every move, but he didn't so much as flinch. Didn't offer up the tiniest snarl.

Shelby's throat closed in fear.

*Go ahead, do it. Go on, Shelby. Don't be a wimp. You've come this far, you can't back out now. Nevada's waiting.*

Biting her lip, she shouldered open the door of the stables, cringing as it creaked and the dog let out a sharp warning bark. Her heart was hammering as she slipped through the crack and felt along the wall to the door of the tack room. She couldn't risk a light, but she knew where her bridle was hung, just this side of the window. Her fingertips grazed the leather reins. Deftly, she removed the bridle from its hook, then, feeling along the wall, edged her way into the stables again and walked swiftly down a cement aisle to the far stall, where her mare waited.

"Easy, girl," Shelby whispered as she unlatched the gate and stepped inside. Her eyes were adjusting to the darkness, and she saw the white splotches on Delilah's rump. The smells of horses, manure and dust filled her nostrils as she eased the straps of the bridle over the mare's long nose and ears.

Delilah, high-strung by nature, snorted and tossed back her head. Even in the darkness, her white-rimmed eyes were visible. "Shhh...It's me." Shelby patted the mare's sleek neck as she tightened the chin strap. "Come on." Carefully, she led her horse along the unlit corridor to a back door. With each step, steel horseshoes rang against the concrete, but still there was no sound of dog or men. As she passed by the windows, she caught a glimpse of the bunkhouse, where the lights were glowing through door and windows.

So far, so good.

Praying the old hinges wouldn't let out any noise, Shelby shoved the back door open and tugged on Delilah's reins.

The mare's nostrils flared as Shelby led her into the dark field, where the air was thick with the promise of rain. Snorting and side-stepping, Delilah minced, as if she, too, felt the electricity of the night. "Take it easy. That's a girl," Shelby whispered, using the fence post to help her climb onto the mare's broad back.

Clamping her knees tight, Shelby clucked softly. "Let's go."

Delilah took off. She broke into an easy lope that accelerated with each stride, eating up the dry earth and range grass, until they were racing through the night.

Shelby's heart soared.

The dog and Ross McCallum were far behind her.

Ahead lay Nevada.

Adrenaline rushed through her veins at the thought of seeing him again. Wind tore through her hair. Thunder rumbled over the hills. The night bristled with anticipation. More clouds choked the moon and covered most of the stars.

Shelby leaned forward. "Come on, come on," she urged, not wanting to waste a second. Soon she'd be with Nevada again, soon she'd touch him, hold him...oh, God, her throat went dry at the thought of what the hours ahead promised.

If he showed up.

But of course he would. Why wouldn't he?

Though he'd hinted that they shouldn't see each other again, she couldn't believe that he'd stand her up.

She hoped beyond hope that Nevada was waiting for her. He was her first—her only—love. She'd dated a few boys during high school, but had never gotten serious, never gone much further than making out once in a while. But with Nevada it had been different from the start. When he'd returned to Bad Luck, the gossip mill had gone crazy, grinding the grist daily about the town hellion who not only had the nerve to show up again, but to somehow land a job as a deputy. He'd already been linked with several women in town, including Vianca Estevan, a local girl with a reputation as tarnished and corroded as Caleb Swaggert's old Dodge station wagon.

But that was long over, Shelby told herself. Now she, and she alone, was the woman in his life.

She gave the mare her head. Delilah responded, powerful muscles stretching and bunching, running faster and faster, her hooves pounding over hay stubble and weeds.

Through the fields, past the skeletal remains of an old cabin and along the base of a ridge, the horse raced freely. Shelby tucked like a burr to the mare's shoulders. Sinuous muscles moved beneath her bare legs, coarse mane twined in her fingers. Thunder rolled over far-off hills.

Delilah crested a final rise. Then, as Shelby's fingers tightened over the reins, the nervous mare began to slow, until, tossing her head, she was walking along a trail that wound downward to a creek on the very north edge of the ranch. Sweat shone on the mare's coat. Bats flew by in a whoosh of wings. The scents of dust and wildflowers mingled in the air.

Oaks lined the creek and their dark shapes loomed large and foreboding. Shelby squinted, searching the darkness for any sign of Nevada, crossing her fingers, silently praying that he would be there. "Please," she whispered over Delilah's breathing and the plop of her hooves. Then she saw it—the glowing red tip of a cigarette—a beacon flaring through the shadowy trees.

"You made it." Nevada's voice had a way of touching her heart.

"Of course I did." She swung a leg over Delilah's back and hopped to the ground. "I said I would."

He took a final drag on his cigarette, dropped it and squashed it under the heel of his boot. "This isn't a good idea."

"So you've said." Wrapping the reins of Delilah's bridle over a sapling, Shelby sauntered up to him. Even in the darkness she recognized his sharp features and aloof stance. Wearing faded jeans and a T-shirt, he was so much more approachable than when he was decked out in his uniform. "I think you're wrong."

"You do, do you?"

"Mmm. What could be wrong about this?" she asked as she stood toe to toe with him and boldly wrapped her arms around his neck.

"It could lead to trouble."

"Maybe I want trouble." she said brazenly, shocked by her own words.

"You don't. Believe me." But his arms locked around her waist, the strength of his muscles comforting.

"You don't know what I want."

"Sure of that?"

"Um-hm."

The creek gurgled and Delilah's bridle clinked softly. Insects hummed and the wind picked up, pushing more clouds over the moon. "You want what all women want, Princess," he said, bending down so that his breath whispered through her hair, his words seemed to caress her ear. Shelby tingled inside. "You want a man to provide for you, take care of you and give you lots and lots of babies."

"Not me," she said, shaking her head.

"Why're you different?"

"You tell me." She tilted her head back, looked upward into his night-shadowed eyes.

His teeth flashed white in an irreverent smile. "Okay. First, you're rich as hell."

"No, I mean—"

"And then you're Judge Red Cole's daughter."

"But—"

"On top of that you're spoiled and sassy and smart as a whip."

She didn't know whether to be complimented or insulted. "Wait a minute—"

"You ace all your tests in school, flirt outrageously with boys you never intend to date, drive that damned yellow convertible of yours too fast and study too hard. Sometimes you act like a spoiled brat and other times you seem a lot older and wiser than you should be." Strong fingers twined in her hair, tilting her head back, forcing her to look at his night-darkened face. "You told me there was somethin' important you wanted to talk about, that I had to meet you, and that was a damned lie—you and I both know it."

"It is important that we be together. Don't you think?"

"I'm just trying to be smart about this."

"Aren't you?"

"Nope. The truth is, I don't know what to do with you, Shelby Cole," he admitted, and for the first time since knowing him, she heard a note of desperation in his voice.

"Liar," she teased.

"I'm serious."

*Oh, if only you were! Love me, Nevada, oh, please just love me!* She started to blurt out the words, but didn't. "I'm serious, too," she said.

"And it scares the living hell out of me."

"Why?"

"Because I can't get involved with you, Shelby."

"You are involved."

Somewhere overhead a night bird flapped his wings, and the wind rustled through the leaves of the live oaks. Nevada kissed her forehead and she felt him tremble. "You and I—"

"Don't say it." She moved a finger to his lips. "Don't say we're from different worlds or anything so—so clichéd as that," she whispered. "I know it. It doesn't matter."

"Of course it does." His mouth moved against her finger, his tongue flicking against her skin, making her shiver. She traced his lips and heard him groan from somewhere deep inside. With the tip of her finger she prodded slowly and he opened his mouth, his tongue surrounding her finger, his mouth gently sucking.

Shelby quivered, her blood running hot and wild. Inside she turned to liquid fire. She wanted to kiss him, touch him, experience the wonder of making love to him.

He pulled his head away. "Don't," he warned.

"Why not?"

"We don't have to go through this again." Releasing her, he swore under his breath and stepped back.

"Nevada—"

Angrily, he jabbed two sets of stiff fingers through his hair. "You don't know what you're getting into here," he said tightly. She saw the tension in his broad shoulders as he walked to the shore of the creek and reaching upward, braced himself against a low branch of one of the oaks.

"Of course I do."

"How?"

"I—I know what happens between a man and woman."

"Do you?" His voice held a sneer of disbelief.

"Yes! I was practically raised on this ranch. I—I watched the bulls with the cows and the stallions that were brought in for the mares. I—I wasn't supposed to," she admitted as she walked up behind him and wrapped her arms around his waist, "but I did."

He flinched. "Well, it's a little different with people."

She laid her head between his shoulder blades, holding him close, hearing him breathe. Dear God, was that his heart beating so wildly, or hers? He smelled of smoke and musk, and his muscles flexed hard at the feel of her. "Different how?"

"Don't play dumb, Shelby. It's not your style."

"Nevada—don't you want me?"

He let out a low groan; then, taking the hand that was flat over his abdomen, he pulled it downward to his fly. She started to jerk away, but he was forceful and flattened her palm over the bulge in his crotch. "What do you think?" he asked and let go.

She didn't. "That...this...is natural."

"Don't mess with me, Princess," he said. "What this is, is dangerous."

"Nevada, I think I love you." The words were out before she could take them back.

"Oh, shit, no. You don't know a thing about love." He turned and faced her again, and this time she saw more than anger in the lines of his face. There was a different emotion in his eyes, a raw pain she didn't understand.

"I know what I feel."

"You're a kid."

"Eighteen next year."

"As I said, a kid." Leaning his forehead against hers, he sighed. "You'd better leave."

"No." She stood on her tiptoes and kissed him softly on the lips, felt his resistance and kissed him again, more slowly this time. His mouth opened, his tongue slipped past her teeth and he wrapped his arms around her. The world seemed to fade away as he kissed her long and hard. Her bones started to melt, her blood heated and she moaned softly when he lowered his head and kissed the corner of her mouth and the slope of her neck. His lips brushed a spot near her collarbone and deep inside she quaked, wanting more— oh God, so much more.

Holding her tight, he rubbed against her. The hard fly of his jeans pressed against her, and through her shorts she could feel him—hot and hard and wanting.

Slowly he backed her up until her rump was stopped by the trunk of one of the trees and he held her there, kissing her, his hands fisting in her hair, his mouth moving magically over every bare inch of her skin.

"This is what you want, Shelby?" he asked.

"Yes."

He kissed her harder, his tongue plunging into her mouth, his breathing raspy. Her chest was crushed, her legs pinned with his and she shivered with passion as he pulled her blouse from her cut-offs and moved a hand against her abdomen, reaching upward, fingers delving inside her bra to find her breast, graze her nipple.

"You're sure?"

"Yes." *Oh, God, yes.* Her thighs flexed involuntarily and she moaned. Unbuttoning her blouse, he slid the strap of her bra down her arm, then lifted her breast and slowly, nearly torturously, teased her nipple with his tongue and teeth.

Deep inside she began to ache. Throb. Want with a hot need she'd never felt before. It felt so right to hold him, to kiss him, to do things she'd never before dared. A part of her knew that she was about to step through a door that would close forever behind her. And yet she couldn't resist.

Arching, she pressed her hips ever tighter to his, feeling his hardness, wanting that smooth skin against hers.

He kissed and sucked. She grabbed his head, drawing him closer, feeling pleasure and pain as his teeth gently scraped her skin and her breast swelled, aching for more of his touch.

"This is crazy," he growled, but didn't stop. She tossed back her head as together, clinging to each other, they slid to the ground. As her back pressed against the earth, he lifted his head and kissed her hard on the lips. He pushed her blouse over her shoulders and reached around her, unhooked her bra and bared her breasts to the night. His mouth and hands were everywhere, touching, kissing, feeling and causing her to shiver with need.

Her heart pounded in her ears. Her fingers dug into his back until he paused long enough to yank his T-shirt over his head and toss it aside. Corded muscles flexed as he pulled her up to meet him. Hard, bare skin brushed hers. Boldly, she touched the flat nipples hidden within a sworling matt of springy chest hair. His nipples tightened beneath her fingertips. Quick as a rattler striking, he grabbed her wrist. "Careful—"

"Of what?"

"Me."

"Should I be scared?" she teased.

"Oh, yeah."

In response she lowered her hand, her fingers skimming his skin to rest at the waistband of his jeans. He sucked in his breath and she felt the tip of his hardness.

"Sweet Jesus," he whispered as she tugged at his button fly and his worn Levi's parted in a rapid series of pops. She began to shove the jeans over his hips when he grabbed her wrists with steely fingers. "There comes a time, Shelby, when no man, and I mean *no man,* can stop."

Swallowing hard, she gazed into smoldering gray eyes and slowly reached forward. He sucked in his breath as her fingers surrounded the thickness of his cock and he closed his eyes when she moved her hand. "Shelby—don't," he warned. "I don't know—oh, God."

He reacted quickly, kicking off his boots and jeans and reaching for the zipper of her cutoffs. It slid down in a soft hiss that seemed to echo through the hills. Effortlessly, he slid the scrap of denim and her panties down her legs, his fingers, pushing off her boots, and before she could take a second breath, she was lying naked with him, feeling the cool breath of wind bring goose bumps to her skin, hearing the rippling sound of the creek rushing past and the crack of distant thunder.

Naked flesh pressed hard against naked flesh. Lips found lips.

Shelby kissed and was kissed and her fingers dug into the hard muscles of Nevada's back. *There's no going back,* her mind warned, but she didn't pay any attention; didn't care.

"God, you're beautiful," he said, staring down at her as he gently nudged her knees aside. "So damned beautiful."

Need and white-hot desire throbbed through her veins. The smell of sex was in the air.

"I love you, Nevada," she whispered fervently.

He closed his eyes. Hesitated.

He couldn't stop. Not now. She pulled him closer and whispered hoarsely into his ear. "I want you. Nevada, please...love...me...."

His arms surrounded her and he shifted, thrusting deep inside her, breaking the fragile barrier of her virginity and holding her close as she cried out.

Nothing would ever be the same.

# Chapter 8

"I carved a heart with your initials in the hitching post outside the drugstore," she whispered, cradled in Nevada's arms, looking upward through the branches of the trees to the rapidly disappearing stars. Clouds had rolled in, the thunder that had sounded so far away was closer and she'd seen forks of lightning sizzling bright in the hills.

"You didn't."

"Mmm." Snuggling against him, she sighed softly and listened to the sound of his breathing as afterglow slowly faded. So this was what it was like to make love to a man, to feel him inside you, to *want* his body joined with yours.

Making love with him had been frightening and exhilarating. Painful at first and then incredible.

"The hitching post in the middle of town?"

"Yep. On the underside."

"What possessed you to do that?"

She shrugged, feeling suddenly young and foolish. "It seemed like a good idea at the time."

"I'd hate to see what you consider a bad one."

She chuckled and knew she was falling hopelessly and gloriously in love.

He kissed the top of her head. "You know, I think it might be considered a crime. Disfigurement of a public landmark, vandalism or—"

She rolled over and shut him up with a kiss. Though she was sore between her legs from their lovemaking, she still wanted to be close to him, to feel him against her. His arms wrapped around her, and he shook his head as she lay on top of him.

"You are somethin'." He pressed his lips to the tops of her breasts.

"What?"

"Don't know. Can't figure it out."

"Try."

"Believe me, I have," he said and then leaned up to kiss her mouth again. Harder this time. Insistent. She opened her mouth and sighed. His hands rubbed her back, settling near her buttocks—work-roughened palms molded to her soft skin. His fingers dug deep. Wind, smelling of rain, rushed across her bare skin, catching in her hair. Somewhere nearby an owl hooted.

Shelby's flesh tingled. He kissed each breast, his mouth pulling on her nipples.

Liquid fire ran through her blood as he suckled, harder and harder. She closed her eyes. Beneath her his manhood stiffened.

"Again?" she whispered incredulously, and before she could ask anything more he shifted slightly, adjusting himself to fill her once more. She gasped as he drove upward, arching his back, his buttocks pinching. Strong hands held her fast and she began to sway, catching his slow-moving rhythm, losing herself in the magic of the night.

Her mind spun with erotic images. Desire caused her to melt inside. He was everything at this moment, her beginning and end. She closed her eyes, lost in desire that pulsed deep inside, the ache that he created and relieved. "Nevada," she cried hoarsely, "oh, God...Nevada..." He moved more quickly now, and she was enveloped by his spirit, caught in the wonder of the night. Her breath came in short bursts, perspiration beaded on her skin, her heart beat frantically and her mind spun out of control.

"I love you."

Had she said it? Or he?

Raindrops began to fall from the sky.

"Nevada, oh, God . . ." Her fingers delved deep into his shoulder muscles.

He groaned; his hands held her fast and he quickened his pace again, driving upward ever faster. "That's it, that's it, oh, Shelby . . ."

A spasm of pure ecstasy shot through her. She jolted. Cried out. With a primeval groan, he let go. Spilled himself in her. Fire and ice, heat deep inside, her skin instantly chilled with the first drops of rain.

She shuddered and fell against him, exhausted.

His heartbeat thundered against her ear. He breathed as if he couldn't draw another breath.

The sky opened.

Cold beads splashed against her bare back.

Nevada stirred, his hands twisting in the wet strands of her hair. "You're going to drown," he teased, still gasping for breath.

"I don't care."

"Well, you will."

"Never." She lay on top of him and laughed as rain dripped down her nose.

Strong arms surrounded her and he kissed her temple. "Oh, yeah, Princess, believe me, you will. Big-time."

"You don't know me."

"Well enough," he said, giving her a gentle slap on her behind. "I think we should grab our clothes and make a run for my truck. I parked it on the other side of the fence, half a mile away."

"Half a mile?"

"Didn't want anyone to catch us."

She laughed at his caution.

"Come on. I'll drive you wherever it is you want to go."

It sounded like heaven, but Shelby couldn't risk it. She was already pushing it; even now her father might have called Lily's place and realized his only daughter had lied to him. For all she knew, he could have phoned the police or, worse yet, his own private search party of ranch hands.

Squinting against the shower, she cast a wary glance up at the dark sky and shivered. Oh, to leave with him now and be forever with Nevada Smith. "I've got to get Delilah back to the ranch and cooled down," she said. "That might take some doing."

The rain increased, the shower intensifying to a downpour. "I'd feel better if you'd come with me," he said. One persuasive hand trailed down her wet thigh.

"I can't. Really." Forcing herself, she rolled off him, grabbed her damp panties and cutoffs and pulled both on. She felt different now, a woman at last as she searched the muddy grass for her boots.

"Shelby—"

"Really. I've got to go back to the ranch."

He didn't respond, just helped her find her ancient cowboy boots. As she tugged them over her feet, he tossed her blouse and bra to her.

"I don't like this."

"I'll be fine," she assured him, though she was already soaked to the skin.

He grabbed his jeans and stood. One hand surrounded the crook of her elbow. "I'd better come with you."

"Don't be silly," she argued but warmed at the thought that he wanted to be with her, to see her safely home—a gentleman's heart in a cowboy's skin. "I got here by myself. I can get home all right."

He wasn't convinced. "It would be better—"

"—if no one knew we were together," she finished for him, ignoring his worried tone. She hooked her bra, then, shivering, stuffed her arms through the short sleeves of her cotton blouse. "Okay?"

He hesitated, swore under his breath, then grabbed her and his lips covered hers in one last, desperate kiss. Rain peppered the ground, and a breeze chilled her bare skin. "Call me when you get home or wherever it is you're staying," he ordered, standing naked in the night, water dripping from his bare skin. "I want to know that you're okay."

"I will," she promised, touched that he cared.

He yanked on his jeans.

Fumbling with the buttons of her blouse, she blinked hard and told herself it was just the rain, she couldn't be crying. Drops of rainwater ran down her nose and chin. Her fingers seemed suddenly thick and useless.

"Let me." Nevada, his fly not yet buttoned, his bare feet becoming muddy, brushed her hands away and carefully slipped each tiny pearl button through its hole. "There you go."

"Thanks."

"My pleasure." His smile was a crooked slash of white in the dark night. "You be careful, Shelby," he said roughly, then took her face between his palms and kissed her hard.

When he lifted his head, she nodded mutely, her heart nearly breaking.

He helped her onto Delilah's back and stood, feet planted apart, arms folded over his naked chest as she pulled on the sodden reins and clucked softly to the horse. Delilah needed no urging. Nose turned to the wind, she took off, scrambling up the hillside, eager to return to the stables.

Casting a final glance over her shoulder, Shelby caught one last glimpse of Nevada's dark form before he disappeared behind the veil of rain and his image was lost to her.

Now it was time to go home.

"Come on." She leaned over the mare's shoulders as they reached the ridge.

The storm burst over her. Wind and water blew across the bent grass. Lightning flashed in eerie, jagged fingers. Thunder cracked and rolled, echoing through the hills.

Squinting hard, Shelby gave Delilah a gentle nudge with her knees. The mare bolted, long legs lengthening, hooves pounding the muddy earth. A burning sensation at the apex of Shelby's legs reminded her of her recent lovemaking with Nevada and she smiled despite the lash of wind and rain. So she was cold to the bone, so she might be found out and catch hell from her father, so the wet horsehair beneath her bare legs rubbed her skin raw, it had all been worth it. She was a full-fledged woman now, thanks to Nevada Smith.

Across the fields Delilah galloped, faster and faster. Shelby blinked and wiped her eyes with one hand while the other held fast to the leather straps and a fistful of the Appaloosa's mane. Without the moon, the night was dark, the vast stretches of grassland seemingly barren and bleak. Shelby rode by instinct, trusting her mount's intuition and her own sense of direction as the acres sped past.

How late was it? Had her father called? What would she face

when she got back to the ranch? What if someone—like Ross McCallum—had discovered her car? Worries she had pushed aside now towered large in her mind. What would she say? Would the Judge believe her if she lied? The truth would kill him.

Shivering, teeth chattering, she felt her blouse flatten against her skin and her hair drip as it tangled in the wind that now seemed bitter and harsh. "Faster, Delilah," she commanded, "Run." Hooves flew and mud splattered upward.

Past the old cabin and by a field where longhorns grazed in the storm, the game mare sprinted.

A jagged streak of lightning fired the sky and Delilah shied, swerving. Shelby pitched forward, held fast to the mare's mane and somehow managed to stay astride. Heart hammering, she righted herself and caught sight of the blue glow of the exterior lights of the ranch, outbuildings shimmering eerily through the rain.

"God, help me," she whispered. The bunkhouse was dark, but security lights still offered a beacon. Thankfully, no illumination came from the stables. No one had noticed that Delilah was missing.

Still Shelby was careful, slowing Delilah and dismounting far out of the pool of light cast by the outdoor lamps. Her boots squished in the new mud. Ears straining for any sound of dog or man, Shelby quietly led her mare into the warm, dry stables. She unbuckled the bridle, slid it off Delilah's head and locked the mare in her stall. All Shelby wanted to do was escape as fast as she could, to sneak into the darkness before she was caught, but she took the time to brush Delilah and cool her down, offering water and hoping against hope that none of the hands would notice any change in the Appaloosa's appearance when they checked the horses in a few short hours.

She hung the bridle on its peg and silently prayed that no one would see it and wonder why it was soaked.

Then she opened the door a crack and slid outside. Most of the trucks that had been parked near the machine shed were missing and she couldn't see the dog anywhere, but she sensed someone— something—watching her.

*You're imagining it,* she told herself as she took off at a dead run through the fields, but she couldn't shake the feeling that hidden eyes assessed her every move. Biting her lip, she silently begged God that her convertible would still be parked in its hiding spot.

Nevada's worries had made her jittery. The storm only added to her case of nerves. She couldn't wait to put miles between her and her father's ranch.

She had to pick her way across the creek and she slid on the slick grass and mud as she climbed the bank. Shoulders huddled against the rain, she sprinted to the spot where she'd parked her car behind the barrier of mesquite trees. The little yellow convertible was just where she'd left it—top down, the interior drenched with rain.

Shelby didn't care. It would dry.

"Thank you," she whispered, just in case God was listening.

Gratefully, she climbed behind the wheel. She wiped the rainwater from her eyes, glanced in the rearview mirror and saw that her lips looked swollen, her pupils huge in her eyes, her hair damp and lank. But she smiled at the reflection. She'd go home, sneak into the house, shower and change and dream of Nevada the rest of the night. Everything was fine.

The engine sparked quickly and she rammed her little car into reverse. She backed up two feet before the wheels started spinning and the BMW slid to one side. "Come on, come on," she said, easing up on the accelerator and then punching it. Again the tires spun, unable to take hold. She threw the car into first and stepped on it. The convertible lurched, wheels whirring wildly, then settled back as she eased off the gas.

"Don't do this to me. Please. Not now." Over and over she tried until the windows were fogged. Sweat had broken out under her arms and she realized she was just digging her back tires into deep ruts. When she opened the car door and stepped outside, her boots sank into the mud.

*Great,* she thought sarcastically, *just damned great!*

She picked her way through the thicket of mesquite to the lane where a fast-moving stream of water was rushing over the gravel and flooding the already-swollen ground. Things were definitely going to get worse before they got any better.

Back at the car, she knelt beside a back wheel and felt beneath the wheel well to discover that the tire had not only settled into a deep rut of its own making, but the entire back end of her BMW had sunk nearly to its rear axle.

She'd never get out without a winch.

"Now what?" she wondered and looked through the sheeting deluge toward the ranch house nearly a quarter of a mile away. She knew how to get inside, knew where an extra set of keys to her father's Chevy pickup was hung, could find a chain in the machine shop and with the help of flashlights, ingenuity, effort and a lot of luck, could wrap the chain around the axle, hook the other end to the trailer hitch, and, barring any further disaster, tow her car out of the muck.

Maybe.

If all the ranch hands had gone into town.

That wasn't supposed to happen. They were paid so that someone—usually the foreman—was on the premises around the clock, but on Friday nights they generally skipped out. She could only hope.

It was risky at best, a disaster at worst, but what other choice did she have?

"Just go for it," she told herself and started running toward the house. She was soaked to the skin and as dirty as a pig rooting in a bog, but it didn't much matter considering the task at hand. Breathing hard, exhaustion only kept at bay by adrenaline, she ran down the lane and slowed before she reached the cattle guard a hundred feet from the bunkhouse. Acutely aware that the watchdog or some equally mean-tempered hired hand might be stirring, she moved stealthily, thankful for the steady pounding of raindrops plopping into puddles, the rush of wind across the hills and the wild gurgle of rainwater running through the gutters.

The dog was still missing, so she walked straight to the ranch house, left her muddy boots on the back porch and stepped into the kitchen. Biting her lip, she reached to the right. Her fingers encountered the extra set of key rings hung on hooks in the wall. Keys jangled noisily. Somewhere outside the dog barked. Shelby's stomach clenched in fear. She didn't waste any time. She snatched every set of keys from the hooks. Stuffing them into the pocket of her shorts, she managed to slide into her boots and softly shut the door behind her.

So far, so good.

Shelby was off the porch and around the edge of the building within seconds. She slunk through the wet shadows and made her way into the wavering pool of lamplight in the yard, where she walked directly to the truck. Glancing over her shoulder and spying no one, neither man nor beast, she opened the door.

Instantly the interior was awash with illumination. Shelby slid behind the wheel and pulled the door shut. The interior light blinked off, but she was shaking, certain she would be caught. Heart thudding, she tried the first key. No luck. She gritted her teeth. The second failed as well. Her fingers were practically useless, her nerves stretched thin when the third wouldn't slide into the lock. What if she'd left a set in the house? What if none of these worked? What if—

"Who the hell are you?" a voice bellowed.

She jumped. Squealed. Fell against the steering wheel.

The horn blasted. The dog began barking wildly from somewhere outside as the door to the truck was ripped open.

The interior light blazed on again. In the harsh glare she stared into the florid, determined face of Ross McCallum. His wet hair was plastered to his head, his eyes mere slits, his expression somewhere between surprise and satisfaction. A silver-barreled pistol was clutched in one big fist.

Shelby nearly peed in her pants.

"Well, lookie here, would ya, dawg! We got us the Judge's little daughter right here in this damned truck."

The smell of sour whiskey blew inside the cab. Shelby's stomached roiled.

"What'cha doin', Shelby-girl, stealin' the old man's pickup?"

"Borrowing it," she forced out, scared witless. She'd bluff him. Had to.

"And why's that?"

"None of your business." This man was her father's hired hand, nothing more, she reminded herself. But the jagged remnants of the conversation she'd overheard emanating from the bunkhouse earlier played through her mind. Inside she was jelly, more afraid than she'd ever been in her life.

"Somethin' to do with that fancy little car you got hid up the lane?" He jerked his head in the direction of the main road, and her heart sank as his eyes roved over her disheveled state—wet hair, nearly transparent blouse, short, drenched cutoff jeans. From behind him somewhere the dog growled. "Yep, I seen it when I came back from town—that paint job has a way of catching in head-lights, y'know." His eyebrows rose as if he expected her to nod in agreement. "I stopped, saw that it weren't goin' nowhere in this storm and figured you'd show up sooner or later."

Her heart sank. He'd been waiting for her. Watching. Probably laughing inside.

He rubbed the stubble on his chin. "So what you been up to, eh? Nah, don't tell me. Let me guess. You've been out whorin' with my old buddy—*Deputy* Nevada Smith."

"I'm just here to borrow the truck," she lied, forcing a false bravado into her voice. "I don't have to explain myself to you."

Nostrils flared in his red, unshaven face. "No, I s'pose you don't." He seemed to mull what she'd said over, and stupidly she felt a ray of hope. "Lookie here, I know ye're in a fix what with the car and sneakin' around your daddy's back and all, but I'm willin' to help you out, get you out of this jam you're in, keep my mouth shut, if ya want."

She didn't believe him. Wouldn't trust him. Kept a wary eye on the barrel of the pistol he still held tight in his fingers.

"That's right." He leaned into the cab, started climbing inside.

"I don't need your help."

"Sure you do, honey," he said, and one big, thick finger reached up to trace the slope of her jaw.

"Get out!"

"Can't do it."

"I mean it, McCallum."

"Oh yeah? And what're ya gonna do?" He pulled himself into the truck and she scooted across fast, to the far side, scrabbled for the door handle. Too late. One big hand surrounded the back of her neck, dragging her close, forcing her head to his.

Oh, God, he smelled foul.

Open-mouthed, he kissed her and she nearly retched with the taste of him. "Leave me alone."

"Oh, no, sugar, I ain't gonna do that. Not now."

Fear congealed her blood. He kissed her again. Set the pistol on the dash. She hauled back to take a swing at him, but he slapped her hand away and laughed wickedly, as if he *enjoyed* her feeble attempts.

She struck again, hard, her palm smacking against his cheek. "Get out, Ross, I swear—"

"You ain't doin' nothin' but givin' me what you give that shit-all half-breed," he snarled. Then he was on her. She fought and screamed and clawed at his face, and through it all he grinned, pushing her down onto the seat.

*Crack!* The back of her head smashed against the passenger window. Pain blasted through her brain. Bright lights flashed, then the world started to go dark. She nearly passed out and he tried to kiss her. She flailed, her fingers raking down the side of his face.

"Shit! I just knew you'd be a hell-cat," he grunted, pinning her beneath him and holding both her wrists over her head in one of his big hands. "And that's just fine with me. I like a woman with some fight in her."

She hauled back and spat. To her horror, he licked the spittle from his face and smacked his lips. His free hand felt between them, groping her breasts roughly.

Sick inside, she fought his weight, felt the hardness of his cock straining against his jeans, heard the horrifying sounds of a belt unbuckling and a zipper being lowered. Oh, God, he was going to rape her!

And there was nothing she could do about it. Nothing.

"Don't," she cried, disgusted at the pleading tone in her voice. "Don't do this thing. Please. Ross—oh, no." She writhed to no avail. He was too heavy, too determined. Something inside her began to die. Tears streamed down her face and she let out horrid sounds, half screams, half sobs. *No, no, no!*

"You're gonna enjoy it," he said through lips that barely moved. "All you hot-blooded whores do."

She tried to knee him, but he was quick. He shifted. Pinned her legs apart. Pushed her hard onto the bench seat. "Come on, baby. Relax a little. You and I, we're gonna have a good time right here in Daddy's truck." He reeked of whiskey. His beard stubble rubbed hard against her face. His hands were rough, his breathing irregular. "You know, pretty baby, I've been waitin' all my life for this."

For the next week, Shelby walked around in a horrible, disbelieving fog. The sickening, ugly events of the night replayed in her mind, over and over. She showered, bathed, tried to scrub the filth from her, but it was always there, lurking just beneath the surface of her skin and hovering in the bleakest corners of her mind. She was listless and lifeless, hiding her secret, refusing to tell a soul. She avoided going to town, missed as much school as she could because of "headaches" and, at night when no one was around, curled into a ball on her bed while rocking anxiously and biting her tongue so that the tears she cried would be shed silently into her pillow.

Lydia was concerned and tried to feed her when the last thing she wanted to do was eat; her father dismissed her change in personality as a phase she was going through.

"Oh, Shelby-girl will be all right," she'd heard him tell the worried housekeeper. "It's just end-of-the-year jitters. She's worried about graduatin' from high school, you know. All girls go through this kind of thing."

"But—"

"Now, Lydia, don't you worry. She'll be fine. You're not her mother now, are ya? You're my housekeeper, and I appreciate how you've stepped in with Shelby, but she'll be fine. Just fine. Give her time to adjust."

That was always the end of the argument, though Lydia's dark eyes had always been black with concern.

Nevada called, but Shelby didn't answer, couldn't face him or hear his voice. She avoided him in town and only once did she run into him a few weeks later.

She'd been driving home from school, her thoughts returning to that wretched night. Nevada, still working for the Sheriff's Department, had pulled her over.

He strode up to her idling convertible and demanded answers she couldn't give.

"What happened?" He stood outside her driver's side window. Shelby had parked on a tree-lined street not far from her house. Oh, Lord, what could she say? She squinted up at him, but no words would form.

Nevada yanked open the door, pulled her out into the bright sunlight, stared at her so hard she thought she would melt under the harsh glare and repeated slowly, as if she were dim-witted, "What the hell happened, Shelby?"

"Nothing," she forced out.

"Like hell!"

"Leave it alone, Nevada," Oh, God, she wanted to tell him the truth, but she couldn't. He'd never understand. No one could know. No one.

"You were supposed to call me that night. I was frantic."

"I forgot." She cleared her throat.

"You *forgot?* You know, I've heard enough B.S. in my life to know when it's being slung in my direction."

"Are you going to give me a ticket or something, because if you are, just do it, and if you're not, I think I'd better get home." It took all her strength to keep her tone even, her words emotionless.

"You're shutting me out."

She didn't respond, watched a car pass as a couple of teenaged boys she knew rubbernecked, thought she was being cited and laughed over the roar of an engine and the thrum of heavy-metal music.

"I've called."

"I've been busy." Even to her own ears the excuse sounded frail.

"It's your father."

She didn't answer.

Strong fingers curled over her forearms. "If it's over, fine," he said, and she wanted to sink into the asphalt. "But at least you owe me an explanation."

"I don't owe you anything," she said tonelessly, though for the first time since Ross's attack, she felt something, a stir of passion deep within her numbness.

His jaw clamped shut. "Then what was it all about—you and me down at the creek a month or so ago?"

"Does it have to be about something?" She stared at the ground, noticed a smashed bottle cap in the gravel on the shoulder. Swallowed hard.

"Shelby?" Oh, God, was there a bit of desperation in his voice?

A part of her wanted to scream that she loved him, that she was sorry, that she knew it was irrational and pathetic to feel so ashamed of something beyond her control, but if she did, she'd have to tell him the truth and she couldn't face it. Not ever.

"Does it have to be about something? Well, yes, Shelby, it does."

"I—I can't explain it."

"Try." The desperation was gone. Replaced with anger.

She took in a deep breath, found no words. A crow flapped its black wings and settled on a telephone wire that drooped through the branches of a gnarled oak tree.

"Look at me."

With all her strength, she raised her eyes, forced herself to meet the questions in his gaze.

"Did I hurt you that bad?"

She wanted to die inside. The truth pounded in her ears. Shame drove it back. "No."

"Then—?"

What could she say? Nothing. So she didn't.

His nostrils flared and his lips twisted into a hard scowl. Storm clouds gathered in his gray eyes. "It's not true, you know," he said, his voice somehow permeating her haze of despair.

She blinked. "What?"

"That I've been seeing Vianca again."

Her heart, already bruised beyond repair, took another sharp blow.

"I—don't understand."

"It's just talk, Shelby," he said, the brackets around his mouth deep and hard. From inside his cruiser the radio crackled.

"It doesn't matter."

"Like hell!" He yanked her close, pulled her roughly against him and kissed her so hard she couldn't breathe, could barely think. When he raised his head, she looked at him through a sheen of tears. "It's you I care for. Damn my soul to hell, Shelby, but that's just the way it is."

She sniffed, the C.B. crackled again—spitting static and orders, his number and then, through the static, "...officer in need of backup..."

"Damn." His grip lessened, he took off his hat and rammed impatient fingers through his hair. "You don't believe me."

"I don't know what to believe," she said, trying to get over the hump of her ill-won guilt and degradation.

"No matter what happens, you're the one." Flinty eyes held hers in a gaze that was hot and pure. "You're the one." He strode back to his car, climbed inside, spoke into the microphone and flipped on his lights and siren. In a spray of gravel and squeal of tires, he was gone.

"Get over this," she told herself, finding some shred of faith in his words, knowing that she had to trust him, to find a way back to that safe haven she'd felt in his arms, to rediscover her own self, her sense of vitality. As she drove to her house, she glanced in the rearview mirror. "Don't let Ross McCallum do this to you," she said, tears streaming down her face, mascara leaving black tracks. "You can't let him win."

She parked near the garage, dashed around the hedge, through the gate and up the back stairs. With each riser she felt a new degree of determination, her battered pride resurfacing, bruised but not broken. Nevada loved her. He'd as much as said so. What had happened that night six weeks ago was long over. It wouldn't happen again. Ever. No man, including a scum bucket like Ross McCallum, would ever terrorize her again.

At the top of the stairs she felt a little light-headed. She walked to her room as the first wave of nausea hit her. Her stomach threatened to empty. She raced to the bathroom, barely making it to the toilet when she heaved.

Everything she'd eaten, which wasn't much, came up.

She fell back on the cool tile, then steadied herself and stood, rinsing her mouth by holding her head under the faucet. What was that all about? But she knew. Deep inside, she'd been worried sick for a couple of weeks.

"Oh, no." She hung her head.

In a second her world splintered and that which she'd tried to deny became impossible to ignore. "Oh, God, no." She ran to her bedroom, picked up her calendar and stared in disbelief. "Please, no," she whispered. "Not this..."

She was late.

Not just by one month, oh, no, it had now been nearly sixty days since she'd had her last period.

"God help me," she whispered and wished for the millionth time that her mother was still alive.

Maybe there was some mistake, maybe her cycle was just off-kilter because it was the end of the year and she'd be graduating in a couple of months. She was tired and worried and stressed out and depressed over the rape and…and…and…She gulped, stared at herself in the mirror. The excuses that she'd clung to for the past few weeks fell away as she gazed with worried eyes at her pasty-faced, nearly gaunt reflection.

It didn't matter that she hadn't found the nerve to buy a pregnancy test either at the local drugstore or farther away, in Austin, where she wouldn't have been recognized. It really didn't matter at all.

There wasn't much doubt about it: Shelby Cole knew she was pregnant.

# CHAPTER 9

*The present*

And now, ten years later, Ross McCallum was back in town. A free man. Shelby shuddered. Lying on her bed, looking up at the lazily circling ceiling fan, she reminded herself that she was no longer afraid. Since the time she'd last seen McCallum, she'd moved away from a controlling father, spent countless hours with therapists and counselors, found her self-esteem and managed to finish college in California. Eventually she'd landed in Seattle where she'd taken the exam to become a real estate broker while earning her master's degree. She'd never finished her thesis, but she was satisfied, successful, and long over the curse of her youth.

She rolled off the bed and flipped on her computer. As it warmed up, she decided to do some checking on her own. First she would try to find Nevada's friend, the private investigator. Bill Levinson. Nevada had told her to figure it out and with a little digging through the Internet, she'd put two and two together to come up with Levinson's name. It wasn't much to go on. But it was a start, and Shelby was tired of waiting for someone else to do what she had to. She hadn't stopped her quest for Doc Pritchart and anyone associated with him—relatives, other physicians, nurses or receptionists. Then there was her father's attorney—what was his name?

Orrin something-or-other. Orrin...Filkins or Fillmore or... She remembered the Judge rustling around in his desk drawer earlier, searching for his Last Will and Testament. Like a shot, she was down the stairs and into his office, where the smell of cigars smoked long ago still lingered in the air. The Judge was nowhere to be seen. Not that she cared. If he found her searching through his private things, tough. As far as she was concerned, he was stonewalling her about her life. Her daughter's life. Let him come unglued if he found Shelby rifling through his things. It served him right.

His laptop was missing as the Judge always kept it with him. But her father was old school enough to have kept a paper trail, one that should lead straight to his attorney. Without any qualms she opened the drawers of his desk, one after another. Finding no legal documents, she scoured the room for a Rolodex or address book or anything with the law firm's name on it. She pulled on the drawers of his credenza, but the sleek cherry cabinet was locked. Surely there was something...a piece of paper, letterhead, business cards ...She scanned the room and spied a ring of keys in a crystal dish near his humidor. She tried three keys before finally finding the right one. Unlocking the first drawer, she ignored a jab of conscience and started rifling quickly through files, some as old as she was. Over the sound of rattling pans, Shelby heard Lydia humming softly, the same Spanish lullaby she'd sung to Shelby as a child. From the corner of her eye she saw movement outside the window—Pablo Ramirez, the gardener who was raking the flower beds. Still there was no sign of the Judge.

Shelby's heart was beating like a drum. Sweat broke out on her forehead. "It's got to be here somewhere," she told herself, then stopped short. Her breath caught as she found a file with her mother's name on it. "What in thunder?" she whispered, her mouth drying of all spit as she realized there were slots for everyone who had ever worked for the Judge, all his relatives and even others...

*Cole, Elizabeth*
Her baby!
*Cole, Jasmine*

*Dee, Ruby*
*Estevan, Ramón*
*Hart, Nell*
*McCallum, Ross*
*Ramirez, Maria*
*Ramirez, Pablo*
*Pritchart, Ned*
*Smith, Nevada*
*Vasquez, Pedro*

The pull tabs read like a census tally for the town of Bad Luck. A cold feeling swept through Shelby, and she suddenly felt as if she was intruding, wading into a dark pool where at any moment she could step off a hidden ledge and sink to unknown and treacherous depths. Then she saw her own name.

Her father kept a file on her?

"Oh, Daddy," she whispered in despair and disbelief.

She heard the squeak of the back door as it opened, then her father's voice speaking in soft tones to Lydia. She froze as she recognized his measured tread and the tap of his cane. Biting her lip, Shelby quickly extracted a few files from the drawer—just enough that they wouldn't readily be missed. Stealthily, she shut and locked the credenza, left the key in its crystal dish and padded out of the room without a sound. Though she was ready to face her father if he caught her in his office, there was no need to tip him off that she was being so persistent, no reason to let him know that she intended to turn the house upside down and inside out as well as comb through every one of his papers in her quest to find out what had happened to her child.

His uneven gait sounded closer. Damn!

Tucking the files under her arm, she left the door slightly ajar and, to avoid running into him, cut through the butler's pantry, dining room and the living room to the foyer, where she beelined for the main stairs. She was on the landing when she heard his voice. She froze. Held her breath. Glanced to the etched-glass windows mounted high over the twin front doors. Outside the world seemed the same, the front lawn, green and lush in this dry, dusty heat, was being watered by automatic sprinklers, while inside the home where she'd grown up, her life was in a tailspin.

"—I worry about her, you know," the Judge was saying. "Shelby's obsessed right now and has the notion that everyone's against her."

"Are they not?" Lydia asked.

"Of course not." Red Cole snorted his disbelief. "Just keep an eye on her while I'm away."

"She is a grown woman."

"I know, I know, but Ross McCallum's back in town."

*"Dios,"* Lydia said. "That man, he is . . . *el diablo.*"

"You bet he is. Satan incarnate." He paused a second and Shelby strained to hear. "My daughter picked one helluva time to show up again."

"I think it is for the best," Lydia said softly. "And you, Judge, you need to tell her the truth."

"Do I?"

Shelby's fingers tightened over the files—what did Lydia and the Judge know that she didn't? Her heart was drumming so loudly that she could barely make out the conversation. She leaned over the rail and could see the silver toes of her father's boots.

*"Sí.* It is only fair. There have been too many secrets in this family."

*Amen,* Shelby thought. She'd have to talk to Lydia.

"Really. Shelby has the right to know," Lydia said emphatically.

So the housekeeper—a woman as much like a mother as any Shelby had known—obviously knew more than she did about her own family. A deep pang of betrayal burned through Shelby's heart. She'd always suspected her father of manipulating her life, but not Lydia, not the woman who had cradled her when she'd been scared, bandaged her scraped knees, and dispensed unwanted advice about friends and school and life as if Shelby had been a daughter to her. Now, it seemed, Lydia wasn't trustworthy. So who could Shelby trust? Not her father. Nor Lydia.

Nevada's rugged image raced through her mind.

*Oh, Shelby, are you foolish enough to think you can trust him?*

"Look, Lydia, I'm doin' my best, tryin' to keep my daughter safe, and that's the bottom line here." Red Cole's voice was thoughtful and then, as if Lydia had raised a disbelieving eyebrow or somehow indicated she didn't believe him, added, "Really. Damn it, I know it's time to come clean about some things, but it's not easy to have to open up your own closet doors and let the skeletons come dancin' out. Oh, hell's bells, I will. In time. My own time."

Lydia's snort of disbelief said it all.

*What skeletons?*

"I'll be at the ranch this afternoon, so don't worry about me for lunch."

"You will eat there?" she said and there was gentle reproach in her voice, undercurrents of a conversation Shelby didn't understand.

"I'll pick up something."

"But the doctor said—"

*Doctor? What doctor? Certainly not Pritchart. Was the Judge sick?* Shelby had trouble believing it. She'd never considered her father anything but healthy, hale and bull-headed.

"I'll handle it, Lydia," he snapped, irritated. "It don't matter a whole helluva lot anyway."

*Oh, Lord, what did that mean?* How sick was he?

His awkward tread became louder and Shelby, lest she be caught with the incriminating folders, dashed noiselessly up the remaining stairs to her room. Once there, she closed her bedroom door, slipped the files between her mattress and box spring and lay down on the bed as if she'd fallen asleep, just in case her father opened her door.

He didn't.

Heart thudding, a thousand questions whirling through her mind, Shelby listened as his footsteps retreated down the hallway to the wing where the master suite was housed. She let out her breath, then, impatiently staring at the ceiling where, above the slow-moving paddle fan, a fly was buzzing, she waited until she heard the door to his room open again and then his heavy tread as he climbed down the back staircase.

As soon as she was certain he wasn't returning, she pulled out the manila folders and nestled into her favorite chair—the over-stuffed seat where once her mother had held her and read nursery rhymes to her.

But she wouldn't think of Jasmine Cole just yet, or how she died. There was time enough for remembering faded images of the woman who had borne her, a woman she'd barely had the chance to know.

She concentrated on the job at hand and opened the first file, labeled with her daughter's name. It was extremely thin, holding only the birth certificate and death certificate.

Disappointment seeped through her bones. Tears burned the back of her eyes. She'd seen copies of these documents more times than she wanted to count.

*What did you expect?* her frustrated mind nagged. *Pictures? The names of Elizabeth's adoptive parents? Report cards from the school she'd attended? Her first awkward attempts at finger painting? What?*

Shelby bit hard on her lip and told herself to forge on. This was just a small obstacle and if her first attempts at finding the truth through burglary hadn't worked, she'd try something else.

She opened the second file, the one labeled *Smith, Nevada*. It held a sheaf of papers, and Shelby thumbed each item feeling as if she were trespassing on private property. Nevada Evans Smith's birth certificate, medical documents, school and army records were included, along with his juvenile history and a private investigator's report about him and his parents—his drunk of a father and runaway mother.

Shelby felt a shiver of apprehension as she sifted through the pages. She glanced over her shoulder, as if she expected Nevada to appear and catch her snooping into his private life, but that was silly. Of course she was alone in the room, and as the big blades of the paddle fan rotated over her head and the fly bounced against the window, she settled back in her chair and started to read about a man she'd once loved but had barely known, the man whom she believed to be the father of her only child.

Absently she rapped on the top of a nearby table for good luck, though surely Nevada was Elizabeth's father; he just had to be. She wouldn't even consider the other possibility. The third file—the one with her name scratched boldly across the tab—she saved for last.

*Caleb Swaggert looked like death warmed over,* Katrina thought as she paused at the doorway to his hospital room and the clipped staccato beat from her high heels no longer echoed through the hallways of Our Lady of Sorrows Hospital.

Without checking with any of the staff, she marched into the geezer's hospital room and acted as if she belonged there.

Skeleton-thin, his skin pasty and hanging without much flesh to support it, his hair reduced to a few gray tufts, Caleb lay on a hospital bed with rails ensuring that he stayed put. His eyes, so brown they appeared nearly black, were sunken into deep sockets. They stared without blinking at a television from which some televangelist was preaching ardently about the wages of sin.

Tubes and wires were attached to various parts of his body, and he appeared less than half a step from the grave. But his poor health and sorry condition weren't surprising. She'd expected as much. It was the proliferation of religious icons strewn around the room that gave her pause. Three new Bibles on a table near his bed, dozens of pictures of Jesus and the Virgin Mary tacked to the wall, statuettes of Christ gathered on the windowsill and on a table holding not only his comb, a box of Kleenex, a water glass, electric razor and box of surgical gloves, but also a miniature nativity scene, though Christmas was half a year away.

The devil sure wasn't gonna get a toehold in here.

In a way, it was spooky.

As for Swaggert, he was as close to death's door as anyone could get without actually crossing the threshold. If she wanted an interview, and she did, then she'd better get cracking before the grim reaper came to collect her interviewee, and the indicator on the old coot's heart monitor became a flat line.

"Mr. Swaggert?" she said, startling him. He jumped, the monitor over his head went crazy for a second, and he turned his gaunt face in her direction. "I'm Katrina Nedelesky." As if she were approaching a skittish colt, she moved slowly toward his bed. *Like this ancient guy is gonna bolt.* Somehow she forced a smile she hoped looked a lot more genuine than it felt. "Remember? From *Lone Star* magazine."

His balding, spotted pate creased with wrinkles for a second before a hint of understanding crossed his features.

"Did you get the contract I sent you?" she asked, edging closer to the bed and trying not to show that she felt nothing but revulsion at the sight of his bony body. She really didn't expect him to remember much. This guy was way too far gone. But she did hope beyond hope that his memory was sharp enough to recall what happened the night Ramón Estevan was shot and killed.

"You're the reporter?" he said in a dry voice that was little more than a croak.

"Yes." She nodded and felt a little better about his lucidity. "You offered me an exclusive about your testimony in the Ross McCallum case."

"I remember." Sure enough, his eyes flickered with a spark of recollection. "We have ourselves a deal, don't we?"

"We sure do."

"And the money—after I'm gone, it'll go to my daughter. Celeste. Celeste Hernandez. I sent you her address over ta El Paso."

"Yes, yes. We've been over this." *About a million times.* "I've got Celeste's name and address on file," Katrina assured him and felt a little twinge of conscience. Whatever else this old codger had done in his life, he at least felt some latent paternal responsibility.

Some people, herself included, weren't so lucky.

Caleb's wrinkled face fell in on itself. "I weren't much of a father to her. Split with her ma before she was born." So this was his feeble attempt at atonement. Some of Katrina's respect for the old codger evaporated, but she figured some fatherly interest was better than none, and even if love for a child came late in life, it was better late than never.

"I want half to go to the church—Our Lady of Sorrows, here, and half to Celeste," Caleb insisted with a dry, cackling laugh. "That is, after ya pay for the pine box they're gonna put me in."

"It's all arranged. In fact, I brought the paperwork with me," she said, snapping open her briefcase and pulling out a crisp manila envelope. "Your copy. I'll just leave it here." She placed it on the table near the miniature baby Jesus in the manger, but Caleb shook his head.

"Put it in the closet, will ya? Might git stole if it's left out."

"By who—er, whom?"

"Cain't never tell," he said, "but I don't trust no one, 'ceptin' our Lord and Savior, Jesus Christ."

"Probably a good idea." She tried to keep the sarcasm out of her voice as she tucked his envelope into a closet where a ragged plaid robe and slippers with holes resided. "I brought a pocket recorder with me," she said as she closed the closet door, "so let's get started."

"Started doing what?" a demanding voice asked.

A heavyset nurse with thick glasses and short gray hair strode into the room. Her name tag read *Linda Rafkin, RN,* and she looked like a bulldog, all flat features and deep scowl. Katrina suspected Nurse Rafkin gave orders and took no prisoners.

"This here's a woman I need to talk to," Caleb insisted.

Rafkin walked to the bed, checked the IV and glanced up at the monitor before placing a disposable cover on a thermometer and placing it gently in Caleb's ear.

"I'm Katrina Nedelesky, and Mr. Swaggert and I have an agreement for an interview—"

"Not here in the hospital you don't."

"It's all right," Caleb interjected. "Let her stay."

"I won't be a bother." Katrina wasn't about to budge.

The nurse frowned. "Mr. Swaggert needs his rest."

The old man let out a cackling laugh that ended in a coughing fit. "I think I'll be gettin' my share," he said as the nurse took his blood pressure, read the thermometer and checked his pulse. "I'm dyin'," he said matter-of-factly. "Nothin' you or any of these damned contraptions can do to change that sorry fact. So y'all git a move on." He waved her out the door. "The young lady and me, we got us somethin' to talk 'bout."

Rafkin paused, sized Katrina up from behind those thick lenses and scowled. "Thirty minutes," she finally allowed, tapping a fleshy finger on the dial of her Timex. "I'm keepin' track." With that she left in a rustle of nurse's scrubs stretched too thin.

"Ignore Nurse Busybody," Caleb said to Katrina when they were alone except for the images of the Son of God scattered about the room. "And mind that ya close the door. We don't want no one to hear what I'm about to say." With feeble fingers, he hit the mute button on the television.

Katrina didn't argue. She walked to the door, swept the hallway with a practiced glance, saw no one lurking near the door, then shut it firmly. Satisfied that they were alone, she pulled up the one uncomfortable chair in the room, inching it closer to the bed. As she took a seat, she clicked on the recorder and set it carefully between two small statues of kneeling shepherds. "I have a lot of questions," she said, "mostly about the night Ramón Estevan died."

"But that's not all?"

"No. We'll get to that night—of course it's very important. I'II want to know when you got to the store and what you were doing, whom you saw, what you overheard, but first I want to start with some background information," She withdrew a pad and pen, just to take a few personal observations as the recorder picked up the conversation.

"Like what?" He was getting suspicious.

"Well, first of all, for research and background purposes, I want a feel for the town, so you need to tell me everything you can recall about Bad Luck and about Judge Cole and his daughter, Shelby."

Caleb blinked rapidly. "Judge Cole? Why? He didn't preside over the murder case. As for his daughter, I think Shelby was out of town when it happened."

"Probably so, but bear with me. This is my story, and what I'm asking is necessary for me to get it right. Believe me. The Judge was married, right?"

"Not at that time, no. He was married, though, a long time ago. To Jasmine Falconer. Purty thing, Jasmine was. Damned purty."

"She died quite a while back. Right?"

"Not only died. Kilt herself." Caleb nodded, the back of his head scratching noisily against his starched pillowcases. "Up and slit her wrists while takin' a bubble bath in the Judge's marble tub."

Katrina cringed at the thought. She had no love for anyone remotely associated with that bastard of a judge, but she still felt an inward revulsion at the picture this old coot painted. Clearing her throat, she asked, "Why would she take her own life?"

He hesitated. Scowled. "Have you met Judge Cole?"

"Haven't had the pleasure," she said acidly.

"When you do, you'll understand." He snorted and shifted on the bed. "Jasmine was a decent woman, not that Red would know the difference."

"And you do?"

Caleb hoisted a skeletal shoulder.

"Tell me about his children," she suggested, forcing a smile she didn't feel.

"Jest one girl. Shelby. Far as I know Shelby's not quite thirty, if 'n I 'member right. Why do you want to know about her?"

"As I said, background. The way I understand it, Shelby Cole was involved with Nevada Smith, the deputy who led the investigation against Ross McCallum. Everyone I've interviewed says those two—Smith and McCallum—had been enemies for years, and they were rumored to have had a bad fight sometime before Estevan was murdered."

The old man thought for a while, and Katrina suspected he might drift off. He rubbed the stubble on his chin and said, "I'd clean fergot about the fight. But yer right. Nevada, he lost vision in one eye, and Ross ended up with cracked ribs and a broken arm or some such thing. They both wound up in the hospital. Trouble was, as I recall, McCallum always had a hankerin' for Shelby Cole."

"And she was Nevada's girl."

"At the time, I guess." Caleb shrugged again, and through the closed door the sound of a hospital cart rolling past, softly rattling, could be heard. "The gossip around town was that she was seein' Smith. Only reason I 'member is because Shelby was the Judge's daughter. Anything Red Cole did at the time was big news."

Katrina believed him.

"So—if I have the facts straight—somehow Ross McCallum ended up nearly dead in a single-car accident south of town. In Nevada Smith's truck. Is that right?"

"Yep. Ross, he supposedly stole Smith's truck the night Ramón Estevan was killed. No one can figure out why. Smith reported it missing, which wasn't too tough as he worked for the Sheriff's Department. Sure enough, a few hours later, they find it piled up against a tree south of town. Ross McCallum was drunk out of his mind, lucky to be alive."

"And Ramón Estevan was already dead. Shot by a .38."

"That's the way it was." Caleb ran a hand across his thin hair, and Katrina noticed the needles piercing his bruised skin, one attached to the tubing of his IV, the other capped, ready to draw blood again, should need be. She doubted the old guy had much left.

Katrina crossed her legs and scribbled on her pad as the recorder kept taping. "As I understand it, Ross didn't have a gun on him."

"Just Nevada Smith's old Winchester—a huntin' rifle."

She stiffened. This was a little fact she'd overlooked. "But not the murder weapon?"

"Nope. As you said, the bullet that killed Ramón Estevan was from a .38."

She made a note, then checked her watch and changed directions. That warden of a nurse would be back soon if she kept her word, and Katrina suspected that Linda Rafkin, RN, rarely broke a promise. "Let's talk about your testimony."

His lips flattened. "Okay."

"You lied on the stand."

He hesitated, then nodded curtly. "Yep."

"You told me on the phone that you were paid to lie and say you saw Ross McCallum at the Estevans' store that night, right?"

"Yep, but I don't know from who, so don't bother askin'. I just got me five thousand bucks for sayin' I saw McCallum in Nevada Smith's pickup at the store that night."

"But you didn't see it?"

"Didn't see much."

"Who paid you?"

"I said, 'don't ask' cuz I don't know. The money was left in a brown sack in a Dumpster behind the Last Stand. I collected it, counted it, and said what I had to. End of story."

"But you perjured yourself. That's a felony."

"I know that, but who's gonna care now?" he asked, and she couldn't argue the point. The wheels of justice turned too slowly to prosecute and incarcerate Caleb before he died.

He yawned and his eyelids drifted downward. He wouldn't be able to stay awake much longer. Katrina asked, "So who do you think killed Ramón Estevan?"

"Don't know. Anyone, I s'pose. He was a mean sumbitch—er, a mean rascal. Got drunk and hit things. Broke out the windows of his own store more than once. And people 'round town didn't like the fact that he was doin' okay with that store of his, thought he was uppity."

"Because he was Hispanic?"

"If that's what they're called now. Mexican. 'Sides that, he was ornery and mean."

"He had enemies?"

"Everyone in Bad Luck has enemies."

"Any that would kill him?" she pressed.

"At least one, I figure," Caleb said, and she wanted to shake the old coot.

"Who?"

"Dunno."

"What do you know?" she asked and tried not to sound irritated.

"It's all in them transcripts." He yawned again, and the door opened. Nurse Rafkin, her eyebrows rising above the tops of her glasses, appeared.

"Thanks," Katrina said, clicking off her recorder. "I'll be back tomorrow."

"You do that," Caleb said, and as she packed up her recorder and briefcase, she felt his gaze roving over her backside. As if he could do anything more than leer myopically at her. It was sick, really, but she couldn't help leaning over and giving Caleb a peek at the way her skirt stretched over her buttocks. Why not give the old pervert one last thrill before he gave up his ghost? She was safe. In his pathetic condition, there wasn't much Swaggert could do about it.

*Whack!*

Nevada pounded a final nail into the fence post, then grabbed the top rail and tried to shake it free. It held. Good. Little by little this place was coming together. He mopped the sweat from his brow and watched his prize mare prance around the south paddock.

A blood bay, with two white stockings and a trickle of a blaze that curved down her face, the horse was worth more than the rest of his broodmares including the gray that, too, was worth some money. And she acted as if she knew it, tossing her head the way a pretty girl flipped her hair off her face. Beyond the paddock was a hundred-and-sixty acres he'd annexed to his own place, a piece he'd bought just last year. Other horses grazed there, mostly range horses, though a couple in the herd were a notch above, just not quite the same caliber as this one.

He slid his hammer into his tool belt and walked the fence, studying it for flaws.

He'd been lucky to annex the old Adams homestead. Old man Adams wouldn't sell to anyone else. He'd been friends with Nevada's father years before and had been a surrogate uncle to Nevada and his cousin, Joe Hawk, when the boys had been growing up. When it came time to retire and move into town, he'd approached Nevada with a deal that was more than fair, in fact, too good to pass up.

"If you don't buy it, I'll hafta put it on the market and pay some real estate broker a fee for a stranger to take over. I got me no kids of my own, and I'd really like you to have it."

Nevada had signed on the dotted line. The property had added pastureland, a stand of madrones, a lake that rarely went dry, a small orchard and a rock quarry. The old ranch house wasn't worth much, as Oscar Adams had let it run down after his wife died, but to Nevada's eye, the two-storied house had potential. More than his own shed of a place did. He'd planned to move there. Once he fixed it up.

*In time,* he reminded himself as he always did when impatience threatened to overtake him, *all in good time.*

Whistling to Crockett, he walked back to the house and considered calling Levinson again. So far, the private investigator hadn't been able to find the girl.

Three days had passed since Nevada had first run into Shelby again, over seventy-two hours since he'd been told he was a father, and still there was nothing. In this age of electronic, nearly instant worldwide communication, he'd learned diddly-squat about his daughter—didn't even know if she really existed.

All he had was Shelby's insistence that the picture she'd been sent was real, that Elizabeth was his daughter and it was just a matter of finding her.

Born a skeptic, Nevada realized that the letter and snapshot could all be part of someone's sick imagination—a cruel hoax—enticement for Shelby to return to Bad Luck.

But why? And who was behind it?

If the letter and picture proved to be a sham, it would kill Shelby.

She was bound and determined to find that girl. Well, for that matter, so was he.

Dusting off his hands, he climbed the front steps to the porch and walked inside where, though it was darker, the temperature didn't bother to drop even one degree. He cracked a window, but there wasn't much breeze.

He'd talked to Shelby a couple of times on the telephone, did his own digging and kept a running dialogue with the private investigator, but so far, nothing.

Whoever had sent Shelby the picture of the girl had been quiet, not contacting her again. Who the devil was he and why had he picked this time to offer up the information he had? Why now? What had happened in the past few months that would make a person show his hand—why would someone want Shelby Cole to return to Bad Luck now? What had changed?

There was only one thing that might propel whoever it was into action: Ross McCallum was being released.

There was no other connection that Nevada could see.

So what did Ross know about it? Nevada wondered and decided it was time to find out. He was about to put a call in to Levinson again when the phone rang.

He answered before it could jangle a second time. "Smith."

There was a pause—hesitation on the other end.

"Hello?"

No response, but the sound of music in the background.

"Can you hear me?"

Nothing. Though it was broad daylight, Nevada felt a presence as black as midnight. Faintly playing in the background was the sound of music with a Latin beat.

"Who is this?" he asked with more authority, and the phone clicked dead. Nevada stared at the receiver for a second. Maybe it had been a mistake, someone dialing the wrong number. Maybe he hadn't heard music at all. There was a chance that he was jumping to conclusions—people misdialed all the time.

And yet he couldn't shake the eerie feeling that assailed him.

He snagged his keys from a hook near the door and walked outside. The harsh glare of the sun hit him full force. He winced and his bad eye ached from a ten-year-old wound—a wound inflicted by Ross McCallum.

Somehow, today, it seemed a fitting reminder.

The bar was noisy, crowded. A lone singer with an acoustic guitar played in one corner, while conversation was a dull hush that muted the lyrics and most of the notes.

After hanging up the phone, he slipped through the tables, hoping to go unnoticed as he pocketed the pre-paid cell and wondered when the blond girl, who looked as if she'd entered this dive with fake ID, would realize her phone was missing. He'd lifted it easily after spying it in the gaping expanse of her unzipped bag. It had been easy enough to reach down and swipe the damned phone while she flirted with a muscular guy at a nearby table.

The call would be untraceable, or so he'd heard.

Neither Blondie nor Mr. Muscles had noticed. Still he'd ditch the pre-paid sooner rather than later, after using it for a little fun, just to send a shiver down Shelby Cole's spine, and ratchet up the worry in Nevada Smith's brain.

He knew he should leave. Now. Before Blondie figured out her phone was missing, but he liked living on the edge, so he ordered another beer and took a swallow that emptied half the glass. Yep. He felt better about himself than he had in a long, long time.

As Blondie turned, she glanced at him, then reached for her bag. He drained his glass and left some bills on the table. He couldn't afford to be recognized or remembered and he'd pushed it too far, taking the phone then hanging around.

He scooted his chair back loudly as she, frowning, said, "Where the devil is...oh!" Quickly, she withdrew a pack of cigarettes, then whispered something to her girlfriend and walked out the back door to a fenced patio where some of the patrons smoked as they drank. Nonetheless, he wouldn't be surprised if she didn't start looking for her phone once she was outside the noisy bar.

He'd dodged a bullet, but not for long. Time to get out while the gettin' was good.

Besides, he had more to do. Lots more. A phone call or two was just the start.

The files yielded nothing more than a little insight into the way the Judge's mind worked. Shelby had read through each one she thought might help her in her quest, but all she learned were the names of Nevada's parents and the fact that he had been a poor student but a stellar recruit in the army. He'd had brushes with the law as a kid, all documented in the Judge's file, along with the newspaper clippings about him leaving the local Sheriff's Department. It was all hazy in Shelby's mind, but it had to do with the arrest and conviction of Ross McCallum. There had been an inquiry because of the stolen truck and Nevada's history with Ross. Though no charges were ever filed against him, Nevada had officially resigned from his duties, and there was a strong indication that he'd been forced to quit. Hadn't her father said something about him being "kicked out?"

She'd turned her attention to her own file. It held nothing personal. Birth certificate, school documents, health records, all very clinical. A few awards. Copies of her applications to colleges, but nothing about her pregnancy or the baby. Though there was a medical note about her broken collarbone when she was seven, and her bout of chicken pox at three, there was nothing about the fact that she'd gotten pregnant and had a child. It was almost as if her father was denying that critical moment in her life.

"Oh, Dad," she whispered, feeling somehow disappointed. But she had managed to find, in all the documents, the name of her father's lawyer. Orrin Findley's signature was on several documents. Shelby had scratched out his phone number and address and decided to visit Findley in San Antonio.

She wouldn't bother with an appointment. No reason to give him the chance to call her father and tip him off. She threw on a cotton dress and sandals, packed a change of clothes in an old athletic bag she found in the closet, and after grabbing her purse and laptop flew downstairs. The Judge was gone again and she had no trouble returning the files to his credenza. She was about to shut the drawer when she saw a file labeled *Our Lady of Sorrows*.

The hospital where she'd given birth.

Without thinking twice, she withdrew the thin file and found two letters—one from the hospital administrator, the other from the board of directors, thanking Jerome Cole for the endowment he'd made in the name of his late wife. There was no amount of money specified, but the date on the letters was two months after Shelby had delivered her baby.

She stared at the letters in disbelief. Could this have been some kind of payoff for falsifying the records? Surely not. And yet...a chill swept through her and she stopped long enough to write down the name of the hospital administrator on the same scrap of paper on which she'd scribbled Findley's name.

Why would her father have gone to such lengths to ensure that she never found out about Elizabeth? Or was it all a coincidence? Maybe the Judge had just needed a tax break, or felt generous or... no way! This was all part of his cover-up. She stuffed the information in her purse and fought a headache that was beginning to pound behind her eyes. "Damn it all to hell," she whispered, fury sweeping through her.

As quietly as possible, she closed the drawer, locked it and replaced the key.

Disturbed by her new knowledge, Shelby walked into the kitchen and found Lydia, back to the room, on the telephone. Soft Spanish music wafted from hidden speakers.

Unaware that Shelby had entered, the housekeeper had stretched the phone cord so that she could glare out the window at the groundskeeper, who was edging the grass. She spoke in rapid, nearly unintelligible Spanish. From her posture and the tone of the conversation, it was obvious that Lydia was angry. Shelby couldn't follow all of the conversation but understood that Lydia somehow felt trapped, and not wanting to eavesdrop, she cleared her throat as she crossed the room and picked a grape from a basket of fruit on the counter.

Lydia whipped around. Her face was red and blotchy, her eyes bright, tiny white lines bracketing her usually smiling lips. *"Niña,"* she said, startled. *"Dios,* you frightened me. Oh—'xcuse me—" She listened again, said a quick, *"Esta noche,"* then hung up quickly, as if she were embarrassed about being caught in a personal conversation while at work. She tapped loudly on the window, causing the gardener to look up. Angrily she shook her finger at him. "That man, he does not know what he's doing. Just a minute."

She was out the door in a flash to accost the man, who listened to her rantings as he withdrew a pack of cigarettes from his pocket and lit up, waiting patiently while she berated him up one side and down the other in Spanish. A few seconds later she returned, her composure somehow back in place, though Shelby still felt that something was amiss here. There were undercurrents she didn't understand. Usually even-tempered, Lydia wasn't known to go off the handle so wildly, especially not when the gardener was obviously doing a decent job. Then again, maybe Shelby was making more of it than was there, considering what she'd recently discovered in her father's file drawer.

"*Hombres!*" Lydia muttered, rolling her expressive eyes.

"Can't live with 'em, can't shoot 'em," Shelby said automatically, trying to lighten the mood. Lydia laughed, her tension seemingly forgotten for the moment.

"*Sí, sí.* That one I will remember."

Shelby slung the strap of her purse over her shoulder. "Is anything wrong?" she asked, hating to butt in, but feeling she should say something. "You seemed upset."

"Upset?" Lydia shook her head and reached into the refrigerator for a foil-covered dish.

"On the phone."

"Oh. Uh, family troubles. My niece, Maria, she is having a time with her daughter. Nothing serious," she said as she set the pan on the counter and opened the foil. The sharp, tangy scents of marinade filled the kitchen as Lydia forked a slab of meat and turned it over several times.

"You're sure?"

"*Sí.*" Lydia avoided her eyes, and Shelby didn't press the issue. At times the housekeeper was very open, others she was extremely private. This seemed to be one of those closely guarded personal times, and Shelby decided to leave well enough alone. "You are going out?" Lydia motioned toward Shelby's bag with her fork.

"Into San Antonio. I don't know if I'll be back tonight."

"Business?" Lydia asked.

"Nope," Shelby said, still trying to keep the conversation light. "A hot date."

"With *Señor* Smith?"

Shelby's smile faltered a bit. "Nah, you caught me. I was just teasing. No date. I thought I'd go into the city and do some shopping." She plopped the grape in her mouth and swallowed it. "And, just for the record, I'm *not* dating *Señor* Smith."

Lydia lifted a disbelieving eyebrow. The older woman knew her too well. "You are taking the day off and are going shopping?"

"Yes, I've only got a couple of things with me and, believe it or not, there seems to be a dearth of boutiques in Bad Luck."

Lydia managed a smile then returned the pan of meat to the refrigerator. "Now *Dios* where is . . . Oh! Here we go." She retrieved a brick of white cheese, set it on the counter and washed her hands. Over the rush of water she said, "Your father, he will not believe that you just left to buy some new clothes. You came back here to find your daughter, no?"

"Yes."

"You were very . . . *específico*—"

"Specific," Shelby supplied.

"*Sí.* Specific." She shut off the tap and wiped her hands on a dish towel. I do not think he will believe that you are now interested in a new pair of shoes or a bracelet."

Shelby plucked another grape from the basket and plopped it into her mouth. "It doesn't really matter, Lydia. He can think anything he wants." She was about to leave, but decided that now was the time to talk to Lydia about the conversation she'd listened to on the stairs. "The other day I overheard you talking to the Judge."

"*Sí, sí*—" Lydia was removing a cheese grater from a cupboard.

"Well, actually, you were talking to him about me and some family secrets. I was on the stairs and you were in the hallway near the foyer."

Lydia froze for a second, then caught herself and began unwrapping the plastic wrap from the cheese. "*Sí,*" she said, obviously nervous.

"What were you talking about—what secrets?"

One shoulder lifted as she began grating. Curlicues of Jack cheese fell onto the cutting board. "There are many."

"Such as?"

"Don't ask, *niña,* for I cannot say." She lifted her head and her brown eyes were filled with a sadness Shelby couldn't begin to comprehend. "These things, they are for you and your father to discuss."

"Not if they involve me."

"As I said, ask him." The housekeeper looked away.

"Lydia."

"I have said enough. Talk to the Judge." She glanced at the kitchen clock. "He will be here shortly."

"But he won't tell me..." Shelby let the argument slide as she saw the determined set of Lydia's jaw. Lydia's loyalty to the Judge was fierce and unshakable, though Shelby didn't understand why. Yes, she was paid well and was given a lot of authority, but it hardly seemed worth dealing with a man as deceitful as Red Cole.

> *Ol' Judge Cole*
> *Was a nasty old soul*
> *And a nasty old soul was he...*

Even as a child, Shelby had suspected the truth about her father—that he was a liar and a grand manipulator—but she'd refused to believe it. Now, it seemed, the scope of his influence and exploitations was far broader than she'd suspected.

"Look, Lydia, I have rights," Shelby insisted, hooking her thumb toward her chest. "If you have any idea where my daughter is—"

The phone rang and Lydia scooped up the receiver. "Hello?" she said, wiping one hand on her apron. "Hello?" Her brow wrinkled and her lips pursed. "Is anyone there? Hello?" She hung up. *"Dios mio!"*

"What?"

"The second time this has happened. No one is there."

"Probably a wrong number," Shelby said.

"Then they should answer. *Idiota!*"

Shelby wasn't about to be deterred. "Listen, Lydia—"

But the housekeeper was looking out the window and knocking on a pane with her knuckles. "That Pablo, he is a lazy one. What my sister sees in him, I do not know. He is my *cuñado, sí,* but he does not know how to work." She gesticulated wildly to the man who barely looked up as he edged the lawn.

"Pablo Ramirez is your brother-in-law?" Shelby repeated. This was news to her.

*"Sí, sí,* you know. Carla's husband." Lydia clucked her tongue in disgust. "It is a wonder the Judge does not fire him!"

"Now wait a minute, Lydia," Shelby said. "I get the feeling that you're dodging the issue here. We were talking about my daughter."

*"Niña,* please, I know nothing. The secrets I was speaking of were about your mother, God rest her soul." She made a quick sign of the cross over her ample bosom. "Those you need to discuss with your father."

Shelby wasn't about to drop it, but for now, at least, she'd back off, mainly because she heard the rumble of an engine. Maybe her father had returned. Well, if he had, she was about to give him a piece of her mind. She walked to the archway, where she could see through the windows flanking the front door, but there was no sign of her father's silver Mercedes. Instead she caught a glimpse of old green paint and spied Nevada's truck through the window.

"All right, Lydia," Shelby said. "You're off the hook for the moment. I'm not going to argue with you now, but if my father won't tell me the truth, especially about my daughter, then I hope you will." She pinned the housekeeper with a determined glare. "It's only fair, don't you think?"

"Sometimes, *niña,* the world is not fair."

"But it should be, Lydia. It damned well should be. Even in Bad Luck."

With that she was out the door just as Nevada's truck ground to a stop near the garage. She told herself she didn't want to see him. Not now. She had too much to do.

He swung out of the truck with a purpose, and Shelby's stupid heart tripped at the sight of him. Why, she couldn't fathom. So what if she sensed an electricity in him, an animal magnetism that was raw and sensual? Big deal. So it got to her at the most basic of levels. So what?

He was the father of her daughter and that was it. Nothing

more. What they'd shared ten years ago was over. Long over. Even if she'd been foolish enough to react to his kiss, it was just female response. Nothing more.

And yet...

He slammed the door of the truck and looked like he could spit nails. His expression was hard, his eyes unforgiving, his lips compressed. Worn jeans. Wide belt. Dusty boots. A navy blue T-shirt that had seen better days. A real twenty-first-century cowboy—as raw and rangy as a West Texas bronco. And just as wild.

She didn't want him, she told herself, but it was a lie. A bald-faced lie. All her arguments to the contrary, the plain, disgusting truth was that she'd never really gotten over him.

Worse yet, she was afraid she never would.

# CHAPTER 10

"Going somewhere?" Nevada asked, striding up to her and motioning to the bag slung over her shoulder.

Shelby braced herself. No doubt they were in for another confrontation. "San Antonio. I'm sick of sitting around here waiting for your friend Levinson to call with more information on Pritchart. I thought I'd try and track down Dad's lawyer and see what he has to say. He probably knows something about what happened."

"I'll come with you."

She was astounded. "I don't think that's necessary."

"Maybe I want to." The words hung heavy on the air, echoing in Shelby's brain as the gardener's clippers clicked somewhere behind her.

"Don't you have things to do here?"

He shifted, and she saw the indecision in his eyes.

"Something happened," she said, and her heart leapt. Maybe he'd found Elizabeth! But, no, he would have said so right from the start.

Shelby saw a movement to her right and realized they were within earshot of the gardener. As if he'd caught her reaction, Nevada took her by the elbow and guided her through an arbor to a bench by the pool, where they were alone aside from a hummingbird that hovered over planters of petunias exploding in vibrant pink and purple blossoms. "What is it?" she asked as they sat down, side by side, his denim-clad thigh brushing against hers.

"Maybe nothing," he allowed, but didn't seem to believe it. "I got a call a while ago and when I picked up, no one answered. It was weird, though, I swear I could hear music or static in the background."

"Pocket dial," she suggested, but her stomach was knotting. She'd never known Nevada to jump at shadows.

"Don't think so and when I looked for a number on caller ID, nothing. 'Private caller.'" He squinted up at the sun. "I don't think it was a telemarketer or a computer, no clicking, no response. Just... nothin' but that faint music... Spanish, I think."

"Wrong number." The knots tightened as she tried to convince herself that she was overreacting. "No big deal."

"Guess so."

"Except..."

"Except what?" His narrowed gaze came back to land on her with full force and she felt the heat radiate from his body to hers.

"Lydia took a couple of those here, at the house," Shelby admitted.

"When?" he asked.

"One was just a while ago. The other, I don't know." She shrugged, trying to stay calm. It was nothing. A couple of hang-ups, so what?

"I don't like this."

"Probably just... you know, a coincidence."

"Too many coincidences for my liking. You showing up here around the time McCallum is suddenly out of prison, to start with. And now the calls."

"You think McCallum is behind them?" she asked, voicing her own worst fears.

"Wouldn't put it past him. And he had a thing for you. We know that."

She shuddered inside, remembering the last time she'd seen him. They'd been leading him away, his shackles clinking, but he'd still had the nerve to turn to her and not only point his fingers as if he were shooting her, but also blow her that cold, hate-filled kiss. Even now, so many years later, she felt that old, icy fear returning.

"If McCallum called," she said, forcing a calmness to her words she didn't feel, "why wouldn't he say anything?"

"Don't know and we can't prove it's him. Yet. But I'm going to have my phone records checked. Yours, too. As well as the Judge's."

"How can you do that?"

His smile was cold as a demon's heart. "I've got my ways. Connections. Let's just leave it at that."

She did. For now. "You'll let me know?"

"Of course. You know, I'm just like everyone else in this town."

"Meaning?"

"Everyone's jumpy now that McCallum's back, and there's talk that he's gonna cause trouble. Rumors that he made some private vow to wreak his own kind of hell around here."

"People speculate. Gossip." But she felt it; that certain terror she fought when she thought of McCallum and remembered his foul breath and rough hands and . . . *No way! Don't go there, Shelby. DO NOT give him the power that allows you to conjure up your old fears! Pull yourself together. It's a few phone calls, nothing more!*

Giving herself a quick mental shake, she reined in her rapidly galloping emotions.

"Look, Shelby," Nevada said and grabbed her hand. "If he's calling me, who cares? Big deal. Bring it on!" His fingers tightened over hers. "But if he's calling you—"

"Hey, wait a minute," she snapped, pulling her hands from his. She absolutely refused to be McCallum's victim, ever again. "All we know is that someone called you and hung up and someone called the house. Not my cell. Not me. And then hung up a couple of times. We've all done the pocket dial thing, so let's not rush to any conclusions, okay? We don't even know if whoever was on the other end of the line was McCallum or some kid playing a prank, right?"

"Right," he drawled, obviously unconvinced.

"So let's not dive into the deep end. Not yet. There's time enough for that later. Just find out what you can."

"Okay. We'll see." He nodded slowly as the hummingbird flew away. "But there's something else."

"What?" Her heart sank.

"Trouble."

"Meaning...?"

"There's a reporter pokin' around, askin' questions, a woman by the name of Katrina Nedelesky. She writes for *Lone Star* magazine, and rumor has it she's going to write a series of articles about the Estevan murder and Ross McCallum's release."

"So it'll all be dug up again," she surmised.

"And then some." A muscle near the corner of his jaw worked. "I've still got a friend in the Sheriff's Department, and they're thinking of reopening the Estevan case."

"To find the real killer?"

The brackets at the corners of Nevada's mouth deepened, and one hand closed into a fist. "We found the real killer ten years ago, Shelby. Trouble is, now he's a free man."

"You think. If Caleb Swaggert lied, maybe Ross didn't kill Ramón Estevan."

Nevada's face became as hard as granite. "McCallum did it, Shelby. I'd stake my life on it." He stood abruptly and walked to the edge of the pool. The seat of his Levi's was worn, one pocket ripping out, his belt hanging low over a tight rear end that she remembered all too well. Broad shoulders pulled his T-shirt tight across his back, the very back where her fingers had dug deep as he'd made love to her. Suddenly warm inside, she dragged her gaze away from him and glanced back to the house. Silently she chastised herself. It was ludicrous to fantasize about him, especially now, when they had to concentrate on finding their daughter.

"Any word from Levinson?" she asked, clearing her throat.

"Nothin' new."

Shelby had been afraid of that. She climbed to her feet and stood next to him in the shade of an aging pecan tree. The leaves shimmered and rustled in a gust of wind. Scolding noisily, a squirrel leapt from one branch to another.

"What about other people involved in all this?" he wondered aloud. "The lawyer—what's his name?"

"Findley. Orrin Findley."

"He's as good a start as any," Nevada allowed, "but there had to be other people who knew about the baby. Who are they?"

She'd asked the same questions of herself. "I spent most of the pregnancy with my father's aunt in Austin. Everyone thought I'd gone away to school, but I was really taking courses online and fighting with Dad. He wanted me to give the baby up for adoption, and I was bound and determined to keep her. Anyway, my great-aunt knew, of course, but she died three years ago."

Nevada's frown deepened. "Anyone else?"

"Sure. Everyone who worked here at the house could have over-heard the fights between the Judge and me. Of course Lydia knew. But then, she knows everything." *More than you do,* her mind teased.

"None of your friends?"

Shelby shook her head and brushed her bangs from her eyes. "Not as far as I know. I didn't tell anyone, and since I left town be-fore I started to show, no one suspected. They all just thought I went off to school early. They could have heard from other sources later, I suppose, but it never came back to me." She watched the play of emotions on his face and felt suddenly ashamed that she hadn't confided in him, hadn't told him that he was going to be a father. All because of her insecurities, pride and jealousy of Vianca. And the rape. She *couldn't* have told him about that. "Look, I'm sorry I didn't say anything to you."

His mouth turned down at the corners. He stuffed his hands into the back pockets of his Levi's. "Water under the bridge now."

"But I should have—"

"Yeah, you should have. But it's too late for apologies, Shelby." He turned and faced her with those damning eyes. "Let's get on with this. What about the people who worked with Pritchart, or nurses at the hospital, someone who was there?"

Bristling slightly, she said, "I've called the hospital, asked for records, but all they have is the birth and death certificates. They show that Elizabeth died."

"There had to be other people. Doctors—your anesthesiologist, aides, someone on the nursing staff or who worked in the maternity ward or pediatric unit."

"I know. So far I've come up with nothing." She lifted a hand to let it fall again.

"What hospital?"

She'd known this was coming. "Our Lady of Sorrows in Coop-ersville."

"Where Caleb Swaggert is?" he asked and she watched as the wheels of his mind began to turn.

"But it was smaller nine years ago. A lot smaller. It was before my father left an endowment to the hospital in my mother's name. Then Our Lady of Sorrows got swallowed up by a bigger system."

His head snapped up. "When did this happen?"

"My father left his endowment right after I had the baby," she admitted. "I didn't know about it until this afternoon, when I saw some of his files." She glanced at the house, caught Lydia watching them from an open kitchen window, then realized that Pablo was nearby, ostensibly weeding the flower garden on the other side of the arbor that guarded the pool. Was Lydia, from the vantage point of the corner window, observing Shelby and Nevada on one side of the arbor, or keeping her ever-vigilant eagle eye on her brother-in-law?

"How much of an endowment?"

"I don't know. I just found a letter of thanks from the board of directors and the hospital administrator. I haven't had a chance to talk to him about it yet."

Nevada's fist opened and closed. "You think it might have been a payoff, for the hospital's part in this."

"Yes." She was sick at the thought, but it was true.

"Hell." He raked impatient fingers through his hair. "Why was your father so against you keeping the baby?"

"The shame of it all," she said with a sigh. "He thought I was hell-bent to ruin my life."

"Were you?"

She looked into the eyes she'd once loved so fiercely, to the man she would have, years ago, walked through hell to be with. "Maybe. Who knows? I was just a kid. But the way I figure it, it was mine to ruin."

"And our daughter's." A thread of accusation wound through his words.

"Let's get something straight, Nevada," she said emphatically. "No matter what, I would never, ever have done anything to hurt my child."

"Except not tell the father."

She felt as if he'd slugged her. "I . . . I thought we got past that, but obviously not." As far as she was concerned, the conversation was over. She started for her car. He caught up with her, grabbed her wrist and spun her around so fast she nearly collided with him.

"Okay, that was a cheap shot, but I want to believe that now we're on even turf. You've told me everything I need to know. Right?"

"Absolutely." *Except about the rape. You haven't come clean about the rape, Shelby.*

"Good." For a minute he didn't say another word, and she felt his fingertips hot against the skin on the inside of her wrist. Her pulse jumped, and as she stared into his face she wished to high heaven that she was anywhere else on earth. Being this close to him was too nerve-wracking, too emotional, too damned seductive. "I—I have to go."

"So do I."

Still he didn't move, and Shelby was vaguely aware of the gardener's rake scraping in the dirt and a bird chirping high overhead, but for a second, while she stared up at Nevada, she felt seventeen again—all youth and innocence and rebellion. It had been so long ago. A lifetime. She swallowed hard, and his gaze drifted to her throat.

"Be careful."

"I will."

"If you get any more phone calls, or there's any trouble . . . Hell, I should come with you."

"I'll be fine. You take care of things here. Talk to Levinson. Find Pritchart."

"Shelby—"

Oh, Lord, was he going to kiss her again? She pulled her arm away and he let go. "I mean it, Shelby. Don't take any chances."

*The most risky chance I ever took was with you.*

"I said I'd be careful and I will be. You do the same, Nevada." And then she headed for her car. She didn't say good-bye, didn't watch as he made his way to his truck and drove off. Behind the wheel of the Cadillac, she blew her bangs from her eyes and adjusted the rearview mirror, where she caught a glimpse of her flushed cheeks and bright eyes. "Oh, yeah, and you're a moron," she chided. "A complete and utter moron." She had to compose herself. She couldn't, wouldn't, let herself fall in love with Nevada Smith again. Hell would freeze over first.

Shep Marson couldn't shake the bad feeling that had been with him for the past couple of days—ever since he'd pulled Mary Beth Looney and Ross McCallum over. Nope, that uneasiness had followed him around like a bad smell and still tailed after him as he pulled into the Estevan driveway and cut the engine of his cruiser.

Officially, Shep was off duty, but he didn't want to go home just yet. Peggy Sue was sure to be as snarly as a cornered timber wolf that he was late, but she'd have to wait. This was important. He hitched his pants up as he strode up the front walk.

The Estevan house, an adobe-and-tile bungalow, was well kept, the dry yard trimmed, petunias and marigolds blooming in abundance in planters clustered in pots on the shaded front porch. Fuchsias trailed bright pink from hanging pottery. A well-used tricycle was parked beside the hose bib. On the window ledge, a gray tabby cat scratched at its ear with a back leg, but at the sight of Shep, it hopped off and slunk around the corner.

As he climbed up the steps, he heard a woman singing over the sound of running water. The hot, spicy scent of something made with chili powder and cumin wafted through the screen door. His stomach growled, and he took out his can of Copenhagen and put a fresh pinch under his lip; then he rapped on the door.

The singing abruptly stopped. The water quit running. He peered into the house, where a television was turned on in one corner of a living room, the sound turned down low.

Vianca appeared, her hair wrapped in a towel, water spots on the shoulders of her sleeveless blouse. "Yes?" she said through the mesh.

No need for introductions; they'd met before. Shep tipped his hat. "I thought I'd stop by and see how you and your ma were gettin' along," he said, then added, "This ain't official business, you understand, just a friendly visit. I figure it's tough on you both now that Ross McCallum's out of jail."

"*Cabrón!*" she spat out, her eyes flashing with anger.

He didn't argue. Most people in Bad Luck considered Ross McCallum a bastard or worse.

Scowling, Vianca slid through the screen door and pointed to a couple of plastic chairs on the porch. "*Madre* hasn't taken it well."

"I can imagine." Lowering himself into a dusty chair next to the one Vianca had claimed, he took off his hat and fiddled with the brim. He was usually a confident man, but Vianca Estevan was the kind of woman who made him squirm. Innately sexy, she had a kind of innocence beneath her tough-as-nails exterior, an innocence that he found damned attractive. She was rumored to be easy; Shep found himself wishing the gossip would prove true.

"*Madre*—she is not well."

Shep nodded; he'd heard the story that ever since her husband was murdered, Aloise Estevan had slipped further and further into confusion. She attended Mass twice a day, was rumored to have a shrine built to Ramón's memory in the house she shared with her daughter and grandson, and was known to speak to Ramón though, of course, he was long dead.

Vianca crossed her slim legs, and Shep tried not to stare at the hem of white shorts that barely covered her butt. He wondered if she wore panties and what color they were, but sucked a little harder on his wad of chew and forced his eyes to meet hers.

"I'm sorry. I know this has been hard for her and it won't get much easier in the next couple of weeks. The department's gonna reopen the investigation into Ramón's death, and so you might have to deal with investigators and probably the press."

"*Mierda!* My father is dead, *Señor*—er, Deputy Marson. *Muerto.* No one can bring him back. And *sí,* it would be good if the bastard who killed him was brought to justice, but"—she shrugged and the towel she'd wound around her head slipped a bit as she leaned her head to one side and pinned him with eyes as black and hot as a Texas summer night—"it would not bring him back to life."

"It's our job," he said. "I thought you'd like to know." She pursed her lips, and Shep found himself wondering what it would be like to kiss her—or more. As hot-blooded as she was, she'd probably be a real she-cat in bed. Lord, she was a randy-lookin' thing, and he felt his crotch tighten just looking at her. She adjusted the towel and her gaze followed a truck lumbering down the street. As she lifted her hands and fiddled with the towel, her blouse gaped a bit and he caught a glimpse of the top of one breast, a warm honey color over a lacy scrap of a red bra. *Red—near scarlet.* Shep hadn't seen a red one up close in years. Lately Peggy Sue had become partial to a white support thing that turned a dingy shade of gray after a few washings. But this—he couldn't help but stare and the spit dried in his throat.

*"Gracias."* Her voice was cold. Brittle.

His head snapped up, and he found her staring at him. Hard. With those fiery black eyes.

Shep held her stare. No need to try and hide the fact that he found her sexy. She didn't so much as blink.

He cleared his throat. "I know you were working at the store the night your father was killed."

*"Sí,"* she said, suddenly guarded.

"You saw Ross McCallum there."

A mute nod.

"Who else?"

"I have told this over and over," she said, "when the investigators first asked questions." Somewhere down the street a dog began to put up a ruckus.

"I know, but refresh my memory."

She hesitated, little lines etching her forehead as she thought. "There was his sister, Mary Beth," she said with a frown, "and, of course, the whore."

"Ruby Dee."

*"Sí."* Vianca's lips curled into a sneer. "Ruby. And Joe Hawk, he was there earlier, much earlier, with...Nevada Smith." She looked away.

Bingo! Shep had thought Nevada and his cousin were there, but hadn't yet looked through the reams of testimony and depositions from McCallum's trial.

"Badger Collins, Etta Parsons....Celeste—oh, she is the daughter of Caleb, the drunk." She snapped her fingers impatiently as she tried to remember. Vianca was on a roll now.

"Swaggert, now Hernandez."

"Yes, she was there and Manny Dauber and Lucy...the woman who now works at the Last Stand." Vianca whispered a stream of Spanish as if it would jog her memory.

"Lucy Pride," Shep supplied, though he knew from the few

scrapes Lucy had been in that she had a record and had used more than one alias. Recently, she seemed to have become law-abiding. Hence, he supposed, the name Pride.

"*Sí*. Pride," Vianca agreed, chewing on her lower lip as she rolled back the years. "There were so many. Maria Ramirez, and Juan Padilla—and your wife was there, too." Vianca pointed out and Shep's jaw clenched tight. It was a shame Peggy Sue's name was even involved.

"Just pickin' up some Tylenol for one of the kids," he said quickly, feeling the need to defend the woman he'd taken as his bride such a long time ago. "Timmy had a headache—the flu, I think."

Vianca waved off his excuse and damn but she wasn't right. Half the damned town had been at the convenience store that night; though without a motive or a murder weapon, the investigation would probably stall.

But the name that kept worming into Shep's brain, that never seemed to go away, was Nevada Smith. He'd worked tirelessly on the Estevan case years ago, insisting that Ross McCallum had offed Ramón while drunk and arguing about a gambling debt. At the time it had all seemed to fit, especially with the witnesses who had seen Ramón and Ross arguing heatedly in the parking lot over two thousand dollars. But even ten years ago, Shep's gut had told him that Nevada was working too hard to pin the murder on McCallum, that there was a personal grudge involved. Maybe that was the ticket—find out what the bad blood between McCallum and Smith was.

He suspected it was about a woman—the princess herself. Shelby Cole was the source of the trouble, Shep would bet his grandfather's silver-plated spurs on it. And he was kinda related to Shelby—a cousin once or twice removed—so he had a personal interest.

"Vianca!" a shrill voice cried. Somewhere deep within the house a door slammed. Small scurrying feet scrambled through the house.

Vianca was on her feet as the screen door burst open and a boy of about four barreled through. "*Tía V, Tía V,*" he cried, his mop of black hair flying as he flung himself into Vianca's arms.

She pulled him off his feet and whirled him around as he giggled wildly. Her towel came completely undone and her black hair tumbled past her shoulders in wild curls. "Oh, little Ramón, you are a devil, do you hear me," she said, kissing his cheeks and tossing the towel onto her recently vacated chair. "A precious little *diablo*." Casting a glance at Shep, she explained, "My brother Roberto's son, and the light of my life." She nuzzled the boy's cheek.

Little Ramón threw back his head and laughed as the door opened again and Aloise Estevan, stoop-shouldered and gray-haired, appeared. Her eyes were haunted and soulless, her once-flawless skin now lined and sallow. Leaning heavily on a metal cane, she looked at Shep, but he was certain she didn't recognize him—probably didn't remember too many folks.

Vianca made quick introductions, but to no avail. Aloise muttered something unintelligible under her breath, and Vianca's expression changed from pure, unfettered glee to despair.

"No, *Madre,* he is not here. Remember? *Padre* is...is gone." She sent Shep a quick glance, and he got the message.

"I'll be shovin' off now," he said, suddenly in need of a beer.

Aloise kept talking, her face expressionless, her vision centered on a world only she could see. The gray cat reappeared, and little Ramón slid down his aunt's slim body to chase after the beast.

Shep tipped his hat. "I'll be talkin' with you again."

"*Sí,*" Vianca said. Almost shyly, she offered him a smile that followed him back to his car and all the way home to Peggy Sue's hot temper and cold bed.

Shelby's trip to San Antonio was a bust.

So far, Orrin Findley had been no help whatsoever. Of course, Shelby had yet to see the man or even talk to him on the phone. She'd spent two days trying to get into his office, but hadn't made it past his drill sergeant of a secretary. Now, as she sat at an open-air café on the River Walk, watching a sightseeing river barge filled with tourists float down the San Antonio River, she remembered the excuses she'd heard.

"Mr. Findley is out of town."

"Mr. Findley is in court."

"Mr. Findley is away from his desk."

"Mr. Findley is in a meeting."

The truth was that Mr. Findley was ducking her. Leaning back in a café chair as a breeze moved the leaves in the branches overhead, she sipped lemonade and tried to hold on to her rapidly escaping patience. The element of surprise hadn't helped; Findley had been indisposed at every turn.

In the meantime Shelby hadn't been idle. She'd spent hours on the Internet, digging for information, and checked in with her real estate office in Seattle, just to make sure her clients hadn't suffered in her absence. The agent she'd left in charge was more than capable and had urged her to "take your time. Everything's handled." Fortunately, Shelby trusted him.

While on her cell to her office, she'd missed Levinson's call and when she'd dialed his number, she'd been connected to his voice mail. "Great," she'd mumbled, asking him to call her, then texting the same message in case that was his preferred method of communication. Anything to get a fast response.

Frustrated, she'd pocketed her phone and walked to the library, where she'd gone through old newspaper clippings on microfiche, hoping to find something she'd missed on the Internet. She read everything she could about Ross McCallum's trial and tried to keep her emotions out of it, refusing to think of the eye contact they'd had that day, the cold-blooded kiss he'd blown her way in the courtroom, or anything else on a personal level, especially resisting the urge to remember the night he'd attacked her. That horrid event she kept compartmentalized, in a locked cupboard on a shelf deep in a far corner of her mind. Those memories were only accessible if she allowed them to be. Not today. Hopefully not ever.

And now he was back... released by recanted testimony. What was up with that? she'd wondered as she'd left the library. She couldn't help but think McCallum's release from prison was what had prompted someone to write the anonymous letter and send the picture of Elizabeth to her. But who? And why now? And where in God's name was her daughter? The heaviness in her heart always increased when she thought of her girl, who was far from being a baby any longer.

In desperation, Shelby had even attempted to call Nevada, hoping that he'd been in touch with Levinson or had learned something, but Nevada, too, hadn't answered. She hadn't bothered leaving a message, figuring he would recognize her number. Besides, she'd be back in Bad Luck soon. She'd visit him in person then.

So what would it take to find her daughter, their daughter? "Where is she?" she'd whispered aloud, wondering if God was listening as she'd glanced up to the sky, where soft clouds floated lazily over the sun, casting shadows and offering no answers.

Now, tears of frustration threatened her eyes, but she blinked them back. There wasn't time for regrets. She had to move forward and she was nowhere near finding Elizabeth. All her digging on the Internet hadn't helped at all.

As she walked toward the river, she thought of her failed attempts at surveillance and how she'd tried to force information from her father's lawyer. Having overheard his secretary book a lunch for him in a restaurant on the River Walk, only three doors down from this shaded café, Shelby had decided to accost the attorney. She planted herself in a chair with a view of the entrance to the restaurant in which he was presumably dining with his client. While waiting, she ordered three glasses of iced tea.

Findley was supposed to have met his client at one. Shelby waited impatiently, but it was pushing three now. Great. Swirling the tea in her glass with her straw, she kept her eyes fastened on the front door of the establishment. Another ten minutes passed and she thought she'd go mad. She was just on the threshold of marching through the front door, finding Findley and having it out right in the middle of the restaurant. "Patience," she told herself and crunched on a piece of ice.

The table next to hers was vacated for a few minutes before a couple, obviously head-over-heels in love, sat down. They scooted their chairs close together and linked hands under the table, their huddled bodies partially blocking her view while several crows and pigeons, wings flapping, vied for leftover crumbs that had fallen to the cobblestones beneath the tables.

*Come on, come on,* Shelby thought as she glanced over her shoulder and hoped that no one recognized her. Ever since Nevada and she had discussed the hang-up phone calls, she'd been edgy. Nervous.

"It's nothing," she whispered now, stirring her tea again as the ice melted, but she couldn't shake the feeling that someone was watching her, even manipulating her. She glanced over her shoulder but saw no one lurking in the shadows, no one sitting on a bench and staring at her through opaque sunglasses.

However, despite the heat, she felt a lonely cold inside...a warning.

*Quit imagining things!*

Just then, before her worrisome thoughts could get the better of her, she saw the man whose portrait had graced the reception area of his law office. She'd caught pictures of him on the Internet as well and was certain the tall, silver-haired man with the dark tan, pencil-thin mustache and Western-cut suit and string tie was, indeed, Orrin Findley. Findley and his client, still engrossed in conversation, sauntered along the river, then up the stairs to the main streets of town.

Shelby left her glass and a few dollars on the table, then followed, all the while trying to keep her quarry in sight without attracting any attention to herself. Quickly, she hurried up the stairs to higher ground, where Findley and the other man parted company at the lawyer's shiny black Jaguar with vanity plates that boasted S A LAW.

As soon as the client crossed the street to his vehicle, Shelby didn't waste a second. "Mr. Findley?" she called, closing the distance between them as he hit a button on the keyless lock and the car beeped in answer.

He turned, and a broad smile stretched across his tanned jaw. "Something I can do for you, miss?"

"I hope so. I'm—"

"Shelby Cole," he supplied, his grin falling away with the recognition. He actually seemed taken aback, a little stunned. "God, you look just like Jasmine."

"You've been avoiding me," she charged on, refusing to discuss her mother or anything other than Elizabeth. "Look, I really need to talk to you about my baby."

"I don't know anything."

"Of course you do. You're my father's attorney, and your firm deals with adoption."

"Legal adoption."

"So what happened to my baby?"

"I don't know. I didn't even know you had one."

"Sure you did, Mr. Findley," she insisted as traffic on the street backed up at the light. "I'm sure my father confided in you."

"Even if he did, it would fall in the category of attorney/client privilege. I couldn't discuss it with you or anyone else."

"But she was *my* daughter and I was told she died at birth!" Shelby planted herself next to the Jaguar's door and wouldn't budge. She barely noticed the pedestrians walking by or the traffic that began to move when the stoplight turned green. Her eyes, behind dark lenses, were focused directly on the smooth lawyer whose smile was more snakelike than the python-skinned boots covering his feet. "I had rights, too. Rights that were forgotten or ignored."

With a quick glance over his shoulder, he scanned the street, then said between teeth that barely moved, "Let me tell you somethin', Miss Cole. I don't discuss business in the middle of the street."

"You wouldn't talk to me in your office."

"Because I had nothin' to say," he drawled, his eyebrows lifting pointedly. "Nothin'." He wanted her to shut up, to keep quiet, to maintain some kind of propriety, but she wasn't about to be snowed by his reputation of good-ol'-boy charm.

"I think you do. You know about the baby, you know about my father's gifts to Our Lady of Sorrows Hospital, and you probably even know why the Judge thinks it's his damned right to run my life by his rules."

"No. What I know is that you should give up this quest you're on. If you've got a baby, she's a child now, living with parents who love her—"

"How would you know that?" she demanded, leaning her hip against a shiny fender and folding her arms over her chest.

"Excuse me?"

"If you don't know where she is, then how can you surmise that she's living with two parents, that they're happy, that she's being taken care of? Unless you're privy to inside knowledge about my daughter—where she is and who she's living with—everything you're saying is supposition, and I think I have the right—no, I'm damned sure I do have every moral, legal and ethical right to find out that my daughter is safe and happy!"

His eyes turned frosty. "Then, Miss Cole, talk to your father," he said as if to dismiss her.

"I've tried that. It hasn't worked. I guess my only other option is to hire my own attorney and go through the courts. You'll be subpoenaed."

Findley's face turned to stone. "That would be difficult, Miss Cole. As I understand it, your baby died right after birth. I believe I've seen a death certificate to that effect in your father's papers. Good day."

He was lying. Shelby would bet her life on it, but he was also practiced in his art of deceit and unshakable in his convictions. As she watched him walk to the driver's side of the Jaguar, unlock it and slide inside, she felt helpless and frustrated.

Yep, she thought as the sleek car eased away from the curb, this entire trip had been a fruitless waste of time.

"You're sure about that?" Ross asked, eyeing the blond barmaid suspiciously. It was just after the dinner hour, and a handful of good ol' boys, regulars from the looks of them, had wandered into the Last Stand after working all day to down a beer or two before driving home to their tired, nagging wives, runny-nosed kids and sorry-ass lives. Hoisting a bottle of Lone Star to his lips, Ross didn't envy a one of them. The way he figured it, each man lived in his own kind of prison.

Lucy twisted off the top of a long-necked bottle of beer and eyed her reflection in the mirror mounted over the bar. She dabbed at a smudge of mascara at the corner of her eye before sliding the second bottle to him. "I heard Shelby tell Nevada myself. They were talkin' a few days ago, right over there"—she nodded toward a booth where a couple of women with long hair, bright earrings and tight jeans were checking out the action—"and she said clear as a bell that the two of 'em, they had them a kid." Lucy propped an elbow on the bar and leaned closer. "Well, let me tell you, he hustled her out the back door real quick, and that's all I heard." She nudged a basket of popcorn Ross's way.

"Well, don't that beat all."

"Thought you'd want to know." She began mopping the counter with a white towel.

Ross did want to know. He wanted to know anything that had to do with Nevada Sum-bitch Smith and Shelby Cole. Lucy was the one friend in town he could count on. Everyone else had treated him as if he had a bad case of lice or worse.

He gulped his beer in one swallow, left Lucy a meager tip and ambled outside. He was itchy—ready for a fight, or better yet, a woman. Just about any woman would do, but at the mention of Shelby Cole's name, he felt a particular satisfaction. He'd only been with her once and, well, in all truth he'd forced her, but he'd love to do it again.

Hell, mounting her had been the rush of his life. Even jabbing his jackknife into Smith's eye hadn't given him the same sense of power and satisfaction that fucking the Judge's daughter had. He'd never felt more like a man than he had pinning the princess to the seat of her daddy's truck and nailing her. He'd been scared as hell, sure, but the risk had been worth the feeling of raw power that had lingered with him for months. Very much akin to the time he'd really gotten into it with Nevada Smith. Nevada Smith had come at him and they'd ended up fighting, one on one. He'd felt no drop of remorse. Not one. Sure he'd ended up in the hospital—Nevada had beat him up good—but he'd given a little back. Smith's vision would never be quite the same.

Now he climbed into his grandfather's truck, and listened as the ancient Dodge's engine ground, barely catching, then fired. The old gears creaked, the tires were bald and the windshield was cracked, but he didn't have too much choice when it came to transportation. At least the sorry-assed pickup ran.

He checked his watch. Ruby Dee got off work at eight, according to one of the locals. He'd checked with a few of the men who knew her years ago. They claimed she worked at the twenty-four-hour store in the next town over, and Ross had called the grocery earlier, investing some of his limited change to find out about her shift.

Now he had plenty of time to drive to Coopersville, a town four or five times the size of Bad Luck and twenty-five miles south.

Lighting a cigarette and checking the rearview mirror to see that he wasn't being followed by the law or anyone else, he drove out of town. Never once did he break the speed limit. No reason to call any attention to his rattletrap of a truck or his expired license.

Less than an hour later, he had parked in the asphalt lot of the market and waited. Shoppers and bag boys pushing rattling carts walked in and out of the store while half-a-dozen cars found parking spaces. Crows flapped around looking for morsels, and a rangy dog meandered through the cars, finally lifting his leg on the tire of a fancy sports car.

Good shot.

On his third Marlboro, Ross looked through the plate-glass window and recognized Ruby as she was getting ready to leave. He watched as she talked to a few of the other cashiers and untied her apron. With a wave to the poor stiffs still manning the registers, she pushed open the glass door and stepped into the sweltering evening.

Ross smiled slowly. He tossed the butt of his cigarette onto the asphalt.

Ruby was still a pretty little thing, and Ross remembered what she was like in bed. That had been years ago, before she'd turned on him, but at the time she'd been a spitfire in or out of the sack. He wondered if she still gave good head. His cock got hard just thinking about it.

She'd cut her hair. It was shorter now, cut in curly mahogany-colored layers that framed a pixie face with huge brown eyes. Some folks claimed she looked like a shorter version of Audrey Hepburn, but Ruby Dee was too full-figured for that.

His hard-on made him squirm. It had been years since he'd been with a woman. *Years*. He was long overdue. He'd been fighting a hard-on since the minute he'd gotten out of prison. Just about any woman looked like a ready piece of tail to him these days. He was so damned horny, he thought he'd go out of his mind.

He waited until she had pulled her keys out of her purse and started to unlock the door of her Ford Escort. Then he was out of the old truck like a shot. Long strides took him past a few maverick grocery carts that weren't in their appropriate chutes, and he circumvented an ancient green El Camino with a FOR SALE sign plastered to one window.

"Ruby," he said and she visibly jumped, turning and holding her keys as if they offered some kind of protection.

She said something under her breath. It sounded like, "God help me." More loudly, she said, "Ross. I—I heard you got out." She looked for the life of her like a doe caught in headlights.

"No thanks to you."

"I—I don't know what you mean." But fear shone in those big eyes.

He leaned a hip against the door of the Escort, making sure she couldn't unlock the car. "Sure ya do, honey. Your testimony sent me to the big house."

"No, Ross, that wasn't the way it was. I—um, I just told the court what I saw. That's all."

"Did ya, now?" Ross knew his gaze was menacing. He reached forward and twined one of her saucy curls around his finger.

She jerked away as if his touch was fire. "Yes, sir, I sure did. You were in Nevada Smith's pickup. Drunk as a skunk. I saw you in it when I came out of the Last Stand. You were pullin' into the parking lot of Estevan's store." She stopped suddenly. "Look, Ross, I don't want no trouble. I don't see any reason to go over this again. You're out of prison now, so what do you care?"

"What do I care?" he repeated, tossing the question over in his mind. "What do I care?" Rage started flowing through his blood. "I lost ten years of my life because you lied, Ruby. Ten years. Two fighting the damned case and eight in prison. Do you have any idea how long that is? Do ya?" When she didn't answer, he glared hard at her. "Well, that's what I care."

"I—I didn't lie."

"You might have seen Smith's truck that night, but I wasn't behind the wheel. The way I figure it, Smith and Estevan had it out, probably over the fact that Smith dumped Estevan's daughter for Shelby Cole. Ramón had a temper—everyone in town knew it. He probably came after Smith with a knife or gun and things got out of hand. Smith blew him away."

"You're out of your mind," Ruby said, her spine stiffening a bit. "Nevada didn't kill anyone."

"Well, neither did I, but I paid, didn't I?" His eyes narrowed on Ruby, and she visibly trembled. A surge of power swept through his bloodstream; he liked the way her skin had turned white at the sight of him. He reached for her, but she drew away.

"Don't touch me, Ross, or I'll call the police. Just because Caleb changed his story and now he's gonna make big bucks sellin' it to that woman reporter doesn't mean a thing. I told the truth about that night."

Ross ignored her show of gumption. He grabbed hold of her arm and his fingers curled over bones so small he thought he might be able to break them with a simple twist. "What reporter? What're you talkin' about?"

"The reporter from *Lone Star* magazine. Katrina Something-Or-Other. She's got herself a deal with Caleb."

"That lying sum-bitch is gonna make money off *my* story?" His temper notched up another degree or two. "Well, don't that jest beat all. First he sends me to fuckin' prison and then he's gonna get rich. Fer what? He's gonna die, ain't he?"

"I—I don't know." Ruby struggled, but he wouldn't let go.

"That really pisses me off." He gave her a shake and she cried out.

"I swear I'll call the cops," she warned.

"Will ya now?" he taunted, moving closer so that there was only a hairbreadth between her cheek and his lips. He could smell her fear, and it worked like an aphrodisiac, making him as hard as a rock. "Seems to me you should be callin' a lawyer instead. You lied on the stand, Ruby."

"I didn't. I said I saw you driving Nevada's truck and I did." With more pluck than he'd given her credit for, she yanked her arm free. Then, rather than bolt like a frightened filly, she reached behind him and inserted her key in the lock. She tried to pull the door open, but he didn't budge. Instead, he grabbed her arm again.

She swallowed hard. "Get out of the way, Ross," she snarled. "And don't ever bother me again."

"Is that what I'm doin'? Botherin' ya?" He liked that idea and smiled inwardly when he noticed how pale she'd become. Despite her brave words, she was about to pass out from fear and that was just fine. In fact, it brought a heady feeling to Ross. One he liked. Maybe he should haul Ruby back to the trailer, liquor her up and—

A police cruiser swept down the street, and Ross let go so fast that Ruby nearly toppled over. Nope, this wasn't the time or the place. He had to slow down a mite and be patient. He wasn't ready for the kind of trouble the cops could bring. Not yet. Ruby could wait.

Besides, he had bigger fish to fry.

# CHAPTER 11

"I found your doctor." Bill Levinson's voice sounded as if he were in the next room rather than thousands of miles away and connected only by Wi-Fi.

"Where?" Nevada demanded. He'd been chewing on a toothpick, but stopped.

"Six feet under."

*Damn.* "What happened?"

"Drank himself to death, it appears. Lived in Jamaica and had a love affair with rum. Been gone about two years."

Another dead end. "You're sure it's the same guy?"

"Checked and double-checked the records. I'll scan 'em in and e-mail 'em to you, if ya want."

Nevada didn't doubt him; Levinson had proven himself trustworthy in the past. But it was best to have the records. "Send 'em," he said. "Thanks."

"Sorry it wasn't better news."

"Me, too."

"Say, I tried to call Shelby Cole. Didn't get through. Left a message on her cell."

"She's out of town. I'm sure she'll get back to you," Nevada said, then asked Levinson to do a little more digging. On Ross McCallum.

172 • *Lisa Jackson*

"Your old pal," Levinson joked. "I'll see what I can come up with, but he's been clean for the last eight or nine years."

"Probably ten," Nevada allowed, "but see what kind of stuff he was into before that."

"I thought you checked this all out."

"I did. But I've been told I'm not objective. And while you're at it, there's someone else—"

"Let me guess. Judge Jerome Cole."

"Wouldn't hurt."

"Never does," Levinson agreed with a satisfied smile in his voice. "You got it."

Nevada hung up, and a bad taste rose in his throat. He walked to the bedroom, where, on a small table, his laptop and printer were set up. Sure enough, within ten minutes, the printer spewed a report and death certificate for Ned Charles Pritchart, M.D., who, as stated by the local doctor, had died of natural causes at the age of seventy-one. Along with the report, Levinson had included a bill.

"Great," Nevada mumbled to himself just as he heard the crunch of tires in the gravel drive. Crockett began to bark his fool head off.

"Quiet!" Nevada ordered as he snapped off the computer and hoped that Shelby had stopped by. He'd been nervous ever since she'd taken off for San Antonio; he had even considered chasing her down and had mentally kicked himself for not finding out where she was staying. Like it or not, he was worried. Even though she'd been away from Bad Luck for years without him worrying about her, things had changed. Now there were anonymous letters, harassing phone calls, McCallum on the loose. Ever since Shelby had driven up Nevada's lane about a week ago, she'd been on his mind and hell, yes, he was concerned about her.

And it wasn't just because she was the mother of his child. Nope. His feelings for her ran deeper than that. In fact, too deep. He didn't want to think about the way she messed with his mind.

Hoping to find her climbing out of that white Cadillac she'd rented, he walked outside to spy a small blue car roll to a stop near the pump house. A woman was behind the wheel. She wasn't Shelby.

Crockett, hairs on the back of his neck bristling, growled deep in his throat and bared his fangs.

"Easy, boy," Nevada warned as he stood on the porch and watched as the woman, one he couldn't place, dragged out a briefcase. The muscles at the base of his skull tensed. He wasn't used to having visitors, and lately he'd had more than his share. This one, a petite, no-nonsense woman with red hair and eyes much older than her years, slung the strap of the briefcase over one slim shoulder and strode up the front walk. A pair of sunglasses had been pushed to the top of her head. At the bottom step she slid the shades off and slipped them into the side pocket of her briefcase.

"Mr. Smith?" she asked and flashed him a thousand-watt smile—as bright as a snowy mountaintop at dawn and just as cold. Nevada was instantly wary. He didn't get many solicitors out here, not even missionary types who wanted to sell him religion, so who the hell was she? And then it dawned on him.

"Yep."

She stuck out a hand. "I'm Katrina Nedelesky. I'm a reporter for *Lone Star* magazine."

Her grip was strong. Sure. Yet there was something tenuous about the way she looked up at him, something he innately didn't trust. Filled with self-importance, she fished in a pocket of her briefcase and retrieved a business card. She slapped it into his open palm. "Just in case you doubt me."

"Wouldn't do that." But he glanced down, skimmed the information, then assessed her slowly. "What can I do for you?" Leaning one hip against the frame of the door, he folded his arms across his chest and slid the toothpick from one side of his mouth to the other.

"I wanted to ask you a few questions about the night Ramón Estevan was killed."

So that was it. He wasn't surprised. "Look, I made a report. Testified on the stand. I think it's all a matter of public record."

"I know, I know, but if I could just come in and talk to you a while...I really would like to hear your side of the story."

"My *side*?"

"Well, your take on things. You were there."

He'd never had much use for reporters, thought they were all snoops and glory-seekers; this one didn't impress him as any more scrupulous than the rest of the lot. Also, there was something about her—the way she stared up at him with such intense eyes—that gave him pause. Had he met her before? He didn't think so. He was pretty good with faces, and yet she seemed familiar.

He motioned to the plastic chairs on the front porch, and as she took a seat Crockett gave off a soft "woof " and slowly slunk down the steps to his favorite spot under the porch. In the fields nearby a few spindly-legged colts pranced and bucked, their coats gleaming in the fading rays of sunlight.

Nevada leaned back, crossed his legs at the ankles and waited. The reporter perched on the edge of one chair as if afraid some of the dust that had settled on the seat would dirty up her black skirt.

"I've got a pocket recorder—" She snapped open her briefcase.

"No recorder."

"But—"

"Listen, I don't think I have anything to say to you. I heard you were interviewing Caleb—in fact he's been crowing about it, talkin' about all the money he's gonna make from some exclusive deal the two of you have cooked up—but there's not a whole lot more I can add."

"You were a major part of the investigation," she argued, and the scent of her perfume teased him. It wasn't cheap, and her clothes looked as if she'd picked them out at Nieman Marcus rather than Kmart; he'd bet his favorite mare that the skirt, boots, knit top and jacket—hell, even her perfume—were imprinted with some famous designer's name. Though her car was inexpensive and had seen better years, Katrina Nedelesky wasn't afraid to spend some bucks on her appearance. A dichotomy, the lady reporter. Nope, he didn't trust one hair on her head.

"You and Ross were sworn enemies," she said with that same gee-I-find-you-fascinating grin. "And you claimed he stole your pickup that night."

"Someone did. Ross ended up in it."

"And nearly died. Plowed it into a tree, right?"

"It's all in the report," he said testily. He didn't like the woman—she was too smooth, too self-impressed.

"But you were friends in high school."

"Not friends. We played on the same football team while he was in school." She was starting to irritate him. He stared at her. Hard. She didn't so much as flinch.

"As I understand it, you were both interested in the same girl." This wasn't just an aside. She'd been leading up to it. "Shelby Cole, daughter of Judge Jerome—er, I guess he goes by Red around these parts. Anyway, the both of you were seeing Judge Cole's daughter."

Nevada's temper, burning slow, snapped. "I dated Shelby for a while."

"And Ross—?" she suggested.

"You'll have to ask him about that." He matched her grin with one of his own. "But that probably isn't the best idea around. Ross has kind of a bad reputation, Ms."—he checked the card he was still holding—"Nedelesky. And a pretty foul temper. So if I were you, I wouldn't push things."

She was just slightly unnerved, but not yet off track. "Is there something I should know about your relationship with Ross McCallum?"

He snorted. "Didn't think I had one."

"You hated McCallum. Everyone I've interviewed in town says so. As teenagers you had a few skirmishes and later, just a few weeks before Ramón Estevan was killed, you and McCallum got into a pretty big fight. Both of you ended up in the hospital. You lost the vision in one eye, and McCallum suffered broken ribs and a separated shoulder, I think. What was that all about?"

"We had a disagreement. It got out of hand. As I said, McCallum's got a hot temper."

"And what about you?"

"I can hold my own. Look, I think we've talked enough. As I said, everything you need to know is in the court records." Nevada stood, signifying that the interview was over.

She didn't take the hint. "So where were you when Ramón Estevan was shot?"

"It's in my report. I was driving around."

"Alone?" She didn't bother to hide the suspicion in her tone.

"Didn't have a partner with me at the time."

She lifted both eyebrows as if she thought this information was somehow important. "The murder weapon was never found. True?"

"As far as I know."

"And you had a gun that was missing—the same caliber that killed Ramón."

"That's right." He shifted from one leg to the other.

"You've never found your gun?"

"Pistol. No, never."

"But your hunting rifle was in the truck along with Ross McCallum."

"It wasn't the murder weapon."

She ignored that. "You were asked to leave the Sheriff's Department shortly after the investigation. Why?"

The muscles at the base of his neck knotted up tight. "I resigned, Ms. Nedelesky. Personal reasons."

"What were they?" The porch was getting dark, and he didn't bother switching on the light. She wasn't budging, so he decided to come straight to the point.

"This interview is over."

"Is it true you railroaded Ross McCallum into prison?"

"He was tried and convicted."

"With witnesses who weren't reliable. Witnesses you provided."

"I said, 'the interview's over'."

Reluctantly she climbed to her feet and picked up her briefcase. "You know, Mr. Smith, there's a whole lot more to this story than just the facts on the surface."

"Is there?"

"Oh, yeah." She nodded as if agreeing with herself while hiking the strap of her briefcase to her shoulder and searching for her keys. "And I'm going to find out what it is."

"Do that," he said.

With a final strobe of that icy smile, Katrina walked back to her car. She swung that tight little butt of hers as if it was something special, but Nevada wasn't interested. The lady was about as safe to cuddle up to as a viper.

By the time she slid behind the wheel, the sun had settled behind the western hills and darkness was fast encroaching. Long purple shadows swept across the fields and the first few stars winked in the sky. Somewhere far off a coyote howled.

Boots planted wide apart, Nevada folded his arms across his chest and observed Katrina's aging rattletrap of a car as she drove off. He told himself not to let her insinuations bother him. She was an opportunist, nothing more. He sensed that she had her own agenda, a personal reason for her interest in Ross McCallum becoming a free man.

So what was it? The taillights of her Escort winked through the trees. His eyes narrowed. *Forget her. She's not gonna dig up anything damaging.* And yet he couldn't ignore the fact that she was a loose cannon. Bothered, he walked inside and reached for the phone. He dialed Shelby's cell. Waited. No one answered.

He didn't bother leaving a message.

A bad feeling settled over Nevada, partially because of the snoopy reporter, but also because he was worried about Shelby and annoyed that Ned Pritchart had died, taking any information the doctor had about Elizabeth to the grave with him. The fact that Doc Pritchart was dead wasn't a surprise, and yet it meant it was one less lead to finding their daughter. His child. Shelby's. It was strange how he'd accepted the fact that he was a father.

And yet, once he finally located Elizabeth—and locate her he would—Nevada Smith didn't have a clue as to what he'd do. For the first time in his life, he didn't have a plan. And it bothered him. It bothered him a lot.

Caleb Swaggert was counting his money in his head. The doctors didn't think he'd survive, he saw it in their eyes when they spoke to him and the unspoken message in their words was, *You're not gonna make it, you old coot. Modern medicine can only do so much.*

But what did they know? Sure he had a bad ticker, and there was his proclivity for whiskey and cigarettes, but hell, he'd weathered worse than this and the service he was getting here in the hospital was top rate. Yeah, he was weak, but he might just make it and he was counting on God to give him a few more weeks, if not years. He glanced at all of the statues of Jesus and Mary that littered the windowsill and his tray and counter, then looked at the Bible verses tacked to the walls. This room was a virtual shrine and surely God would see to it that he had a few more days on this earth to spend the money from the magazine. Oh, sure, he planned on leaving most of it, had drawn up a will to that purpose, but he should at least enjoy part of it.

Right?

He figured he'd go into the Last Stand Saloon, buy everyone in the house a round of drinks or two, leave a large tip with Abelena, the curly-haired waitress with that tight, round ass and full lips. Sure as hell, he intended to celebrate the damned end of his life in style and thank God for his good fortune.

As he was thinking about it, he closed his eyes, decided to send up a hasty prayer and started to drift off. Oh, yeah, Abelena would be thankful, maybe allow him a pinch of that sweet behind....

He dozed peacefully, his breath coming in a little hard, but his thoughts happily dancing through his head. No doubt he was getting a little mellow juice pumped through his IV. Well, that was just fine with him. The happier, the better.

He was barely aware of someone slipping into his room, hardly heard a sound, and cracked an eyelid to see that the room had been darkened. He must've been more asleep than he'd realized. He was drifting again as the person, a nurse or aide most likely, stepped closer.

But he didn't hear her call his name softly as was the usual case. In fact, he thought he detected the smell of beer and smoke, or was it just his imagination conjuring up those wanted scents?

With an effort, he tried to open his eyes fully, but the sedative he was sure he'd been slipped was working full force and it wasn't a bad thing, not at all, to be drifting away on a peaceful cloud of happiness.... Aaah, yes...

A hand clamped over his mouth.

*What?*

His eyes flew open, and he realized no nurse had entered the room, but someone intent on doing him harm. He tried to scream, but that was impossible as his own pillow was forced over his face! He scrambled for the nurse's call button, fingers scraping the bed rails. Where the hell was it?

He bucked, tried to get free, but his body was weak and the strength applied to him was punishing. His lungs were on fire and he tried to gasp for breath, to strike at the offender. Nothing worked. The pressure kept coming. Harder and harder.

Panic surged through him. Adrenaline kicked in.

His old heart was pounding furiously, wildly.

But there was no air. He felt his eyes bulge as he gasped and got nothing.

*Get off me! Let me go! Help! Someone help me! I can't breathe.*

His lungs were exploding. Pain burned through him. He flailed, but what little strength he had ebbed.

*No, no, no!*

*Oh, Jesus, HELP ME!!!!* he silently cried. But it was too late.

Once outside the hospital, the dusk enveloped him. In a back alley he pulled off the scrubs he'd "borrowed" from a locker he'd found open and made a quick zigzag course through the streets of Bad Luck, avoiding street lamps and traffic, and especially surveillance cameras.

No doubt he might show up on the security cameras in the hospital, but they were old and didn't cover every hallway. He'd been careful, watchful, even of people talking on cell phones that could become instant cameras.

Adrenaline fired his blood and he had to force himself to walk slowly and ease between the buildings until he found his vehicle, parked on the street where he'd left it.

Smiling, almost assured he'd just gotten away with murder, he relived those final seconds when the old bastard had been struggling, trying to free himself, his scrawny arms useless, his hands unable to grasp anything.

And no one had come running to Caleb's aid; at least not until it was too late. The act had been quick and timed to happen between shifts. It hadn't hurt that he'd stopped by an old lady's room and unplugged her monitors, so that most of the staff had either been on their way out the door, or trying to save Pearl Landell....Too bad, Caleb.

In less than two minutes, Caleb had breathed his last, his struggles over.

It had been so easy. Almost too easy.

That gave him pause as he slid behind the wheel and fired the engine. He couldn't afford to get too cocky. Not yet. There was still so much to do.

The way the killer saw it, he was just helping Caleb Swaggert along. The grim reaper hadn't been far behind, but now he could take someone else as a victim.

Caleb was already on his way straight to hell.

A million stars were flung across the wide black sky, and a half moon was rising steadily over the hills.

Shelby pushed the button for the sunroof. It opened just as the Cadillac crested the final rise on the road to Bad Luck. The windows were open and a hot Texas wind raced by, caressing her cheeks and tangling her hair. Hot, tired and frustrated as hell, she saw the lights of town glowing steadily ahead and her fingers held fast to the steering wheel. She didn't hear the music blasting from the radio, didn't notice much other than the ribbon of asphalt caught in the beams of her headlights. Two days in San Antonio—for what?

Nothing.

Nada.

Zilch.

Damn it all to hell anyway. She didn't know much more about Elizabeth's whereabouts now than she had when she'd returned to Bad Luck in a blaze of self-righteous indignation and motherly determination.

It seemed like an eternity since she'd received the letter and picture; in truth it wasn't quite a week. So why was it that she felt every day that went by had been wasted, that she'd lost another twenty-four hours when she could have been with her child?

"Where are you?" she asked a daughter she'd never met, but she refused to let a sense of desperation invade her soul. She would find Elizabeth. She had to. She wouldn't rest until she had.

The lights of Bad Luck loomed nearer. Her stomach soured at the sight of the Well Come Inn glowing in neon splendor on the edge of town.

Shelby had planned to drive home, take a late-night swim and let the cool water soak away the aches in her muscles and the headache pounding through her brain, but before she reached the city limits, she eased off the accelerator and took a road that veered west, toward Nevada's ranch. Maybe he'd learned something in the last couple of days.

*Or is it because you just want to see him again?*

Her fingers tightened over the steering wheel at the thought, and she checked the rearview mirror, as she had every ten or twenty miles since leaving San Antonio. She'd been jittery and nervous, half expecting that she might be followed, though that was crazy. Just because someone had called her hotel room right before she'd left and not spoken was no reason to freak out. It was just a coincidence, nothing more. No one was following her.

As she drove past prickly pear and live oaks, she rationalized that she had to face Nevada again, and soon. They were in this thing together—parents of their missing daughter.

*But there's more to it than that, Shelby, and you know it.*

She refused to listen to that nagging part of her mind and pushed the speed limit until she reached the turnoff to Nevada's ranch. Dry weeds brushed the undercarriage of the rental car. Bugs splattered against the windshield. Her heart was pounding with a mixture of dread and anticipation, and for a second she wished she hadn't made this little detour. Her hands felt suddenly damp with nervous sweat. She checked her reflection in the rearview mirror, made sure that her lipstick hadn't faded.

"Ridiculous," she chided herself as the Cadillac bounced down twin ruts grooved deep into the hard pan. She wasn't a high school girl in the throes of her first crush. This was far different. She stared through the windshield. In the moonlight she saw the silhouettes of longhorns in the nearby fields and ahead, lamplight glowing from the windows and open door of Nevada's house.

Her mouth was cotton dry. She parked and was out of the car before the dust had settled. Crockett began to bark, and as she climbed the single step to Nevada's porch, he appeared in the doorway, standing in stark relief, his shoulders nearly touching either side of the doorjamb.

Why was it that she always noticed how all-male he was, how raw and rugged and untamed? Like these dry, wind-blown hills, he was earthy and wild and Texan.

*And the kind of man you should avoid like a coiled rattler.*

"Well, Shelby," he drawled, a slow-spreading grin growing from one side of his jaw to the other. "This is a surprise." His teeth were a white slash against his night-darkened skin. Flinty eyes assessed her. "Miss me?"

"So bad I couldn't sleep at night," she mocked.

"Me, neither." Amusement danced through his eyes, and some of her apprehension dissipated. One dark eyebrow lifted appraisingly. Dimples cut into his dark jaw. "I just never thought you'd admit it."

He was baiting her, and though she warned herself not to rise to it, to avoid the lure, she couldn't help saying, "Get over yourself, Nevada. I have."

"Like hell," he muttered. As she tried to pass, he struck swiftly, strong arms surrounding her. Before she could think twice, she was dragged against the hard, flat wall of his chest. He stared down his broken-more-than-once nose with eyes that burned silver gray in the moonlight. "You, lady, are the worst liar I've ever met, and that's saying something, cuz I've known a lot of them."

"I'll bet." She angled her chin up, refusing to back down, but couldn't ignore the heat he generated, the splay of strong, calloused fingers against the small of her back. "So what're you gonna do about it, Smith?" she taunted.

That irreverent slash of white was back. "You want to find out?"

*No!* "Maybe." Dear Lord, why was she toying with him? She could barely breathe being this close to him, had trouble concentrating on anything but the thin twist of his lips.

One thick eyebrow arched. "Watch."

With excruciating deliberation, he trailed a work-roughened finger down the slope of her neck.

Oh, God, she was melting inside. Heat seeped into her bloodstream, yet she shivered and her heart began knocking in frantic anticipation.

His hand settled over her shoulder, fingers on her back, thumb placed at the hollow of her throat. If he wanted to, he could crush her windpipe and snap her neck. But she trusted him with her life and, stupidly, with her heart.

He pressed warm lips to the crook of her neck and she moaned.

*Stop this, Shelby. He's seducing you and you're falling for it! Stop it now, while you still can.*

Lifting his head, he stared at her. His thumb slowly traced the ring of bones at the base of her throat, rotating in sensuous circles.

*I want you.*

Had he said it?

Had she?

Embers of a long-forbidden fire smoldered. She knew it was madness, being alone with him, touching him, letting the smell of him invade her senses, and yet she couldn't stop, wouldn't think beyond this moment.

Backing her against the wall, he lowered his head. Though she knew kissing him was about the craziest thing she could do, she couldn't resist. His lips touched hers and she quivered. His bare arms, corded and strong, held her fast and her knees threatened to give way altogether. Just as his mouth settled over hers, he whispered, "You are the most aggravating, mule-headed and sexy woman I've ever met."

"And...and you're my worst nightmare."

"I know."

Oh, God, she could barely think, let alone talk. Embers sparked. Desire pounded through her brain and it was all she could do not to grab him and never let go.

He kissed her then. Hard. With his whole body. As if he never intended to stop. His mouth clamped over hers and his body was pressed tight to the contours of hers. Wild, wanton thoughts tore through her brain. Hot as an East Texas wind and twice as willful, a yearning like no other raged deep in her soul. She couldn't breathe. Couldn't resist. She gasped, and through her open mouth his eager tongue pushed past her teeth. Her eyes fluttered shut. Memories of a younger time played through her mind. Oh, God, how she'd loved him then; how she wanted him still.

His tongue teased and flicked against hers, scraping the roof of her mouth as his lips caressed hers. He was everywhere, his hands holding her fast, his breathing as ragged as her own.

*Don't do this, Shelby. This is treacherous.*

She remembered making love to him in a spring storm, his

honed wet body mounting hers, his bare hips thrusting forcefully as he entered her, the smell and feel and taste of him surrounding her then as they did now.

He lifted his head and she clung to him.

"So you *did* miss me," he taunted, twining his calloused fingers through her hair and tugging so that she was forced to open her eyes and stare up at him.

"Not—not a second."

He laughed gruffly. "As bad a liar as you are, Shelby Cole, you sure don't know when to quit."

"What?" she asked, gasping. "And ruin all this fun?"

"You're pushing me, darlin', and that could be dangerous."

"Could it?" She laughed. "I don't see how."

"As I said before, watch." He kissed her again and this time his deliberation was replaced with fervor. Hard, demanding lips met hers, and his fingers found the buttons running down the front of her dress. One by one they were released from their bonds and the bodice opened, exposing breasts held tight by a filmy bra. Her nipples tensed under his touch, hard little buttons pressing against black lace.

Inside she turned to hot tallow and her bones became water.

He buried his face in the cleft of her breasts and his breath was hot and wet, steamy against the skin of her abdomen. She thought of what he could do to her, how long it had been since he'd loved her, and she ached for more.

"You're so beautiful," he said as he kissed the top of one breast, then slid his tongue over the scrap of lace to flick against her nipple. She writhed in his arms, the fingers of both hands running through his hair, yet holding his head fast against her. With a groan that touched the deepest core of her, he bit and toyed with her, never letting up.

Desire sizzled through her brain, thundered in her ears. "Nevada!" she cried in a voice she didn't recognize as her own.

"What, darlin'?" he asked, his breath teasing her skin.

"I—I—"

"I know." Deftly, he lifted her from her feet and carried her through an open doorway to a small, dark bedroom. "Me, too." Together they tumbled onto a soft bedspread and mattress that gave with their weight. They kissed frantically and the need deep within her pulsed hot and wild through her veins. She knew she should stop this madness, that making love to him would be the worst possible mistake of her life, but that wild, rebellious part of her that he'd released ten years earlier was revived and tonight, alone with him, away from the prying eyes of her father and the worries over her child—their child—she let go.

He pushed her dress over her shoulders and tossed her bra onto the floor. She shoved his shirt over corded, muscular shoulders and closed her mind to the doubts that screamed at her. It had been so long, so damned long since she'd loved him. His lips were everywhere and heat uncoiled within her, need pulsing through her blood, want pounding in her brain.

More buttons gave way. Her dress parted completely, leaving her only in panties. His breath worked magic against her abdomen, his fingers rough and coarse. She let out a long, low moan as his tongue rimmed her navel and his hands slipped beneath her, cupping her buttocks, lifting her upward, closer. He kissed her gently, stroking with his tongue, sliding ever lower.

Her mind spun in sensuous circles, and she traced the muscles of his shoulders and arms. He kicked off his boots, his jeans.

*No, no, no! Don't do this.*

His fingers splayed over her lower spine.

"Tell me no."

*Yes, tell him!* "I—I can't."

"Shelby, this is dangerous." His words whispered across her mound, ruffling the fluff of down that covered the juncture of her legs.

Trembling, writhing with want, she couldn't find the words to stop, didn't want to. Tonight was theirs. She closed her mind to yesterday, wouldn't consider tomorrow. His lips were wet, warm as they kissed her inner thigh.

She gasped.

The ache within her yawned.

His mouth brushed closer.

Her heart was thrumming, her mind spinning. The night faded

away, melted into the shadows. He kissed her intimately, and she opened to him, wanting, needing—so hot she couldn't drag in a breath.

She wanted him as she'd always wanted him, the only man she'd ever trusted with her heart, the only man she'd allowed to break it.

His fingers dug into her buttocks, holding her fast as she began to rock, faster and faster, her blood pumping, pulsing through her veins until, somewhere in the furthest reaches within her, a dam broke. Violently. Wildly. Her spirit, so hopelessly trapped in a private misery, flew free. She cried out, her voice powerful where it had been weak only seconds before.

"Nevada—"

"Right here, darlin'," he said and inched up to hold her close. His breathing was labored, the bristles of his beard shadow rough against her cheek, and he kissed her on the lips while his knees parted her legs. She was lost in the wonder and feel of him. "Oh, God, Shelby, I've missed you," he said and then thrust deep into her. Closing her eyes, lost in the warmth and feel of him, she let go, her body moving easily with his, catching his rhythm quickly, as if they had been lovers for years.

"Shelby...beautiful Shelby," he whispered, his voice raw, his body wet with sweat. Faster and faster, like a horse galloping out of control toward a great, yawning abyss, he pushed her, breathing hard, holding her close. Shelby couldn't think, could barely breathe. *I love you, Nevada,* she thought desperately and mouthed the words, though her voice failed her. Lightning splintered behind her eyes. Her body convulsed.

"I can't stop, I can't..." He stiffened, the muscles of his butt flexing, his back curving as he poured himself into her until he fell, gasping, upon her, his breathing ragged, shallow. "Sweet Jesus," he whispered into the hollow of her throat.

She clung to him and blinked against a sudden, unwanted, hot rush of unexpected tears. "I—I'm sorry...I didn't mean..."

"Shh. It's all right." Strong arms surrounded her, and a big hand held her face against his chest, where she heard the steady beat of his heart. She sniffed, refusing to let go; unwilling to let her defenses down for even a second. He kissed her forehead, and she fought the urge to sob against him.

"I was worried about you," he finally admitted as they lay alone in the darkness of his room. Through the partially open window she heard the sounds of the night—a cow lowing, traffic humming on a far-off highway.

"Why?"

"Don't know. But there are things happening that bother me." The mattress squeaked as he rolled over, turned on a bedside light, and she was offered her first glimpse of his bedroom. It was small, compact and functional. An antique dresser and mirror stood at the foot of the bed, and a small, battered table holding a computer and printer had been pushed into a corner. The knotty pine walls were bare save for one window, a horseshoe mounted over the door-way and a rack with brass hooks where his jackets hung beside a closet door.

"You're nervous because Ross McCallum's out of prison. It has everyone jittery."

"Not you?"

She hesitated. Now didn't seem the right time to tell him about the rape, about the fact that Ross might be Elizabeth's father. She cleared her throat and licked her suddenly dry lips. "Me the most of all," she admitted, beginning to sweat. How could she explain? How would he feel about her if he knew the god-awful truth? The pain of the past, the feeling of being used and the shame of it all brought fresh tears to her eyes. "But I try not to."

He shifted, looked hard into her eyes and placed a hand on either side of her face. "I know what happened," he said softly.

*Oh, Nevada, no. You don't. You couldn't.* Her throat clogged. She laughed without a trace of mirth, and the sound bounced hollowly off his walls. "No, I don't think you do."

His eyes locked with hers, and in that heartbeat she realized that he knew her deepest secret. "McCallum raped you, Shelby. And that's why you left."

*Oh, God.* Her world splintered. All the lies she told herself were now exposed.

Her heart squeezed painfully. Tears threatened her eyes all over again.

"What I didn't understand," Nevada said gently, his hands forcing her to look at him, "was that you were pregnant, and until the

Judge brought up the fact that you hadn't told me everything the other day, that I was only working with half-truths, I hadn't figured out that McCallum could be Elizabeth's father."

*No!* "He's not!" She pounded the quilt with an emphatic fist. Fate couldn't be so cr uel. Tears filled her eyes. "I mean...I mean... it...just can't be."

"It doesn't matter, Shelby."

"Of course it does." She wouldn't—couldn't—allow herself to believe that her child, her precious baby, was conceived in the terror and rage of that degrading attack. Her stomach roiled, sweat poured from her face and again she was shaking violently.

"Come here." Nevada folded her into his arms and kissed her crown. "You don't know whether your daughter is fathered by me or by him and it's tearing you up inside."

"No—" she argued.

He grabbed her chin between strong fingers, forcing her face upward to stare into his eyes again. "It's not your fault."

"But—"

"Do you hear me?" he demanded, refusing to let her turn away from him. "It's *not* your fault."

She couldn't stop the tears this time. Fresh, hot and filled with shame, they rained from her eyes. "I—I—"

"Shh." Once more he held her close, and this time she let loose. Burying her face in his shoulder, she wept the bitter tears she'd kept at bay for nearly ten years. She'd shared her secret with only her father when he'd forced the information from her weeks after the horrid night.

She held fast to Nevada, felt the strength of his body surround her. His lips pressed against her forehead, his hands stroked her back as she cried.

"It's all right, Shelby. It's gonna be all right."

If only she could believe him. Trust him. Hang on to those precious words. As the minutes passed, somewhere deep in the farthest reaches of her soul, she found her strength. She had to pull herself together—if for nothing else, then for Elizabeth. Gritting her teeth, she refused to give in to the agony and the fear. Ross McCallum had defiled her once. No one would ever do so again. She'd die first.

Slowly she pulled herself together, and when the sobs finally subsided, she found the nerve to ask, "How did you know?"

"About McCallum?" he asked through lips that barely moved. "From Badger Collins."

Through a sheen of leftover tears, she noticed the granite-hard set of his jaw, his razor-thin lips, the flare of his nostrils—as if he'd encountered a bad scent. "McCallum couldn't keep his mouth shut. Bragged to Collins, who passed the information my way."

She cringed inside. It had been worse than she'd thought. Her dirty little secret, the one she'd only shared with her father when he'd pressed her, had been whispered through the back alleys, bars and church pews in Bad Luck—probably all the way to Coopersville, Austin and San Antonio. The Judge had finally suspected that there was more to her depression than fear of graduation and her pregnancy, and one night, in desperation, she'd confided in him, begging him to keep it beween them, not wanting anyone else to know her shame. Her father, with his pride and reputation at stake, had been ashen-faced as he'd stood at the side of her bed, trying to comfort her and being unable to do any more than pat her on the head and promise to keep her secret.

But it hadn't worked, obviously. Even Nevada had known. All these years, he'd suspected that she'd been violated and raped; all these years she'd hoped he'd never found out.

This time, though she wanted to look away, she managed to maintain eye contact.

"I wasn't sure if it was true or not, so I confronted McCallum myself," Nevada conceded, still holding her close. "He wouldn't admit it, but he seemed so smug and self-satisfied that it didn't take a genius to put two and two together."

"And that's when you and he got into the fight."

"Yep."

"A few weeks before Ramón Estevan was killed?"

"'Bout that long." His eyes held hers, and she had to force the question from her lips.

"There...there was talk that you steered the investigation away from other leads, that you were hell-bent to prove that McCallum did it. That...that you—"

"Set him up? Sent an innocent man to jail?" His voice held no trace of regret, not one iota of remorse. "Maybe my case wasn't strong enough to keep him in jail, but believe me, Ross McCallum deserved to be behind bars." He hesitated, as if he intended to say more, then held his tongue as she brushed the tears from her eyes and pulled away from him. The bedsprings creaked.

Sanity slowly seeped into her brain, and she realized she was naked, lying on Nevada's bed, acting as if they were long-term lovers, people who cared for each other, a man and a woman who trusted each other. But they weren't. They were just caught in the same trap, had made love because of the past rather than the future, had satisfied their frustrations sexually, and though she fantasized about loving him, the truth of the matter was that they were worlds apart, two once-upon-a-time lovers who were on the same quest. Nothing more.

She began reaching for her clothes and he rolled over her, pinning her to the bed with his body. "Wait a minute."

"No, I think I should go. I didn't mean to come in here and... and well... you know."

"Take advantage of me?"

She laughed despite herself, despite the pain knifing through her soul. "Well, yeah, that wasn't really my plan."

"Then it was that I was just too damned irresistible."

"Bingo." She wiped away any trace of her tears. "That's it, Smith. I just can't think straight whenever I'm around you."

"It's a gift I have," he said, and she chuckled deep in her throat. What was it about him that one minute she wanted to slap him, the next make wild love to him and within seconds laugh with him? It was absurd. She struggled into her clothes and he, lying naked on the bed, just watched her.

"What did Findley know?" he asked as she slid into her panties and felt a ludicrous blush stealing up her cheeks.

"Whatever it was, he wasn't saying." She slipped her arms through her bra straps, suddenly anxious to be dressed. "Orrin Findley's going to take whatever he knows to the grave with him. What about you?"

"Not good news." Reaching across her, he grabbed some papers from his printer and handed them to her. "Pritchart's dead."

"What?" She'd been buttoning her dress, but her fingers froze.

"Levinson called a couple of hours ago. He'd tracked a doctor named Ned Charles Pritchart to Jamaica, but the guy drank himself to death. I think Levinson tried to call you."

"I missed his call and couldn't get a hold of him." She was already scanning the few pages, and with each one her heart sank further.

"Two years ago." Her shoulders sagged. "I know it's only been about a week, but I'd hoped that soon we'd..." Her voice threatened to break and she fought the urge to fall apart all over again. No, that just wouldn't do. She had to be strong. For Elizabeth.

"We'll find her." His voice sounded so certain. Wrapping strong arms around her, he drew her backward until she was lying on the bed with him once more, her head cradled against his shoulder. "It might take some time, but we'll find her," he promised and kissed her hair. Why did it feel so damned right to be lying here in this tiny cabin, with a man she'd vowed to avoid for the rest of her life holding her? "Somewhere nearby we've got an ally... or at least a person who wants us to know that Elizabeth's alive."

"But who?" Shelby asked, "and why not just flat out tell me—us—where she is?"

"Good question." He frowned, and she knew intuitively that he was thinking the same thing she was—that this entire scenario might be a heinous joke—that someone, an unknown enemy, might have sent the letter to her, might even now be cackling in delight about their false hopes and agony, knowing all along that they would never find their daughter. The photograph of Elizabeth could be a simple hoax—a snapshot of another girl with Shelby's face photoshopped onto it. It was done all the time.

But she couldn't think that way! Not until she was certain that Elizabeth didn't exist.

The phone jangled loudly, startling her out of her thoughts. Nevada rolled over and grabbed the receiver. "Smith," he answered and then Shelby felt his body tense, saw his expression turn as dark as midnight. "When?" he demanded. "How?" He listened a few more minutes and then said, "I'll be here." Slamming the receiver down, he turned to Shelby. "That was Shep Marson. He's on his way over."

"Why?" she asked, and a chill as cold as death slithered down her spine.

"Caleb Swaggert died this evening." Nevada swung his legs over the side of the bed and snagged his shirt from the crumpled covers.

She didn't move. "That was sudden."

"Yep. That's the problem." He yanked his shirt over his head and plowed stiff fingers through his hair. "It seems that someone couldn't wait a few weeks for the grim reaper to do the job."

"No—"

"That's right, Shelby," he said grimly. "The police suspect that Caleb Swaggert was murdered."

# CHAPTER 12

"Murdered? But...I mean, he was in the hospital and dying and... isn't that leaping to conclusions?" Shelby asked, but the phone call was like a dash of cold water. And here she was lying, barely dressed, in Nevada's bed. And she'd made love to him. Even though she'd promised herself she wouldn't.

"I don't know." Nevada reached for his jeans, yanked them on and buttoned the fly. "But it must be important for Shep to be dropping by."

Shelby didn't like the idea. She was related to Shep distantly, through a cousin, and she'd always considered him coarse, too rough around the edges.

"Let's see what he has to say." She adjusted her dress, caught her reflection in the mirror and finger-combed her wild hair. It didn't help, so she grabbed a brush from the top of the bureau and dragged it through the tangled strands.

"You could leave if you want."

"Why?" she asked him, her gaze meeting his in the mirror. "I don't see any reason to run."

"It could get sticky." His expression was grim. She set the brush down.

"For who? You?" she demanded.

"Everyone."

"I'm not afraid of a little goo." Turning, she pointed the brush at his chest. "Is there something you're hiding from me, Nevada?" she asked, then motioned toward the bed. "Because if there is, you picked a helluva time to tell me."

"I just don't want you to get caught in something you're not ready for."

"And you're talking in circles. If you don't remember, Smith, we just made love, right there." She jabbed the brush in the air over the bed. "And aside from that, we're both searching for our daughter. We've agreed that it's more than coincidence that Ross McCallum is granted his freedom the week that I find out my—*our*—child is alive, not forty-eight hours after I get back to Bad Luck, so I say I want to be a part of this. Somehow McCallum's release, Ramón Estevan's murder and me getting that picture of Elizabeth are connected. Now the man whose testimony was recanted, the man who was the catalyst for freeing McCallum, is dead—possibly murdered. Do I want to be a part of this?" She folded her arms over her chest, the back of the brush tapping against her ribs in agitation. "What do you think?"

His smile was as bright as a dying twenty-five-watt lightbulb. "Fair enough, Shelby. You're in."

"Thank you," she said without a trace of sincerity. She dropped the brush onto the bureau, straightened her dress and hoped he couldn't tell that a part of her—the cowardly part she'd always fought and tamped down—was suggesting she run like hell. She'd never liked Shep Marson, didn't want to deal with him now, but she had to do this if she intended to find Elizabeth, and above all else, Shelby was determined to locate her child.

Within ten minutes, headlights flashed through the trees and Crockett began barking, only to be cut off with a sharp word from Nevada as he and Shelby emerged from the house.

Shep hauled his body out of his pickup, and Shelby let out her breath, relieved that he hadn't arrived in his cruiser. He wasn't even in uniform, but as he reached the weak illumination thrown by a single bulb on the porch, she noticed his expression was set, his eyes deep in the sockets of his fleshy face. A mustache covered his upper lip, and as his eyes met Shelby's, the muscles near the corners of his mouth pulled tight.

" 'Evenin'," he drawled, tipping his head, a wad of chaw bulging in his cheek. "Shelby, I heard you were back in town. What's it been now? 'Bout six, maybe seven days?" His eyes dragged over her and her wrinkled dress. Nevada hadn't bothered tucking in his shirt and his feet were bare, but if Shep noticed, he had the decency not to comment.

"Not quite a week," she hedged, her nerves on edge. She'd never trusted Shep and wasn't going to start tonight on this dusty porch.

"You're staying with your pa, the way I heard it."

"That's right."

"What's this about Caleb?" Nevada cut in. He was standing next to Shelby, his arm nearly touching hers, but not quite. He was tense, like a boxer ready to deflect the first blow.

"Found dead by an orderly. Half an hour before, he'd been drinkin' juice and braggin' to one of the nurses that he was gonna leave this earth a rich man. Then all of a sudden, he's gone. Looks like someone might have helped him get to those Pearly Gates he's been findin' so fascinatin' lately."

"But he was already dying," Nevada pointed out. "Why would anyone bother?"

"Good question. One I'm workin' on. Caleb, he had a lot more enemies than friends."

"Why do you think he just didn't die?" Shelby asked.

"The doctors, they're the ones who were surprised it hit so suddenlike. They thought he'd have a few more weeks. But we'll see. The ME will take a look. We'll see what the examination comes up with. Maybe this is all fer nothin'. Maybe Caleb did just give up the ghost, but until we know that fer sure, we're checking his IV for any traces of somethin' that shouldn'ta been there, doin' an autopsy, checkin' the hospital records and security cameras to see who'd come to see him this afternoon. But you know how it is up ta Coopersville, security at the hospital is kinda lax." He hitched his pants up a bit, then spat a stream of tobacco juice out of the side of his mouth and over the rail of the porch at a dried bush.

"What's the motive?" Nevada asked.

"Who knows? Maybe someone didn't like the fact that ol' Caleb was talkin' too much." Shep pinned Nevada with humorless eyes.

"Someone pr'bly didn't like it much that he was singin' like a birdie to that reporter woman."

"Who?" Nevada asked.

"Well, that's what I was hopin' you might tell me. McCallum, he's already free; if it weren't for ol' Caleb recantin' his story, Ross would still be doin' time, so it don't seem he would be likely to kill our boy. Caleb didn't have any family aside from that daughter of his, and we already checked. Celeste hasn't left El Paso for over a month." He bent down and scratched Crockett behind an ear before straightening again. "So we've been checkin' all the people who've visited Caleb in the last week or two. Your name came up." His gaze was uncompromising as he stared at Nevada.

"I saw him at the hospital."

"Why?"

"Just wondered why he changed his story," Nevada said, every muscle in his body taut. "Turns out it was all for a buck. So he could die and leave his daughter with a sizable inheritance." He glared at Shep. "Is your stopping by an official visit?"

"Hell, no. Just two ol' boys who used to work together talkin', that's all," Shep said, lies slipping past his teeth as easily as a cottonmouth gliding through a swamp. Shelby didn't believe him for a moment. "I'm just wonderin' who would want to do the old boy in."

"I'm still bettin' on McCallum."

"But then, you're kind of a one-note song now, ain't cha?" Shep spat again, then curled his lower lip down thoughtfully. "As I just said, the way I see it, Ross should be kissin' the ground Caleb walked on. Without Swaggert's newfound piety, he would never have cleansed his soul and set the record straight. Ross would still be up ta the big house."

"But Caleb's testimony sent him there in the first place."

"With more than a little nudge from you." Shep's eyes gleamed, two pinpricks of light that seemed almost evil in his big face. "Now if you remember anything else that might help out, you give me a call." He tipped his head toward Shelby. "Always a pleasure, Shelby. Give the Judge my best." With that, he swaggered off the porch.

He climbed into his pickup and fired the engine. The smells of dust and exhaust mingled in the air as Shep drove off, putting the old truck through its gears. From nearby a horse neighed, then quieted.

"He thinks you killed Caleb," Shelby said as the night grew still.

"Why would I do that?"

"I don't know, but Shep seems convinced."

"He's grasping at straws." Nevada turned toward the house. "Come on in, I'll buy you a drink."

"I think I'd better go," she said, shaking her head. This night had already been too emotional, and she needed to put some distance between Nevada and herself, needed some time to clear her head.

"You could stay."

His words seemed to hang on the air, suspended by invisible cords. "I—I don't think so." Oh, God, it was tempting. To lie in Nevada's strong arms, make love to him again, wake up sated in the morning and watch sunlight play upon his face and bare skin at dawn. Her throat turned to sand.

"I don't bite."

"Sure you do," she teased, arching an eyebrow. "I remember."

"You're wicked, darlin'."

"Am I?"

So swiftly that she couldn't step back, he grabbed her with those damnably strong arms and pulled her hard against him. "Decidedly so." His fingers dug into the muscles of her forearms, and his lips crashed down on hers. Hard. Hot. Promising passion. She closed her eyes, and for a moment her bones melted. "Decidedly so," he repeated, lifting his head, his eyes as dark as the night.

"I—I'll take a rain check."

One side of his mouth lifted into that crooked, cocky grin she remembered from her youth. "I'll hold you to it." And then he released her. She nearly stumbled backward, but somehow grabbed her things and made it to her car. She drove by rote, seeing his profile in her rearview mirror, his feet wide apart, his shirttails flapping in a small breath of wind, his profile all male.

For the love of God, what was she getting herself into? She was losing her sense of purpose, letting herself fall in love with him all over—no! Her fingers suddenly gripped the wheel so hard they ached. She wasn't falling in love with him. That was a ludicrous notion. She had gotten caught up in the moment, that was all. Emotion had overrun common sense, and she'd ended up in bed with him. What they had done had hardly constituted love. So he'd brought her to orgasm. So he'd held her. So he'd told her everything would be all right. So what? It wasn't the first time those things had happened in this universe.

*No, but it's the first time they have happened to you!*

She set her jaw and reminded herself that it couldn't occur again. She couldn't be derailed. Her purpose was simple—to find her kid.

Come hell or high water.

She drove toward Bad Luck and noticed headlights in her rearview mirror, twin beams that, no matter if she stepped on the accelerator or eased onto the brake, stayed the same safe distance behind.

"You're imagining things," she told herself and tried to remember when she'd first noticed that she was being followed. Was it just after she'd turned onto the road from Nevada's lane, or had it been later, a rig that had been waiting at one of the forks in the road? "It's nothing," she said out loud but kept her eyes glued to the mirror.

She slowed to the speed limit as she approached Bad Luck, expecting the car behind to catch up to her. Instead, before the streetlights could illuminate the make or model, it turned off, probably headed to the driver's intended destination.

"Stop it," Shelby growled at herself. She wasn't usually so edgy, didn't take much stock in any kind of cloak-and-dagger stuff.

She was just too wound up because of being with Nevada and Caleb's death and her fruitless search for Elizabeth. She needed another course of action, another avenue to explore. Inside the city limits, she surveyed the dusty little town where she'd grown up—a town filled with secrets and lies, a tightly knit community of friends and enemies. She drove past the pharmacy and the feed store, then took a right to cruise past Estevan's Market, still open, Spanish music wafting into the street. Vianca strolled out the door, lit a cigarette and cocked one knee, leaning like a stork against the plate-glass windows. She drew on her cigarette, flicked her ash and watched sullenly as Shelby drove by.

All in all, the Estevans' store had changed little in the ten years since Ramón Estevan was killed, and Shelby tried to imagine what had happened ten years ago.

From what she understood, Ramón had been working alone that night, waiting for his son, Roberto, to relieve him. Vianca had worked earlier in the evening, then gone home to see to her mother, but had returned just before Roberto was due to arrive. She had spoken with her father; then, before Roberto drove up, Ramón had walked into the back storeroom to smoke a cigarette and wasn't seen again until nearly three hours later. His body had been found in the Dumpster behind Walt Sawyer's mechanic's shop in an alley a quarter of a mile away. A .38-caliber bullet was lodged deep in Ramón's brain. The murder weapon had never been recovered.

According to the Judge, who had told Shelby what had happened, dozens of suspects and witnesses had been questioned about the murder. Ramón, though successful and very visibly Hispanic, wasn't popular with everyone. Rumored to be so tight he squeaked, he made as many enemies as friends and was said to have had a nasty temper. Few people dared cross Ramón. Some of the Anglos in town thought him "uppity" and didn't like the fact that he and his family worked all hours and prospered when many of them, less industrious than the Estevans, had languished. Ramón Estevan's success had caused more than one case of envy.

Ross McCallum had been vocal in his dislike of the "snotty-nosed Mexican." Badger Collins had broken out one of the store's windows years before, and Nell Hart, a waitress in the local diner, had been run out of town for seeing Ramón on the sly. She'd left not only because Ramón had been married at the time, but also because he was Hispanic and her family, staunch white Protestants, had been humiliated on several levels.

Prejudice oftentimes seemed to seep into the water system in Bad Luck. Even Shelby's father, the Judge, a man who was supposed to mete out justice fairly to each citizen regardless of race, color or creed, had disapproved of Nell's behavior. It seemed beyond ridiculous now. Probably had then, too.

It had been years ago, of course, when Shelby was a young girl, before her mother had died. Attitudes had softened somewhat since then. But, even now, just beneath the surface of civility, simmering under a facade of political correctness, old grudges and intolerance still existed in this small town. Bigotry didn't die overnight.

At the next stop, she turned right and wheeled past the hardware store and an electrician's office only to ease off the gas pedal as she reached a quaint, two-storied structure on Liberty Street. As old as Bad Luck itself, the building housed her father's suite of offices. She pulled into the vacant parking lot, letting the Cadillac's engine idle near the back door, and wondered what secrets the ancient structure held. Suspecting she wouldn't be so lucky as to gain entrance, she cut the engine and climbed out of her car anyway then checked both the front and back door. Each was locked firmly, and there were small stickers in the windows warning anyone foolish enough to break in that the building was protected by a security company. Shelby would have to wait.

But she wasn't ready to give up. Not yet. She drove to the Estevans' Market as it was the only store open, walked inside and paid for a cup of self-serve coffee. Vianca was behind the cash register.

"Anything else?" she asked without much inflection. Red lips pulled tight over her teeth, and if looks could kill, Shelby would already be coffin-bound. Vianca handed Shelby a paper coffee cup.

"This'll do.... No, wait." It had been hours since she'd eaten, and Shelby had been so keyed up she hadn't noticed that she was hungry, but now her stomach rumbled and she couldn't resist the candy display. She grabbed a bag of peanut M&Ms. "Add these in."

"*Sí.*" Vianca rang up the items, her perfectly manicured nails moving swiftly over the keys while her expressive eyes avoided Shelby's. "One eighty-nine," she said.

Shelby handed her a five-dollar bill, waited for her change and walked to the counter where three chrome coffeepots marked with differing blends sat. She poured decaf into her cup and split open a packet of powdered creamer. The door opened again, but Shelby, stirring her coffee, barely noticed.

She lifted the cup to her lips, tasted the hot brew and wondered how she was going to get into her father's office. She could try to break in, or steal his keys, or pay him a visit and then hide in the restroom or—

"You're Shelby Cole!"

Shelby jumped at the sound of the woman's voice. Hot coffee slopped over the rim of her cup, burning her fingers as she looked up and stared into the eyes of a petite woman she didn't recognize.

"Katrina Nedelesky," the woman said, extending her hand.

"The reporter."

"Right. *Lone Star* magazine." She took Shelby's palm in small, strong fingers and gave it a quick, perfunctory shake. "I'd like to talk to you."

Shelby glanced up to the curved security mirrors mounted near the ceiling. In the distorted reflection she saw Vianca watching from the cash register. "About what?"

"Everything. You've probably heard that I was doing an exclusive with Caleb Swaggert, but he died this evening."

Shelby stared into the woman's blue eyes. Though she'd never seen her before, there was something about Katrina that was familiar, and a long-buried memory threatened to surface, but, like her own image in the security mirror, it was misshapen and just out of reach. "I don't know how I could help," Shelby said, feeling the weight of Vianca's gaze upon her back.

As if Katrina finally got the message that this wasn't the place to discuss the Estevan murder, she said, "I'll call you. You're living with your father, aren't you?"

"Temporarily."

"How long will that be?"

"I'm not really sure." She took another sip of coffee and felt beads of sweat gather on her scalp.

"Then I'll give you a call."

The door banged open and Roberto, Vianca's brother, stormed in. He was rattling off Spanish so quickly that Shelby couldn't understand more than a few words, but his face was red, his hands shaking as he shoved them through his hair, and the one word that kept cropping up was *madre*. Though Shelby couldn't make out much of the conversation, the names McCallum and Swaggert were hard to misinterpret. At one point Roberto said something about a *cabrón*, but Vianca cut him off and sent a harsh glance Shelby's way.

Roberto didn't take the hint and railed on in Spanish, the names Swaggert, Smith and McCallum punctuated by curses. Vianca's face drained of color. She began speaking wildly, slung the strap of a beaded leather bag over her shoulder and flew out the front door. Roberto was still muttering in short bursts of angry Spanish.

Katrina watched the drama with elevated eyebrows. "I wonder what all that was about," she said, following Vianca's hasty exit with her interested gaze.

Through the smudged glass, Shelby saw Vianca slide into the interior of her old El Camino and tear out of the parking lot. "I couldn't hazard a guess."

"I bet I could. Isn't her mother kind of... well, to put it kindly, a little off?" she whispered, risking a look in Roberto's direction.

"As in off her rocker?" Boy, this woman bothered Shelby.

"Exactly."

"I've never met her."

"Well, I've been talking to quite a few people here in Bad Luck. The word is that Aloise—that's her name, right? The mother's name?"

"I think so."

"That she's a few cards short of a full deck."

"As I said, I don't know the Estevans," Shelby replied, and again Katrina focused those hard blue eyes on her. "So, how about tomorrow?" Katrina asked. "I could meet you in the early afternoon."

"I really don't think there's anything I can tell you."

Katrina smiled. "You might be surprised," she said with a mirthless gleam in her eye—as if she was hinting that she knew something Shelby didn't, something important. "See you then."

"Call first."

"Oh, I will." Katrina turned and walked to the counter while Shelby tried to shake the feeling that the reporter was just plain bad news.

The Estevan house was in an uproar. An ambulance, lights strobing the night, was parked haphazardly on the street, a police car idling nearby, one officer on the radio, the other, presumably, in the house.

A child was crying and voices shouted as Shep pulled up and climbed out of his truck. He'd been off duty for a couple of hours and had lingered in the Last Stand sipping suds and listening to Lucy flirt with some of the regulars while country music crept through the bar and Shep kept coming up with excuses not to go home to his sorry-assed house and pregnant, cranky wife. Peggy Sue was really putting the screws to him these days, insisting he get a vasectomy and nagging him about officially running for sheriff. On top of all that, she had a hundred and one reasons why she wouldn't let him touch her, wouldn't even let him cop a quick feel. "Not until you git yourself fixed," she'd insisted through clenched teeth, "and while you're at it, take Skip in with you. He's drivin' me nuts, barkin' and tryin' to run away cuz the Fentons' springer is in heat agin."

No amount of talking had dissuaded her. She was pregnant, it was Shep's fault and all men—including male dogs, it seemed—needed to be neutered. Well, no one was gonna make a soprano outta Shepherd Belmont Marson. Not yet.

As he started up the steps, pushing his way through a small crowd of neighbors who had gathered on the lawn, Vianca flew out of the house and down the steps. Packing little Ramón on one hip, tears streaming from her beautiful eyes, she tried to quiet the screaming toddler while she herself looked about to collapse.

"What's goin' on here?" Shep asked. On his way home, he'd heard that an ambulance had been dispatched to this address, one he'd known by heart. He'd pulled a quick U-turn and hadn't thought twice about his own family.

*"Madre, oh, poor, poor Madre. She is . . ."* Vianca broke down altogether as two paramedics rushed from the house. They carried a gurney with Aloise Estevan strapped to it. Her face was the color of paste, her bony fingers clutching a rosary, her lips moving in silent prayer. Vianca chased after the paramedics, and Shep's heart nearly broke for the poor girl. Still clutching her nephew, holding his little body close to hers, she tried to grab her mother's hand as the paramedics shoved the gurney into the back of the ambulance and the onlookers whispered among themselves. *"Madre . . . oh, Dios, Madre . . ."*

Quickly but efficiently the paramedics climbed into the back of the ambulance with the stretcher. As they tended to Aloise, the doors were slammed shut, the driver hurried to step into the emergency vehicle and, within seconds, it took off. Colored lights flashed and the siren screamed through the dusty streets as the ambulance raced away.

"I'll drive you," Shep said to Vianca and placed a comforting arm around her slim shoulders. Good God, she felt good—such smooth skin. "Can someone take care of the boy?"

"No—"

"I'll see to him," an elderly woman in a bathrobe and slippers offered. "I live three doors down and—"

"No!" Vianca spat. Her expression turned as hard as concrete. "Ramón stays with me."

"But it might be a while," Shep said.

"Roberto will come for his son." She was emphatic. "He will close the store and come to the hospital."

"But..."

"We are family. Maybe you do not understand."

Little Ramón was still clinging to his aunt. His head was buried in the crook of her neck, and his chubby arms held on tight.

"Fair enough," Shep said, realizing she wasn't going to budge. He turned to the crowd and lifted his hands to get their attention. "You can all go home now. Everything's all right." He didn't wait for the throng to disburse, just guided Vianca toward his truck and helped her inside. She strapped herself into the passenger side of his bench seat, did the same for her nephew in the middle, and Shep experienced a pang of guilt. He should go home to his own family. Peggy Sue was sure to be tired after chasin' Donny and Candice around all day. She was always grumpy and worn out when she was pregnant and now, carrying their fifth, she had to deal with the older kids, Timmy and Robby, who were fast becoming holy terrors. Timmy was already in trouble; Shep had caught him smoking dope with his friends once or twice already, though Shep had shoved the kids up against the side of the garage and hadn't let on to Peggy Sue. Then there was Robby, always hanging out with those damned Dauber kids. In Shep's opinion, Robby had never been quite right, not from the day the kid was born. He just seemed about two beers shy of a six-pack. Or maybe three. Not that he'd ever admit it to a soul. Candice was a cutie, but Shep had caught her pushing her little brother around, and Donny was a sniveling, sickly whiner—no backbone in that kid. And now there was another one on the way. Shit. Shep couldn't think about his kids right now. Didn't want to.

The smell of Vianca's perfume filled the cab, and he slid a glance her way, saw a tear glide down the slope of her cheek and wished to hell he could kiss it away.

"So what happened?" he asked as he threw his truck into gear and edged around a couple of straggling neighbors still strolling back to their homes.

*"Madre,* she ... she swallowed too many pills."

"Pills?"

*"Sí.* For sleeping."

"On purpose?" he asked as he took the back streets out of town. His internal radar was instantly on alert. "Cop radar," he called it. To Shep's way of thinking, it looked like someone had helped Caleb Swaggert on his way to see his maker and now Aloise Estevan had OD'd? How was that for a coincidence? Too much of one.

"No, oh, no." Vianca was shaking her head to his question about her mother's medication. Her eyebrows drew together and her pretty red lips pursed. "She ... she gets confused. Sometimes, if I am not there, she forgets that she has already taken a dose and then she takes more. This time ..." Her voice trailed off and he let his suspicions fall away. There was just nothing nefarious about the old lady's overdose. It was just an accident, made by a confused elderly woman, if he was to believe Vianca, which, he told himself, he did.

Vianca made a quick sign of the cross over her breasts and sighed loudly as she looked out the window to the passing night-darkened landscape.

Shep tried not to stare at the woman next to him, attempted not to smell her sensual perfume. It just wouldn't do. Nor would the hard-on he felt deep in his britches. Nuh-uh. He'd turn his thoughts elsewhere, he told himself. Putting Vianca and her sexy, hot body out of his mind was the right thing to do. Nonetheless he couldn't help wondering, as the big truck headed through town toward Coopersville, what Vianca was wearing beneath her black T-shirt and tight jeans.

Maybe not a damned stitch.

Oh, man, he was really hard now.

Or maybe she was wearing that red bra again. She seemed pretty perky, so it might be that the scarlet lace was holding up her glorious boobs.

Or, she could have thrown on a black one. Oh, man! He imagined her breasts spilling out of a scrap of ebony lace where her nipples peeked through.

Hell, his old cock was really straining now, uncomfortably so. To cool off he turned his thoughts to his kids and stared through the bug-spattered windshield to the oncoming headlights, drove twenty miles over the speed limit and reminded himself that he was married.

Like it or not, Peggy Sue, once the best damned baton twirler in all of Blanco County, was his wife.

# CHAPTER 13

"I think we need to talk," Shelby said, flying down the front stairs. Her father was at the door, sliding his arms through the sleeves of his suit jacket and she was still in her pajamas, her hair wild from a fitful night's sleep.

He chuckled without so much as the trace of a smile. "Since when do you have anything to say to me?"

The muscles at the base of her neck tensed. "Since I don't have any other options."

"Can it wait?" He checked his watch and scowled. "I've got to stop by the office, then the ranch before a breakfast meeting in Coopersville with some investors."

"I think you know where Elizabeth is."

He adjusted his jacket and reached for his ivory-handled cane propped in the umbrella stand near the front door. "We've been over this before."

"I know, but I think you're lying. She's alive, and you know where she is."

"Let it drop, Shelby."

"I can't!" She grabbed his sleeve, her fingers digging into the lightweight fabric. "Don't you see, Dad? This is important. The most important thing in my life. I have to find Elizabeth and I'll do anything—*any*thing—to find her. That's why I'm begging you to help me." She was desperate, at the end of her rope. Her father was the only link she had to her child. "Please..." Her throat caught. "Please, Dad."

He sighed. "There's nothing I can do, Shelby." His old shoulders slumped and he seemed tired, suddenly ancient. "Let it rest. You're young. You'll marry a nice young man and you'll have more children. I told you I had some men I wanted you to meet. There's a lawyer up in San Antonio. Thirty-two. Never been married. Good-lookin' and smart as a whip. If you ask me he'll get into politics and—"

"No!" Her fingers recoiled from his sleeve and she took a step backward, her rump touching the newel post at the end of the staircase. "You don't get it, do you?" She stared at him as if he were a stranger. "You don't know what it's like to know you have a child somewhere and not be able to locate her."

"I know what it's like to have a child you love so much you want only what's best for her."

"Even if she disagrees?"

"Even if she despises me for it." He picked up his briefcase and opened the door. "When Lydia gets in, tell her I won't be back in time for dinner. I don't know what time I'll get home, but it'll probably be late." As he walked out the door, Shelby knew he'd never help her. She was on her own if she wanted to locate her daughter.

*Not entirely alone. You've got Nevada. He's on your side.*

Or was he? Could she really trust him?

A headache nagged at the back of her brain. Too little sleep and too many worries had kept her up most of the night. Why had she flirted with Nevada? What had possessed her to kiss him? And, oh, Lord, why had she made love to him? What they'd shared before was long over; they both knew it, and yet she hadn't been able to stop herself.

She walked into the kitchen and poured a glass of orange juice. Yes, he seemed to be trying to help her locate their daughter, but what then? What if they did find her? Hadn't he suggested that it would be better to leave Elizabeth with her adoptive parents?

The juice soured in her stomach. She hadn't really thought that far ahead. First she'd find her daughter and then she'd figure out what she was going to do.

The phone jangled loudly. She scooped up the receiver. "Hello?"

"Oh, *niña,*" Lydia's voice was muffled. "I thought I would catch your father."

"He already took off. Early meeting. Said he might not make it for dinner."

"He works too hard. Pushes himself. If he is not careful..." Her voice faded again and then she cleared her throat. "I called because I will be in late this morning. Aloise is in the hospital."

"Aloise Estevan?" Shelby asked, surprised. She'd thought it would take an act of God to keep Lydia from her chores. Even then, the Almighty might have a fight on His hands.

"*Sí. Sí.*"

"Is she all right?"

"I do not know. She took the pills. Too many."

"What pills?"

"Again, I do not know, but when Vianca called, I said I would look after little Ramón for a few hours so that Vianca and Roberto could be with their mother and talk to the doctors this morning..."

"Of course." Shelby took another swig of juice.

"But if you need me at the house I will bring the boy along..."

"Oh, no... everything's fine here," Shelby said and twisted the phone cord to look outside at the pool. The surface was like glass, reflecting the blue of the early morning sky. "Take your time." She hung up, polished off the rest of the O.J., then, as she was completely alone in the house, hurried outside, stripped off her pajamas and dived into the pool.

The water hit her in an icy blast.

She kicked upward, hit the surface, took a breath and began swimming, stroking to the far end of the pool. As she cut through the water she concentrated, not on her swimming, but on her life and how it had changed. Somewhere she had a daughter. But where? Nearby? Or far away? Or was this all a hoax? Oh, God, who would be so cruel and why?

She reached the edge of the pool, somersaulted under the water and began swimming the length again. Faster and faster, knifing through the bracing water. Her mind, no longer fuzzy with sleep, was suddenly acutely clear. A picture of Elizabeth, the only photograph she'd ever seen, floated through her mind, and as she reached the end of the pool that image changed to that of Nevada and she remembered how easily she'd made love to him last night. It had seemed so natural, so right... oh, she couldn't think about their lovemaking; not now. She had more important issues.

*Think, Shelby, think. You're a smart woman. How are you going to find your child? There's a way. You just have to find it.*

Again she reached the edge of the pool. She flipped onto her back and began an easy backstroke, staring up at the sky. *Dollars to donuts, the Judge knows where your daughter is.*

> *Old Judge Cole*
> *Was a nasty old soul*
> *And a nasty old soul was he.*
> *He called for his—*

The phone rang and Shelby missed a stroke. Maybe someone had news about Elizabeth!

She cut to the side of the pool, hoisted her naked body out of the water and ran, dripping, into the kitchen. Snagging the receiver, she said, "Hello?"

There was a loud *click* on the other end.

"Hello?" she said again, but knew whoever had called had hung up. "Hello?" She felt a moment's anxiety—there had been too many calls when no one answered—but then chalked it up to a misdial, though the person on the other end could have had the decency to apologize. "Jerk," she muttered under her breath, then dashed up the back stairs to her room. Within fifteen minutes she'd showered, changed into shorts and a sleeveless T-shirt, slapped on a little lipstick and mascara and was down the stairs again. In the kitchen, she mopped up her wet footprints with a towel and then, realizing that she might not be alone again in the house for a long while, started the coffeepot and headed straight to her father's home office. Today she'd go through every one of his files. If there was anything to be learned about the whereabouts of her daughter in the Judge's office, Shelby would find it.

\* \* \*

"Jerk!" the word ran through his mind as he wiped the pre-paid cell phone free of fingerprints, then drove to a winding road leading into the hills outside of town. Dust plumed behind his truck and that was a bit of a worry, but it was a chance he had to take. Hopefully no one would see him. Out here, there were no damned security cameras, no tourists, no damned eyes following him. At least he hoped not. He checked the sky and saw no small planes fly over his head.

Good.

All he wanted to see out this way was a rabbit or a coyote. Nothing human.

He forced himself to be as careful as possible, to rein in his temper so he could still accomplish what he had to. But it was tough; his temper had been known to get the better of him, time and time again.

Beneath the baking sun, the truck ground along, sliding a bit over a spot where the thin gravel had given out altogether during the last gully washer. Still, the tires held and he shifted down to the topmost rise. As he reached his destination, an old bridge spanning the deepest gulch in this part of the county, he swiped the sweat from his eyes. Heat shimmered in waves ahead of him and the engine idled hot and fast.

Using all his strength, he flung the pre-paid cell through the open window. The phone caught in the sunlight, like the flash of a trout snagging a hook, twisting as it hurled to the canyon floor to hide somewhere in the scrub brush and, he hoped, never be found. He'd learned somewhere that a pre-paid cell phone was untraceable, but wanted to make certain, so after calling Shelby Cole from a rest stop on the other end of town, he'd driven here, seven miles north, to ditch the phone, far away from the cell tower that had caught his last signal.

Just in case.

He'd loved hearing Shelby's voice on the phone and the fact that it was getting a little more irritated was all the better. He knew, deep in his gut, that she was getting scared and that was perfect. Made his day.

As did punching in Nevada Smith's number and hearing the

pent-up anger in that bastard's voice. Man, oh man, he just loved yanking Smith's chain.

Yeah, he'd have to find him a new phone...maybe one that could be traced to someone special.... Wouldn't that just be a hoot?

As he turned the pickup around and he remembered Shelby's voice, it whispered through his mind, tantalizing and cruel. Just the way it should be. "We'll see who's a jerk," he muttered under his breath as he nosed his rig toward Bad Luck and hit the gas.

So much to do. So little time.

"Idiot!" Nevada mentally kicked himself up one side and down the other. What had he been thinking? Making love to Shelby Cole! "Fool! You get what you damn well deserve." He tossed a forkful of hay into the manger and watched as the broodmares buried their noses in the feed. What was it about Shelby that he couldn't resist? Years ago he'd convinced himself that he'd been fascinated with her because she'd been Judge Cole's only daughter, forbidden fruit, the great taboo.

But now?

"Son of a bitch," he grumbled, whistling to Crockett and sauntering outside to the sweltering Texas afternoon. God, it was hot. Waves of heat shimmered in the distance, and horseflies buzzed near his head. Dust clogged the air, and yet he loved it here. Once a Texan, always a Texan, he'd heard more than once. Well, in his case, it seemed true. Though for the life of him he couldn't understand why. All morning long he'd been bothered with thoughts of Shelby, kissing her, touching her, the feel of her skin glistening with sweat as it pressed hard against his. He couldn't resist making love to her last night, and damn it, he doubted he ever would again.

Swiping his brow with one work glove, he walked to the machine shed, where the heat seemed to settle. Wasps droned in their nests in the rafters, and the smell of oil competed with the ever-present odor of dry dust. Outside a horse nickered softly. Nevada kneeled near the flatbed trailer and scowled at the bald tire that had gone flat in the past few weeks. He jacked the trailer up then found his wrench and began working on the lug nuts. All the while his thoughts ran in circles about Shelby and their daughter. Or Ross McCallum's daughter.

His stomach turned sour. Bile rose in his throat, and his right hand clenched the wrench so hard that his knuckles showed white through his skin. McCallum should never have gotten out of prison. Never.

Nevada spun one lug nut off and caught it in his left hand. He settled the wrench over the next one. Something was going on in Bad Luck. McCallum was out of jail. Shelby was back in town searching for a daughter she'd thought died at birth. Caleb Swaggert was dead—maybe murdered—and now Aloise Estevan was in the hospital, having nearly killed herself taking an overdose of pills—or so he'd been told at the hardware store this morning. Somehow these events had to be connected. In a town the size of Bad Luck, where nothing much ever happened, it was far too much of a stretch to believe that these incidents were unrelated.

He yanked off the tire and hauled it out to his pickup, then tossed it into the bed.

Who had sent Shelby the picture of the child? *Who?* The thought tormented him as he walked to the house. If he could locate that person, then everything else would fall into place. He was sure of it.

Inside the kitchen, he washed his hands, then walked into the bedroom and found his wallet and keys on the bureau. Glancing at the bed, now made, he felt his damned groin tighten. In his mind's eye he saw Shelby, naked, lying beneath him, her skin white, her eyes as clear as a Texas sky, her hair fanned around her head, the night filled with promise. His jeans were suddenly too tight as he remembered making love to her, and he noticed the scent of her perfume lingering in the air.

He couldn't shake the feeling that she was in some kind of danger, that she'd been lured here with the photo of her daughter as bait. But why? The back of his neck prickled as his thoughts skated to Ross McCallum. Was he behind all this? An ex-con who'd raped her, a man who should still be locked away.

Nevada changed his shirt and slapped his wallet into the back pocket of his jeans. Scooping up his keys, he made his way outside and told himself he was going into town to get the flat repaired. But he had other reasons as well. Reasons that surrounded Shelby Cole, the Judge's princess of a daughter—the mother of his child.

The single-wide trailer was a pigsty. Ross crushed his cigarette in an old Jiffy Pop pan and felt the afternoon heat begin to bake the interior.

He'd been living in this old tin can ever since he'd gotten out of the big house. At first he'd tried to fix the place up since his no-good sister, Mary Beth, refused to help him out anymore. Probably because she was out lookin' for another no-good to make her next husband.

So Ross had cleaned the inside as best he could, but the trailer wasn't a whole helluva lot better than his prison cell. Long-neglected paneling was falling off the walls, the carpet was worn bare and all the faucets were rusty. Cobwebs, dust and dead insects had collected on the windows, and the countertops had faded and cracked. The furniture was worn, broken and just plain shot. He'd managed to get the electricity turned on, but the plumbing was giving him fits and it was hotter than Hades during the day. Night wasn't much better, and as glad as he was to have gotten out of prison, he needed to improve his lot in life.

And he had just the ticket.

Caleb Swaggert was dead and now there wasn't anyone to give that reporter-gal the inside scoop on what happened the night ol' Ramón Estevan had been killed. What better story than straight from the horse's mouth, from the man who'd been set up and sent away for the murder?

Yep, he'd have to contact the reporter and work himself a deal. And then there were some other old debts that needed to be repaid. He had yet to square off with Nevada, but that day was comin' and fast. Like a fuckin' freight train.

He hadn't paid a call on Shelby Cole yet, but the time just hadn't been right. He would, though, and soon.

Ross smiled to himself and walked outside to the two weathered steps that constituted the front porch. Some of the garbage had been strewn around the place last night, and Ross thought it was about time he got himself a gun to take care of the coyotes or whatever the hell it was that was marauding around here after dusk. Aside from that, it would feel good to have a rifle in his hands again. A man wasn't really a man without a gun. He surveyed the dry landscape. A few scraggly trees, dry grass and hard land. How the devil had his grandfather ranched here and supported himself, his wife and five kids?

He'd have to find himself a rifle, and soon. Maybe he'd get himself a dog as well—a pit bull or rottweiler would be just the ticket. He needed protection. A lot of strange things were going on in Bad Luck these days. He rubbed the back of his neck, felt the sting of a bee and slapped the hornet hard. Buzzing angrily, it dropped to the rickety step. Ross was quick, grinding the varmint beneath the toe of his boot and feeling a spurt of satisfaction race through his blood.

Yep, he thought, his neck smarting, a lot of strange things were happening in Bad Luck, Texas, and unless he missed his guess, there were gonna be a few more.

Shelby slid the last file into its slot in her father's credenza and silently berated herself. She had read through each one, slipping a few folders at a time up to her room, then studying them and finding nothing that would help her. Whatever secrets the Judge was keeping, they were still safe, unable to be uncovered by any of the papers he'd locked in his den, nor able to be located by cross-referencing names and dates on the Internet.

Lydia had come to the house sometime after noon, and other than offering to make Shelby some lunch and explaining that Aloise had taken too many sleeping pills, the housekeeper had kept to herself. Her eyes had been red, her usually sunny expression decidedly missing, and Shelby had thought she'd heard Lydia sobbing softly.

All in all, it had been a fruitless and disturbing morning.

It was nearly two thirty by the time Shelby locked the credenza and pocketed the small ring of keys that her father kept in the dish near his humidor. Surely one of the keys would open the door to his office downtown, and maybe there she would find more information, anything, that would help her find Elizabeth. She'd take the keys to Coopersville this afternoon, find an out-of-the-way locksmith who wouldn't recognize her, then return the original set to the den. After that, the Judge's office would be at her fingertips. Hoping no hint of guilt showed on her face, she walked from the den to the kitchen. The keys jangled softly deep in her pocket.

Lydia was crying again, dabbing at her eyes with the corner of her apron and muttering softly in Spanish to herself as she carried a plastic container filled with cleaning supplies toward the dining room.

"Lydia, is something wrong?" Shelby asked as she poured herself a cup of coffee.

"What? Oh, *niña*. No." Lydia cleared her throat and disappeared through the archway. Shelby followed.

"You've been crying. Look, I'm not trying to pry, but I'm not blind or deaf. Something's bothering you, Lydia. Something big."

The housekeeper offered a frail smile as she set her bucket on the floor. Last week's birds of paradise arrangement was beginning to wilt on the table, though the crystal, rarely used, sparkled behind the glass doors of the buffet. "I am just upset to hear of Aloise. She is... well, a friend, and a relative."

This was news. "You're related to the Estevans?"

"*Sí*—well, not to Ramón's family." Lydia's mouth puckered as if she'd just tasted something sour. "That one, he was a... *tirano*." She made a quick sign of the cross over her ample bosom.

"A tyrant?"

"*Sí*. Worse. He was *always* the boss. Everything had to go his way. If not, then he would... *reventar*, like a volcano, yelling and screaming with anger." She threw her hands over her head, either showing how the man vented or appealing to God. "Ramón, he was not a nice man. But..." She cocked her head and sunlight streaming through the dining room windows caught in the silver strands of her hair. "... He was Aloise's husband and she is cousin to Pablo, my brother-in-law."

"Pablo—the gardener?" Shelby asked, leaning against the archway and sipping her coffee. How had she missed this bit of information? Why hadn't she paid attention?

*"Sí."* Lydia removed the vase with the dying flowers, which suddenly seemed morbid. Her father's canonization of a woman to whom he was not always faithful wasn't so much about love, Shelby decided, as about guilt.

"Aloise and me, we grew up together in the same village in Mexico, not too far from Mazatlan—you have heard of this resort? It is by the ocean."

"Yes."

"Later, all the families moved. Closer to the border," Lydia explained. "But that was very long ago, when we were both girls."

"And from there you both moved to Bad Luck?"

Setting the vase on a counter of the china cabinet, Lydia nodded, but the corners of her mouth tightened perceptibly. *"Sí.* Our families moved here." She turned back to the table and began spraying lemon oil on the dark surface, working as if she intended to rub the polish right through the dark wood.

"And Pablo is Maria's father." Why hadn't she known this when she was growing up?

Again Lydia nodded, but this time her shoulders stiffened slightly and she avoided Shelby's eyes. "She is his only daughter, but he has three boys as well. Enrique, Juan and Diego."

"Lydia, what's going on here? The other day you were upset because Maria was having trouble with her daughter. Today you're crying because Aloise Estevan nearly killed herself, and I didn't even know you were related." Before she could answer, Shelby added, "Then there was that conversation I overheard between you and the Judge. The one about the secrets that I should know about."

Lydia picked up a bottle of Pledge and avoided Shelby's gaze. "I told you to speak to your father."

"I've tried. Over and over." Shelby set her cup on the counter near the vase. "He won't tell me diddly-squat."

"He will. In time."

"I don't have a whole lot of that."

"None of us do," the housekeeper admitted, blinking rapidly.

Shelby felt as if she was finally getting through to the woman who had practically raised her, and she wasn't going to let up.

Touching her gently on the shoulder, Shelby said, "Look, Lydia, whatever it is that Dad's hiding, you've got to let me know about it. The secrets in this house are getting to all of us."

"Oh, *niña,*" Lydia whispered, her dark, tormented eyes filling with tears, "please, please, for my sake, do not pursue this. I can tell you nothing."

"You mean you won't."

"It is no different." Lydia attacked the job of polishing the mahogany table as if her life depended upon it. Sweat beaded her brow, and the flesh beneath the cuff of her short sleeve wiggled as she worked.

"The Judge won't tell me anything." Shelby was so frustrated, she wanted to shake the housekeeper, but as she saw the pain in Lydia's dark eyes—no, it was more than pain, more like fear—and the lines of sadness near her mouth, she said only, "If you know anything about Elizabeth, please, tell me. You're a mother. You know how important it is for a mother to be with her child—"

"*Sí,* but I cannot."

"For the love of God, Lydia, she's my daughter! My only daughter. Please—"

The doorbell pealed. Soft, dulcet tones that were as intrusive as if they'd been the report of a shotgun's blast.

"Excuse me," Lydia said and dropped her dusting rag, wiping her hands on her apron and, in a rustle of nylon panty hose, hurried to the foyer.

"This discussion isn't over," Shelby insisted, trailing after her like a tracking dog on the scent of an escaping felon.

As the housekeeper opened the door, Shelby's heart sank. There, standing in the middle of the front porch, just as she'd promised she would be, stood Katrina Nedelesky. Her grin was neatly pinned in place and she was just removing her sunglasses.

When she turned her blue eyes upon Lydia, the housekeeper gasped and her face drained of all color. "*Espiritu Santo!*" Lydia crossed herself yet again.

Shelby asked, "What's wrong?" but wondered if she really wanted to know. She felt the tension in the air, saw the fear in Lydia's eyes. "You two know each other?"

"No." Lydia drew in a deep, shaky breath and touched her fingers to her hair. "No."

Katrina's eyes narrowed a fraction and her smile seemed all the more fake. "I'm Katrina Nedelesky," she said, extending her hand. "And, no, we've not met before."

"This is Lydia Vasquez," Shelby introduced. "I thought you were going to call before you showed up."

"Oh, yeah." Katrina grimaced. "Sorry about that. Guess I forgot."

Shelby wasn't buying it for a minute. She'd bet Katrina didn't forget much.

Lydia mumbled a quick "pleased to meet you," took the woman's hand, then dropped it as if it actually had burned her skin.

Katrina turned that incredible smile toward Shelby. "You know, since I landed here in this part of Texas, just about everyone I meet tells me I remind them of someone."

"Is that so?" Shelby asked. "Who?"

"No," Lydia said. "This is foolishness."

But Katrina just turned those incredibly blue eyes on Shelby. "Can't you guess?"

A cold sensation started at the base of Shelby's skull and dripped down her spine. She knew in an instant that she wasn't going to like what Katrina had to say.

"Don't you know what it is?" Katrina rolled her eyes and then sighed theatrically. "Well, I hate all this high melodrama, so let's just get this over with. I'm your sister, Shelby. Well, half sister really. The Judge is my father, too."

# CHAPTER 14

"I think you'd better come in and explain all this," Shelby said, unable to keep the suspicion from her voice. Shell-shocked, she stared at the woman standing on the front porch, searching for any sign of resemblance between Katrina Nedelesky and the Judge. Okay, so they both had startling blue eyes, but so did millions of other people. Katrina was a redhead, as was the Judge, but who knew if her short tresses were a natural shade or dyed. One thing was for certain, Shelby didn't trust her. Not one iota.

"I take after my mother," Katrina said as if reading Shelby's thoughts.

"Convenient."

"True." She flashed that irritating, smug smile that was already getting on Shelby's nerves.

"Why haven't I heard of you?"

"Because I was Judge Cole's deep, dark secret."

Shelby was only vaguely aware of Lydia, but the housekeeper was still at the door, staring at Nedelesky as if she were a ghost, confirming the truth far better than the slight, confident woman standing in the shade of the porch's overhang.

"Then what took you so long to show up?"

"Timing, Shelby. Timing."

"And now's the right time."

"Bingo."

Well, it wouldn't hurt anything to hear Katrina's story, though Shelby had her own agenda. Through her pocket, she felt her father's key ring press against her thigh. She needed to drive to Coopersville, get duplicates of the keys made and replace the originals before she was found out. "Come on in," she invited, pushing the door open wide and attempting to hide her skepticism.

Though she'd always known her father attracted women, and he certainly hadn't been celibate in the past twenty-odd years, she'd believed that he'd been careful, discreet, and would have taken precautions not to father any children out of wedlock, if only to protect his reputation as well as his pocketbook. Katrina's claims could well be just a scam, a publicity ruse, and she was older than twenty-one or twenty-two. Ace reporter though she might allege to be, Katrina Nedelesky was an opportunist clear and simple. And in that respect, Shelby grudgingly thought, she was very much like Judge Jerome Cole. "We can talk in the living room."

"Lead the way."

As Katrina entered, Lydia, ashen-faced, her forced smile tremulous, muttered something about getting refreshments, then gratefully retreated toward the back of the house.

"Nice place," Katrina remarked, hiking the strap of her briefcase onto her shoulder. With the confidence of someone who knew that she belonged, she took in the gleaming marble floors, the sweeping staircase and the pieces of art mounted on the walls. Finally, her gaze inched across a rosewood table covered with pictures of Shelby and her father.

"Yes, very nice," she commented, touching a silver frame as her eyes met Shelby's in the mirror. A fleeting kaleidoscope of emotions—envy, anger and despair—showed in those blue depths before being quickly masked.

*She wishes she was me.* The thought struck Shelby hard, like a fist to her stomach. Was it possible? Could she really be spouting the truth? Was Katrina her half sister?

"This way," Shelby said, peeling off toward the living room and leaving the image of two women with varying shades of red hair and blue eyes behind her. She opened the French doors and walked into the living room, where bowed windows overlooked a rose garden and furniture in muted earth tones was strategically placed around a marble-faced fireplace, another rarely used shrine to Jasmine Cole.

Once Katrina was inside the room, Shelby closed the doors behind her and leaned against the glass panes to look the younger woman square in the eye. "Let's get one thing straight, right up front," she said. "Everything we discuss is off the record. If you dare print a word of it without a signed, written release from me, I'll sue you and that rag you write for from here until tomorrow."

Katrina wasn't bullied. "Look, Shelby, all the magazine is interested in is Ramón Estevan's death, Caleb Swaggert's testimony, why he recanted it and who could possibly have killed him—Ramón, I mean. If it turns out that Caleb was murdered, then they'll want information on that as well."

"I can't help you there. I don't know anything about the Estevan murder."

Katrina eyed a white piano tucked into an alcove. "That's not why I'm here."

"Well, then, that brings up an interesting point." Shelby crossed to the dun-colored love seat and sat on an overstuffed arm. "What do you want?"

Frowning slightly Katrina stared through the window to the rosebushes with their heavy-headed blooms. "Okay, the deal is this—I'm not just a freelance reporter." Katrina admitted, turning away from the view and dropping onto an antique settee. "I'm working on a book."

Shelby's heart dropped. She should've seen this coming. "About?"

"The Estevan mystery, of course. That's at the center, but it's also a story about Bad Luck and all the town's secrets." Katrina's eyes brightened.

"Including this...claim you have that you're my father's daughter?"

"Yes."

"Maybe you'd better explain that." Shelby wanted to believe this woman was a con artist, nothing more, someone who was trying to set her father up, but the fact that her own stomach was knotting, her mind spinning ahead with a million questions, convinced her that there was more to Katrina than met the eye. "So why is it you think the Judge is your father?"

From the corner of her eye, Shelby spied a gleam of silver through the windows. Her father's Mercedes was rolling up the drive, its shiny finish catching shafts of sunlight that had pierced the lacy branches of the trees. "Wait. I think you'll get a chance to tell the Judge himself." Apprehension swept through her. "Looks like he's had a change of plans and has come home." The keys in her pocket seemed to burn through the fabric and scorch her leg. Should she try to replace them in the den before her father found them missing?

Katrina's smile didn't even falter. "Good. This will only make things easier."

Shelby doubted it. Since landing in Bad Luck, things hadn't gotten easier for Shelby. Instead they'd become more complicated, much more complicated. "I'll tell Lydia to send him in here," she said, standing and heading out of the room, just as she heard the housekeeper's footsteps in the foyer.

Carrying a silver tray that held crystal glasses and matching pitchers of lemonade and iced tea, Lydia had nearly reached the French doors when she, too, caught a glimpse of the Judge's Mercedes slowing to a stop in front of the garage.

"*Dios,*" she whispered, shaken. The tray wobbled.

Shelby was through the doors in an instant.

Glasses and silver platter shifted.

Shelby was quick, grabbing an edge of the tray, but it was too late. Tea and lemonade slopped over the sides of the pitcher. The glasses toppled, crashing to the floor. Ice cubes slid across the marble. Lemon wedges flew. Iced tea splashed over Shelby's face and blouse as she held onto the tray.

The front door opened. Judge Red Cole, leaning heavily on his cane, stepped into the foyer. "What the devil's the matter with you two?" he asked, his face flushed, sweat trickling down from his hairline.

"Oh, Judge, I am sorry." Lydia gulped as she tried to pick up the rapidly melting ice cubes. "So sorry. I—we did not expect you home so early."

"My meeting in San Antonio got postponed."

"I will get a mop."

"What's going on here?" Red Cole demanded.

"There's someone here I think you should meet," Shelby said as she handed the tray to Lydia's unsteady hands, then wiped at the liquid running down her face.

"Who in tarnation—?" His gaze moved from Shelby to the French doors, and from the corner of her eye Shelby spied Katrina standing on the other side of the paned glass.

"For the love of God," her father whispered, his jaw suddenly slack, his shoulders slumping beneath his suit jacket.

Shelby knew then that Katrina's claims were true. The reporter from Dallas was her half sister. Her throat was instantly as dry as cotton, her mind spinning with nearly twenty-five years of lies. "I think we need to talk, Dad," she forced out. "Straight talk this time."

The Judge stared at the younger woman in the living room. "You're right, Shelby-girl," he admitted softly, his expression bordering on tragic, his gaze never leaving Katrina. "We do need to talk. And I guess it had better be now."

*So Caleb Swaggert was murdered*, Shep thought as he squinted through the bug-splattered windshield of his Dodge pickup.

Someone had wanted the old man dead—someone who hadn't been patient enough to let his deteriorating health take its course. *Who?*

With the question still nagging at him, Shep drove into the driveway of his house and noticed that the satellite dish mounted on the roof was listing again. He should adjust it, as well as tack down a few new asphalt shingles while he was up there. Well, the roof, paint, satellite dish and all the other domestic chores that Peggy Sue had listed and tacked to the refrigerator with a magnet would have to wait. He just didn't have time for that right now—not when he had another murder on his hands. The D.A. was gonna want an answer and so would the sheriff. Pronto. This was the time for Shep to make a name for himself.

Caleb Swaggert's doctors were certain the old man had been helped into a grave, and the autopsy that had been ordered was nothing more than a formality. Bruises on Swaggert's scrawny neck indicated that someone had held him down, probably after putting a pillow on his face. Evidence of petechial hemorrhaging in the geezer's eyes seemed to confirm that Caleb had suffocated. But who the hell would want him dead? Who would risk facing a murder rap just so that Caleb went to his grave a week or two before he was scheduled to be knocking at the Pearly Gates?

He stopped his truck in front of the garage, climbed out and felt the heat of late afternoon press against his chest. Sweat ran down his back and under his arms. It seemed to him that as the years and pounds piled on, the summers in Texas just got hotter and more uncomfortable. Peggy Sue's minivan was parked inside the garage, so she and the kids were home. Why the fact that his family was waiting for him depressed him, he didn't understand, but it did put him in a foul mood.

The laundry hanging from the clothesline didn't help, nor the fact that most of the tomato plants had wilted in the garden. Nothing about this place that he'd called home for nearly twenty years was the least bit endearing to him. In fact, this dusty house that desperately needed paint seemed more of a trap than a sanctuary these days. The phrase that a man's home was his castle had never rung so false.

Extracting his tin of Copenhagen from his back pocket, he thought of Vianca Estevan, as he had on and off all day. Shit, she was more woman than Peggy Sue ever thought of being. And he'd lay odds ten to one that she was a hellcat in bed.

He pinched a chaw, stuffed it behind his lower lip and stopped to scratch Skip's ears as the dog pulled at his chain and tried to jump on Shep's uniform. "Down, boy, there ya go," Shep said, feeling a jab of guilt that the retriever had to be tethered and checking to see that Skip had water in his dish. It didn't seem right to tie him up just because he wanted to do something as natural as dig under the fence and service the neighbor's bitch. What was the harm? It was only what the dog was made to do.

Boy, howdy, did he know it. The hour or so he'd been with Vianca in the hospital had made him hornier than a bull in a field of heifers in season. In the hospital last night, Vianca had turned to him, cried on his shoulder, and he'd felt her trembling lip against his shirt, noticed her firm breasts pressed against his abdomen, and smelled the perfume in her hair. It had been all he could do not to wrap his arms around her, kiss her and promise her that everything would be all right. But he hadn't; he'd remained stoic and outwardly detached, all the while hoping his damned hard-on wasn't visible to the rest of the worried loved ones hanging around the waiting room.

As for old Aloise, she'd been whisked off to the psychiatric unit and there had been talk, because of her age, that she would have to be transferred down to Austin, where there was a geriatric psychiatric unit. Vianca had refused. When the doctor had suggested that Aloise might be better off in a nursing home, Vianca had nearly spat on the man.

"Not *Madre,*" she'd said, shaking her head and explaining that she wanted to take her mother home as soon as possible. Roberto had finally shown up, and Shep had made good on an excuse to leave. Vianca had turned those big brown eyes of hers toward him and said a sweet *"Gracias,* deputy. For this I owe you." He'd corrected her, insisted she call him Shep and walked down the corridor of the hospital and out the door, certain that his feet never once touched the floor.

"Shep!"

His daydream was interrupted and he straightened at the sound of Peggy Sue's shrill voice. He felt the muscles at the base of his skull knot while he gave his dog a final pat and vowed to have him neutered the next week. "You'll be fine," he assured the dog.

Turning, Shep discovered his wife standing at the back door, her eyes narrowed on him. "Did you stop at the store and pick up the hamburger and onions like I told ya?"

*Shit.* "I plumb fergot," he admitted and watched her mouth draw into an *I-figured-as-much* frown. Little lines framed her mouth and appeared between finely plucked eyebrows. "But I'll run down to the market and grab some now."

"Well, you just do that, would ya, 'cause I can't very well watch the kids, cook, and be at the market at the same time." She looked tired and beaten down. Lined and discouraged. As sick of her lot in life as he was with his.

"I'll be back in a jiff." He was surprised at how anxious he was to leave. There had been a time when all he wanted to do was get home, turn on the news, read the paper in his La-Z-Boy with the dog at his side, then wrestle with the kids while he heard her rattling around in the kitchen, cooking for the family while humming in that sweet voice of hers. On his way to the truck he wondered how long it had been since he'd heard her sing anything. A year? Two? Ten?

Hell, he couldn't remember the last time.

He climbed into the cab as Donny and Candice raced out of the house, dust rising beneath their sneakers as they ran to the truck.

"I come, too!" Donny cried.

"No, me!" Candice pushed her younger brother out of the way, and Shep felt a surge of pride that his little girl showed some pluck while his whiney-assed son started crying and sniveling. God, that kid was a pain. The older boys hadn't been such wimps.

Shep reached over and opened the passenger door. Both kids tumbled inside. "Be good," he growled, but they didn't pay him any notice and he had to remind them to buckle up. They sniped all the way to Estevan's Market and Shep, handing Donny his hankie for Donny's perennial runny nose, promised them each an ice cream if they'd stay in the cab while he grabbed the groceries. He was hoping for a glimpse of Vianca, of course, but she was nowhere in sight.

An Hispanic boy of about twenty with pockmarked skin and downcast eyes, a kid Shep only vaguely recognized, was manning the till and Shep suspected the kid was probably an illegal. Not that he cared. The boy seemed nervous as he eyed Shep's uniform and handed him back change from his twenty without saying a word.

"Vianca here?" Shep asked as he grabbed the paper sack.

The boy shook his head.

"Nope? Know when she'll be back?"

Again the mute shake of short black hair. This time he also shrugged.

"She still at the hospital?"

The boy stopped. Nodded. "*Sí.* Hospital," he said, showing off a gap between his front teeth.

"What's your name?"

The kid froze. "Enrique."

That was it. Shep remembered now. Enrique was one of the Ramirez kids. Related to the Estevans somehow.

"Thanks, Enrique." Shep knew it was foolish, but he felt a wave of disappointment that he hadn't been able to see Vianca. She'd been an obsession with him these past few days, and he couldn't resist trying to catch a glimpse of her at any opportunity.

Maybe it was the heat. Or his age. Or just plain restlessness. He couldn't figure it; he'd never thought he'd want to cheat on Peggy Sue, but damn it, a man had needs.

He returned to his sun-baked truck and cranky kids, then handed each child an ice-cream sandwich and warned them not to spill any in his truck. He told them it was their duty to eat every bit of their treats before they got home. "Don't tell Mom that you had ice cream before dinner, or that you waited in the truck," he warned as he backed out of the lot and pulled into the street. "And you'd better eat your dinner tonight or she'll be suspicious. You know your mom. Sometimes, I swear, that woman's got eyes in the back of her head."

"I eat it all," Donny promised solemnly, and Candice threw him a look that silently called him a kiss-ass.

Shep jammed the Dodge into first, tried to avoid a pothole and nosed the truck down the street.

He drove past the Last Stand and noticed Ross McCallum, as big as life, swagger out of the bar and stand in the shade of the awning out front. The hairs on Shep's forearms prickled.

"Son of a bitch," he said under his breath.

"Mommy doesn't like it when you swear." Candice licked her lips, flicking away a piece of chocolate with her little tongue.

"Don't tell her." Shep had no time for his daughter's precociousness. Not now.

"But—"

"I said, keep yer mouth shut, Candy, and eat yer damned ice cream."

"Yeah!" Donny chimed in and Shep wanted to cuff the kid. He didn't. Instead he drove slowly and kept one eye in the rearview mirror as Ross lit a cigarette and sauntered over to a rattletrap of a pickup that had seen far better years. "He's up to no good," he muttered under his breath again, "no damned good."

"You did it again!" Candice cocked her little head at a superior angle, mimicking Peggy Sue's holier-than-thou attitude.

Shep didn't respond, just watched as Ross eased his truck into traffic and headed north, out of town. If it weren't for the fact that he had the kids with him and that the hamburger was probably already cooking itself in the hot cab, Shep would've followed the bastard. He doubted he'd gotten a license yet.

Shep turned the corner and eased off the gas at the traffic light where the temperamental air-conditioning finally kicked in. Why was McCallum back? Why didn't he move on, relocate in a town where his reputation wasn't known—where people didn't know him capable of hellish crimes? What was it that dragged him back to Bad Luck?

Tapping a finger nervously on the steering wheel, Shep started through the intersection when he noticed Nevada Smith's rig driving past the bank, heading toward the center of town. Nevada was at the wheel, his dog on the passenger side, head out the window, tongue hanging out. Nevada's rifle was mounted on the rack behind his head, mirrored aviator glasses covered his eyes and his jaw was hard and set as if he was expecting a fight.

Yep, Nevada Smith looked like a man with a purpose, and as if by instinct, he turned onto the street that ran in front of the Last Stand, following Ross's lead northward.

Again, Shep paid more attention to his rearview mirror than he did to the oncoming traffic, and he told himself that it was just coincidence—that in a town the size of Bad Luck, spotting a couple of enemies within a few minutes of each other wasn't that big a deal.

But he wouldn't forget it either.

McCallum and Smith had always been dangerous together.

Shep stewed about seeing Smith tailing McCallum all the way

home. He barely noticed that the kids were fighting as he swiped at their faces with his handkerchief. Avoiding anything close to a washing, they scrambled out of the hot truck, dashed across the backyard and up the steps. Once out of the Dodge, Shep stuffed the hankie into a back pocket, and brought the dog inside with him. Skip slunk to his bed in a corner of the living room.

The house was stuffy. Fans only blew hot air around.

" 'Bout time," Peggy Sue said as he entered the kitchen. The skillet was already set on a burner, tomatoes and lettuce chopped on a cutting board, corn tortillas dripping oil on a rack, ready to be filled. "And next time don't give the kids any ice cream," she added without missing a beat. "You know it ruins their dinner."

How she knew he'd bought the kids a treat, he didn't bother to guess. Peggy Sue had a sixth sense when it came to that kind of thing. "I'll keep that in mind," he said dryly, and she shot him a look that said she didn't take kindly to his sarcasm.

He handed her the small sack of groceries and she started in, breaking the meat into small chunks and firing up the stove. As the hamburger sizzled, she minced the onions, then tossed the pieces into the skillet.

Shep reached for a beer in the refrigerator and wondered why all those years ago he'd been so hot for Peggy Sue. She'd been different then, before the kids. Demanded less of him. He popped the tab of his Coors and headed for the living room, where Timmy and Robby were playing a video game. Half-grown, they either spent their time acting like little kids, fighting over the controls of the game, or looking at copies of *Playboy* or *Penthouse* they'd hidden on the top shelf of their closets under old boxes of baseball cards. These days they didn't seem to know if they were eight years old or eighteen.

"We're watchin' the news now," he announced, frowning at Timmy, who was lounging in Shep's worn recliner.

"After I kill this guy—"

"Now! Turn that danged thing off."

The phone jangled loudly and Peggy Sue shouted, "Get that, would you? Someone's been callin' and hangin' up all afternoon."

The boys ignored her and Shep grabbed the receiver. "Marson," he said.

There was a moment's hesitation. Robby let out a whoop. Some video bad guy had just bit the dust.

"Anyone there?" he asked again.

A muffled voice said, "The gun that killed Ramón Estevan is at the rock quarry at the old Adams place. In the cave."

Shep's blood ran cold. "What?" he asked. His pulse jumped. "Who is this?"

*Click!*

"Hello?"

The line was dead.

"Hello? Damn it!" He stared at the receiver a minute, then hung up. His hands were sweating and his heart was pounding like a damned tom-tom. He strode through the house, stopping at the pantry for his favorite flashlight with the big head. "I'm goin' out," he said as Peggy Sue lifted the skillet from the stove and began to drain off the grease.

"But it's nearly dinnertime." Her eyes narrowed, and she set the pan aside as he flicked on the flashlight, making sure it didn't need batteries. "Who was on the phone and whatcha plannin' to do with that?"

"I got me an anonymous tip."

"About what?" She was suddenly really interested.

"I'm not sure yet," he said, not wanting to let on to anyone, not even Peggy Sue. Not until he checked it out. "Might be nothin'."

"But you don't think so."

"I just don't know," he called over his shoulder as he strode outside. The screen door slammed shut behind him and he couldn't help but wonder why the tipster had disguised his voice. It had been whispered and rough and yet, he thought he might recognize it. Had there been the hint of a Spanish accent in the caller's message? He'd thought so, but the kids and television had been so damned noisy, he'd barely heard the words. Was the person on the other end of the line afraid for his life? Or was there another reason to hide his identity?

Whatever the reason, he was going to check out the tip. Adrenaline raced through his bloodstream at the thought of what this might mean for him. For his family. He had a few hours before sunlight faded, and he planned to make good use of them. He'd get himself a metal detector and find the damned gun himself.

*If it's really there, son. This could be a cheap trick, you know. A prank.*

"Tough." Shep would see it through. Obtaining a search warrant wouldn't be much of a problem, even if he did it after the fact. He knew enough judges in Blanco County who trusted him and would turn a blind eye, even fudge a little. Once everything was on the up-and-up, he'd take the evidence to the lab.

*If you find the damned weapon. You're getting the cart before the horse.*

Still, this was going to be his collar. His alone! Hell, yes!

Shep Marson stepped quicker than he had in years. He was either on a wild-goose chase or he was about to solve a ten-year-old crime and claim his fifteen minutes of well-deserved fame!

Maybe he would run for sheriff after all.

*Sheriff Shepherd Belmont Marson.*

It had a nice ring to it. A damned nice ring.

The call had been made from, and would be traced to, the only phone booth in town. But no new prints would be found, the caller thought. Gloves had been worn, street cameras avoided, anonymity guaranteed. Shep Marson would take the information, find the gun and run with it.

By the end of the day, Nevada Smith would be behind bars and spend the first night of the rest of his miserable life in prison.

Mission accomplished.

That thought alone should have brought satisfaction, even pleasure, to the caller.

It didn't.

The caller had done what was necessary. That was all.

But there would be no savoring of revenge as had been expected. No, instead of the sweet taste of satisfaction, there was only the bitter tang of regret that lingered long after the phone call from the old phone booth had been disconnected.

* * *

"That's right," the Judge was saying as he stood leaning on his cane in front of the cold fireplace. "Katrina is my daughter."

Shelby felt as if all the underpinnings of her life had been pulled, one by one, out from beneath her. As if by the sheer force of gravity, she sank into a chair covered in apricot-colored velveteen. "But why didn't you tell me?"

"I meant to," he said, but she wasn't sure she believed him. "But time slipped away. At first you were too young. Then there never seemed to be the right moment, and later I was afraid that it might turn you against me, disrupt your life—" He lifted a hand. "All excuses, I know."

"And what about me?" Katrina demanded. She'd reseated herself on the settee, but the starch had drained from her spine and instead of coming on like gangbusters, she seemed smaller and more vulnerable when facing the Judge. She cleared her throat. "Were you just going to let me go on thinking that my father was some kind of drifter, a cowboy who had blown through town, gotten my mother pregnant and taken off on her?"

"I thought it would be best."

"For whom?" Katrina whispered.

"All of us."

"So I spent the first sixteen years of my life not knowing the truth."

"Which is what?" Shelby asked. "Who's your mother?"

Raising her eyebrows, Katrina glared at the Judge, silently encouraging him to tell the truth.

"Sweet Jesus." He drew in a long breath, then braced his shoulders. "I got involved with a woman, a waitress named Nell Hart," he admitted.

*He kept a file on Nell Hart.* Shelby had read it. She saw a movement through the French doors and realized Lydia was mopping the floor, edging closer.

"I thought—I mean, I heard she was involved with Ramón Estevan and that's why she left town."

"I didn't even know you knew of her."

"It's a small town, Judge."

"Anyway, this was when you were very young." Guilt riddled his expression, and for the first time Shelby understood him.

"When Mom was still alive?" she whispered, a dull roar thundering in her head.

"Yes. While I was still on the bench."

Shelby blinked hard, turned disbelieving eyes to Katrina perched on the edge of Jasmine Cole's settee. A cold understanding dawned, chilling her soul. "Are you telling me that... what? Mom found out and..." She swallowed, her head ringing with denial.

"Your mother was upset," he said, nodding slowly and sniffing as if he were about to cry. "She, um, wanted a divorce and I refused. Told her it would ruin everything. So she demanded that I pay Nell off, stop seeing her and send her packing."

"But Nell was already pregnant," Katrina finished bitterly. "With me. I changed my name to Nedelesky a few years back when I got married and kept it after my divorce."

"Your mother couldn't stand the fact that Nell was pregnant," the Judge continued. "It was one thing that I was unfaithful, another that I'd fathered another child. I should have seen it coming, I guess, forced her into some kind of therapy, or... hell, let her have the damned divorce. Instead she..."

"Killed herself," Shelby supplied, her insides twisting, her stomach threatening to empty when she remembered the rumors that she'd lived with while growing up. "An accident, you said, and Doc Pritchart agreed." Horrified at the depths of his duplicity she shot to her feet and advanced upon her father. "The story I was told was that Mom drank too much at a party, was feeling sick and took the wrong medication by mistake—sleeping pills instead of pain relievers, a whole handful of 'em—but there was always a question about whether it had been intentional or an accident."

"It was a mistake," the Judge insisted as Shelby angled her face up to his. "Your mother didn't commit suicide, not on purpose. She left no note, said no good-byes. She just messed up." His spine stiffened and he drew himself up to his full height, transforming himself before Shelby's eyes from a weak, guilt-riddled old man to the strong, determined, manipulating son of a bitch who had sired her.

"She wasn't the first to make a mistake, now, was she?" Shelby threw out, stunned and feeling bereft. Alone. Motherless. "And why should I believe you anyway? All my life you've lied to me through your teeth." She was vaguely aware of Katrina, knew that she should hold her tongue, but she couldn't stop herself. "Well, it's over, okay? The secrets stop now, and there's one you haven't given up yet."

"This isn't the time," the Judge warned, slanting a glance at Katrina who sat, transfixed, on the other side of a glass-topped coffee table.

"No more excuses. I want to find Elizabeth, Dad. And I'm going to do it even if I have to take out an ad in the *Coopersville Gazette* or even"—she threw an arm out toward Katrina—"the next issue of *Lone Star* magazine."

"Who's Elizabeth?" Katrina asked.

"Elizabeth Jasmine Cole. My daughter. I thought she was dead. I was told she died right after birth, but it turns out that she's alive."

"Holy shit!" Katrina's mouth fell open.

Shelby skirted the coffee table and stared at the younger woman, this intruder who was her half sister—stared her down. "Now listen to me, you're not to print a word of this, not one word, until I tell you it's all right. We had a deal, remember?"

"But—"

"Not until I give the word, or I'll sue you so fast your head will spin!" She turned on her father again. "Think about it, Judge—either you tell me where Elizabeth is, or I unleash the press and none of this family's secrets will ever be safe again!"

With that she was out the door and nearly tripped over Lydia and her mop bucket.

"Oh, excuse me," she said automatically.

"No, no, it was not your fault." Guiltily, Lydia picked up her pail and carried the dirty water and mop quickly out of the foyer. Shelby watched her escape to the kitchen and realized that the housekeeper had been eavesdropping. But why? Idle curiosity? Or did she somehow have a stake in all the secrets as well?

As she stood with one hand on the doorknob, she saw her father watching her from his spot in the living room. What kind of man was he? A lawyer. A judge, for crying out loud, and yet a man who bulldozed his way through life without regard to anyone else's feelings, a man who had abandoned his child and expected her to do the same.

No way in hell!

"I've got to get out of here."

"Where are you going?" Lydia asked from the back of the house. She was still, obviously, listening.

"It doesn't matter! Anywhere away from here." Shelby yanked the door open. Despite her hard words and determination, she felt a sense of unreality and betrayal as she strode across the lawn and grasshoppers flew away from her path. She'd known her father lied to her, bent the law to his own needs, played by his own misguided set of rules, but she'd never expected this—that he would hide his own child, deny his own flesh and blood, inadvertently cause his own wife's demise, all for the sake of saving his already-blackened reputation.

Well, all that was over.

Shelby's head was pounding, her muscles tense, her stomach twitching. She had to get away, to think, to put everything she'd just learned into perspective.

"Just take your time," she told herself as she climbed into her rental car, twisted the ignition and, as the engine fired, opened the sunroof. She could run to Nevada, fall into his arms, unburden her soul and let him hold her all for the sake of hoping that he would tell her everything would be all right and they would find their daughter.

But she didn't.

This was her fight. She wasn't going to play the helpless female victim and throw herself at a man.

Nosing the Cadillac north, toward the ranch and the Cole family cemetery, she gunned the engine. The ranch had once been her sanctuary, then later a place she'd avoided for ten long years. All because of Ross McCallum and how he'd defiled her.

But all that had changed, she decided, sliding a pair of sunglasses onto the bridge of her nose and clamping her fingers more firmly around the Cadillac's hot steering wheel while the sun burned in the hazy sky.

Shelby Cole wasn't going to allow any man—not her father and certainly not that snake McCallum—to ever manipulate or abuse her again. She'd damned well die first.

# CHAPTER 15

Like storm clouds gathering over the eastern hills, the sense that something was wrong kept building in Nevada's mind, causing the muscles in his shoulders and back to tighten. He drove down the lane to the old Adams place, the addition to his current spread, and told himself not to borrow trouble. But the fact that he'd seen Ross McCallum and Shep Marson in Bad Luck within the span of a heartbeat didn't bode well, not well at all.

As the lane forked, he glanced in the direction of the gravel pit that was located on the property, thought he spied a cloud of dust, but again told himself he was overreacting. He was hot, tired, and had been fighting the urge to call Shelby Cole all day.

He guided the truck to a stop by an ancient cottonwood that stood near the barn and whistled to Crockett as he climbed out of the cab. As the sun beat down, he unloaded sacks of grain from the pickup and hauled the bags of oats into the barn while Crockett barked his fool head off at a woodpecker drilling in the copse of live oaks that shaded one of the machine sheds.

Once inside the barn, Nevada stacked the sacks of grain, and, sweating, tried to shake the uneasy feeling that things were going to get a lot worse before they got better, a whole lot worse. He'd never been one to worry too much about the future and took life in stride—except when Shelby Cole was involved. Then he worried like nobody's business.

As the horses wandered into the barn, nickering and snorting, he measured rations of oats, spilled them into the mangers and managed to pet a few sleek coats as the mares began to feed.

Being this close to the animals usually calmed him, but not today, not when so much trouble was brewing. He felt it, almost smelled it in the air, and every muscle in his body was tight, as if readying for a fight.

He patted the bay's shoulders and walked outside, into the heat again. After refilling the water troughs and satisfying himself that the stock had been tended to, he headed along a weed-choked path to the old house with its sagging porch. He unlocked the front door, stepped inside and was greeted with cool, if musty, air. A staircase ran up one wall; a parlor, still papered in a faded rose print that was probably pre–World War II, was little more than an alcove. Down a short hallway was the kitchen—the biggest room in the house and complete with wainscoting, a wood stove and a hand pump at the rusted sink. The bathroom was an add-on, just off the kitchen at the end of the screened-in porch.

Oscar hadn't improved the place, but Nevada thought he just might. Someday he'd gut and remodel the kitchen, add another bathroom upstairs between the two bedrooms and move in. Eventually.

But first things first. On the top of the list was to locate his daughter.

*And what then?* He scowled and opened several windows, letting the hint of a breeze waft through the empty rooms. *What about Elizabeth? What are you going to do about your daughter? And what the hell are you going to do with Shelby?*

In his mind's eye he saw them here, Shelby and their daughter, living with him and the old dog and…He stopped dead in his tracks. What the hell kind of fantasy was that? He and Shelby were from two different worlds, far removed and getting farther by the day. She'd grown up privileged and when things got bad, left town and made a new life for herself. He'd never known his mother, been raised by a drunk of a father, and been hell on wheels in high school. If it hadn't been for a stint in the army, he might never have straightened out.

He and Shelby were worlds apart. Always had been, always would be. They might have a daughter together, but they damned sure didn't have a future. That's just the way it was.

Outside, he rounded up his dog, noticed storm clouds growing thicker, and again sensed an underlying current of tension in the air, like the crackle of electricity unseen. But felt.

He drove home, again fought the urge to call Shelby and cracked open a beer. Stripping off his clothes, he made his way to the bathroom, stepped under the shower's weak spray, and while cool water washed over his tense muscles and splashed on his face, he finished his beer, then twisted off the shower, left his empty bottle on the vanity and walked naked to the bedroom.

He'd just pulled on his jeans when his cell phone rang. As he'd left it on a table in the living room, he walked barefoot through the house while buttoning his fly. Snagging the phone, he saw the caller ID read PRIVATE CALLER.

"Hello?" he said. No response.

The warning hairs on the back of his neck lifted and though he knew he was alone, he looked around the first floor. "Hello?"

Nothing.

"Can you hear me?"

Silence, but the caller was there...listening. Waiting. *For what?* "Who is this?" Nevada asked, peering through the windows and feeling as if someone was watching him, from a distance and yet close enough to do harm. "Why are you calling? What do you want?"

Still no response and yet Nevada could sense him, somewhere out there, waiting and anticipating, enjoying every moment of Nevada's frustration. So Nevada quit railing and just held the phone to his ear, straining to hear anything that could help him ID the caller, though he knew in his gut it had to be McCallum. Who else? The silence stretched across the wireless connection, seconds clicking by. Nevada heard only his own heart beat and then, finally a whispered threat. "Your life is over, Smith," a raspy voice declared, "and hers is, too."

Nevada didn't ask who he was talking about. They both knew the threat had been leveled at Shelby Cole.

"You touch one hair on her head, you jerk-wad, and I swear, I'll personally rip your throat out."

"Try, bastard."

*Click!*

The phone went dead. "Son of a bitch! You goddamned coward!" Frantically, Nevada attempted to call up the number again, to reconnect, to find some way to find out who had been on the other end of the connection, but he failed. No caller ID was listed, no number or name available. He might never know. He'd already been in contact with the cell phone company and they'd been no help with the earlier calls. It didn't take a rocket scientist to realize this connection, too, would prove impossible to pin down. Whoever was calling was smart enough to keep his anonymity. Nevada pocketed his phone and felt that too familiar sense of foreboding creep through his body.

Someone, most likely McCallum, was getting his rocks off with the calls. But why all the taunts and teases? What was up with this sick mind game? McCallum, no Rhodes scholar, had always been in-your-face and physical. The phone taunts were a new wrinkle.

As the warm air dried his skin, Nevada wondered for the dozenth time if Ross McCallum's release had anything to do with the reason Shelby had been lured back to Bad Luck. Was the ex-con behind it? If not him, then who?

*What if it isn't McCallum making the calls? What if there's another player involved, someone who knows where Elizabeth is?*

He walked to the front of the house and stared through the screen door to the coming storm. Dark and malevolent, the roiling clouds threatened.

Just like the caller.

Realizing he might be stepping into an intricately baited trap, he ignored the warning signals and put a call into Shelby's cell. No answer. Great. He didn't bother to leave a message and dialed the Judge's house from memory. On the third ring, Lydia Vasquez answered.

"Cole residence," she said, her accent still thick.

"This is Nevada Smith." No reason to beat around the bush. "I'm looking for Shelby."

"Oh, *Señor* Smith, I am sorry, but Shelby... she is out."

"Where?"

"I...I do not know. She left here an hour ago. Maybe longer. She said she..." Lydia lowered her voice. "She was very upset."

"About what?"

Lydia hesitated. "I do not know."

"Sure you do, Lydia." He wasn't about to be put off.

Lydia cleared her throat, and Nevada wanted to reach through the phone and shake some sense into her. "Where is she?"

She muttered something under her breath, something in Spanish. "I have no idea, really. She said something about just wanting to get away. I...she worries me."

*Me, too,* Nevada thought. *She worries the hell out of me.*

Slamming the receiver into its cradle so hard that Crockett, startled, leapt to his feet, the scruff around his neck standing straight on end as he barked loudly, Nevada swore loudly.

"Hush!" Nevada walked outside and stood on the porch. Some of the mares lifted their heads, noses to the wind, ears flicking anxiously as if they, too, sensed danger.

The bad feeling that had been nagging at Nevada all day got decidedly worse. Light was already fading as the sun was buried behind a thick bank of steel-colored clouds and the smell of a coming storm charged the air.

*Finding the murder weapon here would be just too damned easy,* Shep thought as the beam from his flashlight swept the cavern floor. Why would someone call now, ten years after Ramón Estevan had been sent to his maker? It just didn't make any sense. Who would want to tip Shep off? And why call him at home? Why not the Sheriff's Department? Nope, this just didn't feel right.

He nearly stumbled on an old pile of debris, the remains of a long-dead campfire. Charred stones surrounded a pile of cold ashes. Swearing under his breath, his right hand reaching for his sidearm, Shep moved the beam along the floor of the cave. It was starting to get dark outside and bats, ever restless this time of day, were as noisy as hell as they swooped overhead, streaming out for the night, making Shep's skin crawl. The cave was man-made, dug by Oscar Adams's grandfather, an overzealous prospector who wasn't happy selling stone and gravel and who had hoped to find silver or gold or God-only-knew-what-other precious metal in the hills within the confines of his property. Littered with bat droppings, bleached bones from an old kill, a deer from the looks of it, probably dragged in by coyotes or dogs, the floor of the cave gave up no clue.

*This could all be a wild-goose chase, a prank or hoax.* God knew there were enough people in Bad Luck who would like to see Shep chase around in circles, like a stupid dog trying to catch his own tail.

He threw the beam of light over the rafters, startling more bats before he saw it.

There, on the top of one beam, was a plastic sack. Shep sucked in his breath. Using his handkerchief, he carefully removed the package and sure enough, through the folds of clear plastic, he recognized the shape of a .38. A slow smile crept across his face. He didn't doubt for a minute that this was Nevada Smith's missing pistol, department-issued and probably the weapon that killed Ramón Estevan.

*So who had planted it here? Who would call him now, ten years after the fact? What the hell was this all about?* The gears in Shep's mind cranked, fueled by a dozen questions, but he couldn't stem the thought that he was about to crack the Estevan case.

Did it really matter who had called and tipped him off? The evidence was here.

Setting the gun back where he'd found it, Shep made tracks to his truck and, using his cell phone, called for a search warrant. The judge, Peggy Sue's uncle, didn't ask many questions as he was in the middle of supper. He gave Shep his okay on the spot. Grinning like a damned Cheshire cat, Shep phoned his partner, ordering an investigative team to the old mine. Might as well do this right—by the book. Well, kind of. His partner didn't ask too many questions either and Shep hung up, feeling better than he had since the last time he'd seen Vianca.

Unless he missed this guess, depending on the ballistics tests and fingerprints, he'd soon be able to prove who killed Ramón Estevan.

Her father's ranch was relatively unchanged. The main house had weathered and sported a new roof and shutters, but the low-lying bunkhouse and outbuildings looked as if they'd been frozen in time, still just as she'd remembered them.

Every muscle in Shelby's body was tense as she climbed out of her car. From her father's house, she'd driven to Coopersville, stopped at a locksmith's kiosk and waited as the man with a hand-rolled cigarette clamped between his lips had created a duplicate set of keys for her. She'd paid him in cash, believed that he had no idea who she was and had driven directly here, where now she squinted, using one hand as a visor while surveying the stables, barn and interlocking corrals. Her chest tight, her throat dry, she remembered that night, so long ago when Ross McCallum had raped her.

There was no reason to sugarcoat the vile act, and her stomach convulsed at the memory of his hot, sweating body pinning her against the bench seat of her father's truck. "Bastard," she muttered, walking across the gravel of the parking lot. No dog barked to herald her arrival and only a few vehicles were scattered near the buildings. Shadows were beginning to lengthen over the asphalt and the sky was darkening, clouds blocking the sun, the promise of a storm on the horizon.

Horses and cattle grazed in nearby fields as she walked directly to the stables, found a bridle and saddle, and caught the first horse she found in a paddock just outside the door to the tack room. She'd never seen the sorrel gelding before, didn't bother searching for anyone to get permission to ride him. It didn't matter. Everything on this ranch belonged to her father—acres of land, sun-beaten buildings, miles of fence line, equipment and even, to some extent, the men who worked here. Again her stomach roiled.

It had been years since she'd ridden, but she saddled and bridled the gelding and without thinking twice, took off through the open gates to the fields beyond. She rode trying to clear her mind, biting back the overwhelming feeling of betrayal that had been with her since learning that she had a half sister, a child her father had denied, a secret he'd hidden. How many more were left to uncover?

The gelding galloped eagerly, turning up dust, chasing away pheasants and grasshoppers that flew from his path, racing past grazing longhorns who barely lifted their heads as the horse and rider flew by. From the corner of her eye Shelby spied ranch hands rounding up a small herd of maverick calves. They turned to watch her horse gallop past, then went back to their tasks.

Unerringly, she rode directly to the family plot, the cemetery where generations of her ancestors had been buried. The grounds, surrounded by a wrought-iron fence that was beginning to rust, were untended, some of the gravestones toppled over, others crumbling.

Shelby dismounted, tied the gelding's reins to the fence and opened a gate that creaked as she passed through. Long, dry grass brushed her legs, and burrs clung to her shorts.

In the newer section of the plot she found her mother's grave, one of the few that looked as if someone had cared. No weeds encroached on the headstone that had been engraved long ago with Jasmine Cole's date of birth as well as the date of her death. Inscribed over an etched bouquet of flowers and ribbons were the simple words: *Loving wife and mother.*

"I'm sorry," Shelby whispered, her throat clogging at the thought of the pain her mother had endured. Being married to Jerome Cole would test any woman's spirit; loving him had been a curse.

Shelby had no flowers, no token of remembrance, and she felt a sensation akin to guilt for not returning to this gravesite in so many years, but the truth of the matter was that she hardly remembered her mother. The images of the woman who had borne her that were ingrained in her memory were more likely from snapshots she'd seen, a few family videos she'd watched and memories embellished by stories she'd heard from her father or Lydia.

She listened to the sound of a songbird, hidden and warbling from a clump of mesquite, as she stared dry-eyed at the ground. "I wish I'd known you," she admitted. "Oh, Mom, I think you would have helped." There was no gravestone for her baby. She'd flung ashes—she now didn't know from what—over the hills, thinking her child had died. There had been no stone set into the graveyard because, she'd thought, her father had been so ashamed of his unwed and pregnant daughter. Now, she realized, there was no stone because her baby hadn't died. Thank God. "I will find you, Elizabeth," she vowed, her throat thick. "I will."

Tossing her tangled hair from her face, Shelby stiffened her spine, left the cemetery and noticed the crackle of electricity in the air, the threat of rain.

She untethered her horse, mounted and took off over the hills more determined than ever to find her own child. She rode by instinct, knowing she had one more place to visit before she turned back.

Her heart beat crazily as she passed the old cabin, so dilapidated that she hardly recognized it. Most of the old timbers had fallen, the roof had caved in, and aside from the rock chimney, it was little more than a pile of century-old memories. She kneed the gelding and his legs stretched longer as he loped through the dry grass and weeds. Wind bearing the scent of rain screamed by, pressing hard against Shelby's face as she guided the sorrel along a ridge and down a gully to the creek where she and Nevada had made love.

She swallowed hard at the memory, the feel of his hands and lips on her body, the cool caress of the rain. She'd told him then that she'd loved him and never since had she felt the same about any man.

She'd believed—oh, God, how she'd prayed—that the baby she'd conceived that night belonged to him, that the child was evidence of their love, that she wasn't the daughter of Ross McCallum.

But did it really matter? As Shelby searched for her child, Elizabeth's paternity became less and less of an issue. Reining up, she noticed dark spots of sweat on the gelding's coat. "Good boy," she whispered, patting the game horse's neck. She dropped to the ground and walked along the creek bed, her mind spinning with thoughts of Nevada, her heart pounding with the same love she'd felt ten years earlier.

"Silly woman," she muttered and settled onto a rock to stare at the dry creek bed. A jackrabbit bounded into the woods, and a hawk circled high overhead.

Shelby reached into her pocket, and her fingers scraped against the set of keys she'd had made. She pulled out the new set, gleaming and rough-edged, held together with a bent paper clip. What would she find in her father's office? Her stomach clenched. More damning secrets?

Would she finally be able to locate her daughter?

Or would she discover evidence of other moral and ethical lines that had been crossed? What about Lydia? Why wouldn't the housekeeper confide in her? And why was Ross McCallum a free man now, let out of prison at the same time she was contacted about Elizabeth?

Shelby had been in Bad Luck a little over a week, and she felt as if the entire time she'd been spinning her wheels, chasing after ghosts, no closer to finding her child than she had been when she'd first driven into town. Stuffing the keys in her pocket, she was about to leave when she sensed, rather than saw, someone approach, not from the ranch, but from the other direction, where government land abutted the north end of the property—the direction Nevada had used to gain access years ago.

She stood as she saw him walking swiftly, long, jean-clad legs eating up the ground. Her silly heart lifted at the sight of him and she told herself, yet again, that she was the worst kind of fool—a smart woman who knowingly fell for the wrong kind of man.

"I've been looking for you," Nevada said as he neared. His lips were flat against his teeth, the brackets surrounding his mouth severe, the lower half of his face covered with the dark shadow of his beard. A muscle worked near his temple, and he looked as if he could strangle a grizzly bare-handed.

"On foot?"

"My truck is parked back there a piece." He hitched his chin toward the north, the same direction he'd parked it so long ago.

"You thought I'd be here?"

"No, I thought you'd be at the Judge's house, or somewhere in town tracking down dead-end leads looking for your daughter, or maybe even on a side trip out of town, but I was running out of places, so I gambled and came here."

"The back way."

"Didn't want to take a chance that the Judge might be at the ranch and throw me off." He grabbed her arms in strong, angry hands and pulled her close. "When I called the house, Lydia said you'd left upset, that you had to get away, and so I remembered that you used to either swim or ride whenever you wanted to work out a problem. You weren't at the house, so I thought you might have come to the ranch to ride." His gaze drilled deep into hers. "And if you rode the hills, I figured you might come here." He lifted a shoulder. "It was just a lucky guess." Some of the tension seemed to drain from him and he rested his forehead against hers. "Damn it, Shelby, I was *hoping* I'd find you here."

"Were you?" Her bad mood faded as she stared into his eyes, both gray, one pupil slightly larger than the other. "Any particular reason?" She couldn't help baiting him.

"Don't jerk my chain."

"Wouldn't dream of it," she said sarcastically.

"Like hell." His fingers tightened again, dug deep into her forearms as the Texas heat seemed to rise from the dry ground. "You'd take any chance you could."

"Geez, Nevada, don't you ever get tired of hauling that massive ego of yours around with you?"

"You're doing it again," he warned.

"Sorry." She lifted an eyebrow and tried not to respond to the warmth of his body, the flame of desire in his eyes. "I just can't help myself."

"Me neither," he admitted, and his lips crashed down on hers so swiftly that she couldn't draw a breath. The stubble of his beard brushed her skin, and as his tongue pressed hard against her lips, his arms surrounded her and she opened herself to him, just as she always had, just as she always would. Nevada Smith was in her blood. Now and forever. It was her blessing as well as her curse.

Closing her eyes, she kissed him with the same wild abandon she had as a teenager. Her blood heated, and deep inside she hungered for more. She felt his weight drag her downward to the carpet of dry grass and wildflowers. Her fingers climbed up his arms, touching the sinewy muscles that bunched at his shoulders. Skin stretched taut over hard flesh, and he groaned when she tore off his T-shirt.

He lifted his head and she kissed his chest, her hands running down his back. She kissed a nipple buried deep in the springy coils of his chest hair and he groaned, then curled his fingers in her hair and pulled her head backward so that his eyes could clash with hers. "What is it about you?" he demanded as the wind picked up, ruffling his hair. "Why can't I stop?"

"Why can't I?"

"I'm serious, Shelby. This is insane."

"Absolutely."

"Emotional suicide."

"Yep."

He released her hair. "You don't care."

"That's where you're wrong," she said with a sigh as the leaves in the branches overhead rustled over the soft nicker of her horse and the thudding of her heart. "I care, Nevada," she admitted. "I care too damned much. *That's* the problem."

"Same one I seem to be havin', darlin'," he admitted.

She didn't dare believe him, refused to fall back into that ravine of sorrow and pain, and yet she couldn't stop loving him. Staring deep into her eyes, he kissed her hard. As he removed her T-shirt and shorts, his strong, calloused hands scraping off her clothes, sent tingles of delight through her limbs.

A million reasons to push away from him crowded through her mind, but she shoved them aside and reveled in the feel of his honed, masculine body rubbing against hers. His hands and mouth were everywhere, touching and caressing, causing goose bumps of anticipation to rise on her skin and stirring a whirlpool of hot desire deep within her. Somehow he managed to kick off his boots as she opened his fly in a series of quick pops.

"You're askin' for trouble," he warned.

"So? Am I gonna get it?"

Nevada's chuckle was as deep as the coming night. He kicked off his jeans, revealing his rock-hard body and muscles sculpted from hours upon hours of hard labor. "Oh, yeah, Shelby. You're gonna get it big-time." They fell to the ground.

His lips found hers again. Hot, hungry, anxious. He tasted faintly of alcohol and smelled of soap. Their tongues touched and locked as he unhooked her bra and her breasts spilled into his hands. Work-roughened thumbs caressed her nipples in circular strokes.

The world started to spin, the sounds of the hillside faded. Shelby kissed him as wildly as he kissed her. She wanted him. Now. Forever. Or just for the moment. It didn't matter. He kissed the crook of her neck and something inside her broke. A hot tide of desire swept through her veins.

"Hold on, Shelby," he whispered as he lowered himself and ran his tongue over already puckering nipples.

She shuddered and bucked. He slid her panties over her buttocks, tossed them aside, then touched her with expert fingers, opening her, massaging a spot deep inside that made her wriggle and cry out. Pleasure, with just a hint of pain, made her want more, oh-so-much more.

"Nevada," she whispered hoarsely, the world spinning crazily, her every need centered between her legs.

"Let go, darlin'."

"Oh, God, I can't—" She closed her eyes. Swallowed. Felt a spasm building as he rolled her over and forced her to straddle him. In one thrust, he drove upward, his thick erection filling her. She cried out, holding on to his shoulders as his hands were planted firmly on her hips, forcing her to move with him, causing a thrill to erupt deep in her soul as he slid in and out and she melted around him.

Faster and deeper he moved, his breathing as shallow as her own as the sky darkened and sweat sheened her body. "That's it.... That's my girl," he whispered hoarsely as she convulsed and the sky seemed to splinter behind her eyes. "That's it.... That's it." He was breathing hard, his hips flexing as he grabbed her and jerked violently upward. "Oh, God..." She fell against him and his arms surrounded her, held her tight, as they both fought to take in air and quiet their jackhammering hearts.

She nestled her head into the crook of his shoulder and felt his lips brush against her forehead. Minutes passed as she clung to him. Finally her head began to clear. Only when his breathing had slowed did she lever up on an elbow and feel the wind climb up her spine. Her hair fell to one side of her face as she gazed at him.

"Okay, cowboy, was there something you wanted?" she asked, swallowing a smile. "Or were you just out looking for a desperate woman who looked like she couldn't resist you?"

"That was it." he said, a slow, steady smile crawling across his jaw as clouds roiled overhead.

"I figured as much."

He squeezed her, let out a long sigh, then kissed her temple. "I've been thinkin'," he admitted.

"Uh-oh, *now* we're in trouble."

His chuckle rumbled through the gulch. "You mean more trouble."

"Yes. That's exactly what I mean." She touched the tip of his nose with her finger and, quick as a rattler striking, he grabbed her wrist.

"I'm serious. I want you to move into my place."

"What?" She searched his face with her eyes, looked for any trace of love, felt her heart rise in anticipation. "Why?"

"For protection. Until all this is over. Until we find Elizabeth and sort everything out."

Her lovesick heart fell onto the cold, hard stones of reality. "Protection?"

"I got another phone call today. Of course no one was there. Wouldn't answer. So I waited him out and he threatened us, both of us, saying our lives will be over."

"Empty threat," she said.

"Maybe, but I have a feeling that we need to be careful."

"You mean *I* need to be careful," she clarified angrily as she reached for her clothes. "Why? Because you think I'm some helpless woman who can't take care of herself?"

He grabbed her arm again, pulling her hard against him. Staring up at her, he said slowly, "You were the one who was raped, Shelby. I just want to make sure that history doesn't repeat itself. I saw McCallum driving through town today."

"It won't," she asserted. "But not because of you, Smith. I don't expect any noble act from you. I'm not a damsel in distress, and I certainly don't need a white...or for that matter, black, knight coming to my rescue."

"What do you need, Shelby?" he asked, his eyes as serious as they'd ever been.

"Other than to find my daughter, I don't know," she said, glaring at him. "But more to the point, what is it you need, Nevada?"

"I wish I knew."

"So do I." She whipped her hand away from him and started dressing. What had she been thinking, making love to him all over again? As if she were one of those idiot women with no mind of her own whenever she was kissed by Mr. Right or, as in this case, Mr. Oh-So-Wrong. Throwing on her T-shirt, she fumed inwardly, then hiked her shorts up to her waist.

With a soft chink, both sets of keys fell out of her pockets.

"You're losing your—"

She scooped up the damning key rings and stuffed them both into her pocket. Nevada was watching her with suspicious eyes. "Wouldn't want to lose these and end up stranded at the ranch," she said glibly.

"Shelby—" He reached for her again and she rolled away.

"Look, I've had kind of a rough day already. I don't need any more grief, okay?" She was on her feet and starting for her horse. The sooner she put some distance between herself and Nevada Smith, the sooner she'd think straight again.

"Hey, what just happened here?"

Struggling into his jeans, he caught up with her, grabbed her wrist and spun her around to face him. His face was etched with concern, and if she was one of those goosey women she detested, she might actually be led to believe that he loved her. He didn't, of course. Certainly he cared, she wasn't stupid enough to deny what was painfully evident, what he'd just admitted, but love her? No way. Not Nevada Smith. Never Nevada Smith.

"I found out that the reporter who's been poking around town, rattling everyone—"

"Katrina Nedelesky?"

"That's the one." She lifted a finger and winked as the shadows of night started to fall. "Well, it turns out she's not just a freelance reporter for *Lone Star* magazine. Nor is she just a woman intent on writing a tell-all, part-fiction, part-fact book about Bad Luck."

"What?"

"No, indeed," Shelby insisted. "She just happens to be my half sister, daughter of Nell Hart, a waitress the Judge had an affair with, then paid to leave town before their love child was born."

"Wait a minute—"

"And that's not the worst of it. Uh-uh. It just gets better and better," Shelby said, speaking so rapidly that the words tumbling out of her mouth were beyond her control. "Nell Hart's baby, Katrina, is the reason my mother committed suicide. That's right, she didn't accidentally overdose one night after drinking too much. No, she was so depressed and suicidal that she took a lethal dose of sleeping pills and booze and then...and then my father...the goddamned Judge covered up any hint of scandal, never recognizing his own daughter, never acknowledging that his wife, my mother, was in so much emotional pain that she would take her own life."

"Oh, honey—"

"Don't!" she said as he reached for her. "Just don't touch me and don't tell me everything's going to be all right and don't ever... don't ever tell me what to do."

Over her protests he folded her into his arms, held her tight against him and didn't flinch as the first sob burst from her throat. Tears tracked from her eyes and her fingers curled in his chest hair as she fought to control her runaway emotions. "Oh, for the love of God," she finally sniffed, "I didn't mean to break down like some pathetic, weak female. Damn it, Nevada, why does this always happen?"

"Don't know." His arms tightened over her and he laughed. "But believe me, Shelby, of all the things I've ever thought about you, 'pathetic, weak female' has never entered my mind."

"Good." Swiping at her nose with the back of her hand, she shook her head to clear her mind. Darkness had settled over the countryside, and far in the distance a coyote howled. "But if I indulge any more displays like this, you'll have to change your opinion."

"I doubt it." Arms linked behind her, he leaned backward to meet her eyes. "But I'm worried about McCallum."

"Don't be."

"Shelby—"

"I'll be fine," she promised, refusing to be intimidated and giving him a quick peck on the cheek. "He'd be a fool to try anything with me again."

"Yeah, well, as far as I know, he hasn't earned any intelligence awards lately and besides, we're not talking about a rational man."

"I'll be careful." She broke out of his embrace and reached for the reins to her horse, just as the first few drops of rain fell.

His smile fell away. "You don't have to be tough, you know."

"Sure I do, Nevada." She climbed into the saddle and stared down at him for a long minute. "We both do."

Katrina rubbed the kinks from her neck and stared at the four walls of her tiny room in the Well Come Inn. Dingy walls and yellowed, once-beige drapes surrounded a bed that sagged in the middle like a broken-down workhorse.

She'd turned the television on earlier. It sat in the corner, muted, a sitcom she didn't recognize offering up laugh tracks every few seconds or so. Lying on the back-breaker of a bed, her laptop balanced on her thighs, she tried to compose her notes, put them in some sort of order, while a glass of tequila sweated on the nightstand. She'd only taken one sip, and the gawd-awful stuff had burned its way down her throat.

Tired, restless and feeling like shit after her run-in with her jerk-off of a father, Katrina considered going back to the old ways and scrounging up a joint. Surely even in this backwater town there was a dealer who could hook her up with a few ounces of marijuana or cocaine.

"Don't even consider it," she muttered, angry with herself. She'd tossed out the drugs along with her ex-husband, and nothing was putting her back on that one-way track, not even a run-in with the almighty Judge.

Taking another sip from the tequila, Katrina heard rain beginning to fall hard against the motel's roof and thought there was surely a better way to slowly kill herself, then wrote down the poem she'd heard earlier that day at the Last Stand Saloon. It was a knock-off of a nursery rhyme. At the time she'd thought it was funny, but it hit a little too close to the bone now.

How'd it go? Oh, yeah.

*Ole Judge Cole was a nasty old soul,*
*And a nasty old soul was he.*

That was it. She started typing again, her fingers flying as she heard a thud and an angry shout from the next motel room, a woman yelling in Spanish and a man answering back sharply. *Great,* Katrina thought, wondering if she'd be the victim of a random bullet fired because of a domestic squabble. But that was the end of it.

The noise level from the television elevated with a local commercial for a weight-loss concoction and Katrina, though her concentration was about shot, kept working. She'd been promising the magazine her story but had kept putting them off, claiming she was polishing it, and with Caleb Swaggert's death, she wanted to add a new angle, the slant that he might have been murdered in order to keep his mouth shut.

This was a distinct possibility.

Caleb Swaggert certainly was no Karen Silkwood. In fact, he could've been an out-and-out liar just trying to line his daughter's pockets, but there was the distinct possibility that he'd known too much, was shooting his mouth off and pissing off someone who had decided to take the old man's fate into his own hands and silence Caleb for good. If that was the case, Katrina, too, might be in danger.

*Wonderful.*

The thought that someone might be out to get her had been her companion for the past few days, and as the rain pounded the roof, she glanced around the cinder-block walls of Room 18 and shivered inwardly. *Nothing ventured, nothing gained,* she reminded herself. All good reporters faced their own mortality. Look at those guys who stayed in war-torn countries just for a story, the people who approached burning airplanes, or interviewed despots, all for the sake of fame.

And yet . . . she wasn't fool enough to want to give up her life for the sake of a story. Fame was important; money even more so. But it wasn't worth dying for. Though she would like nothing better than to expose Judge Jerome "Red" Cole for the son of a bitch he was, even satisfaction wasn't worth her neck. That's why she'd bought the gun—a small, silver pistol that fit neatly into her palm.

God help her if she ever had to use it.

She turned her attention back to her computer screen, and heard nothing from the room next door. A nightly drama flickered from the television screen, but she thought of Shelby Cole. The princess. Her half sister. *Unwed mother.* Now *that* was interesting. It wasn't such a big deal that she'd gotten pregnant. It happened every day, but the fact that she'd hidden it. Why? The Judge, true to his loathsome, self-serving self, had not only denied Katrina her birthright, but had done the same with his own grandchild, Shelby's daughter.

Who was the father of that baby? Katrina wondered and made yet another note to herself. Shelby seemed hell-bent to find the kid, but wouldn't it be a hoot if Katrina managed to do it first? After all, she had connections.

She smiled to herself and nearly jumped out of her skin when there was a knock at the door.

"Who is it?" she said, shoving the computer aside and climbing to her feet. The gun was in her purse if she needed it.

"You the reporter-woman?" an unfamiliar male voice called from the other side of the dead bolt.

"Yes." She reached for her handbag.

"Good. I'm Ross McCallum."

Her heart stood still.

"You hear me?"

"Y-yes." *Oh, God.* This was either the opportunity of a lifetime or her worst nightmare. Her pulse began to skyrocket as she unclasped her purse. "What can I do for you?"

"Why don't you open the door so we can talk?"

*Nothing ventured, nothing gained,* she reminded herself yet again, the old adage suddenly becoming her litany. With one hand on her purse, she used the other to throw the dead bolt, unhook the chain and swing open the door.

There he was. Backdropped by the blue glow of the streetlights and the now sheeting rain, Ross McCallum appeared as bad-assed as any of the pictures she'd seen of him. Sullenly, with a primal, almost predatory look in his eyes, he leaned against the doorjamb. She refused to be intimidated. "Mr. McCallum," she said, coolly.

"You know who I am."

"In this town? Uh-huh. And it's kind of a coincidence, you know, I was just about to call you and suggest we meet."

"Were ya, now?" He snorted in disbelief and his humorless gaze stared straight through her, silently charging her with the lie.

"That's right."

"Well then, let's get down to it." Glancing past her to the bottle of tequila on the bureau, he added, "The way I figure it, now that old Caleb Swaggert's dead and no longer able to give you that interview you were working on, you might want to work a deal with me."

So that was his game. Good.

"Possibly."

"Possibly?" he repeated. "Hey, I can give you a better story than Caleb ever could. I'm the one who was framed for the murder—remember, the guy who did time? I'm thinking you could give me the same deal you worked out with Swaggert."

"Hold on a minute." She had to barter with him; she wouldn't be bullied. "Your testimony's already a matter of public record, whereas Mr. Swaggert was changing his, risking perjury charges. I can't offer you a dime until you can assure me that you have something more to add, something different, and even then I'll have to talk to my editor at the magazine, see if he'll go for it."

"Look, I did my time and spent over eight years paying for a crime I didn't commit, so don't fuck with me."

"Then don't fuck with me," she shot back, ignoring a drip of fear she felt just looking at him. "Let's hear what you've got to say, off the record. If I decide it's worth paying for and printing, I'll call my editor." She held McCallum's gaze and didn't let on for a second that her insides suddenly felt like half-set Jell-O.

One side of his mouth curving upward, he raised a surprised eyebrow. "All right, missy—"

"Katrina," she corrected. "Or Ms. Nedelesky. Your choice."

He hesitated, obviously not used to taking orders from a woman, or anyone else for that matter. "Katrina, then. Why don't you buy me a drink?" He hitched his chin toward the nearly full bottle on the bedside table.

"Fair enough." After throwing on her jacket and twisting the lock, she grabbed her purse and walked out of the room, the door swinging shut behind her as McCallum stepped out of her way. "Let's go to the Last Stand." As eager as she was for his story, she wasn't going to lock herself into a motel room alone with him. The bar was just across the street, and there would be plenty of witnesses should he become aggravated, threatening or violent. The truth of the matter was that though she was playing it cool, the thought of an exclusive on Ross McCallum's story made her inwardly salivate.

"Someone might hear us," he protested as she flipped up the hood of her coat and started through the rain.

"That's a chance I'm willing to take." Holding her purse firmly in her right hand, she dodged traffic and puddles, even had to leap across the water rushing along the side of the street as it gushed into the storm drains.

McCallum caught up to her at the door of the bar, where three smokers huddled under the awning, and even held the door open for her. Country music, conversation and the smell of beer and stale smoke greeted her as she stepped inside.

Though she'd been in town a short while, she recognized some of the regulars. Manny Dauber and Badger Collins were shooting pool in a back corner. A group of Hispanic men watched a baseball game on the television set mounted over the bar from their stools. Half-a-dozen women were scattered at different tables, laughing, drinking and generally checking out the action. Ruby Dee was one of them, and as Katrina and Ross passed her booth, she visibly shrank and stared at the neon beer sign hanging in the window. Lucy Pride was tending bar and keeping an eye on the front door, watching everyone who entered. She winked at McCallum as he and Katrina made their way to a corner booth near the busboys' station.

More than one interested glance was tossed in their direction, and Katrina felt the mood in the bar shift, as if a silent undercurrent of electricity had followed them inside.

"What can I get ya?" Lucy asked, appearing the minute Katrina set her purse on the bench seat next to her.

"The regular," Ross ordered.

"Just a Coke." Katrina wasn't going to lose her edge.

"You got it." Lucy disappeared.

"Kind of a lightweight, aren't you?" Ross observed, leaning back on his spine and eyeing her.

"This is business."

"Could be more."

"I don't think so." She leaned forward. "So why don't you tell me why you think I would be interested in paying for your side of the story."

He grinned wickedly. "Because I know who killed Ramón Estevan," he said.

"And yet you spent eight years in jail."

"I was set up. Framed. Caleb Swaggert said as much, right? Wasn't he paid to finger me?"

Lucy reappeared with the drinks. As he grabbed his beer glass Ross said, "Run a tab. The lady's buying."

"That's right," Katrina agreed, her interest piqued, though she thought McCallum was shooting blanks.

"You got it." As hidden speakers from the jukebox began playing an old Patsy Cline hit, Ross took a swallow from his drink and Lucy, spying new patrons entering the Last Stand, hurried back to the bar.

"Okay, I'll bite," Katrina said, swirling her drink and watching a single maraschino cherry bob between the ice cubes. "Who killed Ramón Estevan?"

Ross didn't bat an eye. "Nevada Smith."

"Wait a minute. He was working for the Sheriff's Department at the time. It was his truck you were in, and what possible motive would he have?"

"He hated Estevan. The old man had a bad temper. Everyone in town knew that."

Katrina sipped her Coke. Waited.

"Well, before Smith got involved with Shelby Cole, he was hanging around the Estevan house, seeing Ramón's daughter."

"Vianca."

"Yep."

"So—" Katrina prodded as Patsy crooned and the air in the bar seemed to thicken.

"The old man didn't like the fact that Nevada basically dumped his daughter for Shelby Cole." Ross took a long swig from his beer and frowned. "Estevan had a temper. If you don't believe me, ask anyone in town."

This she already knew. Caleb Swaggert had alluded to Ramón Estevan as being a "hot-headed Mexican," and a few of the other townspeople Katrina had interviewed had seemed to agree, though it was hard to tell.

"So Nevada Smith and Shelby Cole were dating about the time Ramón was killed."

Ross's eyes slitted. "Yep."

She did the math quickly and figured Nevada Smith was the father of Shelby's child. Well, wasn't that interesting? The very man Ross McCallum was trying to blame for the murder, the one who had seen that Ross took the rap for Estevan's death, was the father of Shelby's child. "Curiouser and curiouser," she muttered, taking a sip from her glass. "You have any proof?"

"No more than he did when he set me up."

"Wait a minute—you're serious? You really think he 'set you up'? You mean that he framed you?"

"Isn't that what I just said? Call it anything you want, but that's what happened." Ross finished his beer and motioned to Lucy for another. "Now, listen, have we got a deal or not?" He leaned forward, elbows on the table, empty glass between meat hooks of hands. "I ain't spillin' my guts without gettin' paid. At least as much as what you were givin' Swaggert."

McCallum glanced at the television and she caught his profile. Katrina decided he wasn't bad-looking. Of course he dressed like a hick in his faded T-shirt, worn jeans and scruffy boots, but it was his attitude, the rage that simmered just beneath the surface, that stole whatever leanings he had toward handsome and twisted them toward dangerous.

"I'll see what I can do," she promised, thankful for the weapon hidden in her purse. "What's your number? I'll call you."

Ross's smile was slow and evil. "Don't have a phone, but don't worry, honey. I'll catch up ta you again." He offered her a wink that made her blood run cold.

"Good," she said, fishing in her purse and finding a twenty-dollar bill that she left on the table. Her fingers brushed the barrel of her little gun and she wondered if she'd ever have the guts to use it. "Until then." She managed a grin to match his, but walked out of the bar on legs made of rubber.

She knew as the rain let up and she picked her way through the puddles that Ross McCallum belonged behind bars.

# CHAPTER 16

"I don't care what you have to do, Levinson, just help me find my kid," Nevada growled into the telephone a few days after meeting Shelby at her father's ranch. He was hot, tired and as frustrated as hell. Two of his mares were off their feed, the tractor had died in the south paddock and he thought he'd seen Shep Marson's truck rolling out of the next drive—the lane to the Adams place, now his property—the other afternoon. But he hadn't been sure. The sun had been wicked. Low, harsh, blinding rays had glinted off the pickup's fender. By the time Nevada had put his old truck through its gears chasing after the intruder's rig, the truck had been little more than a speck in front of a wake of dust.

Nevada had been left with the feeling that something bad was about to happen. Worse yet, he was worried sick about Shelby. Sure as shootin', she was gonna get herself into trouble. That thought nagged at him and he took it out on Levinson. "There's got to be a way to find her."

"Doin' my level best." Levinson's tone was flat. Noncommittal.

"So am I." Nevada had visited the hospital where Elizabeth had been born, bribed an administrative aide into finding out who had been working in the maternity ward that week, talked to as many doctors, nurses and aides as he could locate, but no one had been on duty the night Shelby Cole delivered her baby. Or no one was talking. He'd spent hours himself on the Internet looking for adoptions, info on lost children, anything, but to no avail.

"I'll keep workin' on it."

"Do. And check out some of these people." Nevada listed the names of the hospital workers he hadn't been able to locate—people who might have been working on the night Shelby gave birth.

"Will do."

"And don't forget Ross McCallum."

"Oh, I won't," Levinson said with a smile in his voice. "I intend to find out everything about that ol' boy that I can."

"Good."

There was a pause; then the private investigator said, "While I'm at it, I thought I might try to locate your mother."

Nevada's jaw turned to granite. "Don't bother."

"I just thought, seein' as you're tryin' to locate your daughter, it might be a good time to—"

"Forget it." Nevada was firm. The woman who'd borne him had walked out the door when he was too young to remember her. He could only figure that she just plain hadn't wanted him—for what reason, he couldn't imagine. As a boy he'd tried to understand her rejection, and deep in the darkest regions of his soul he suspected that somehow he hadn't been good enough, though in his rational mind he knew there were more concise, concrete reasons that she'd left. She'd been young. Her husband had been a drunk. She'd had to escape to survive.

But she'd abandoned Nevada.

As far as he knew, she'd never looked back. She could be dead. Wasting away in a nursing home. Living the high life in a villa on the Mediterranean. It didn't much matter. She wasn't a factor in his life, but she was one of the singular reasons that he intended to find and connect with his own child.

If Elizabeth and whoever had adopted her would let him.

If he even found her. His fist clenched around the receiver.

"Let me know if you change your mind," Levinson said.

"I won't."

Nevada hung up and felt restless, like an anxious stallion who senses an invisible predator lurking nearby. Shoving his fingers through his hair, he told himself that he was just imagining things, but he couldn't shake the feeling that something bad was about to go down. And there wasn't a damned thing he could do about it.

"Blast it all to hell," he growled, wishing he had a Marlboro, though he'd given up the habit years before. He needed something to settle him down. Being in the same county with Shelby, knowing she was close by, worrying for her safety, knowing McCallum was up to no good and not being able to find his kid were driving him out of his mind.

The phone rang and he tensed. Probably the damned anonymous caller again. He grabbed the receiver and barked a gruff, "Hello."

"Smith?"

He recognized the voice. The tension in his shoulders tightened. All his attention focused on the conversation as he leaned a jean-clad hip against the counter. "Judge Cole."

"I think we should meet," Shelby's father said without preamble.

"Why?"

"You'll find out when you get there."

"Get where?"

There was a second's hesitation, and Nevada wondered what Red Cole had up his sleeve.

"My office downtown," the Judge decided. "Ten o'clock tonight."

Nevada glanced at his watch. It wasn't quite eight. "Why don't you just tell me whatever you want to over the phone?"

"Don't ask questions. Meet me there."

"Don't see why."

"It has to do with Shelby. And Ross McCallum."

The warning hairs on the back of Nevada's neck prickled upward; then he reminded himself whom he was dealing with. He wouldn't put it past Red Cole to play the melodramatic trump card just to force the issue. "And you can't tell me over the phone?"

"Nope."

"Look, Judge, I'm not buying into all this cloak-and-dagger crap. Whatever it is you have to say to me, just spit it out."

"I will. At ten."

The phone line clicked, then went dead.

Nevada hung up and checked his watch. He had two hours to kill before his date with the devil.

"I need to talk to you." Vianca's voice had been firm on the phone. Though Shep had been at the office, he'd felt the top of his ears turn red and had imagined everyone within earshot could hear her. He glanced nervously around the room with its once-green walls. Where there used to be a wide-open space littered with desks, now the room was chopped up by cubicles made of portable and supposedly soundproof walls.

"It is . . . it is concerning my father's murder," Vianca had said, and he'd recognized the hesitation in her voice.

"I'll be right there." Just the sound of her voice had caused his spirits to rise. The paperwork he'd been going over was instantly forgotten.

"No! I am still at the hospital. Come later. To the house."

His foolish pulse had skyrocketed.

"Now I must work at the store, then see to *Madre*. She is coming home from the hospital today."

Shep's inflated ego nose-dived. So the old lady would be there. No chance of being with Vianca alone.

Yet Vianca's request had hung with him the rest of the day, flitting through his mind while he'd visited the lab and gone over the case files of the Estevan murder.

Now, as he nestled his truck against the curb across the street from the Estevans' bungalow, he smiled inwardly. He was about to get lucky—one way or another. He could feel it, like the promise of a prairie storm in the air.

He'd taken the time to shave, even gone so far as to brush his teeth and put on a clean shirt before driving across town and fighting with his conscience. He had business here, true enough. Even if Vianca hadn't called, he needed to interview all the members of Ramón's family yet again. But the reason his boots gleamed, his breath was fresh and he'd even gone so far as to spray on a couple of shots of Right Guard under his arms wasn't because of his job. Nope. It was because he wanted Vianca to see him for the man he was.

He glanced at his reflection in the rearview mirror and slicked down the ends of his mustache, frowning as he noticed more gray than red in the bristles. Hell, he was pushin' fifty. His gut hung over his belt, his hair was thinning and he'd never in his life cheated on Peggy Sue. Never thought he would, what with her being so pretty and all, but here he was, feeling like a schoolboy again. All because of Vianca.

To be honest, Peggy Sue had changed. Lost interest. Was always too tired for a quick roll in the hay and somehow, over the fifteen years they'd been married, had forgotten how to laugh.

Shep sighed and wondered if he was about to screw up the rest of his life. He knew he had a reputation for being a mean sum-bitch when it came to his job, and in all fairness, it was deserved. Something he'd once been proud of. Hell, he'd cracked more heads, punched more bellies, snapped his share of guilty spines with his billy club often enough. He'd even gone so far as to "adjust" the evidence if he needed it to convict the right man and had looked the other way when one of his friends had broken the law.

He had his own set of rules and they were flexible. For the right price. He didn't see it as a bad thing to take a few dollars off a friend for a favor. Hell, if he hadn't cleaned up that mess when the Johnson kid, who, all liquored up and pissy, had been shooting at stop signs and somehow killed old man Cowan's prized bull, the kid would've ended up in jail and probably never would have finished college. Shep had talked to him hard, slapped him around a little, told him what a piece of shit he was, then accepted a token of appreciation from his father.

It had all ended up fine. Cowan's bull had been insured and the Johnson kid became an accountant—a straight-arrow, even married a Methodist girl and had him a set of twins. And Shep's oldest son, Timmy, had gotten the braces he needed.

The Johnson thing had worked out. Had it been payola? A bribe? Who the hell cared? In Shep's mind, justice had been served, it hadn't cost the taxpayers a dime. The worst thing about the whole business was that old man Cowan had eaten the thickest, toughest steaks this side of Amarillo.

It wasn't that Shep was dishonest. No, sir. He was just practical. A practical man saw to things.

But he'd been faithful to Peggy Sue. Not so much as copped a feel from any other woman. Not that he hadn't had the opportunity. There had been plenty of women interested in him. Plenty. But he hadn't wanted to risk losing his wife and kids.

Until now.

Until Vianca.

He drummed his fingers on the steering wheel and watched a stray dog, tail tucked between his legs, hurry down the street. Shep opened the door and stepped into the muggy air. It wasn't just Vianca needing to see him that put a lift in his step. No, sir. He'd called in all his markers on this case, and the boys in the lab had come through, rushing the ballistics and fingerprint tests on the .38 he'd found in the old mine on the Adams place. Sure enough, the tests had established that the gun was indeed the weapon that was used to kill Ramón Estevan. As expected, the .38 was registered to Nevada Smith and the only set of prints on the gun were Smith's. Not one other smudge.

The lab boys had checked the plastic in which the gun had been wrapped and found no traces of prints, nor hair samples, nor any other trace evidence that would help them. How long the gun had been on the rafter was yet to be determined and might not ever be discovered, but for now, Nevada Smith was the number-one person of interest in this case.

And that bothered Shep. He'd thought a lot of bad things about Nevada, had even suspected that Smith had bribed Caleb Swaggert and Ruby Dee to testify against Ross McCallum. There was definitely some bad blood between Smith and McCallum. But murder? A frame-up? Shep found that a bitter pill. In his own way, he respected Smith.

But he'd been wrong before, and right now Nevada Smith's ass was on the line.

He climbed the steps to Vianca's house, and the thought nagged him that someone else had known about the gun; the anonymous tip had come from somewhere. Had Nevada shot off his mouth? Bragged? Or inadvertently, maybe even drunkenly, revealed the whereabouts of the weapon? That didn't seem right.

As he reached the porch, the cat jumped from its spot on the windowsill and disappeared around a terra-cotta pot of blooming bougainvillea.

Shep rapped on the screen door and peered into the darkened interior. The television was switched on, glowing in one corner, turned to a station airing a Spanish program.

"*Momento,*" Vianca called from inside. Shep's pulse shot to the stratosphere at the sound of her voice.

She was at the door in an instant, her dark eyes sober as she held the screen open. "Thank you for coming."

"No problem." He pulled off his hat and held the brim in fingers that were sweating.

"Here, let me—" Taking the hat from his hand, her fingers brushed his, and he felt a tingle all the way up his arm to the spot where his shoulders connected to his spine. The smells of spices and cigarette smoke mingled with the scent of her perfume. "Would you like something to drink? I have soda or coffee or—"

"I'm fine," he lied, his mouth completely dry of spit. Her hair was dark and shiny, soft curls framing a heart-shaped face. Luminous eyes stared at him above a straight, short nose and the fullest lips he'd ever seen. She was dressed in jeans that looked painted on, a wide black belt with silver trim and a hot-pink tank top that stretched over her breasts. "You said you had information on the case."

"Yes...just a minute. I need to check on *Madre*. Please, have a seat." She motioned toward the couch in the room where the television was glowing. Self-conscious, feeling old and oafish, he edged past a small shrine set between the dinette and living area. A painted picture of Jesus, his heart visible, was backlit by bright light. The table beneath the painting was covered in a lace cloth topped by flickering candles and several framed photographs of a smiling Ramón Estevan.

The whole business gave Shep the creeps. He'd been born and raised a Methodist and didn't completely trust the Catholics... well, for that matter he didn't trust the Lutherans or the Mormons. He wasn't even sure about the Baptists, but held his tongue on that one, being as Peggy Sue's folks were part of that particular flock.

Taking a seat on a plaid couch that had seen better days, he followed Vianca with his eyes. Her jeans were so tight, he had no trouble envisioning the crack of her tight little ass and wondered what it would feel like to run his fingers or his tongue along that sexy little cleft.

She stepped into a small bedroom, and he spied the foot of a double bed with a hand-knit afghan thrown over it and two mounds visible where Aloise's feet were covered. Presumably the old lady was resting, and within a few seconds Vianca reappeared. She offered Shep the tiniest hint of a smile as she closed the door softly behind her.

"Now," she said, taking a seat next to him on the couch and folding her hands between her knees. "There is something I must tell you." The smile faded. She was stone-cold sober and beneath her dark skin she seemed to pale slightly.

"What?"

"It is about Nevada."

Shep was instantly wary. A long while ago, Nevada and Vianca had dated. The word was that she'd never gotten over the fact that he'd left her for Shelby Cole.

Vianca drew in a shaky breath. "I lied about him before. I did not want to see him get in any trouble. Oh, *Dios.*" She licked her lips nervously, and Shep thought he might go mad. His damned cock was as hard as a rock. "I saw him that night. The night my father was killed. At the store."

"So you said. But it was earlier. When he was with his cousin. Joe Hawk."

"No, he came back later. Alone." Her voice was so low, he could barely hear it. Those gorgeous lips rolled in on themselves and tears sprang to her eyes. "I, um, I was in love with him and I did not want anything to happen to him. I could not believe..." Her voice cracked, and she placed a small hand to her mouth.

"It's all right. Just tell me what you saw."

"We were alone in the store. The three of us. *Padre,* me and Nevada. There was an argument. My father...he did not like Nevada. They...they had words, angry words, and Nevada left."

"Left the store?"

"*Sí.*" She reached for a pack of cigarettes on the table, shook one out and lit up. Her fingers were unsteady as she flicked a lighter. Shep had the urge to help her, but resisted, waiting until she was able to hold the flame steady and was able to draw in a calming breath of smoke.

"Was he driving his truck?"

"I did not see—I was too upset." She rubbed her arms as if suddenly chilled and blinked back her tears.

"What happened then?"

Swallowing and looking away, her eyes focusing on the picture of Jesus, she took another drag, then set her cigarette in an ashtray. "A little while later, my father walked out of the back of the store and never returned." Her voice had risen an octave, and she began crying in earnest. Shep couldn't help himself. He placed a comforting arm around her shoulders, intending just to hold her until the storm passed, but when she inched up her chin, offering up those sweet, red lips, he kissed her, gently at first, just to show her he cared, but when she responded, her mouth opening to him, her tongue slipping anxiously between his teeth, her breasts—oh, Christ, those incredible breasts—pressed against him, he couldn't help himself. She smelled and tasted like smoky heaven.

His tongue found hers, danced, mated, stroked.

She moaned softly, kissed him feverishly and didn't stop him when he pulled the tank top out of her jeans and his nervous fingers climbed up her ribs. She gasped when he reached into her bra, and for a second he thought she would slap him away. Instead she placed one small hand over the fly of his pants and squeezed.

Hell, he thought he'd lose his wad right then and there.

"Wh-what about your mother?" he asked as she slid his zipper down.

"She is asleep."

"She could wake up." He was on fire. He wanted her more than he'd ever wanted a woman, but this was dangerous. The old lady could walk in on them at any second.

"No. She will not." Vianca glanced up and held his gaze. In her eyes he saw desire and something else, something calculating that was so quickly disguised, he thought he'd imagined it. "Sleeping pills," she said, parting his pants and reaching into his jockey shorts.

He groaned at the touch of her fingers, thought for a split second about stopping this madness. But then she leaned down and kissed him, her luscious wet lips caressing his shaft.

Vianca started working her hot magic, and Deputy Shep Marson quit fighting. His hands dug into her hair and he held back, not wanting to end this incredible moment and knowing deep in the stygian regions of his soul that he was about to cross a barrier he'd never before scaled. He was not only going to cheat on Peggy Sue; he was going to do it for as long and often as he could.

Shelby tossed the beads of water from her hair, hauled her body out of the pool and wrapped herself in a towel as the moon rode high in the night sky. Less than half an hour earlier, Lydia had taken off, but not before explaining that the Judge had called and he wouldn't be home until late, that he had a meeting in San Antonio and might not be home until the morning. The gardener had left a couple of hours ago, and Shelby had forced herself to wait until darkness had settled over Bad Luck to break into her father's office.

Dabbing her face with a towel, she now climbed up the back stairs to her room and was already pulling the straps of her swimming suit off of her shoulders as she closed the door. Quickly she stripped off the wet suit, flung it over the shower curtain rod and found her bra and undies. Smoothing her hair into a wet ponytail, she snapped a rubber band in place, then stepped into her favorite jeans, tossed on a black T-shirt and pulled on her running shoes. She found the set of keys she'd had made in Coopersville, her watch and a small flashlight, tossed them along with her wallet into a small fanny pack and flew down the stairs.

She felt a sense of urgency, as though if she didn't take this opportunity, it wouldn't come again. Out the back door, down a brick path to the Cadillac. Within two minutes she was in the rental car and cruising into town.

The past couple of days had been torture. She'd spent every waking moment wondering how and when she was going to use the copies of the keys she'd made, what she was going to do about the newfound half sister she didn't trust, and how she was going to deal with the plain, sorry fact that she was falling in love with Nevada Smith all over again.

"You are an idiot," she muttered under her breath and snapped on the radio.

Lyle Lovett's voice crooned through the speakers.

*"That's right, you're not from Texas, that's right, you're not from Texas—"*

"That is right, Lyle. I'm *not* anymore." And yet a part of her denied that awful fact. She was from Texas, always would be, and though she embraced the great Northwest, there was a deep-rooted heritage here that she couldn't ignore. Angrily, she flicked the radio off. Her nerves were too jangled to listen to any music right now—especially lyrics that seemed to mock her and her hard-won independence.

In the past forty-eight hours, Shelby had been going not so quietly out of her mind. Frustrated, hot, tired and sick at the thought that with each day she was spinning her wheels getting nowhere, that she was no closer to meeting Elizabeth than she had been on the day she'd arrived in Bad Luck, Shelby was ready to make good her threat to the Judge and Katrina. If something didn't break soon, she intended to go straight to the newspapers, the radio and television stations, even a dozen different private detectives, to anyone, anywhere. It didn't matter. She just had to find Elizabeth. And soon.

She pushed a button and the driver's-side window slid down. Warm evening air invaded the Cadillac's interior just as through the windshield the lights of the center of town appeared ghostly blue.

For all her anxiety, Shelby hadn't been sitting idle. She'd put in a few calls to Seattle, spent time faxing information to the agent who was handling her real estate listings, tried to reach Orrin Findley again and waited with limited patience for her father to leave Bad Luck for a few days.

It hadn't happened. Until now. In fact, he'd spent more time in the office than normal and the few times Shelby had cruised by his office, even late at night, she'd spied his Mercedes in the parking lot and seen light from windows of the office, though the shades had been drawn. Once, as she'd driven past, he'd been standing on the front walk, leaning on his cane, smoking a cigar and talking with the same two goons she'd caught him with on the first day she'd come into town.

She'd prayed he hadn't seen her as the Caddy rolled past, but he had, of course, and when he'd asked her about it later, she'd made up the excuse that she was looking for Katrina. She wasn't sure he bought it, but he didn't make a scene or call her on the lie.

Now, as she reached the commercial section of town, her stomach tightened. Several cars passed, and the drivers were people she didn't know, who didn't recognize her. Music filtered from the Last Stand and there, big as life, walking toward the main door, was Ross McCallum.

*No.*

Her blood turned to ice.

He paused to light a cigarette, cupping a meaty hand around the flame, and Shelby turned her head away as she drove past. Maybe he didn't see her, didn't recognize the car, but as she checked her rearview mirror, she spied him standing in front of the saloon, his eyes trained on the rear of the rented Cadillac with such cold intensity that she shivered. All the horror, pain and humiliation of that long-ago night reared its ugly head and sweat broke out between her shoulder blades. "Don't let him do this," she warned herself. She wouldn't be defeated, nor deterred. Ross couldn't do anything to her ever again. Ever. She would make sure of it.

She drove as if she were heading straight through town, just in case he had any idiotic ideas of following her. When the lights of Bad Luck had faded behind her, long after she'd crossed the bridge out of town, she took a side road, doubled back and came through Bad Luck from another angle.

Her hands grasping the wheel in a death grip, she eased through the back streets of town and eventually wound her way to the old building where her father spent most of his days.

The parking lot was empty. No sign of Etta Parsons or the Judge's secretary's vintage car, if she still owned the thing. Nor was Red Cole's Mercedes anywhere in sight. The office was dark. Silent.

Good. Using the back streets and alleys, Shelby swung past the office one more time. Still no one. "Just do it," she grumbled. Convinced that no one was going to show up, she parked four blocks away, on a side street behind the laundromat and dry cleaner, catty-corner from the building where Doc Pritchart had once housed his clinic. Unfortunately, there was always the chance that someone would spot her car and mention it at the diner, or coffee shop or even the Last Stand tomorrow. The way gossip passed around this small town in two days, the entire population of Bad Luck might know that she'd been in town tonight, but it was a chance she had to take.

Quickly she locked the car, then started jogging through the sultry, sticky night. The air was thick and pressed hard against her chest—a far cry from the brisk, salty atmosphere of Seattle. It seemed like years since she'd left the West Coast, and yet it hadn't quite been two weeks.

*Time flies when you're having fun,* she thought as she veered through back alleys, trying to avoid the main street and hoping to draw no attention to herself. Never in her life had she willingly broken the law. *You can do this,* she told herself. Smaller minds broke into houses and offices every night of the week.

At the street running behind her father's office, she hesitated behind a hedge, just long enough to see that the coast was clear. No one had pulled into the lot in the ten minutes since she'd driven by. *It's now or never.*

Avoiding the pools of light cast by the streetlights, she ran directly to the back door of the building. Her fingers were sweating as she inserted two keys that wouldn't budge. The third one turned as easily as if it had been oiled.

*Click.*

The dead bolt gave way. She worked on the knob with another key and the lock sprang open. A twist of her wrist and the door swung inward.

Within a split second a security alarm started softly beeping, telling her she had only a few seconds to shut the damned thing off before it began blasting an alarm that was probably loud enough to wake the dead or, worse yet, silently dialed the local police, who would arrive en masse along with screaming sirens and flashing lights.

*Oh, God, where is it?* She took two steps, bumped into a desk and swore under her breath.

*Beep! Beep! Beep!*

Sweating from every pore in her body, she snapped on her flashlight, swung the beam through the small reception office, along the wall, over a calendar, past a light switch and finally spied a control panel mounted near a closet. Whispering a quick prayer, she walked around Etta's desk and directly to the alarm.

What were the code numbers? Her father's birthday. She pushed the buttons and pressed enter.

*Beep. Beep. Beep.*

*Oh, damn! What now?*

In a panic, she tried her mother's birthday. After all, the Judge did keep the birds of paradise on the table and flowers on Jasmine's grave.

*Beep—beep—*

*Oh, hell!* She was rapidly running out of options. Out of desperation, she punched in her own birthday, and the beeping suddenly stopped. The office was still, aside from the hammering of her own heart.

Thank God. Her heart quieted, but sweat still ran down her nose and her knees weren't all that steady. Giving herself a swift mental kick, she walked unerringly to the pebbled glass door of her father's office and opened it. The room smelled faintly of cigars.

Shelby quickly drew the blinds. A hat tree stood in one corner, one of the Judge's trademark black Stetsons hooked over a curved wooden arm, a forgotten golf sweater slung over another hook. His desk was functional. Metal topped with Formica. A humidor filled with cigars, ashtray and telephone graced one corner. On the opposing side were three snapshots, including a small wedding photo of the Judge and Jasmine, a picture of Shelby at eight and her graduation photograph.

So her father seemed to care—had even used her birthday as his security code. She never would have guessed. She stared at the pictures for a few seconds, then reminded herself that she couldn't, *wouldn't* be blindsided by some meaningless nostalgia. Driving unwanted emotions from her mind, she went to work.

The drawers of the desk were locked, but she found a small key on her new ring that worked. Pencils, paper clips, matches, letter opener and such were in the first drawer. Big deal. The second drawer in the stack offered up recent paperwork, mostly having to do with the ranch and none of which looked interesting; the third housed a partially consumed fifth of Jack Daniels and an extra stash of cigars.

So far she'd used up ten minutes and found nothing. Wiping the sweat from her forehead, she started with the credenza. It opened easily and was much like his cabinet at home, everything neatly marked and, not surprisingly, some of the names she'd found at the house were duplicated here.

*Bingo.*

She found Dr. Ned C. Pritchart's file and eased it open with anxious hands. The manila folder was thin, only a few notes, nothing significant except that his last known address and date of death had been written in. So the Judge had known Pritchart was dead but had let her go on looking for him, running down blind alleys and wasting precious time.

"You snake," Shelby said, disappointed, though she knew she was being foolish. Her father was and always would be the grand manipulator. For reasons of his own, he didn't want her to find Elizabeth and would put up every roadblock he could to stop her. The man who had denied his own illegitimate daughter would do the same with his granddaughter. "Thanks a lot," Shelby whispered as she forced herself back to work.

Nevada's file was next.

She opened it on her lap, the beam of her flashlight racing over the pages. The folder was filled with dozens of notations, mostly about Nevada's wayward youth, but there were other pages as well, pages with personal memos. Judge Cole didn't pull any punches and was scathing in his remarks about the "insolent juvenile delinquent" who had been hell on wheels as a kid and yet the Judge had hired later. On one page there was a note that Judge Cole suspected his daughter was pregnant and that the "motherless son of a bitch Smith" was the father of his grandchild.

"So who's the real bastard here?" she asked as she closed the file and with shaking fingers found her own folder. She glanced at her watch. Nine forty-five. She'd been here twenty minutes, and each one that passed made her more edgy. A clock ticked from a corner bookcase, traffic moved slowly outside, but other than that the dark office was silent, eerily so. How many not-so-honest deals had been consummated in this room? How many lives changed forever?

Ignoring her case of nerves, she opened the thick file inscribed with her name. Her entire life seemed to spill out with the pages. Copies of the same report cards, employment records, medical reports she'd seen in the file at home, but there was more here. In the back of the folder was a handwritten diary, a listing of the significant events in Shelby's life and little asides put in by the man who had sired her. She swallowed hard as she read each note, starting with her birth, going through her grade school and high school years, including her mother's death, and yes, not only her pregnancy, but her rape, the latter being squeezed in as her father hadn't learned of the act until he'd confronted her about her pregnancy.

Tears threatened her eyes, but she drove them back, refusing to cry. After the pregnancy there were other notations as well, her schooling and jobs, but the most interesting note was a cross-reference to Lydia Vasquez, the Coles' housekeeper.

Why?

Because Lydia had been the only mother she'd ever known? The woman who had taught her to sew, cook and arrange flowers and had brought home her first box of tampons? Lydia had bandaged her knees when they'd been skinned, offered advice that Shelby had rarely listened to and had filled the big house with laughter and funny stories about her family.

Yes, they were linked, but Shelby sensed there was more to her father's hastily scratched notation. She only had to figure out what it was. Probably nothing. But then again ...

Shelby slapped her file onto the desktop, then searched for Lydia Vasquez's folder, found it and wasted no time in dragging it from the drawer to lay it open on the desktop.

There were dozens of notes on Lydia, since she had worked for the Judge for years. Her legal papers had been copied and paper-clipped together and there were various pages mentioning all of her relatives, including Carla and Pablo Ramirez and their children. Each child was duly noted as well. There was even a cross-reference to the Estevan family, who were also related to the Ramirezes.

Shelby stared at the file. Why would her father take such meticulous notes on these people? In the back of her mind, she felt a cold comprehension beginning to build. There was something more here . . . something ugly.

She skimmed the names of the children again jotted down in the Judge's cramped handwriting—Enrique, Juan, Diego and Maria. Four kids. Three boys, one girl. She'd known them all growing up. Maria was the oldest and the boys had come along later, stair steps. She'd not been allowed to play with Maria, though. It had been one thing for Lydia to practically raise her—the Judge had found that just fine—but when it came to actually making friends with the Spanish-speaking children, Judge Cole had drawn the line, which Shelby had often ignored.

She'd remembered Maria, a bright-faced, smart girl who had left school early on. Shelby couldn't remember why.

She was about to turn the page, then stopped and gazed at Maria's name again. Didn't Lydia say that Maria's daughter was giving her so much trouble? Her *nine-year-old daughter?* Hadn't Lydia been crying on the phone with Maria? Shelby's heart nearly stopped. So what? *Don't jump to any far-fetched conclusions,* she told herself. It's just a coincidence.

But she twisted in her father's chair and, holding the flashlight between her teeth, searched the file drawer until she found a folder for Maria. It was thicker than those of her brothers.

Holding her breath, extracting the folder, Shelby drew in a deep breath. The file fell open and there, shimmering in the flashlight's pale beam, was a color picture of a child—one taken for school, Shelby guessed.

"Elizabeth," Shelby said, tears filling her eyes as she gazed upon a girl with teeth too big for her small face, a blue ribbon sliding out of curling brown hair, freckles evident on tanned skin and turquoise eyes staring straight at the camera.

Shelby's heart cracked for all the years she'd wasted, but she managed a tremulous smile through her tears. "Dear God," she whispered, sobbing in relief.

After ten years of lies and deception, she'd finally located her daughter.

# CHAPTER 17

Shelby scraped her chair back, tucked the damning file under her arm—then heard a truck's engine slow and stop in front of the office on the deserted street.

*Great,* she thought. Someone else who might recognize her. Not that it mattered, she supposed. Unless it was Ross McCallum.

Her heart nearly stopped.

*Don't panic, Shelby. Ross has no business here; you're just overreacting. Get a move on. Go to Lydia's. Demand to know the truth.*

Stuffing her own file into the cabinet, she flicked off her flashlight, slid the drawer shut, locked it as well as the desk. She didn't want to tip off her father that she knew the truth, not yet. Not until she'd seen her baby, talked to her, decided what she was going to do. If the Judge caught wind that Shelby had discovered Elizabeth's whereabouts, he was certain to sabotage her efforts again.

"Bastard," she said, rounding her father's desk as her eyes adjusted to the darkness.

She couldn't take any chances of being caught. Not yet. A door slammed right outside the office.

"Blast it all," she whispered.

Adrenaline sped her out of the Judge's office and toward the back door that she'd used to enter. Headlights flashed against the window facing the parking lot.

Her heart nose-dived as she realized her avenue of escape had been cut off. Peering through the blinds, she recognized her father's Mercedes as it ground to a stop near the fence. *No!* What was he doing here? Lydia had said he would be out of town the entire night.

Frantic, Shelby realized she had to take a chance and leave through the front door or confront her father on the spot, when the knob to the opposing door rattled. Then there was a sharp knock.

So the Judge wasn't just stopping by to pick up something or make a late-night phone call or do a little paperwork when it was quiet here. Nope, he was meeting someone. This was no time for a showdown.

Without thinking, Shelby ducked into a storage closet and clutched her precious file to her chest. The closet was close, shelves of papers and supplies nearly touching each of her shoulders, and the temperature inside seemed about a million degrees. Sweat ran down her forehead as she heard the back door open.

"What in thunder?" her father's voice boomed. "Damned fool contraption." Heavy, uneven footsteps crossed the reception area at the sound of pounding. Shelby heard the sounds of locks opening, saw a crack of light under the door as the overhead fixture was flipped on. "So you made it."

"Been waitin' for ya."

*Nevada? Oh, God, Nevada was meeting her father?*

Shelby couldn't believe it. Didn't want to.

"What was it you wanted to talk to me about?" Nevada demanded.

"You haven't come inside yet?"

A pause. "The door was locked, Judge. You just let me in."

For a second neither man said a word. "You didn't see anyone come or leave?"

"I just got here."

Shelby was dying inside. Somehow her father had divined that she'd been around.

"Goddamned Etta," the Judge growled. "Doesn't have enough sense to lock the damned back door or set the fool alarm. What's the use of a security system if you don't turn the fool thing on?"

Shelby's heart pounded. Her palms were itchy with sweat. At

any moment her father could fling open the door to the closet, snap on the light and expose her.

*So what? Breaking and entering is nothing in comparison with his crimes of falsifying records, fraud, kidnapping and whatever else.*

"What was it you wanted to talk to me about?" Nevada demanded. "You said something about Shelby and McCallum."

*Oh, God.* Shelby clenched her jaw so hard it ached.

"Come into my office where we can sit down."

*No!* Shelby wouldn't be able to hear either of them if they moved, but the sound of footsteps retreating indicated that they had, indeed, moved.

This was her chance to escape. She waited a few seconds, then eased open the closet door to a room awash with light. Etta Parsons's desk, complete with a vase of daisies and pictures of her grandchildren, was lit up like the proverbial Christmas tree. Shelby looked through the crack over the hinge in the closet door and saw the back of Nevada's head and shoulders through the open door to her father's office. Sitting opposite him on the other side of the desk was the Judge. His view of the reception area was complete.

She was trapped unless she wanted to expose herself.

"I know you railroaded McCallum into prison," the Judge said, his voice surprisingly clear.

Shelby's heart missed a beat.

"The evidence pointed his way."

"Did it? Well, hell, it doesn't really matter, does it? We both know the man deserved what he got."

"He killed Estevan."

"Did he?" There was a long hesitation. Shelby was sweating bullets. She saw the cords in the back of Nevada's neck become more pronounced. "We don't know that for a fact, but we do know that he raped Shelby, and for that he deserved what he got. Even more."

*What is this all about?* Shelby's fingers twisted the folder in her hands.

"That's why you railroaded McCallum. You found out about the rape and got into a fight with him. Landed the two of you in the hospital and cost you some of the vision in that eye of yours. But that wasn't good enough. The night Estevan was killed, you somehow figured out how to get Ross in your truck and claim that it was stolen. Your gun turned up missing. Estevan was shot with the same make and model."

"And you think *I* did it."

"Could be."

"Why?"

"Convenience. To set Ross up. Besides, Estevan was a mean, uppity prick who roughed up his wife and daughter every once in a while. You were involved with Vianca at one time." Shelby's gut twisted. Was this all possible? Did Nevada manipulate the law as much as her own father did? All because of the rape?

"This is bullshit."

"Conjecture."

"The bottom line is that Ross McCallum killed Estevan," Nevada said. "I didn't set it up, Judge. That's your kind of game, not mine."

"Well, we'll just see, won't we? There's a leak in the Sheriff's Department, and I already heard a rumor that the murder weapon's been found."

Nevada, from what Shelby could see, didn't so much as flinch. "The .38?"

"*Your* .38. It was registered to you. Uncovered in the rock quarry at the Adams place, the one you own now."

"Now wait a minute—the gun was at the quarry?" Nevada sounded surprised.

"In a cave or mining shaft." The Judge leaned forward, and Shelby's heart beat like a drum. "It's your gun, was found on your property, has your fingerprints on it and is already proved to be the weapon that killed Ramón Estevan."

"Is that so?"

"The D.A.'s pressing for an arrest, and you don't have an alibi."

"Or a motive." Nevada was on his feet. "As I said, Judge, I didn't kill Ramón Estevan. My guess is that McCallum did it and got out on a technicality because *some*one paid Caleb Swaggert to frame him."

*Her father? Her father had bribed a witness?* Shelby's mind was reeling.

"Someone came up with five thousand dollars for the old guy. I figure it was you."

Her father stared at Nevada as if he were sighting a gun. "You can figure from now until forever."

"And the judge who sent McCallum up the river was an old golfing buddy of yours, wasn't he?" Nevada was on his feet in an instant leaning over the desk. "You pull so many strings in this town, Judge, you can't keep 'em all straight. You're like a damned puppeteer who's tangled the strings of all his marionettes." Jabbing a finger at the older man's chest, he said, "I didn't kill Ramón Estevan, and you and I both know it."

"Someone did."

"Maybe it was you," Nevada accused him. "Now get to the point. Why the hell did you think it was so important we meet?"

"I want you to leave my daughter alone."

Through the crack in the door Shelby saw Nevada bristle.

"Why?"

"She doesn't need you complicating her life." Anger fired through Shelby's blood. Who was her father to control her?

Nevada didn't move a muscle, and the clock ticked over the thudding of Shelby's heart. "Wait a minute," he said and dropped back in his chair. "You've had it in for me for years, Judge. You always claimed it was because I got into trouble with the law as a kid, but I've had the feelin' that there's more to it than that, more than you've ever admitted."

"I only want what's best for my daughter."

"According to you. Maybe Shelby has a different opinion." Nevada was leaning low on his back, one booted heel resting over the opposite jean-clad knee. "I suspect this goes way back."

The Judge looked away.

"What is it, Red? Why do you hate me so much?" Nevada asked, and the air in the closet was too thick, too tense to breathe. Shelby's nerves were twisted as tight as guitar strings about to break. "Why do I have the sneaking suspicion that your aversion to me has to do with my mother?"

Oh, God, what was Nevada saying? The Judge's face drained of color.

"Don't tell me you got it on with my old lady?"

"No!" The Judge's fist smashed against his desk. Shelby jumped. Nevada didn't budge.

"Then what the hell is it?"

For a long second, Judge Cole stared at his fist and then slowly moved his gaze up to Nevada's face. "If I tell you, you've got to promise to leave Shelby alone."

"Can't do it."

"Sure you can, you no-good son of a bitch. Because no matter what I think of you, I know you want what's best for Shelby, and you're just not it. You're the goddamned hot-blooded son of a whore and a drunk who couldn't keep his hands off other women, even those above his station."

Shelby didn't move. Couldn't.

"Meaning?"

"My wife, you bastard," the Judge said. "Why the hell do you think she took her life? Because I had an affair with Nell Hart? Because I fathered an illegitimate kid? Shit, no. She got back at me for that. With your father."

Shelby's ears were ringing, her world spinning out of control, her knees suddenly as steady as pudding. She tried to put the information together. Was her father saying that Nevada was her half brother? That—oh, God—she was fathered by...Her stomach turned to acid. It was all she could do not to throw up. *No! No! No!*

"It was after that, when Jasmine realized what she'd done, that she...that she died."

"Killed herself," Nevada clarified and the Judge didn't answer. "You sick, self-important prick!" Nevada was over the desk in an instant. Standing above the Judge, looking down on him, Nevada reached for the older man's throat, then clenched his hands into the air. "You're lying."

"I wish I was," the Judge said, his shoulders slumping as if suddenly all of the wind in his sails had died. He reached into his desk drawer and withdrew his fifth. "But I didn't call you here to bring this all up. I just wanted to let you know that you'd better cover your ass. Unless I miss my guess, you'll be charged with Estevan's murder."

"And you care?" Nevada spat out.

"No, Smith, I don't really give a shit about what happens to you. I just want to find a way to get McCallum back in prison where he belongs."

"And you want me to help you?" Nevada sneered.

"He raped Shelby once. What's to stop him now?"

"Me," Nevada growled as the Judge twisted off the cap of his bottle of Jack Daniels. "If he so much as looks at her, I'll kill him."

"Talk like that will land you in jail."

Nevada leaned closer to his old enemy. "So be it. The only reason I decided to meet you here is that I want to know about my kid."

"Yours or McCallum's?"

"Doesn't matter. Where is she, Judge? You know. You paid off Doc Pritchart, saw that he left town and somehow got to everyone who worked the night shift when Shelby delivered. On top of that, you left Our Lady of Sorrows a nice endowment, just for insurance so no one would dare say anything. But it's time to come clean, Judge. Where's the kid?"

"I don't know."

"Like hell," Nevada muttered, every muscle in his body tense.

"I found her." Shelby had heard and seen enough. She forced the words from her throat and walked from the closet and into the light of Etta's office. In three steps she was once again in her father's sanctuary, where both men stared at her, each clearly shocked to see her.

"What the hell are you doing here?" the Judge thundered.

"Getting to the truth."

Judge Cole's face fell.

"I came here to get information." She brandished Maria Ramirez's file like a sword, slapped it on the desk next to her father's fifth of whiskey, then stared straight into Nevada's eyes. "Elizabeth's being raised by Maria Ramirez."

The Judge blanched. "No." But his protest was feeble, an obvious lie.

Shelby explained, "Maria's related to Lydia."

"I remember Maria," Nevada said, his eyes narrowing thoughtfully.

"Leave it be, Shelby," her father protested.

"Can't do it." Whipping out her cell phone, Shelby held it under her father's nose. "Do you want to do the honors, or shall I?"

"You're making a mistake."

"I don't think so."

Determined, she punched out the familiar numbers of Lydia's home phone. "We're going to deal with this now. I'm going to call Lydia this very minute and find my child. I'm not going to waste another second. As for all this mess between my mother and your father"—she motioned to Nevada—"we'll sort it out later. They're both dead now, so as painful as it may be, it's over. As for Ross Mc-Callum—believe me, I can deal with him."

"You broke in here," her father accused her as the telephone began to ring on the other end of the connection.

"You bet I did, Judge. And I'd do it again." It was Shelby's turn to lean across the desk. Sweat dripped onto the top of her father's humidor from her chin. She didn't care. Didn't even notice as she glanced from her father to Nevada and she heard someone pick up on the other end. "Come hell or high water, I'm going to meet my daughter."

"Ramón, no! *Dios,* do not! Oh, Holy Father..."

Shep sat bolt upright. Reached for his sidearm and wondered where the hell he was when he discovered he was bare-assed naked.

"Do not, no, no, no—Ramón!" Aloise was screaming and crying in the next room and he...oh, shit, he was alone and naked as a jaybird in Vianca's bed. He must've fallen asleep after screwing her from here until tomorrow. The bedroom still smelled of smoke, sweat and sex.

As the cobwebs cleared from his head, he grabbed his clothes and mentally kicked himself up one side and down the other. The digital clock on the nightstand read one forty-five, soft Spanish music was wafting from the radio and the double bed was empty except for him. What had gotten into him, staying here with Vianca? Peggy Sue would be worried sick.

How would he explain...oh, hell! He heard Vianca's smooth, silky voice trying to quiet her mother and the old woman having none of it. She was upset and her dead husband's name kept cropping up between the broken, disjointed pieces of conversation and prayers.

Stepping into his jockey shorts and slacks, Shep discovered his wrinkled shirt tossed over the edge of the bureau. What had he been thinking? His truck was parked outside, and here he was fucking his brains out while Peggy Sue couldn't get a good night's sleep and would be up at dawn, fighting morning sickness and dealing with the kids.

He was a fool. There were no two ways about it. Here he wanted to be the next sheriff, had the Estevan murder about tied up so that he would be a hero, and he'd been willing to throw it all away for a blow job and a quick roll in the hay.

He was just about finished buttoning his shirt when the moaning stopped and Vianca, wearing nothing but a red, shiny robe, flew into the room. She stopped short at the sight of him fumbling with his buttons. "You are leaving?"

"I have to."

"But it's early."

"No, Vianca. It's late."

Her lips, no longer shiny, drew into a little pout and her eyes, darker with the mascara that had rubbed onto her skin, silently accused him of using her. "I want you to hold me." She pouted and he sighed.

"Just for a second." Opening his arms, he drew her close, sighed onto her crown and wished to holy heaven that things were different. If he was twenty years younger, if he didn't have a passel of kids with another on the way, if he wasn't married to a good woman who trusted him, if he'd already been elected sheriff...He kissed her forehead. "I've got to go."

"You will be back?"

He hesitated and saw tears begin to form in her eyes. "Sure I will," he heard himself say, but she didn't smile and those dark, suspicious eyes of hers seemed to pierce his very soul.

Carrying his boots to the front steps, he walked outside to air that was as warm and sticky as honey. Halfway down the steps he heard Vianca lock the door behind him. He had to put all thoughts of her out of his head for the moment. Vianca's testimony that she'd seen Nevada at the store alone on the night that Ramón Estevan was killed and also in the hospital the day that Caleb Swaggert died was just what he needed to nail Smith's hide to the cross.

He had some details to attend to, wanted to write up a report, talk to the D.A. himself and then, if things went as expected, arrest Nevada and charge him with the crime.

His scalp itched as he crossed the street, and he felt more than one twinge of guilt. This was all too easy and smacked of a setup. Why would everything fall into place so easily now, after all this time?

Unlocking his truck, he stepped inside. Despite a grudging respect, Shep didn't much like Nevada Smith, never had. Smith was just too damned cocky and arrogant for the son of a whore and a drunk. But Shep didn't see him as a cold-blooded murderer either.

*Stranger things have happened*, he told himself as he cranked on the ignition and the Dodge's engine roared to life. He had a job to do and he damn well planned to do it. If Nevada was innocent, he'd get his chance to prove it.

Shep didn't much believe that a man was "innocent until proven guilty." That right was just way too convenient and overused by the bleeding-heart liberals who weren't out in the trenches fighting the bad guys. Let a man prove he was innocent, rather than the other way around. It was just a damned sight easier, to Shep's way of thinking. He found his can of Copenhagen, put a pinch under his gum and pulled away from the curb. A final glance at the Estevan house made him smile.

Vianca was standing at the window, staring after him, as if she couldn't wait to see him again.

Shep felt a moment's pride, all of his guilt over Peggy Sue and the kids temporarily forgotten. He'd ridden Vianca like a stallion. Of course she'd want more.

Katrina rubbed her eyes. Criminy, she was tired. Her back hurt, her neck hurt and she didn't know when she'd be able to get some more sleep. Not that the sagging mattress in this flea bag of a motel could give her a moment's rest. And forget the fact that the bed, ancient enough to be equipped with "magic fingers," was supposed to give her a massage. She couldn't wait to move out of this place.

She thought of the Judge's mansion, *her father's* house, with its manicured lawns, tile floors, shimmering pool and expensive furniture and artwork. What a joke. While her half sister had grown up privileged, Katrina had been raised in a two-bedroom bungalow in a tiny town near the Oklahoma border. They'd had enough money to scrape by, but nothing, *nothing* like the palatial lifestyle of Shelby Cole.

Katrina had done her research. Shelby had been pampered. Her damned horse—an Appaloosa named Delilah—that Shelby had ridden while growing up had cost more than Katrina's mother's Chevrolet station wagon. And her little car—a BMW. Damn it all to hell.

Katrina stood and cracked her back. She peered through the blinds of her room at the WELL COME INN sign and frowned as the first rays of gray light were visible in the eastern sky. Life hadn't been fair, but it was about to turn around. Big-time.

The story for *Lone Star* was just the tip of the iceberg. She intended to write a book, an exposé on Judge Cole that everyone who was anyone in Texas would drool over. There were enough skeletons in the old man's closet to ensure that the pages would be juicy.

She turned away from the blinds.

She alone had had an interview with Caleb Swaggert, and now she was getting insight from Ross McCallum, who swore he'd been set up—by Nevada, no less.

"Tsk, tsk, Daddy," she muttered, rotating her neck and wondering if she could just close her eyes for twenty minutes, then go back to work.

She'd survived on a couple of hours of sleep last night and large quantities of caffeine. She'd learned more and more as the days had passed and the townspeople of Bad Luck had grown more accustomed to her. As a means to her end, she'd even readopted the drawl she'd worked so hard to get rid of in college. But it fit here. Fit as well as one of the trademark black Stetsons on the Judge's aging head.

"Bastard," she muttered and wondered when Ross McCallum would call again. The man was a snake with sharp fangs and a coiled body, ready to strike. Yet she needed him. He was the key to the Estevan mystery. She was sure of it. If Ross didn't call soon, she'd have to tuck her little gun in her purse and go looking for him.

Her blood turned to ice at that thought. The truth of the matter was that Katrina didn't like dealing with McCallum. He was just plain bad news. But she'd swallow back her fear and do whatever it took.

She turned back to her laptop placed on the motel's cheesy table. She was just beginning to stretch her notes into story form, the tale of an egomaniac of a Texas judge who would soon rue the day he'd ever cut off his illegitimate daughter. And Shelby—maybe it wasn't her fault that she was the pampered princess. But face it, the girl was a fool. How could anyone in this day and age get knocked up and believe that her baby had died? Idiot. Shelby was a woman who had the world by the tail and didn't know it. As far as Katrina could see, Shelby had carved out her own life up in the Northwest. God, why would she want to live in that dreary, coffee-soaked area of the country, when everything she could ever want, *everything* was here? Not only would she eventually inherit unlimited wealth, but she also had a loving if stubborn and crooked father.

Katrina swallowed hard and blinked fast. She wouldn't cry, damn it. She picked up her glass, drained the remaining sip of Mountain Dew from it and crunched on a couple of melting ice cubes. Jerome Cole was a jerk. A man who hadn't cared one iota for his second-born. A man who hid his granddaughter from the kid's mother. A man who deserved everything he got.

Katrina only hoped she was the person who could give it to him.

Ross slammed his empty glass on the bar. The crowd at the Last Stand had definitely thinned, just a few old drunks still hanging around, but the gossip that had fueled most of the conversation still rattled around in his head—conversation concerning the reporter-woman, the Judge and Shelby Cole. Conjecture had it that Katrina was the Judge's illegitimate kid and she was back here with her own ax to grind.

Funny, she hadn't mentioned it to him when they'd had their little chat the other night. Maybe it was time to pay her a visit. But first, he had his own agenda—a special game he played.

Quickly, he motioned to Lucy and she managed a thin smile. Hell, she'd always liked him. Tonight, Lucy looked shot. Her lipstick had faded, her eye makeup was long gone. She swabbed the bar's surface as Ross handed her a twenty for the four beers he'd consumed. She made change quickly and he left her a decent-enough tip, but pocketed the coins.

"Say 'hi' to your sister when you see her," Lucy said, and Ross mumbled that he would. It was a lie. They both knew it. He didn't much like Mary Beth and she felt the same about him. They'd only banded together because, as kids, they'd only had each other. Workin' on that old scrap of land for a grandfather who spouted off verses of the Bible as easily as he beat them with his belt, they'd cowered together. Until Ross had noticed Mary Beth was growing titties. Until he'd kissed her and put his hand down her pants at the age of twelve. Mary Beth had screamed bloody murder, Grandpa had beat him within an inch of his life and then taken him down to the irrigation ditch where he'd nearly drowned Ross while the family dog looked on.

He'd pushed Ross's head under the water until Ross's lungs had burned and he'd come up gulping and gasping only to be held down again. "Get thee out, Satan," Grandpa had yelled. "Get away from my grandson!" Swallowing warm, stagnant water, spitting and coughing, Ross's head had been dragged upward so that he could see the sky for a few seconds before he was plunged into the ditch again. Over and over again, until Ross had passed out and woken up on his bed, feverish, his grandmother, dark-eyed and sullen, tending to him without saying a word.

"You leave your sister alone or I'll strip you down and take you to a place where the scorpions nest," his grandfather had warned later while slathering butter on a slice of homemade bread, then drizzling it with honey. With rimless glasses, a bald head, and several missing teeth, Gerald McCallum was an imposing man whose wife, children and grandchildren never raised their voices to him. His word was law. "I ain't kiddin'."

Ross had believed him.

He'd never laid a hand on Mary Beth again.

From that point on he'd been more careful, and his sexual fantasies about his sister had been transferred to other girls. He'd gotten laid at fifteen, but found no thrill in it; the girl, seventeen and horny, hadn't been a challenge and Ross liked a challenge. The harder a woman said no, the more he pushed. Using his football player's body and promises he never intended to keep, he usually got what he wanted.

Until Shelby.

She was the only woman he'd had to force into his way of thinking. And, he'd guessed later, she'd liked it that way. Otherwise she would've told her pa and there would have been hell to pay. Ross suspected Shelby liked it rough.

Now Ross shouldered open the door of the bar. Outside, the air felt muggy and oppressive, the night as dark as his mood. He thought of Shelby again and would gladly have given his last dime to get her alone. He remembered the rape vividly, had replayed it over and over in his mind as he'd lain in his bunk in his cell for those long, lonely eight years he'd spent behind bars. He'd told himself that she'd really wanted it, that she'd fought him only because she had some hang-ups about sex; the next time she'd be begging him.

He made his way to his rattletrap of a truck parked near the corner, climbed inside and frowned. When he got some money from that magazine, he'd get himself a new truck and a rifle—which he might just have to buy through the black market. He wasn't really sure about the laws about ex-cons owning a gun. He wasn't really a con, though, the way he'd been sent to prison on trumped-up charges.

But just to be on the safe side, he'd get himself a gun through the want ads. Same way he'd get himself a dog. The car would be different. He'd get all legal and then go out and get the flashiest set of wheels his money would buy.

And one way or another, he'd have Shelby Cole again. It was goddamned written in the stars.

Inside his truck, he twisted on the ignition, then turned on the radio. Nothing. "Fuck!" He banged on the dash with his fist until the temperamental speakers crackled to life, then wheeled away from the curb. John Cougar Mellencamp was rocking.

*"I was born in a small town..."*

"You and me both, buddy."

Ross noticed the pharmacy as he drove past, and the feed store down the way. You couldn't get much smaller than Bad Luck. With the music blaring, he spat out the open window and drove to the very edge of town where there was a pay booth that was still operational, one of the few. He'd run out of minutes on the stolen cell phone, one of those that wasn't registered, so the lonely pay phone would have to do. Mounted on the highway by a vacant building that had once housed a machinist's shop, the booth was tucked far enough away from prying eyes that Ross felt safe. There were no security or traffic cameras anywhere close. He snapped off the radio just as ol' John wailed on about living, being taught the fear of Jesus and dying in a small town.

Isn't that what had happened to Caleb? Found Jesus and then died. But Ross didn't think the old coot had managed to get to heaven. Nope. Caleb was probably roasting in hell right now, and that was just fine. Perfect. That's what he got for lying through his false teeth and helping send Ross up the river.

And it had been so easy to kill him. Slip into the room while he was sleeping when no one was paying attention, stuff the pillow over his head and watch his pathetic, skinny arms and legs flail as he struggled and failed to take another breath.

The old guy shoulda thanked him. The way Ross saw it, he saved Caleb a whole lot of pain and suffering. No amount of chemotherapy or surgery or radiation was gonna pull him through. Ross had just helped nature along. And it had felt good. Damned good.

He'd feel even better if he could do the same for Ruby Dee and Nevada Smith. Both of those lowlifes deserved to die after setting him up.

Softly whistling the refrain of "Small Town," Ross drove through a gate that sagged open and parked his truck behind the vacant metal building. Out of sight from the street, he climbed out of the truck. It was dark here, aside from the dim light in the booth, and as he walked to the phone Ross jangled the change in his pocket. Dialing quickly, he turned his back to the street and waited as the call connected. He couldn't quite swallow the smile that stretched across his chin because he liked nothing better than to rattle Nevada Smith's cage.

One ring.

Two.

Three.

Hell, was the guy asleep or dead?

*Or getting it on with Shelby?*

Ross's smile fell away. He lost count of the rings, and when the answering machine picked up, he didn't bother to listen, just hung up and wished he hadn't lost all his coins.

His thoughts turned dark as he considered Smith with Shelby Cole. His stomach clenched, and he decided he couldn't keep pussyfooting around, making anonymous calls and just toying with Shelby.

Nope. It was time to see her again.

On his terms.

# CHAPTER 18

"*You* sent me the picture," Shelby said, staring at the housekeeper with new eyes. Shelby, Lydia and the Judge sat at the patio table near the pool of the Judge's house. Nevada leaned against an exterior wall, his body rigid, his expression grim, his gaze boring into Red Cole's fleshy face.

"*Sí, niña.*" Lydia nodded slowly and took a puff from a cigarette that she'd left burning in the solitary ashtray. Smoke curled toward the sky. Dawn was fast approaching. Already birds were singing morning songs and the first rays of sunlight were dancing across the pool's smooth surface. "I sent it. *Sí.* And I lied about it." Lydia's eyes became downcast for a brief moment before she slowly lifted her chin in near defiance. She met the silent accusations in her employer's eyes and said directly to the Judge, "And I would do it again. It was not right that Shelby did not know about Isabella... Elizabeth. She is her daughter."

"Why didn't you tell me before?" Shelby asked, still stunned by the deceptions and lies that clung, as diaphanous and ever-growing as Spanish moss, to this house she'd once called home.

"I asked her not to," the Judge admitted. Then, prodded by an angry look from Lydia, he amended his stance. "Actually, I threatened her."

"*Threatened* her?" Shelby repeated and saw Lydia's dark eyes snap.

"With deportation?" Nevada guessed.

Lydia's lips pursed. She took a final pull on her cigarette, then jabbed it out in the tray. "I—I was not worried about myself, but Carla and Pablo, the children and..." She shrugged. "And Isabella. They would all suffer."

"You would deport your own grandchild?" Shelby's stomach turned sour. This was too much. Shaking inside, she shoved back her chair and refused to look her father in the eye. "What kind of a monster are you?" she asked.

"A sick one." Lydia, finally getting some starch in her spine, stood and carried her ashtray into the kitchen. "Tell her," she said over her shoulder. "She has the right to know. She is your *hija,* your daughter. She deserves to know the truth. No more secrets. No more. I...I cannot deal with them."

"What's she talking about?" Shelby asked, but began to understand. The Judge looked old. Tired. Hadn't there been some reference to her father's health before? Hadn't she overheard Lydia and the Judge talking about it?

"Oh, hell, I've got cancer, Shelby. Not the same as Caleb Swaggert's, but terminal." Before she could ask, he waved her question aside. "Prostate, not that it matters. Advanced. Surgery's out." He leaned back in his chair, the bags under his eyes more defined. "The doctors are giving me a year...maybe two, but that's it."

The bottom of Shelby's world fell out. "No...I don't believe it. In today's world there are so many treatments." She looked to Nevada for encouragement, but he only shrugged. Her father dying? She'd considered it before but never had she really thought she'd lose the man who had run roughshod over her and manipulated her life for as long as she could remember.

"Accept it, Shelby," Jerome said slowly. "I have. If you hadn't come back because of Lydia's doing, I would have called you myself eventually. You're going to inherit everything I have, you know. The ranch, oil wells, this house and—"

"No!" Shelby said, her voice raw, her emotions splintered. "I don't want to hear this. Not now. Not on the day I'm going to finally be reconnected with the daughter you told me died, the daughter you hid from me. Okay? I can't deal with the fact that when I'm finally going to get to know my daughter, you...you might be dying." Her heart was pounding and she felt tears of anger burn behind her eyes.

"You have a lot to face," the Judge said, standing slowly, his jaw covered with a day's worth of silvering whiskers. Leaning heavily on his cane, he swept his tired gaze to Nevada. "And so do you, Smith. Like as not you're going to be arrested for Estevan's murder. The D.A.'s got a pretty tight case against you, or so I've heard." His old eyes narrowed. "You ready for that?"

"I told you. I had nothing to do with it."

"Well, that may be. Then again, you might be lying." He frowned, used the tip of his cane to squish an ant that had been foolish enough to wander close to him on the veranda. "Either way, you'd better be ready, so get yourself a good lawyer. You know there's a woman in San Antonio, knows Orrin Findley. Has her own firm. Strandill, that's her name. She's a big woman—near six foot tall—and got a tongue on her you wouldn't believe. Doesn't pull any punches and isn't afraid of nothin'. Scares the living hell out of the D.A. She and that partner of hers—oh, hell, what's his name." He snapped his fingers and shook his head. "Joe or John Crawford, can't remember which. He's as small as she is big—always smilin' that one. Looks innocent but he's tough as nails. They're a helluva team, let me tell you. I could put in a good word for ya."

Nevada's expression didn't change. "Don't bother."

"Strandill and Crawford. They're supposed to be the best."

"Forget it. Right now I'm gonna meet my daughter."

"Ha." The Judge started toward the house. "Someone's daughter, you mean." He didn't wait for a reaction, just hiked his way across the tile and opened the door to the kitchen. "What's a man got to do to get a fresh cup of coffee around here?" he asked Lydia, and Shelby's heart tore into a thousand pieces. Judge Jerome "Red" Cole had actually offered Nevada a kind of olive branch in suggesting the name of a defense attorney. Not that Nevada needed one. Not for a second would she believe him capable of murder.

The door closed behind her father. Dear God, was she gaining a daughter only to lose a father—a man whom she despised and yet knew deep in her heart had tried his best to provide for her? A womanizer, a liar, a cheat, the grand manipulator?

She swallowed back any shred of pity for the man who had sired her. He'd spent too many years attempting to ruin her life.

"Let's get out of here," she said to Nevada, already walking across the tile and past half-a-dozen pots overflowing with summer blooms. Elizabeth's plane was due to land at the ranch within the hour. "I'll drive."

Nevada didn't argue, just followed her past a rose garden and climbed in the passenger side of the Cadillac, then slid a pair of sunglasses onto his nose. Shelby drove away in a cloud of dust, pushing the speed limit, taking corners faster than they were meant to be.

"Still a lead foot," he remarked as they crested a rise just before turning north at the outskirts of town.

"Scared?" she asked, sliding him a glance.

"About your driving?" One side of his mouth lifted in amusement.

"About this whole Estevan thing."

"Not for me." Tilting his head, he looked at her over the tops of his shades.

"What? You're worried about me?" she said with a snort. "Well, don't be. I'm a big girl, I can handle myself."

He didn't say another word, just turned to watch the countryside fly by out of a bug-spattered windshield. The car sped past miles of fence line, acres of range grass, copses of pine and oak gilded by the early-morning sunlight. Cattle and horses grazed in pastures irrigated by above-ground sprinkler systems or ditches.

Her stomach was in knots, her mind racing ahead as they turned into the lane to the ranch. What if Elizabeth hated her on sight? What if Maria resented her? What if... oh, hell it didn't matter. She would find a way to work things out with her child, but dealing with Nevada was another issue altogether.

*He might not be Elizabeth's biological father. Face it, Shelby, this nine-year-old girl might have been sired by Ross McCallum.*

Her fingers clenched over the steering wheel. No way in hell was that possible. God wouldn't play such a cruel trick on her, not now, not after she'd come so far.

Through the gates and over the cattle guard she drove, barely slowing as they approached the main house and outbuildings, the very area where Ross had caught up with her ten years earlier.

"So she was in Galveston all this time?" Nevada asked.

"Yes." Shelby nodded and eased up on the gas. "According to Lydia."

"And Lydia's silence was bought by your father," Nevada clarified as she pulled up near the machine shed. "In exchange for the right to stay in the country and work for him, Lydia and everyone else who knew about the baby had to pretend that Elizabeth had died."

"That's about the size of it."

"Nice guy, your father."

"Always has been," Shelby mocked as she slowed to a stop and cut the engine. She slid out of the already-warm interior of the Cadillac and walked up a cement path to the door of the ranch house where she'd stolen the keys to her father's pickup so many years before. A morning breeze swept through the canyons, and horses and cattle dotted the landscape. The ranch foreman, Jeb Wilkins, met Shelby on the front porch. She'd never liked the man, remembered when he was just a ranch hand and, along with Ross McCallum, had, she thought, leered at her, talking behind her back, laughing at the Judge's little "princess." He'd been here that night playing cards with Ross McCallum.

Shelby's lips tightened over her teeth. This morning Jeb was all business.

" 'Mornin', Shelby," he said, flashing a smile of yellowing teeth. "If ya like, I could ride with ya to the airstrip," he offered.

"No need," she said as he handed her a set of keys, then pointed to the truck with an extended cab.

"If you're sure?"

"Positive."

"Just want to help out."

"The lady can handle it." Nevada held the man's gaze with his own unwavering stare.

Jeb nodded. "Fair enough, then. I'll see to the gate." Shelby snagged the keys from his outstretched hand, walked to the oversized truck and climbed behind the wheel. Nevada sat next to her on the wide bench seat and stared through his shaded glasses at the twin ruts leading to the airstrip as Jeb, true to his word, unlatched the aluminum gate and helped it swing open.

"Don't be disappointed if she doesn't like you," Nevada said, once the ranch house was behind them.

"I won't."

"Sure you will." He eyed the surrounding countryside. High overhead, a hawk circled.

"I know this will take time." The pickup bucked as they hit a pothole.

"It's gonna be tough."

"Thanks for the two-dollar psychology," she snapped, her nerves frayed.

"Anytime, darlin'," he drawled with that damned sexy smile stretching across his face as he turned his attention to the dusty calves who lumbered beside their mothers as the cows grazed or chewed their cuds.

"You know," she said, bringing up a sore subject as the airstrip came into view, "for a man who might be facing a murder charge, you sure don't seem worried."

"I'm worried enough."

"But—"

"I didn't do it, okay?" He turned to her, his lips suddenly blade-thin as his temper got the better of him. "I don't know how the gun found its way to my property. McCallum stole my truck that night. The .38 was locked in the glove box. After the wreck, it turned up missing, so either someone took it out before he slid off the road and wrapped the pickup around that tree or it was taken afterward. Either way, I didn't have it and I didn't kill Estevan!"

"I know that," she said, her throat rough.

"Good. We'll worry about it later. Right now, I think we'd better meet your daughter."

"And yours," she said, slowing as the truck neared the cement landing strip that ran along a flat area of the ranch.

"Maybe." His eyes held hers for several long, heart-stopping seconds. "But you gotta face facts, Shelby. This child could have

McCallum blood in her veins. That doesn't make her any less your daughter."

"I know," Shelby admitted, her heart growing cold, her eyes locking with the steely gray of his. She was still clutching the steering wheel. Oh, God, she wanted this child to belong to Nevada. "I—I just can't believe it."

"It's not the kid's fault." He grabbed her hand then, his big, calloused fingers closing over hers, and she felt the strength of his grip, realizing that he wasn't just talking about Elizabeth, but himself as well. He had suffered the pain of a mother's rejection, the shame of circumstances he couldn't control. Her heart ached for him and what he'd suffered. "Okay, Shelby," he said, glancing through the windshield to the sky. "It's showtime. Your daughter's here."

Shelby's head whipped around. She saw the plane, just a speck in the sky. Her stomach squeezed and sudden doubts assailed her. What if Elizabeth rejected her, what if they didn't like each other, what if—

Nevada's hands grabbed her shoulders, and before she could think, he dragged her across the pickup and kissed her hard on the lips. All her misgivings scattered as his lips pressed against hers. He finally lifted his head. "For luck," he explained, his voice rough as he released her. "You can do this, Shelby. I know it. You'll be the best damned mother that ever lived."

"I hope so," she said, still stunned at the passion that had transferred from his skin to hers. Tears threatened her eyes. "Oh, God, Nevada, I hope for once you're right."

"Aren't I always?"

"No. Never." Laughing nervously, she scrambled out of the cab as the sound of the plane's engines broke through the stillness of the summer air. Holding a hand over her forehead as a visor, Shelby, with Nevada at her side, watched the craft glide into a landing. With a bump of tires hitting the tarmac, the plane was down.

Her child was here. They would finally meet.

Shelby's heart squeezed. She bit her lower lip. Fought tears. "Elizabeth," she whispered as the plane taxied to a stop. Within minutes, three people emerged. The pilot helped Maria and a spindly-legged girl in denim shorts and a matching jacket hop to the ground.

Tears stung Shelby's eyes. A morning breeze smelling of dust and cut grass teased her nostrils and ruffled the girl's tangled, shoulder-length hair.

Shelby didn't protest when Nevada placed a steadying arm around her shoulders, and silently she told herself she wouldn't break down. Wouldn't shed a solitary tear.

Elizabeth clung to Maria. Her face was white, her eyes wide and round, her steps unsure. Oh, Lord, this was going to be tough.

"Hello," Shelby forced out as they neared, and Maria, one arm around the girl she'd raised, flashed a halting smile.

"Shelby," she said. "I remember." Maria's eyes moved to Nevada. "And you, too."

"Everything okay here?" the pilot, carrying luggage, asked. Tall and lanky, his sunglasses barely masking his impatience, he checked his watch. "That's it for the luggage. If you need anything else, let me know. If not, I've got another run to make."

"We'll be fine," Nevada said. "Thanks." He shook the pilot's hand, but his eyes never left the gangly girl—the nine-year-old who might be his daughter.

"Isabella," Maria said to Elizabeth. "This is *Señora* Cole, the woman I told you about."

Elizabeth looked scared to death. She clung to Maria and shook her head. "No," she whispered, and Shelby's heart cracked.

"But you have always wanted to meet your mother."

Elizabeth's face twisted in despair and she began sobbing, speaking rapidly in Spanish.

"No, no, she is your mother, but she did not..." More Spanish as Maria leaned down and held Elizabeth closer still. Shelby's heart broke into a thousand pieces, and were it not for Nevada's strength her own legs might have given way. "Shh, shh..." Maria said and Shelby finally pulled out of Nevada's embrace.

"I know this is hard," she said to the girl. Bending over, she looked her child in the eye. "Very hard. For all of us. But believe me, I won't do anything to hurt you or make you feel uncomfortable. I love you, Elizabeth, and—"

"Isabella," the girl cried.

"Yes, yes, Isabella." Slowly, so as not to frighten her, Shelby gathered her into her arms. The girl was as stiff as a board. "Whatever you want to be called. I..." Shelby's throat caught and she took in a shuddering breath. "I just want you to know that I missed you and I love you and I'm glad you're here now. If I'd known where you were earlier, I would have come for you. I would have brought you...here." She wanted to say she would have brought her home, but they were in Bad Luck, Texas, a place she no longer considered her home and certainly not Elizabeth's.

"See," Maria encouraged the child. "Finally you have your wish. To meet your mother. And I am here with you." Shoving her bangs from her eyes, Maria straightened and said to Shelby, "Isabella, she has known she is...adopted."

"What about my father?" Elizabeth asked, squinting up at Maria, then swinging her glance in Nevada's direction. "Where is he?"

*Oh, God, now what?* "You'll meet him soon," Shelby said.

"For now, I guess I'll just have to do." Nevada stuck out a big hand, shook Elizabeth's small palm and offered her one of his blindingly irresistible smiles. "We'll catch up with the old man later."

"Sure. Right. We'll work things out," Shelby said, her arms feeling empty as she let go of Elizabeth. She would have loved nothing more than to hug her daughter, to hold her close and never let go, but right now it would be best to take things slowly, let Elizabeth get used to the idea that she had a new family. "Come on. I'll drive us all back to the ranch. From there we'll switch cars and head into town." She forced a smile she didn't feel as Nevada threw the few bags of luggage into the bed of the truck. "You can meet your grandfather."

"*Abuelo,*" Maria said reassuringly. "Grandpapa. Come. We'll all go meet him together."

Elizabeth didn't smile, and Shelby didn't blame her. As it was, the girl had no idea that her grandfather wanted nothing to do with her, had pretended she was dead and now was going to die himself. A tremendous pressure threatened to squeeze the breath from her lungs, but Shelby refused to give in to it. It was just life—a life of challenges, problems that would be dealt with. At least now she had her child.

Finally.

With Nevada at her side, Shelby watched as Maria helped Elizabeth into the backseat of the big truck. Elizabeth was nervous and avoided looking directly at Shelby, or Nevada for that matter. *Hang in there, she'll come around. She* has *to,* Shelby told herself, forcing a smile she didn't feel and pretending her heart wasn't bruised in a billion places.

Once inside the truck, Shelby rammed it into gear and hit the gas, swinging wide, turning around in the sun-bleached stubble and driving back to the heart of her father's ranch. Nevada didn't say much, just stared through the window, his jaw set as if in stone, the crow's-feet near the corners of his eyes prominent as he squinted and leaned an elbow through the open window.

God only knew what thoughts were rattling around in his mind as the sun continued to rise in the sky. Was Elizabeth his? Or Ross McCallum's? The sickening taste of bile rose in the back of Shelby's throat.

*Be patient. Take it slow*, she told herself. *Time is on your side. Things will work out. Don't borrow trouble. Time heals all wounds.* But the platitudes that ricocheted through her mind seemed hollow and empty, sentiments that should be pasted into a get well card for a mental patient rather than used as her own life's guides. Already there had been too much lost time; it could never be recaptured, and every minute Elizabeth rejected her was one more minute thrown away.

Hazarding a glance in the rearview mirror, she saw blue, suspicious eyes staring at her as if she were some kind of witch. Great. Just damned great. *Give me strength,* Shelby silently prayed, then noticed Nevada stiffen on the seat next to her as the outbuildings of the ranch appeared. He swore under his breath, his eyes focused dead ahead.

She was about to ask what was wrong, but as her eyes followed his gaze, she felt as if she'd been kicked in the stomach.

Parked near the stables and glinting in the morning sunlight was a cruiser from the Sheriff's Department. Deputy Shep Marson, in full uniform and reflective sunglasses, leaned against one fender, his eyes trained on them.

Shelby swallowed against a suddenly dry mouth.

For a split second, Shelby wanted to crank hard on the wheel, turn the truck around and tromp on the accelerator. Sweat dotted her brow, and her insides turned to stone. No one had to say a word.

With a horrible sinking sensation, Shelby realized that Nevada Smith was about to be arrested for the murder of Ramón Estevan.

# CHAPTER 19

"This is insane," Shelby said, glowering at her father in the billiard room of their house. "I watched as Shep cuffed Nevada and hauled him away." Her heart had twisted, her blood was still boiling and she'd wanted to punch Shep Marson in his big belly. There had been a look of satisfaction on his beefy face as he snapped the cuffs on Nevada's wrists, then held Nevada's head down as he'd nudged him into the backseat of his cruiser.

"Smith was never any good, Shelby," Judge Cole said. "Face it."

"Can't you *do* something?"

The Judge barked out a mirthless laugh. "So now you want me to pull some strings, do you?"

"Yes!" she said, then lowered her voice. Her daughter and Maria were upstairs resting after a stiff, formal greeting from the Judge.

"I offered to call the Strandill firm."

"But Nevada didn't kill Ramón Estevan! You know it and I know it."

"It's the evidence. It's all pointing his way."

"What about the testimony? No one saw him with Ramón that night."

"Vianca's changed her story."

"Then she's a damned liar! What about Ruby Dee? She saw Mc-Callum with Ramón that night." Shelby glanced up to see Lydia puttering in the kitchen. The woman had to be dead tired and jangled, just as Shelby was. But the housekeeper had changed, dressed neatly in her standard black dress and crisp white apron, her graying hair pinned away from her face. She was humming to herself as she always did as she began marinading pork tenderloins, preparing for the first family dinner only a couple of hours in the future.

"I can't stand this," Shelby ranted. As desperate as she had been to find her daughter, now she had to help Nevada—for no matter what, whether he turned out to be Elizabeth's biological father or not, Shelby loved him. With all her stupid heart. She *loved* the damned man. "I'm not going to sit around and do nothing while Nevada's being set up for a crime he didn't commit." Torn, she realized she could do nothing more to cement her relationship with Elizabeth tonight. She had to be cool. Earn her daughter's trust. And Nevada needed her. She marched out of the room, and as she breezed through the kitchen, she said to Lydia, "Look, I have to go out for a while, but if Maria or Elizabeth, er, Isabella need me, please call my cell. I'll be back soon."

"Do not worry," Lydia said with a smile.

"I'm afraid that's all I do," she grumbled. "And you"—Shelby yelled to her father as she grabbed her purse—"why don't you try to get to know your granddaughter!" With that she was out the door.

Flipping off the television in her cramped, dingy motel room, Katrina smelled a story. A bigger story than McCallum's release. The local news had reported that Nevada Smith had been arrested and charged with Ramón Estevan's murder.

Katrina wasn't buying it. Oh, sure, it was the line of bull Ross McCallum had been pitching her way, and she'd learned that the murder weapon that had been used in the Estevan homicide had been found on the piece of property Smith owned, but the only reason the local cops had found it was because of an anonymous tip, not because of any prime investigative work within the Sheriff's Department. Not in this podunk, backwater town.

Katrina was a firm believer that if it looked, smelled and sounded like a setup, then by God, it was a setup. But who was behind it and why?

Who would most benefit from Nevada Smith's incarceration? Who would get money, satisfaction or revenge? Who wanted him to pay—or take the fall?

Lying on the sagging bed in her black panties and bra, she flipped through her notes and drummed her fingers on the night table. She considered those people closest to the crime—the Estevans, of course. Aloise, Roberto and Vianca, along with Roberto's wife. Ross McCallum had already served time for a crime he swore he didn't commit. Nevada Smith had been involved with Vianca at one time, but so had other men, and Roberto had never gotten along with his father.

Judge Cole—Daddy Dearest, as Katrina had come to think of him—didn't like the "uppity Mexican" and he hadn't been alone. Many of the people in town objected to Ramón's way of making money. But who hated him enough or would profit enough from his death to actually pull the trigger? Who would kill him and when, ten years later, the man convicted of the crime was set free, call with an anonymous tip about the whereabouts of the murder weapon— or better yet, plant the damned weapon himself?

Katrina didn't know, but she intended to find out. She rolled off the bed and slid into a T-shirt and shorts. Stretching her back, she slid into flip-flops, then sprayed gel through her hair, ran her fingers under the tap, and finally jammed them through her hair, creating some lift. As if anyone in Bad Luck would know the difference. God, it was hot here. Splashing some water over her neck and forehead, she let the drops evaporate rather than towel them off, then found her purse. Starting for the door of the motel room, she stopped dead in her tracks, opened her handbag and peered inside.

The pistol was still at her fingertips. Good.

Clasping her purse shut, she walked outside to the coming night. The air felt as thick and sticky as tar. The cars that rolled down the street moved slowly, as if they, too, were sluggish from the heat. Once again, storm clouds, swollen with rain, were rolling in, bringing darkness a little earlier than was usual. Katrina locked the door behind her and only hoped a new rain would bring some relief from this damned, incessant heat.

She was bound to be disappointed.

The first raindrops plopped on the Caddy's windshield, streaking the dust. Shelby flipped on the wipers only to smear the glass and make it impossible to see. She'd cranked the air-conditioning on full blast and had rolled the window down, but she was still sweating like a pig, furious that Nevada had been arrested, torn because she wanted to be with her daughter and yet she had to find a way to prove Nevada's innocence.

"A few more minutes won't hurt anything," she told herself as she drove through town and checked her rearview mirror. Ever since turning onto the road to drive into town, she'd had the eerie feeling that she was being watched, or that someone was following her, though, now, looking into the mirror, she saw no suspicious headlights tailing her. "All in your head, Shelby. All in your head." Since paranoia seemed to run in the Cole family, she wouldn't panic.

Not yet.

She had too many other things to worry about.

Tired, stressed-out, anxious about Nevada and Elizabeth, she only imagined the sinister headlights tracking her down. No one was following her. And yet...she continued to check her side and rearview mirrors, and the tension in her shoulders didn't abate.

She'd spent the past two hours trying to locate Nevada and Shep, hoping to do something to stop the slow-moving wheels of justice from crushing the wrong man. She'd checked with the county jail and the Sheriff's Department, called Shep's home and even tracked down Ruby Dee, but had gotten nowhere.

"I don't think Nevada killed him any more than you do," Ruby had said nervously at the door of her apartment in Coopersville, "but there's nothing I can say or do to prove it." She'd touched Shelby on the shoulder. "Just be careful, okay? Ross McCallum's in town and he..." She'd stared straight into Shelby's eyes. Fear radiated from her. "To be honest, Shelby, he scares the hell out of me. He's not someone to mess around with. Stay clear of him."

"I intend to," Shelby had said, but if proving Nevada's innocence meant facing McCallum again, so be it. A part of her quivered and turned to ice inside, but she wouldn't give up. Couldn't. Her fingers curled around the steering wheel in a death grip. Beneath her skin, her knuckles showed white.

Shelby loved Nevada. That was the damned plain truth of it. Those initials carved into the underside of the hitching post by the pharmacy meant just as much today as they had when she'd foolishly notched them into the wood ten years earlier.

She drove by Estevan's Market, where she saw Maria's brother, Enrique, manning the till. Then farther on, past the Last Stand, where music thrummed through the sticky evening air, and past her father's office, where less than twenty-four hours before, she'd learned about Elizabeth's whereabouts.

"This is no use," she said, seeing headlights in her mirror again. She took a corner, and the truck followed. Her jaw clamped, whether in fear or anger with herself, she didn't know. She turned down a side street. The truck didn't make the turn. She felt a rush of relief and told herself not to be so paranoid. "Silly," she said, snapping on the radio and listening to a soft country-and-western ballad as she wound through town.

At the stoplight another vehicle began to follow her. Big deal. She didn't pay much attention. Driving with one hand, she let the other elbow rest on the open window, where raindrops fell on her bare skin. She drove past several houses and ended up slowing in front of the Estevan bungalow, where lights were glowing. Though she and Vianca had never seen eye to eye, Shelby was desperate to help Nevada and fast running out of options. Maybe Ramón's daughter could shed some light on his death.

"Here goes nothin'," Shelby told herself as she parked her car and got out. Somewhere down the street a dog barked, and as she climbed the steps a cat shot out of nowhere and dashed across the porch. Raindrops peppered the roof.

Shelby rapped on the door, and it opened almost immediately. Vianca stood on the other side of the screen. "Yes?" she asked, red lips pursed in irritation.

"I'd like to talk to you. About Nevada."

"He was arrested. There is nothing more to say."

"There's a helluva lot more to say," Shelby argued as the shorter woman on the other side of the screen stood on her tiptoes to peer over Shelby's shoulder. Vianca's eyes slitted as her gaze followed a truck slowly driving past.

"What?" Suddenly her skin crawled. "So you bring the devil with you," she muttered unkindly. Shelby looked over one shoulder, and her blood turned to ice water. Ross McCallum's old pickup pulled up to the curb.

"Oh, God, no."

"Get inside." Vianca threw open the door, and Shelby didn't need any urging. She heard McCallum cut his truck's engine.

*"Dios,"* Vianca said, locking the screen and the door. She whirled on Shelby, who stood in the middle of the living room. "What is this all about?" Vianca said, then sputtered a stream of angry Spanish. Vianca's mother lay on a couch, an afghan spread over her frail body.

"Do not swear," Aloise whispered. "Do not take the name of the Lord in vain."

"I do not, *Madre.*"

Appearing as weak as a ghost, Aloise seemed to lose her concentration and turned her glazed eyes toward the television, where a muted sitcom flickered.

"What do you want?" Vianca demanded, facing Shelby again.

"Your help."

*"My* help?" Vianca walked to the coffee table and reached for a cigarette.

"Nevada didn't kill your father."

*Bam! Bam! Bam!* The front door actually shook on its casing and Shelby didn't doubt for a second that Ross McCallum was on the other side. Ross McCallum pounded on the front door.

Vianca nearly dropped her cigarette then lit up. "What does he want?"

"I don't know, I didn't realize he was following me until I got here."

"Go away!" Vianca called through the door.

"Hey, now, I jest wanna see Shelby. We're old friends," Ross said through the panels. His voice was a rasp.

Shelby walked to the door.

"Leave me alone, McCallum. I've got nothing to say to you." She closed her mind to the slide show of pictures that slipped through her brain, snapshots of the night he'd caught up with her at the ranch, climbed into the cab of her father's pickup, pressed her against the seat. . . .

"I will call the police!" Vianca said.

"You just do that, okay? But remember, I didn't kill your old man."

"Ramón?" Aloise asked, turning to stare at a small table complete with pictures of her late husband and five or six candles burning beneath it and an elaborate back-lit portrait of Jesus Christ.

Vianca managed to pick up her cigarette. "You have to leave, Shelby. *Madre*, she is ill and I cannot help you—"

"Just tell me what you remember about the night your father was killed."

"Nothing. I remember nothing. It was a long time ago."

"Ramón?" Aloise said and turned dark, haunted eyes up at Shelby. "Ramón?" she repeated.

"He's not here, *Madre*. Remember?" Vianca took a nervous drag on her cigarette, then let out a cloud of smoke. "She gets confused sometimes."

"Shelby, come on out!" Ross called, knocking loudly. "Hey, can't you and I be friends?"

"He's drunk." Vianca said, then more loudly toward the door, "I am not joking—I will call the police if you do not leave. Now!"

"No way, José," Ross said and laughed at his own little joke. Vianca swore roundly in Spanish as Shelby took in the small house with its tidy furniture and shrine to Ramón. "Hey, what have you got against me, Vianca? I didn't do it, remember? I'm a free man."

"A free man who is trespassing on private property! Oh, for the love of the Holy Mother!" Vianca walked to the front door and threw it open. Through the screen Shelby saw the angry, rough-hewn features of the man who had raped her.

"Leave, McCallum," she ordered with more ferocity than she felt. "I don't ever want to see you again. Not tonight. Not ever."

His smile was vile. "Is that so. You know, Shelby-girl, I've been waitin' ten years for you. Ten *looong* years."

Her stomach threatened to upchuck. "Get out!" she said. "Just get the hell out, now!" Her insides were shaking. "Leave now and don't you ever bother me or Vianca or any of her family ever again. You got that?"

"Fiery, ain't ya?" His lips curled in disgust. "You know, these people"—he motioned broadly to everyone in the house—"they're not your friends. Don't you see? They stick to their own kind." His gaze settled on Vianca. "And you, I think you've got some ex- plainin' to do. I saw you that night, didn't I? When your old man was killed? You were there. I was drunk, yeah, and I stole the bas- tard's truck, but you were there, too. . . ." His eyes narrowed, and Vianca looked suddenly as white as porcelain. "I forgot until now," he said, his expression dark. "But you were in the truck. . . . That's right."

Vianca's mouth opened and closed again and she actually put a hand over her chest as she backed up.

"Well, shit a brick," McCallum said as if he was putting all the jagged, unwilling pieces of the puzzle of that night together. "You're the one who killed your old man, aren't you?"

"No," Vianca whispered weakly, her eyes as round as saucers.

Was it possible? All this while? Was Ross telling the truth? "Why?" McCallum said and then smiled. "Oh, I get it, you were tired of him roughing you up, weren't you?"

"Get out of my house!"

"You won't call the police." McCallum was no longer shouting. "You won't call them because you're afraid I might tell them something that will incriminate you. Right now Nevada Smith's set to take the rap, but you, Vianca, you're the one. That's the reason you've been cozying up to Shep Marson and don't deny it, 'cause I saw you two together. You want someone on the police force on your side. Is that how he found out about the gun? Did you tell him?"

"*Dios!*" she muttered and made a sign of the cross over her chest. Tears were running from her dark eyes.

"Is that true?" Shelby asked, shocked. Her head was spinning, disjointed pieces of the night Ramón Estevan's life was ended com- ing together. In the living room Aloise began talking again, a mono- tone of Spanish sprinkled with her husband's name.

"This . . . this is nonsense!" Vianca insisted, some of her old fire returning as she notched up her chin. But her eyes were still wide and when she crossed the room and tried to light a new cigarette, her hands were visibly trembling.

"Nonsense? Really?" Ross leered through the screen.

That was it! Shelby had heard enough. She reached into her purse and pulled out her phone. She was dialing 9-1-1 when Vianca noticed.

"Wait? What're you doing? No!" Springing at Shelby, Vianca knocked the phone out of her hands. "No police!"

"We have to call them."

"No!" Vianca insisted.

"Listen, Vianca, even if you killed your father, it could be self-defense. If he was hurting you or..."

"No! Go away!"

McCallum leered through the screen. "That's more like it," he said.

Shelby flung him a "drop dead" look. "Go to hell, McCallum!"

"Maybe I will," he said, then smiled evilly. "No, come to think of it, I've already been there, haven't I? But now it's somebody else's turn, ain't it? Nevada, he finally got his."

"And you set him up, didn't you?" Shelby shot back, no longer afraid of this man. She stepped closer to the door and with only the flimsy mesh separating her from her rapist, she said, "If you framed Nevada, I swear I'll hunt you down and see that you get the justice you deserve."

"No... don't." Vianca was shaking her head vehemently.

But Ross ignored her. "Well, come on, little girl," he said to Shelby, his face a mask of anticipation. "Let's see what you've got. If I remember right, you were the hottest piece of pussy I ever had. And that daughter of yours... now, isn't there a chance she might be mine?"

"You keep her out of this!" Shelby warned. Her pulse was pounding and fear was growing deep in her heart, not for herself, but for the daughter she'd just met.

As if she finally understood the tenor of the conversation, Vianca made a hasty sign of the cross over her chest and turned the color of paste.

From the couch, Aloise stirred again and began to rave in Spanish.

"Come on, Shelby. What are you waiting for? Still holdin' out for Nevada? Well, let me clue you in, Shelby-girl—he ain't comin' back."

"Go away!" Vianca ordered.

The television flickered eerily. Rain drummed on the roof. Aloise mumbled her dead husband's name.

"No, siree, he's gonna pay for puttin' a bullet in ol' Ramón's head."

"He didn't do it!" Shelby cried.

"Well, someone sure as hell did, otherwise Aloise wouldn't be a widow now and Vianca'd still have her father slappin' her around and callin' her the cunt she is!"

"No!" the old lady cried. "No! No! Ramón, do not!"

"Shut up!" Vianca ordered, not to McCallum, but her mother.

Wait a minute. What had Ross said? That Vianca had had access to the gun that killed Ramón?

"Ain't we havin' fun?" Through the screen, his features were even more malevolent.

"You *are* a bastard," Shelby accused him, seeing movement from the corner of her eye as Aloise hoisted herself off the couch. "You deserved every day you spent in prison."

"*Madre,* no!"

"Ramón," Aloise screamed, as if she were witnessing her husband doing something vile. "Oh, *Dios,* no, Ramón, no! Do not!"

"Shhh! *Madre,* please," Vianca begged, suddenly picking up the phone as if she was going to make good her threats and call the police.

"The children. Do not hurt the children." Aloise was sobbing now, screaming, spouting off streams of Spanish.

Vianca dropped the phone and dashed to her mother. "Do not speak. No more. No more."

For a split second, Shelby looked at the older woman. Ross ripped the screen from its hinges. *Crash!* The door splintered. Vianca screamed. Reaching through the screen, he unlocked what was left of the frame.

"Get out!" Shelby ordered.

It was too late. He was in the room.

"Get the hell out, McCallum," she said again.

"Make me, Shelby-girl. You just make me." Smelling of booze, he leaped forward. Shelby dodged. A huge hand caught hold of her wrist, spun her around.

"Let go."

"No way, honey. I've been waitin' too long for this and you—" He pinned Vianca with his cold eyes. "Don't you do anything foolish, or you and your mother will end up in jail for killing your pa."

"Stop this," Shelby ordered, yanking her hand back to no avail. His fingers were a manacle. She tried slugging him with her free hand, and he sucked in his breath and caught her wrist, holding them both in one hand.

*"That* was a mistake."

"Do not do this!" Vianca cried. "Leave us alone, *por favor.*"

"Just you wait, bitch," Ross growled. "Your turn will come. All of you who set me up, you'll pay."

Shelby struggled, but he was stronger. He pulled her close and she smelled the odors of sweat and beer, all mingled together. "God, I've missed you," he growled.

She kneed him. Hard. Rammed her knee right into his groin.

A startled hiss swept through his teeth and he doubled over. "You goddamned bitch!" he swore, but still held her tight, forcing her nearly to the ground. Desperately, she tried to squirm away, but it was no use. Fueled by anger and pain, he only held her tighter.

Through the open door the sound of a siren's shriek reached her ears, but it was too late. Ross's thick arms tightened around Shelby so tightly she thought she would be crushed.

"Let me go, you cretin," she ordered and kicked hard, but he didn't seem to feel any pain.

Aloise collapsed. Vianca was at her side on her knees, crying and sobbing hysterically.

*"Madre, oh, Madre."*

"You can't do this, McCallum," Shelby said. "You'll go back to prison. I've got witnesses."

"It'll be worth it. Besides, you wouldn't send the father of your kid to prison."

"You're *not* Elizabeth's father." She fought him and stumbled, fell back against the wall. Her shoulder exploded in pain. Candles flickered. Tumbled. Wax sprayed and the flames caught on the lace cloth, igniting it.

Shelby slid down the wall.

Ross slammed her head against the floor.

Pain burst behind her eyes. She fought to stay conscious.

Through the curtain of blackness that loomed before her eyes, Shelby heard Aloise as the older woman began to pray, crying as she crawled toward the fallen shrine while Vianca, tears streaming down her face, tried to shepherd her out of the house.

*"Tía V?"* a frightened voice cried, and Shelby, trying to throw Ross's dead weight from her, saw a small, round-faced boy in the hallway.

"Little Ramón, get away—oh, Sweet Jesus!" Vianca was hysterical. She climbed to her feet and swept the crying child into her arms as the flames found the curtains. Crackling and hungry, spewing smoke, the fire climbed toward the ceiling. "Come on, Shelby," Ross said, hauling her to her feet. She wobbled, swung at him and missed. Smoke filled her nose and lungs. She began to cough. Still she fought, and Ross threw her over his shoulder. "You and I got to get out of here and find us a more private place."

"No," she yelled and then felt something crack hard against the back of her head before she gratefully lost consciousness.

"Holy shit!" Shep heard the report, flicked on his siren and lights, did a police U-turn in his cruiser and pressed hard on the accelerator.

Nevada, in the cage of a backseat, was thrown from one side of the car to the other.

"Hang on," Shep ordered as the lights of Bad Luck loomed ahead. "Slight change of plan."

He didn't elaborate and Nevada was thankful for any relief. He'd been booked and questioned, and they'd been on their way to the county jail when a call came over the radio about a fire, changing Shep's course.

Other sirens screamed through the night. Fire trucks, an ambulance, a city cop car all raced toward one section of town.

Nevada's stomach clenched as Shep flew through the back

streets and screamed around corners. Smoke filled the air. Flames rose sky-high from a house on the east side of Bad Luck.

The steady rain had little effect on the inferno, and Nevada's gut tightened. In an instant he knew where they were going, had pinpointed the source of the blaze.

"What happened?" he demanded.

"Hell if I know. But your friend McCallum's been spotted," Shep said, rounding a final corner and standing on the brakes. Nevada's gut clenched. His gaze took in the horrifying scenario. Vianca stood on the lawn holding a small child to her. Aloise, her mother, was being escorted by paramedics to an ambulance, but the woman looked out of it, as if she didn't understand what was happening.

Firemen barked orders and battled the flames, trying to keep the conflagration confined while police and dogs attempted to force the crowd away from the blaze. It was a hellish nightmare.

The little bungalow was engulfed. Then he saw the Cadillac. Shelby's white rental car. Parked at the curb, not too far from Ross McCallum's beat-up pickup. Oh, Jesus. No! His stomach plummeted.

"Let me out," he ordered as Shep opened the door and stepped into the mayhem.

"No way."

"I mean it, Shep. Shelby's here somewhere. So's McCallum." Fear drove Nevada. Though handcuffed, he tried to shove open the door.

No dice.

Shep shook his head. "Well, you'll just have to think about that, won't cha?"

Frantic, Nevada watched in horror. Firemen stretched giant hoses across the street. From the huge nozzles, geysers of water plumed into the night, shooting gallons of water over the flames.

Nevada squinted against the night and the intensity of the fire, scouring the street and yards of neighboring houses. A crowd had gathered, police were controlling the onlookers, hospital workers were seeing to the Estevan family. Where the hell was Shelby? Oh, God, she couldn't be with McCallum! He felt the tendons in his neck stand out, was certain he was about to explode.

"Let me out, Marson!"

"Forget it, son." Shep started to close his door.

"You'll get your confession."

The deputy stopped. "What?"

"Let me out. Unlock the cuffs and I'll give you what you want." Nevada was desperate, didn't care about the consequences.

Shep hesitated and looked over at Vianca, who, holding her nephew close to her, stared back at him with anxious, haunted eyes. Men shouted. Women screamed.

"Do it, Marson."

"Okay. I'll let you out. But the cuffs stay on. And if you cross me, Smith, I swear, I shoot first and ask questions later. Deal?"

"Deal." Nevada didn't quibble. Didn't care. He had to find Shelby. Shep unlocked the door and Nevada took off, stumbling through the crowd, not caring that people parted and stared at him. He jogged, slipping over hoses, his blood pumping, his brain screaming. He ran along the fence to the back of the house and ignored the shouts of men trying to stop him. Ahead he saw someone moving through the shadows.

With speed borne of fear, he followed. Sure enough, he made out Ross McCallum's shape in a thicket of live oaks. Ross was struggling, hauling the body of a woman over his shoulders.

*Shelby.*

*Oh, darlin', don't be dead. You can't be,* he thought desperately. *I love you, Shelby, and I can't, I won't, lose you again.*

Shelby opened her eyes and felt instantly sick. A man was carrying her, trying to climb a fence, and rain was drizzling from the night sky. Coughing, she smelled smoke, felt dizzy and started to scream as flames illuminated the night and she realized she was with Ross McCallum.

"Shut up!" He was breathing hard, and she kicked and fought as he mounted the fence while holding her wrists in one big hand. She was slung over his shoulders. Kicking and squirming, trying to fling her body from his, adrenaline firing her blood, she fought.

"I'll kill you," she screamed as he started over the fence. Her head banged against a tree branch. Again the world tilted. But she wouldn't give up. Not without a fight. She had too much to live for, too much to do. There was Elizabeth and Nevada...oh, God, she had to help Nevada. She swung her head around—head butting the side of his.

"For the love of God—" He managed to land on the other side of the fence, where he dropped them both to the ground and, straddling her, tried to subdue her. "Now listen to me—if you want to live and you want that daughter of yours to grow to be a woman, you'll do as I say."

"Leave Elizabeth out of this!" She started sliding away from him.

"Only if you come along quietly, Shelby. Otherwise I'll hurt her," he said, and she knew he meant it. Sweating, his eyes reflecting the fire's horrifying light, he put one hand to her throat. "You wouldn't want me to do this to her, now, would you? And the other—what I did to you before, you wouldn't want your daughter to suffer through that. Or would you?"

Shelby fought back the paralyzing fear that threatened her. Through gritted teeth, she vowed, "I swear, McCallum, if you so much as touch a hair on her head, I'll hunt you down like the lying dog you are and kill you with my bare hands."

"Try, Shelby-girl." he said, spittle evident in the corners of his mouth. "You just damned well try."

For the love of God, he was enjoying this, savoring the power he wielded over her.

She stared up at him and saw the pure joy in his eyes, but beyond that, above him, poised on the fence, there was a man. *Nevada!* Her heart took flight. Nevada pounced.

In a jangle of chains he landed on McCallum.

*Oof!*

"What the fuck?" McCallum yelled, his legs buckling slightly.

Shelby rolled away. Nevada, face twisted in fury, swung his arms over Ross's head, and the chain holding his handcuffs together covered the convict's windpipe.

"Get off me!" McCallum screamed.

"Never." Nevada jerked hard on the cuffs. Pulled back. McCallum squealed in terror and pain.

Nevada's face pulled into a mask of tension. He jerked.

Ross's eyes bulged white. He clutched at the chain slicing through his neck and cutting off his air supply. Spittle sprayed.

Shelby was on her feet as the men rolled together on the wet grass beneath the trees. *Oh, God, Nevada, be careful.* She searched around for a weapon, heard Ross's painful cries.

"Die, fucker!" a slow Texas drawl commanded. Over the fence Shep vaulted, his sidearm aimed at the two men.

"No!" Shelby cried, certain Nevada would be shot.

*Crack!*

The pistol fired.

Both men slumped forward onto the ground.

Numb, shell-shocked, Shelby screamed and ran to the two entwined bodies. A bullet hole was dead center in Ross McCallum's forehead. His eyes were blank. Nevada lay beside him, but shifted, throwing his arms over the dead man's head as his chains jangled. Shelby fell into his waiting arms and began to cry like a damnedfool woman. She couldn't stop herself.

"Shh," Nevada said, drawing her farther into the few scattered trees and away from Ross McCallum's lifeless body. "It's over. Finally."

"Promise?" she asked, and Shep turned his back on them, giving them a bit of privacy.

"Oh, yeah, I promise."

"You're a liar, Nevada Smith," she sniffed, clinging to him. "You're the worst. And...and...and, damn it, I love you."

"Do ya now?" he drawled. "Funny thing how that worked out," he said, touching a bruise on her head, "because I was just thinkin' I love you. I just don't know what I'm gonna do about it."

She couldn't help but grin. "I have a few ideas, cowboy."

"I'll just bet you do," he said, linking his arms around her back and kissing her soundly. "And once I get a few details cleared up, I intend to examine each and every one of them."

"I'll be waiting," she promised.

"I know." His eyes turned serious in the darkness. "Oh, darlin', I know."

# EPILOGUE

Rays from a late summer sun glinted off the pool's clear surface. Sitting on the terra-cotta lip, Shelby tentatively slipped one toe in and glanced at the cloudy heavens.

"Chicken?" her daughter teased from the far end of the pool, and Shelby grinned widely. How had she ever thought Elizabeth, now Isabella, could have been fathered by Ross McCallum when each day she looked more like Nevada Smith? Tests had confirmed his paternity, of course, but now it all seemed so petty. "Come on, Shelby," the girl, dressed in a bright orange bathing suit encouraged her. She had yet to be called "Mom," but that would come in time. If Shelby could somehow find her patience.

"Oh, all right." Shelby tossed off her cover-up and slid into the water, swimming beneath the surface and skimming the bottom of the pool. Who would have thought things would turn out so well? She and Nevada had married and moved into the big house while her father was off on a world cruise—his last, he claimed, though Shelby hoped there was still time to bury all the old hatchets and become a family before the Judge decided to leave this earth for good.

Nevada, cleared of all charges once Vianca had started talking, still owned both his places, and he wanted to build a more modest home there, raise their children and live a simple life.

Shelby wasn't sure that was possible. Though she'd moved from Seattle for good, working a deal with her assistant for the current listings, life was still a whirlwind and didn't seem to be slowing down. Elizabeth and Maria lived with them and slowly Elizabeth, who had agreed to be called Liz, was growing accustomed to her new home. Thank God for Maria's patience, for the woman planned to marry a man she'd met in Galveston, but they had agreed to wait until Elizabeth was settled and had accepted her new family. The plan was for Isabella to have two families that would blend, that she would feel loved by everyone.

Maria, as well as Lydia and Pablo and Carla, would always be a part of Liz's life. Norman Rockwell, it wasn't. But it looked like it was going to work for them and that, Shelby figured, was all that mattered.

Under the water, she grabbed Liz's toes, and the girl shrieked in delight, then began churning her way toward the shallow end of the pool. The chase was on, and Shelby caught up with her daughter just as Liz reached the pool's steps. They laughed and gasped as Nevada, wearing Levi's and a shirt with the sleeves pushed over his elbows, strode out of the kitchen. Even after all these years, Shelby's breath caught in the back of her throat at the sight of him.

"Well, it's official," he announced. "Shep's running for sheriff and since he solved the Ramón Estevan murder, he might just be a shoo-in."

Shelby shook her head. "Sheriff Shep just doesn't have a good ring to it."

Nevada laughed as she squinted up at him, shading her eyes with one hand.

"He's as good as the next guy, I suppose." Shelby stared up at her husband and was grateful for Vianca's confession. She had admitted to "borrowing" Nevada's gun on the night that Ross had stolen it, and had told the court that when her father started slapping her around for a mistake she'd made while making change, she'd followed him to the back of the store and threatened him with the gun, never intending to use it.

She'd prodded him with the barrel, had made him walk to the Dumpster, just to scare him, but her mother had witnessed the fight and had gotten involved. Ramón had tried to slug Vianca, and

Aloise had pulled the trigger. In the shock of it all, she'd lost whatever hold on sanity she had. Vianca had hidden the gun in an abandoned warehouse and later planted it in the cave, calling Shep anonymously, hoping that Nevada would be accused of the crime, as she was afraid an all-out investigation would find her mother a murderer when, in fact, in Shelby's estimation, Aloise was only protecting her daughter.

Vianca hadn't cared who took the rap for her father's death—either Ross or Nevada—just as long as Aloise was free.

"I don't know. Shep has a tendency to bend the law," Nevada said, squatting down and ruffling his daughter's wet head. Elizabeth giggled. She adored her father. "And he's got his own problems. Peggy Sue isn't letting him in the house these days."

"Yes, but I heard they were 'dating' again."

Nevada made a sound of deprecation. "Yeah, well, we'll see if she can forgive and forget."

"At least he's not seeing Vianca anymore." Vianca had moved away two months ago, as had Katrina Nedelesky, who was writing a book, supposedly already shopping the idea around. If Shelby had her way, the rift between father and daughter would be mended, but so far, neither Katrina nor the Judge had started reaching out. It might never happen.

"Come in," Liz encouraged him from the far end of the pool. "Swim with us, 'Vada."

"Yeah," Shelby teased. "Join us. "She couldn't help herself and splashed water up at him. A dark stain spread up the leg of his Levi's.

"You're askin' for trouble, darlin'," he said, one side of his mouth lifting upward.

"Of course I am. I just wonder if you're man enough to give it to me," she teased.

Nevada's grin was positively wicked. "Tell ya what," he drawled. "Let's find out."

"Oh, yes, let's," she agreed.

Quick as a cat pouncing, he jumped into the water, reached down and grabbed her legs. She squealed, and he pulled her under the water. She popped up again and laughed. From the far end of the pool, Liz giggled, then began heading their way, water churning as she plowed across the clear surface.

"I'll get you back," Shelby warned.

Nevada's laugh started deep in his throat. "You'd better," he said. In his wet clothes, he dragged her close and kissed her soundly. "You'd damned well better, darlin'."

"Or what?"

"Or I'll have to teach you a lesson."

"Another one?"

"As many as you need," he said as Liz landed and grabbed him around the waist.

"I don't know." She tilted her head to one side. "This might take awhile."

"Well," he drawled. "I'm sorry. All I've got is the rest of my life. If that's not long enough, you'll have to find someone else."

"Never," she said. "After all I went through with you, I'm *never* looking at another man." And she meant it. With every breath in her soul. He kissed her again and Shelby knew this life, this love, was forever.

**Please read on
for a very special
Q&A with Lisa Jackson!**

**How did you come up with the idea for *Unspoken*?**
The concept for *Unspoken* was a little unique for me because it started with the hero, Nevada Smith. I saw him and the first scene clearly in my mind's eye and I knew instinctively that he, down and out, had gotten involved with the wrong woman, a woman of higher social status, the daughter of a judge, no less. Usually my books begin with the germ of a plot when I read or see something that intrigues me, but not in this case. As I was thinking about a new book, I saw the hero clearly. I knew who he was and what he was about before I started writing, so that part was easy. The heroine, Shelby Cole, showed up a few days later. Once again, the scene with Shelby came thundering into my vision, and the story evolved from the characters.

**Who was your favorite character in the book?**
Hands down my favorite character is the hero. Nevada Smith is and was the heart of *Unspoken*. Yes, I liked the other characters but Nevada really made the plot move. I saw him so easily from the get-go. I even had a private reader say, "Does he have to be so dirt poor? Couldn't we clean up his place, add some nice books and give him a little more sophistication?" My thought: "No way." This is who he is because of what happened to him. This is his life.

Shelby Cole is my second favorite character. She's strong, determined, and doesn't back down to her controlling father.

My third favorite character is the town of Bad Luck, Texas. The name says it all and the whole feel of Bad Luck shapes the characters.

**Was the novel easy or hard to write?**
*Unspoken* was one of the easier books to write, probably because I knew the characters from the beginning. Right from the start I sensed what they were feeling and what life had in store for them. Also, it helped I grew up in a very small town so I was comfortable with the setting. Yes, I spent my younger years in a logging town in Oregon, far from Texas, but small-town Americana is small-town Americana.

***Unspoken*** **was one of your "lighter" suspense novels. There wasn't a serial killer. There really wasn't much violence. What made you decide to take your stories in a darker direction?**

Each book I write has its own tone. Some are more violent and gruesome. Some are more romantic or erotic. Some are edgier and darker. Some are more of a mystery. Some are more psychological. The book itself, the plot and the characters determine the course and flow of the story. I try not to put in gratuitous sex or violence. No sex just for the sake of sex, no violence for the sake of violence, at least not in my opinion. When I write, I let the characters dictate how the story flows. Sometimes stories are just more psychological, more twisted and dark. Sometimes I want to write something more complicated, or more over-the-top, or darker. At times a serial killer is involved, but I like to shake things up and not create a pattern for my books. Each one is unique. The level of suspense, mystery, romance, or tension depends, again, on the story.

**Do you think the book lends itself to a sequel or are you pretty much done with these characters?**
I would love to revisit Bad Luck, Texas, and see how the characters are doing, but at this point there is no sequel planned, no second story nagging at me. As I said, I love Nevada and Shelby but their story is finished. There are other characters in the town who might one day come to mind, but not at the moment. That said, I have learned over the course of my life to "never say never." Life is funny. I don't foresee another tale about these characters, but you never know.

**What's next for Lisa Jackson?**
This summer I have several new books on the shelves!

In June 2019, the paperback edition of *Liar, Liar* will be available. This is the story of Didi Storm, a Las Vegas impersonator who is so desperate she is willing to sell her own child to his father, only to be involved in a double-double cross that leaves both her and her infant missing, presumably dead. Twenty years later, on the heels of a book released about her, Didi is seen leaping from a skyscraper in San Francisco. Her daughter, Remi, witnesses the horrible act and vows to find out what propelled the woman to suicide. Is it her mother? Or is someone impersonating an impersonator, and why? All the pain of her mother's disappearance returns and during her investigation, Remi is confronted by Noah Scott, now a man, and once the boy that she'd thought she'd loved and is also connected to the horror that went down in the desert twenty years earlier. *Liar, Liar* really is a twisted tale of lies, deception, and death.

*Paranoid* is next up and is a July 2019 release. In the book, Rachel Gaston Ryder is a single mother raising two rebellious teens. The kids' father, Lucas Ryder, works with the local police department and, as far as Rachel is concerned, is pretty much useless. But then she has a lot more problems than a cheating ex. She is considered by almost everyone in her small town as the girl who, as a teen, inadvertently killed her brother in a dangerous game and literally got away with murder. Through the intervening years, her guilt had never subsided and only becomes more acute when she receives cryptic messages that say, "I forgive you," as if her brother is reaching out to her from the grave. But that's crazy, isn't it? Luke is dead. She knows that. Right? But as the messages continue and one after another of his acquaintances are victims of a vicious killer, Rachel starts to doubt herself and the truth blurs. Can she find out what really happened that night before she, or someone she holds dear, becomes the next victim?

In August 2019, on the heels of *Paranoid,* the next book in the Montana "To Die" Series will be in stores and online. *Willing to Die* picks up where *Expecting to Die* left off after Regan gave birth to her new son, Tucker Grayson Santana. Since the boy's birth, she's had a bad feeling, almost an omen, that whispers across her skin. She's not wrong. The horror starts with the murder of her sister in San Francisco and trails after Pescoli to Grizzly Falls, where a pathological killer from her past puts Regan Pescoli in her sights. The killer isn't satisfied to just kill Pescoli and be done with it. This murderer wants her ultimate victim to suffer in the worst way possible for a new mother.

For more information on these or some of my other books, log onto lisajackson.com or visit me on Facebook or Twitter. I'll look for you!

Best,

Lisa Jackson

Please read on for an exciting sneak peek of
Lisa Jackson's
**WILLING TO DIE**
coming soon wherever print and e-books are sold!

# PROLOGUE

*Near San Francisco, California*
*July Fourth*

Dead.

Her son was dead!

Cold to the bone despite the summer's heat, she couldn't breathe, had to gasp for air.

Her throat clogged with grief, pain, and a deep, intense fury.

Standing alone in this cemetery where gravestones stood in sentry-like rows, she clenched her fists and wanted to rail to the heavens where, across the night sky, fireworks burst in thunderous booms and great sprays of light.

The demons that had tormented her mind hadn't lied.

As bitter as the harshest Montana winter, desperation cut through her heart. Blinking against tears, she dragged her gaze from the inscription on the small marble stone at her feet.

A low-lying fog was rolling in, swallowing the lights of the city situated on the far shore of the bay. The iconic Golden Gate was partially obscured, only the bridge's tall towers knifing through the fog to a black sky glittering with stars, a backdrop to the fireworks. She watched another shooting star rise high, streaks of fiery glitter bursting, then fizzling before her eyes. For a few awe-inspiring seconds, the pyrotechnics bedazzled, then faded, their short life spans over in quick, brilliant bursts. Over almost before they'd begun.

Like her son's brief life.

Her heart tugged so painfully she fell to her knees. She'd known this was possible, perhaps even probable, that he'd died, but throughout these past lonely years, she'd held out a glimmer of hope that he'd survived, that they would be reunited, that she would feel the warmth of his arms around her neck as she held him close. "Oh, baby," she whispered.

Once again she turned her attention to the small gravestone, a tiny marker in a sea of larger, more elaborate tombstones. In various shapes and sizes, some tall, some ornately carved, others more plain, the headstones stood unmoving, hulking along the slope that curved downward to the city and the dark, black waters of the bay.

*Why?*

*Oh, God, why?*

Closing her eyes, she drew in several deep breaths.

*Don't question. It is what it is.*

*More importantly: What are you going to do about it?*

Jaw clenched, she thought of those who had wronged her.

Those who had used her.

Those who had abused her.

Those who had taken out their animosity against her on the innocence of her child.

Still on her knees, she reached forward and traced the dates inscribed on the frigid stone with the tips of her fingers. Barely four years from date of birth to date of death.

Her heart cracked with the pain. "Oh, honey," she murmured, her throat catching as thoughts of that unlikely birth swirled in her brain. The agony of labor, the fear of the unknown, the rush in her blood at hearing the newborn's cry, and then the emptiness as her son was stolen from her, taken from that isolated delivery room. She'd heard the whispers in the hospital.

"... deeply disturbed."

"... mentally unstable."

"... severe psychosis."

All spoken in hushed tones. As if she couldn't hear.

And now this.

She squeezed her eyes shut and brought to mind the manipulators who had made the decisions, those who had determined that she was "unable," or "unwilling," or "incapable." More words she wasn't supposed to hear. And then there was the harshest of all: "unfit." Her teeth gnashed as she remembered the callousness with which that word was tossed about. How would they know? Yes, she'd been unstable—she knew that—though the word "insanity," which she'd heard throughout her life, surely was extreme. She wasn't "insane," and never had been.

Especially not tonight.

No, as the rockets screamed into the sky, blooming in wild explosions of color and light, she'd never felt more sane. She'd spent so much time searching for her son only to find him buried here—that bit of hope she'd felt at the thought of reconnecting with him, of seeing him, of explaining to him and holding him... that tiny flame of expectation was now dead. Extinguished. And in its place rose a new emotion, raw and acrid.

Vengeance.

Swallowing the lump in her throat, she gazed at the small grave marker again and now, dry-eyed, thought of what lay ahead. "They'll pay," she promised her child, hoping that he would somehow know. Her fingers twisted in the drying grass of the hillside, the long blades and dandelions that were tucked close to the marker and had escaped the gardener's mower clutched in her fingers. "Every last one of them. I will hunt them down and, I promise you, they will pay." In her mind's eye she saw them all. As she pushed herself upright, a series of smaller fireworks exploded over the bay, flashes of kaleidoscope colors disappearing in fading fingers until the darkness was unbroken again.

She knew who they were, those who had betrayed her.

She knew where they lived.

She also knew she had the element of surprise on her side.

And she would destroy them all.

Tossing the dried weeds from her fingers, she dusted her hands. She had a mission.

As she headed down the hill, stepping carefully between the marble and granite sentinels of the dead, she plotted just how to wreak her vengeance against them.

A sense of cold satisfaction displaced her desperation.

She turned at the locked gate, then climbed atop the wrought-iron fence and looked back over her shoulder. Spying the tiny gravestone, she whispered, "I love you," and waited for an answer that didn't come.

Armed with her new purpose, she hopped lithely to the ground, shoved her hands into the pockets of her jacket, and felt the cold reassurance of the Beretta Pico, a small .380. Jaw set, she strode through the darkness, avoiding streetlights as the explosions burst overhead.

No one would stop her now.

No one would dare.

# CHAPTER 1

*San Francisco, California*
*Six Months Later*

Brindel wanted a divorce.

Correction: She *needed* a divorce.

From Paul Latham...make that *Doctor* Paul Latham. He always did.

Self-important bastard.

Glancing out the bathroom window to the night beyond, the lights of the city pinpoints, the view even from this room stunning, she was ready to give it all up. But of course, Paul wouldn't go down without a fight. Not that it was about her or love. She actually laughed at that ridiculous thought, then took a sip from her second—or was it her third?—glass of wine. Didn't matter. She finished the last drop, considered pouring another, then decided against it, leaving the glass on the marble counter. Whatever love she and Paul had shared nearly two decades before had shriveled and died long ago, like a worm on a hot sidewalk. All that was left was a hard, heartless shell of their marriage. No, the reason he would fight her was that he wasn't a man who could lose. Not in his life, not in his marriage, not in his job, and especially not to her.

She shook her head. She'd been such a fool. She'd suspected

early on, and discovered a few years into the marriage, that he'd expected her to raise his two sons, Macon and Seth. Which she had. Both disgustingly like their father.

Angrily she swiped off her makeup, scrubbing carefully, though she noticed a few irritating and stubborn lines on her face that needed a good shot of Botox. Afterward, she massaged cream into her skin, then brushed her hair until it gleamed. It now was blonder than her natural shade and streaked to hide any hint of gray, then cut in the most fashionable style money could buy, perfect layers framing her face to fall softly to her shoulders.

A glimpse of her closet showed off racks of shoes—heels, pumps, sandals, running shoes, a pair for every occasion displayed on lighted shelves that were slightly elevated. Neat rows. Each pair worth a small fortune.

How had she thought footwear costing thousands was worth the price of this hollow marriage? Along with the shoes, deeper into the wide walk-in were racks and racks of dresses, slacks, suits, sweaters, you name it, all designer, all expensive, all hung neatly, the gowns encased in plastic to protect them, purses, too. From the corner of her eye she caught a glimpse of the white gown she'd worn at her wedding—well, her second wedding if anyone was counting—and she saw the sparkle of beads, the cut of French lace, and cringed inwardly as she remembered wearing that gown and feeling as if her life, finally, had turned a favorable corner as she'd swept down the aisle to meet her handsome, successful groom. Despite his flashes of anger while engaged, his need to dominate, the warning knell from her sisters, she'd been determined to give herself and her toddler daughter a new, "perfect" life.

She'd had no idea how wrong she would be.

And now...now she needed to do something about it. Before it was too late. As it was, she was already over forty, for God's sake, her kid nearly grown. She stepped out of her robe and let it puddle on the floor. Turning sideways to the full-length mirror, she noted that her belly was flat and hard, her breasts high with the help of surgery and enhancements, her nipples pert and dark, her legs long and lean, even showing a bit of muscle, her posture erect. She was still very attractive, could compete with women ten, maybe even twelve years younger than she...well, maybe. If she had to. Not that she was looking for a new man. No way. At least not until she was single. She didn't want the hint of impropriety on her part. She'd already spoken to one of the best lawyers in town; she just hadn't pulled the trigger and filed for divorce yet.

"Tomorrow," Brindel said, mouthing the words as if her husband, who was in the next suite, could hear her.

More than slightly buzzy, she finally took out her contacts and finished getting ready for bed, which was basically undressing to slip between the soft sheets completely naked, a practice her husband had once found exciting, then disgusting, then had totally ignored. That had been before the remodel of the second floor into two master suites. His and hers. It had seemed perfect at the time, but now was claustrophobic. Silk wallpaper, coved ceilings, crystal chandelier, huge four-poster bed and private bathroom with its grand walk-in closet, all part and parcel to her jail cell.

And Brindel needed freedom.

More than anything else.

She'd only stayed as long as she had because of her daughter...and now...well...

She slid beneath the thick duvet, felt the polished cotton smooth against her skin, and turned off the bedside lamp. Her appointment was at nine, when she was certain her husband would be in the midst of his rounds at the hospital attached to the medical school, a short walk through the park from this house. She'd tell her attorney to file the papers and then let the chips fall where they may.

Smiling at the thought that she was finally doing *some*thing, well, actually the one thing he would abhor, she burrowed under the covers and drifted away, her dreams lulling her only to be interrupted by...what? The sound of footsteps? Oh, God, surely Paul wouldn't try to come into her room and slide into her bed....Physically shuddering at the prospect, she opened an eye to darkness, the room lit only by the glow of the bedside clock.

Was that breathing she heard? Soft and low over the pounding of her racing heart?

She swallowed back her fear and stared, eyes narrowing, fingers curling at the edge of the duvet.

For a second she thought she saw movement—a shadow crossing in front of the armoire—but realized it was the mirror mounted over the antique, reflecting the sway of branches from the window on the opposite wall.

*Don't be neurotic. You have one more night and then you start the fight for your freedom . . . and half of Paul's estate. He owes it to you for giving him almost twenty of your best years. In her mind she calculated what she might receive, less attorney's fees. Three million? Maybe four? She'd earned every penny of it being married to the jerkwad.*

*And it would be enough to last her the rest of her life.*

Slightly calmer, she still listened for any sound that he might be stealthily walking down the hallway to her bedroom door, but she heard nothing . . . all her imagination. Her nerves were strung tight, that was it. Because of her meeting in the morning. She was alone. Safe. In her own damned bedroom. Closing her eyes again, she started to breathe easier.

And there it was.

The whisper-soft scrape of a footstep. Then another.

And a new smell. Musky and male and . . .

Brindel's eyes flew open and she gasped, saw the muzzle of a gun just before it was pressed to her forehead.

*What??? NO!*

She opened her mouth to scream.

Her attacker pulled the trigger.

An ear-splitting blast.

Then nothing.

"No, no, noooo!" Ivy threw a hand over her mouth to keep from screaming.

The carnage was horrible. Mind numbing.

Backing up quickly, the image of death seared forever in her brain, she wondered how everything could have gone so terribly wrong.

She knocked over a small table near the door, a vase with a single rose sliding to the floor, while on the bed . . . oh, sweet Jesus, on her mother's feminine bed . . .

Death.

A small dark hole in the smooth forehead, blood coagulated

around the entrance wound, spatters of red on the creamy skin. And the eyes, God, her mother's eyes, sightless and open, seemingly accusing.

Blood on the ruched duvet and the lamp shades, flecks on the thick, white rug covering the ancient hardwood. "Oh, God, oh, God, oh..." Her stomach threatened to heave as she turned and fled, down the narrow hall with its long runner, pictures of the family placed perfectly on the hallway... and to the next room and the second body, lying facedown, the back of his head a mangle of blood, bone, and brains visible through a huge gaping wound that had destroyed the graying hair that had once been thick, his pride and joy. She backed up, ran into the wall, banging her shoulder as she raced through the familiar rooms, the acrid scent of blood chasing after her, the horrid images burned in her brain.

As she ran, Ivy retched, threw a hand over her mouth and tasted blood. Salty... or was that her tears?

*Get out. Get out, now! Don't step in any of it, don't get it on your shoes. Run like you've never run before!*

Images blurred in her vision, the old globe in the library, the books, never read but stacked in neat rows to the high ceiling, the mullioned windows overlooking the city, lights winking through the beveled glass. The banister—*don't touch it!*—smoothed by over a century of hands sliding along it.

She was gasping as she hurried down the runner of the steps, her feet flying, her hair streaming behind her as she reached the marbled foyer—*NO! Not out the front! What are you thinking? There could be people on the street. Old man Cranston walking his aging dachshund, or the Miller girl who was always running the streets at night, or a stranger... no, no, no! The back. You need to go out the back door, through the backyard, to the alley. Then, if no one's around, cut through the park. Fast. Run, damn it!*

She skidded around the bottom of the staircase and through a short hallway toward the rear of the old home.

A creak in the floorboards overhead made her stop short.

Was someone up there?

Someone still alive?

Or the killers?

Who? *Who?*

Holding her breath, she strained to listen over the frantic trip-hammering of her heart.

Was that a footstep?

A noise on the stairs?

Oh. Dear. God.

She didn't wait to find out, but flew through the darkened kitchen, her knee banging against a bar stool near the center island. "Ow!" Cutting off the scream, she saw the knife block resting on the marble top. Without a second thought, she yanked the butcher knife from its slot and raced to the back door.

Another creak on the stairs.

*Shit!*

Fear raced through her bloodstream as she found the doorknob and yanked on the door, the reflection of her own silhouette visible in the glass panels, the cold of winter rushing inside. She thought she saw movement behind her—the killer!

*Oh, Jesus. No!*

Ivy raced down the back porch, slipping on the last step.

She caught herself, but dropped the knife. It clattered against the brick path and she left it, flew through the back gate and didn't bother to stop as the gate slammed closed behind her. Running down the narrow, crumbling alley for all she was worth, she splashed through a puddle and scared a cat hiding near the garbage cans. It hissed and backed away, white needle-sharp teeth visible in the dim light of a security lamp on the neighbor's back porch.

Another screech.

The gate opening on its rusting hinges?

The damned cat scared again?

The killer chasing her down?

She didn't bother to look over her shoulder. Panicked, she sped headlong into the street.

A passing car honked and swerved, barely missing her, street water spraying beneath screeching tires.

She stumbled. Caught herself. Ran.

"Idiot!" a male with a deep voice proclaimed, rolling down the window of his white Volvo to make certain she heard.

She didn't care. Reeling back from the street, she kept going, scrambling away.

Adrenaline propelling her, she raced between two parked cars and along the sidewalk. She didn't quit running at the gates of the park, but sped inside. Heart in her throat, she flew along the path. At a bend in the sidewalk, she veered into the undergrowth, away from the pools of light cast by the lampposts that lit the groomed path. Crouching, breathing hard, she scrabbled into rain-drenched thickets, where trees, shrubbery were her salvation. Her skin prickled. Rain slid down her bare head and under the collar of her jacket. She barely noticed, her fear was so intense, the images of the dead bright behind her eyes.

*Don't panic.*

But it was too late. Rational thought had disappeared, chased by pure terror. Was it her fault? When she'd agreed . . . ? How the hell had this happened?

She swallowed back a dose of guilt and took stock of her situation.

Ivy had played in this park as a child, knew all the hiding spots, and thought she might be safe, if just for a few minutes, long enough to catch her breath and gather her wits.

What now?

Where could she go?

Where could she hide?

Teeth chattering, body trembling, she tried and failed to dislodge the bloody images of the dead bodies from her mind. Her parents. Slaughtered in their beds. Unsuspecting. The brutality and unfairness of it all was too much and she started to cry, tears burning down her wet, cold cheeks. This wasn't supposed to happen, she thought wildly. No, not this. Not now. Not ever.

*Calm down. Just calm the hell down!*

She couldn't. Bile filled her throat. Her insides revolted. She threw up violently, the contents of her stomach emptying onto the bark dust by a thick-leaved rhododendron bush. Then again. This time bile came up and after wiping her nose and mouth with her sleeve, it was all she could do to prevent herself from dry-heaving. She scuttled backward, deeper into the bushes, distancing herself from the sour pool of vomit, creeping over rocks.

Hiding here was no good.

She'd be found soon.

Those who had killed might still be looking for her.

There was a good chance, she knew, that she was the ultimate target.

With that sizzling thought, she rimmed the park, keeping near the brick fence until she reached the far side. From her hiding spot, she had a clear view of the central fountain, lights directed at the rushing water tumbling over jagged rocks. No one stood gazing at the wet stone, no one appeared on the fringes of light.

And yet she felt the weight of someone's gaze, someone who was hiding just like she was, someone who would think nothing of taking her life.

*Get a grip. No one's there.*

*Think.*

*Come up with a damned plan!*

Her insides quivered and she nearly jumped out of her skin as the leaves rattled nearby. Biting back a scream, she scooted closer to the fence as a fat raccoon waddled from the cover of the bushes and padded around the base of a lamp near the path. She let out her breath and tried to pull her thoughts together. So far, it seemed, she hadn't been followed. The sounds of the city surrounded her, the even rumble of engines and whine of tires as traffic passed on the other side of the brick wall enclosing this block of greenery. Cigarette smoke drifted to her nostrils and she heard muted voices as people passed on the sidewalk on the other side of the brick barrier separating the park from the rest of San Francisco. A quiet cough. A far-off bark. In the distance a foghorn moaned. Yet no hurrying footsteps running toward the park.

*Please, God . . .*

Attempting to calm herself, to slow her racing heart, to force the fear back into the farthest reaches of her mind, Ivy frantically reviewed her options. She knew she had to escape. Now!

Going back to the house was out of the question.

Calling the police would be a major mistake.

Notifying anyone she knew would only put her in more jeopardy.

She could trust no one. Not a soul.

It wasn't supposed to happen this way! When she agreed to . . . oh, God. Her mother was dead. Killed.

Hands shaking, she slipped her fingers into the pocket of her jacket, felt her phone and the wad of cash that she'd hidden there. Four thousand dollars. Enough to escape and disappear.

Footsteps sounded. Someone moving fast.

Hurrying through these blocks of greenery.

Her heart lurched.

She bit her lip, trained her gaze toward the sound.

Her ears and eyes straining, her senses on alert, she heard the rapid footfalls, then spied a runner cutting through the park, slim and sleek, a man in reflective running gear striding easily, his breath fogging, earbuds visible as he flew past.

She couldn't stay here any longer.

It wasn't safe.

She was a sitting duck.

Ivy slipped through the dense, wet foliage, easing her way to the entrance on the far side of the park and out. Flipping the rain-soaked hood of her jacket over her wet hair, she walked rapidly through the city blocks where skyscrapers knifed upward into the dark sky, patches of warm lights visible in a few apartment windows, security lights in businesses.

By instinct, she headed downhill, toward the waterfront where, she hoped, she'd find a way to leave this city and her painful past forever. A bus out of the city. That's what she'd do. Find a bus and buy a one-way ticket.

She didn't care where.

Just as long as it was far, far away.

# Connect with
# U s

Visit us online at
**KensingtonBooks.com**
to read more from your favorite authors, see books
by series, view reading group guides, and more.

for sneak peeks, chances to win books and prize packs,
and to share your thoughts with other readers.

**facebook.com/kensingtonpublishing**
**twitter.com/kensingtonbooks**

*Tell us what you think!*

To share your thoughts, submit a review,
or sign up for our eNewsletters, please visit:
**KensingtonBooks.com/TellUs.**